R0700027063   07/2022

**PALM BEACH COUNTY
LIBRARY SYSTEM
3650 Summit Boulevard
West Palm Beach, FL   33406-4198**

W9-DCF-253

a Sitting in St. James

a Sitting in St. James

RITA WILLIAMS-GARCIA

THORNDIKE PRESS
A part of Gale, a Cengage Company

GALE

Copyright © 2021 by Rita Williams-Garcia.
Thorndike Press, a part of Gale, a Cengage Company.

ALL RIGHTS RESERVED
Thorndike Press® Large Print Striving Reader Collection.
The text of this Large Print edition is unabridged.
Other aspects of the book may vary from the original edition.
Set in 16 pt. Plantin.

LIBRARY OF CONGRESS CIP DATA ON FILE.
CATALOGUING IN PUBLICATION FOR THIS BOOK
IS AVAILABLE FROM THE LIBRARY OF CONGRESS.

ISBN-13: 978-1-4328-9049-0 (hardcover alk. paper)

Published in 2021 by arrangement with HarperCollins Children's Books,
a division of HarperCollins Publishers

Printed in Mexico
Print Number: 01   Print Year: 2022

For my ancestors
Alexander and Mahalia Lloyd
and Dean and Mariah Edwards

PROLOGUE

Patience. There is no story without history.
Ante 1678

Before the spread of smallpox and influenza, before the land was claimed in the name of a French king, before the land and its abundant rivers passed from French to Spanish to French hands, the land, the boot of the territory, thrived with Native peoples as diverse as its soil, trees, vegetation, waterways, and creatures. The people who populated the land thrived! The Caddo to the west, the Tunica-Biloxi to the northeast, the Natchez at its heart, the Atakapa and the Chitimacha to the south, and the Muskogee, the Choctaw, and the Houma to the east. And throughout the land, the Alibamu, the Apalachee, the Bayogoula, the Chickasaw, the Coushatta, the

Ouachita, the Quapaw, the Quinipissa, the Yatasi, the Yazoo, and many more. This fertile land, with its wide southern mouth, surging rivers, still lagoons, bayous, swamps, and marshes couldn't be kept to itself, for to follow the great river called Messipi by the Anishinabe people was to find the land and its wealth. So the French, the Acadians, then the Spaniards came by the hundreds, and then thousands. Like the river that carried them, they couldn't be stopped. They learned the land from its diverse people, exchanged gifts, and negotiated the ownership. Yes. Some native to the land remained and brought their cultures into a rapid mixing of French, Spanish, African, and Caribbean people. But many were pushed into the shadows, the marshes, and the piney woods, and many were ultimately removed from the land.

While the land changed hands, finally, from Napoleon Bonaparte to Thomas Jefferson, one Bayard Guilbert, who had fled the Haitian Revolution with his wife, had secured a narrow tract of land to begin his life yet again. Although the land was granted to him, it didn't hurt that he offered a bit of gold to the governor's clerk for his administrative trouble. The land grant was about twelve hundred acres, wedged between wealthier planters. Those acres were not as much as he had owned in the former Saint-Domingue, but they were enough to grow and rotate sugarcane, a decent plot of cotton, some timber, and tobacco near the river's banks. Here, he gave himself and his generations the greatest gift he could afford: he made himself anew in this country, *la Louisiane.* Like a pig rooting in the dirt for turnips, he could sniff his fortune in the soil without having to till or clear the fields. Before enslaved people, mules, horses, cattle, wagons, plows, and cast iron kettles were purchased, or a house facing the river was erected, "Vié Pè," as the Black Creoles called him, or "Ol' Pap," as the Africans called him, tasted the promise of cane juice, hogsheads of molasses, and golden-brown crystal in his clay-rich soil. Although he might have been no more than a yeoman farmer in France, his birthplace, Bayard Guilbert would make himself a lord on this moist earth, as he had done in Saint-Domingue — the land his former slaves and now the emancipated Black men and women call "Ayiti." Long after Bayard Guilbert was gone, the grandchildren of the Africans, Caribbeans, and coloreds on the Louisiana plantation called their children inside after darkness fell, saying the old planter still walked barefoot, stepping on the little things in the way of his big feet. "Run quick! Run quick! Ol' Pap walk de earth!" or *"Galopé, piti! Galopé!* Vié Pè *apé maché la tè!* Vié Pè *apé maché la tè! Be ware!"*

As a young man in France, he couldn't marry his love, the daughter of a vineyard owner, for he was a nobody, young and hardworking. But through time in Saint-Domingue, his brown crystals by the hogshead gained him substantial prosperity.

Bayard Guilbert had plans to return triumphantly to France and claim the object of his affection. Through associates, he learned that the daughter of the vineyard owner had married, given birth to a girl, and then, eight years later, had died. Bayard Guilbert wouldn't be stopped by death. If he couldn't have the woman, he would have her daughter. Kidnap the girl, if necessary. Time. Distance. Impossibility. These things didn't matter to Bayard. He worked each day with the daughter of his love in mind. He bided his time. The girl was now thirteen. He braved seafaring pirates and returned to France to take his prize. Through careful inquiries he learned that in the wake of the French Revolution, the girl had become a discarded remnant of the queen's court. She was within his grasp! He went about finding her.

At that time Bayard was but thirty-five. His suntanned face made him stand out among French men on the streets of Paris, but where he was not fair and handsome, he was virile and formidable.

He found an inn, a bath, and suitable clothing. Not attire so grand he'd look like a mongrel in a poodle's collar.

Bayard wisely dispatched a person who could inquire further among social circles he was not comfortable in. It was still dangerous. The blood of King Louis XVI hadn't satisfied the people. The Terror and revolutionary thirst were in the air. *Blood. Blood. Blood.*

But what of the girl? Thirteen. Perhaps an improvement upon her mother? It didn't matter. Bayard Guilbert was fixed on his new object. This girl. She would compensate him for what he had been denied in his youth. Second, her French blood, her association with the very thing he despised, the aristocracy, would erase his humble background, and his children's children would never be denied entry into society or looked down upon. Yes. He would have her.

1793

Bayard paid a poor farmer handsomely for a perfect head of cabbage. Perfect in color, size, and shape. He then cut the head from its neck in one clean blow and sharpened the hardened neck's rim with his knife. He hired a broker of sorts and gave the man instructions on how to present the gift. *She is a child; she would like a gift and a game.* He had his broker purchase a satin box from a fancy milliner. His broker asked no questions and placed the cabbage in the box with its neck facing up and tied it neatly with a wide satin ribbon. A note, dictated by Bayard, and improved upon and hand-written by the broker, was to be given to the girl. Bayard Guilbert possessed neither persuasive charm nor social grace and couldn't risk frightening the girl with his illiterate scrawl and his gruff manner; he relied solely on the broker to obtain his life's object.

A brief meeting at the convent where the girl had been deposited was arranged between her and the broker. The sneer the girl gave the broker said this meeting wouldn't be long or an easy one. The broker smiled anyway, introduced himself, and asked if she was Sylvie Bernardin de Maret Dacier of the Bernardin de Maret vineyard.

"I am," she snapped. She looked down at the box in his hands. "Is this from the Family?" she asked of the box. He noted she wasn't demure or hopeful, like a poor child, but that she had asked assuredly, if not accusingly, with the scrutiny of a grand inquisitor.

"No, mademoiselle," he said. "I am here for Monsieur Bayard Guilbert, who sends you this gift." If it was Bayard's design to enchant this Sylvie Bernardin with the box, he had miscalculated. The broker extended the box to her and then laid it on the table, since she wouldn't take it from his hands.

"Hmph," was all Sylvie said. She untied the ribbon, lifted the satin-covered lid, and peered down her small but pointed beak of a nose at the cabbage, still green and perfect. She looked at the broker and placed the lid back on the box, dismissing him with dispassion. "Good day, monsieur."

"Mademoiselle," the broker said. "You are too hasty."

"Hasty? I've given you more than you or your master can repay. Even now, I overspend my courtesy."

She turned to leave, but he rushed ahead to block her exit. He had counted on the money Guilbert promised, and this snit of a girl was not enough to keep him from it.

He bowed before her, clasping his hands. "Humblest of all pardons, Ma-

14

demoiselle Bernardin de Maret Dacier. My master asks that you closely examine the contents in hand. I beg you, mademoiselle. It will be the worst for me if you refuse."

She was miffed, but it was also true that she was bored, having been confined for nearly two years in the convent for her safety and separated from her dearest friend, Marie-Thérèse Charlotte.

Sylvie huffed through her nostrils, a sign she had relented; removed the lid from the box; and took the cabbage head. Her expression of impertinence and boredom hadn't changed.

The broker read her face and spoke quickly. "My master only asks that you run your finger swiftly along the cut stem." He demonstrated the gesture in the air.

Sylvie huffed again, fluttering her eyelashes before doing as the broker had demonstrated. She ran her finger swiftly around the hardened edge. She drew blood, dropped the cabbage, then sucked her bloody finger.

The broker said, "My master commanded me to say, 'Better to stick your finger than lose your head.' " Clearly, he had her. At the least, he had succeeded in wiping away her impertinence.

"Mademoiselle Sylvie Bernardin de Maret Dacier, you are an orphan, no longer under the protection of the Royal Family. Monsieur Bayard Guilbert is the lord of profitable sugar plantations in the New World and he sends me to make his offer of protection and marriage. Do you accept?"

At thirteen, she knew it was improper for a girl to decide her own fate, especially in affairs of marriage, even with the smell of spilled blood in the streets. In good times she had expected a proper negotiation for her dowry — a prosperous vineyard and manor house with so many cottages, a fair annual income, and her mother's jewelry. While she didn't expect the same royal situation due Marie-Thérèse Charlotte, her imprisoned friend, she was certain to receive an advantageous negotiation on her behalf. But hastily she must decide: convent, guillotine, or plantation lord's wife? For the moment, she was safe, hidden in the convent in a novice's habit. But even she had heard the shouts for blood in the streets. And for how long would she be safe?

The broker smiled. He had her answer. Without intending to, Sylvie touched her neck.

He held out his hand. "You must come now."

She stood firm and crossed her arms. "No," she said. "First, he must register me as his wife. The vineyard must stay with my family. And I must see the contract."

He couldn't believe her demands. Her mouth. "Are you blind to the thirst for blood? There is no time for a contract."

"Then there is no bride."

He didn't know which he feared more, this thirteen-year-old girl or his master. He wanted to slap her, but he dared not touch her.

The broker changed his tone. "I will do as you ask, mademoiselle, but what you ask will take time. Please be ready to leave when I call tomorrow, or the next day."

"Come with the marriage contract in

17

hand. You tell your master I can read and will read it carefully. And for the marriage contract I am Sylvie Bernardin de Maret Dacier." She recited her date of birth, the name of the convent, the names of her parents and grandparents, the name of the vineyard and its region. She made him repeat everything back, her arms crossed, her brow lifted in complete insolence. Then she sent him on his way.

Sylvie's heart remained proud, and she even congratulated herself on delivering her demands. That wave of triumph, however, dissolved swiftly. The nun who served her bread, potatoes, and green vegetables that evening relayed to Sylvie a horrific sight that left her shaken. A young girl, believed to be a friend of the court, had been dragged away screaming for her life.

Although hungry, Sylvie could not eat.

Two days later the broker returned with a sheet of rolled-up paper and a plain dress. One fit for the scullery maid's daughter in the queen's country home. It was not the gown of a nobleman's daughter. Sylvie was put off by the look of it —

a heavy linen dress, too big for a girl with buds for breasts and barely hips.

The broker anticipated her expression and said, "It isn't safe to walk the streets in high fashion."

Yes, she thought. *The young girl seized by the mob was likely dressed as a young lady and not a peasant.* Still, Sylvie couldn't help herself. Even when she took the garment, she gave the dress the look she had given the cabbage, the broker, and anyone for that matter she deemed beneath her notice. "Where does it come from?"

All he could think of was how he wanted to be outside the bed chamber on her wedding night to enjoy her screams. This thought made him patient with her. "Mademoiselle, the master offers you protection and you care where the dress comes from. Change and leave all behind. As you can see, I have your contract," he said, holding up the rolled paper.

19

Sylvie appeared before the broker wearing the scullery maid's dress and carrying a small, plain bag. The convent doors closed swiftly behind them, a reminder or omen. Once again, young Sylvie Bernardin de Maret Dacier had left one place of protection for another.

She looked at her soon-to-be husband, who had not been waiting in a carriage but on foot. He was a man surely the age of the queen. Thirty-eight. Forty? Big. Tall. Sun-brown skin. Dressed well, but not what she expected in a lord. He didn't try to make himself or the circumstance appealing. Though he had recently bathed, his hair clung to his face. His teeth jutted from his lips.

"May I present Mademoiselle Sylvie Bernardin de Maret Dacier." The broker turned to her. "Mademoiselle, Monsieur Bayard Guilbert."

She waited to hear more. Perhaps a title. Where he was born, or some sort of succession. The realization of it, that she would be absorbed into this giant of a man — and the smallness of his circumstance — made her both woozy and then sober.

He bowed.

With the doors closed behind her, she had no choice but to follow the man and the broker to the office of the registry. Once there, she asked the attending clerk to see the registry. It was all she could think of, the most pressing evidence of her existence. Who she was. Granddaughter of the baron of Bernardin de Maret vineyard; her father, Captain Dacier, a military nobleman with the favor of the court.

"The vineyard. It must stay in the Bernardin de Maret Dacier line and pass to my issue. But you, my lord, cannot own it."

The broker's eyes shone as he waited for the master to smack her down. This he would enjoy as much as if he had laid the blow himself.

The master said, "Write it in the contract." He neither smiled nor flinched.

The young clerk, unlike the girl, feared the master. He wrote quickly while the girl peered over the proceedings, making sure her words were represented as she dictated them. "Monsieur clerk," she said. "The vineyard is to be looked after by and profited to the convent until the heir appears."

Sylvie, acting on her own behalf, had played her card. Besides a printed contract filed with the registry and a secret token stashed on her person, she was out of luck and options. She was still a girl, and in her girlish heart she nursed a hope that members of the Royal Family would learn who she was attached to and obtain her release.

The ink hadn't dried on the writ of marriage contract when Bayard took the thick parchment paper and herded the girl to the church. He presented the paper. The priest said the words. She gave her pledge. He grunted his. The broker witnessed the ceremony, received his gold pieces, and was on his way.

In the dark of night, the former Sylvie Bernardin de Maret Dacier followed Bayard Guilbert to the stinking part of town where the ship they would set sail in had been docked.

On the ship, he said, "You have a bag.

You were told to bring nothing."

"I'm to have nothing? Nothing of myself?"

He didn't reply. He had done his whoring during the day and settled his business and waited for the girl to be delivered to him. With her in his possession he had no reason to linger. Not even for a meal at an inn. When they were aboard the ship and she was queasy from its motion, he said, "There is no need for these old things from that old place. You are coming with me to Saint-Domingue. For you, a new place. A new life."

At first opportunity for privacy the new bride had stashed the signet ring bearing the seal of the Bernardin de Maret vineyard in the hem of the frock that served as her wedding dress, and now, her only dress. She stole a glance at a locket portrait of her mother and also inserted it in the hem of her frock. She intended to place the signet ring in the hands of her firstborn child when he or she came of age. Her instinct hadn't failed her: this husband, this Bayard Guilbert, took her bag, didn't bother to look inside or empty its contents to discover her treasures. He threw the bag overboard into the murk.

She screamed.

"Go," he said dispassionately. "Go, then. Get your dead old things."

His dispassion stopped her cold. She didn't want the guillotine or whatever torture was saved for friends of the royals. She also wasn't brave enough to jump into the indigo abyss after her mother's jewelry, a hairpin the queen had given her, lace gloves, and cloths she would need to attend to herself. Sylvie had no choice but to follow the man, her husband, to their cabin, on a ship bound to Saint-Domingue.

Book I

Book I

I

Patience. Even as time leaps three score and seven years, all that lies between that time and now will be made known. Patience.
July 1860

"Thisbe," Madame said to the dark-skinned girl standing to her right. "Go out to the gallery. Tell me what he is doing." Her French was clipped, but notes of wicked humor peppered the command. Madame Sylvie didn't speak the more relaxed Louisiana French or French Creole. Having lived nearly sixty of her eighty years in St. James, Louisiana, she still only spoke the French of her childhood spent in her family vineyard and in Queen Marie Antoinette's Petit Trianon and in her country hamlet. Madame did not consider herself Creole, and this was

27

true — Madame and her husband were French born. Her son, Lucien, however, like white Catholics born to French or Spanish parents on Louisiana soil, proclaimed himself a proud Creole, much to Madame's objections and disdain. For how could her son be what Black Creoles also called themselves?

"Yes, Madame," the girl answered. She left Madame's salon through the opened shutter doors and stepped outside onto the wood-planked gallery. The gallery faced the river but didn't wrap around the two-story house. She couldn't see her family's cabin in the quarter, or the rows of green cane stalks stretching without end behind the house. Her clearest views were front-facing, of the river, the live oaks that lined the path and served as a walkway, the garden, the far-off manmade pond, and the garçonnière where Madame's grandson, Byron, stayed. To see the cement monument to Bayard Guilbert, the site that Madame's son, Lucien Guilbert, had last night threatened to take action, Thisbe went to the upriver end of the gallery and leaned, holding on to the railing with one hand.

The wide-hipped roof gave her plenty of shade, but she cupped her other hand above her brow to tamp down the sheer might of the July sun that cursed and blessed the small plantation. She saw enough to report to Madame: Monsieur Lucien sitting on his white horse, overseeing the work at hand. Four Black men, men he had earlier claimed he couldn't spare from the cane fields, digging at the obelisk that bore his father's name. Thisbe hoped one of the four men was her father, but she could see he wasn't among them. It had been months since she had visited with her family, although they were housed in the quarter, not more than five hundred feet behind the big house, or Le Petit Cottage. Still, it was a comforting thought to imagine her father being close enough to wave to her, although she dared not wave back while she served Madame Sylvie.

Twenty seconds hadn't yet passed, but Thisbe, aware her Madame wasn't a patient woman, returned to the salon to report back.

"And?"

"Monsieur Lucien watches the men dig

Monsieur Bayard's stone, Madame Sylvie." These words, eleven in total, were the longest utterance the girl would speak in Madame's presence that day. That being the case, she purposely extended each sound before she returned to a vault of relative silence. Still, she hoped for more opportunities to speak. French, Louisiana French Creole, English, pidgin English. It didn't matter. Perhaps Madame would ask which men and if they found anything.

"Digging!" Madame Sylvie threw her head back and laughed, each cackle catching in her throat and mouth, a sound like dishes breaking. "So close, my son. So close!"

Thisbe bent to aid Madame, but the much older woman waved her off and lifted herself up under her own power, gripping the arm of her favorite perch, a faded rose brocade throne with a curved mahogany frame and legs. The little throne was a gift from her husband. A joke and reminder of her former surroundings at Le Petit Trianon. After her years of service as plantation mistress, Sylvie wanted nothing more than to sit on this little chair and to be served. Madame Sylvie, the *maîtresse,* was petite at eighty, but not frail. Still, in spite of being waved away, Thisbe remained close and helped her mistress out onto the gallery.

"And Beee-rohn?" Madame's tongue turned her grandson's name, Byron, after the English poet, into a French confection. "Do you see him? Does he stand at the big tree and wait?"

Thisbe peered toward the grand live oak, the centerpiece of Le Petit Cottage. She and Madame knew the grandson's routine since he had returned home from West Point. Lately, it was to close the commissary at noon, walk to the live oak, and then stand like a guardsman with his hands behind his back for as long as an hour. Sometimes ninety minutes. There were so few customers to buy goods at the commissary. Who had cash? After his hour or so of standing, Byron would then walk back to the commissary in no hurry.

"My fan!" Madame said.

Thisbe was light on her feet in her shiny black leather ankle boots. Her skirt barely rustled when she pirouetted and

31

disappeared into the salon. She was quick about retrieving the ivory-handled fan and rushed to the gallery to give the fan to Madame.

Was he guarding the plantation? This didn't seem likely. But why stand there? Madame and servant looked toward the big tree and waited for something about the routine to change.

Byron's first two years at West Point straightened his spine and opened his chest. He knew his grandmother sat out on the gallery watching, which was precisely why he kept his back to the house, even though she couldn't see his expression. These were private, pleasurable moments for him. Who would want to be spied upon from afar and then picked apart later in the dining room? With his back turned, he was to himself. With his face lifted, eyes closed, the kiss of a breeze rising off the Mississippi swirled around his nape and ears and was gone. A memory. A smile. And now longing. Indescribable longing. And waiting.

For all practical purposes, Byron was an engaged man. The negotiations had been made between his father and Colonel Duhon, the father of Eugénie Duhon. The wedding would take place two years from this past June — five days following Byron's graduation from West Point. He and Eugénie had met three times, but mainly wrote letters. There were no mothers — both having died shortly after childbirth — to press for a shorter and more involved engagement. The two young people, however — Byron, soon to be twenty, and Eugénie, seventeen — were agreeable to the discreet and extended family arrangement, with a proper announcement forthcoming at the right time.

In every way, Byron was a dutiful son. Most important, he was the Guilbert legal heir. (Rosalie, his quadroon half sister, and any other half siblings that had been farmed to other plantations or sold to settle debt had no legal claim to the plantation.) It was Byron Guilbert whose steps in life mattered. In spite of his innermost conflicts, Byron would do what was expected of him. He would marry Eugénie Duhon and assume the management of Le Petit Cottage so his father could drink bourbon, gamble at race-tracks, and read the old poets. Byron would produce heirs, preferably two, as neither his father nor grandfather had much luck in producing white heirs. In time, he would hand off the plantation to the next legal son, or daughter's husband if it came to that. He found the idea of producing legal heirs amusing. A legal heir, maybe two, would be all that he could muster, as he didn't share his father's or grandfather's lust for Black women, or for women of any color, for that matter.

To refuse or escape his life didn't occur to him. Neither of these choices was an option. But this moment, this reverie of stirred air and memory, made the impossibility he harbored within that much sweeter.

Lucien Guilbert climbed off Zuk, his pet name for Sucre, or Sugar. His maneuver from saddle to both feet on ground, inelegant. He had had nearly as many white horses named Sucre as he had had wives. He patted Zuk's butt and released her to the stable boy, a grandson of his own half brother Henri and the boy led the white horse off to graze. Henri. The only brother he had known. If Lucien stopped to consider the loss that Henri's wife and children felt after their husband and father ran away, it was only for a flicker in time. Thirty years later, the only injured person betrayed and bereft by the thoughtless act of the runaway, according to Lucien, was Lucien.

"*Bonjou,* monsieur." The house servants, Marie and Louise, dipped in unison and greeted Lucien as he entered through the front doors and strolled into the main room. Marie and Louise, twin sisters, owed their being to Lucien Guilbert. Nearly twenty years ago his business associate from France visited Le Petit Cottage and took their mother by force as she slept in the dormer set aside for house servants. (This incident and more pushed Madame to make certain the house servants lived in the quarter.) The monsieur, the father of Marie and Louise, made a point to visit his daughters when he returned to the parish of St. James.

Lucien grunted and walked past the

twins, leaving clumps of dirt on the floor and rugs. He stomped heavily up the stairs.

Madame Sylvie and Thisbe returned to the salon, expecting the visit, Madame on her throne, Thisbe at her side. The sound of Lucien's boots irritated Madame. She despised the dirt he brought into the house.

He entered the room of feminine decor, plastered in fading wallpaper.

"How goes the harvest, son?" Madame Sylvie asked.

Lucien didn't answer. His tan face seemed to darken.

"Not well?" she answered herself. "If things went well, you would dance for me. Then bathe, put on your good suit, and make plans for the racetrack or Madame Suzette's for tea," she continued matter-of-factly. "Whoring and gambling always put your father in a good mood. Sometimes not so good." She sought to make him laugh. She failed. "Son, my son. Why don't you believe me when I tell you it's not buried under the monuments?"

He walked over, mainly to track in

more dirt, and he kissed her on the cheek. "I got off old Zuk and helped to heave that stone myself. I had to try," he answered. "On the chance . . ."

"On the chance I lied? Lucien! You should believe me. I have no time for lies."

His laugh was muffled and angry. "I doubt if there's gold at all."

She clapped and laughed. "Don't give up! Not when the game is now fun!" Sylvie was in her glory. Color rose in her face. She felt young.

Lucien felt the opposite. A weary calm of resignation. "I've pulled hands away from the cane and wasted a day."

"You'll make up what you lost. You always do."

This was far from true. Lucien expected this willful ignorance of reality from his mother.

Sylvie changed her tone. "When the time is right, I will take you to your father's gold. All sixty-three thousand dollars' worth."

"Why wait, when your mind is sharp as the knife at my throat? You know every inch of these grounds. Tell me where it's buried and be done."

"And I will! I will," she sang.

Thisbe took in their exchange. She had a way of fixing her head, a slight downward tilt, so as not to favor either speaker or make eye contact. She had become skilled at taking in each word regardless of what was said, while not giving the appearance of listening. As always, she absorbed all that was given, with no plan of how to expend her store of knowledge. Her practiced perfection at invisibility was an art. Her posture, her stillness, and her blankness were as dear and urgent to her as breath itself. These simple arts became her tools for surviving one day, and then the next.

II

The master, or *maître* (in name only), had not been able to win these skirmishes with his mother. He didn't like to give her the satisfaction of his anger or frustration — a trait he learned from her! Defeated, he wished her a pleasant day and left the house to take refuge in his office, a small cottage close to the privy and the commissary. When he left, Marie and Louise rolled up the rug in the main room and brought it out on the lower porch to beat with their brooms.

Lucien removed his jacket, sat at his desk. He didn't open last week's letter from the Sisters of Mercy School for Girls, or the one that arrived before that. Somehow, he would find money for the good sisters to board and educate Rosalie, his only daughter. The good sisters did not hold Rosalie's mixed blood against her — unlike the girl's grandmother — but the Sisters of Mercy expected payment, and soon.

Instead of acknowledging his debt to the school, Lucien spread out his newspapers — the *Sugar Planter,* the *Louisiana Democrat,* and *Le Mésachébé* — which he perused in that order before they were used for kindling or taken outside to the privy.

He didn't know which took the worse toll on him: watching his men dig only to come up empty or waging the age-old battle with his mother, and also walking away with nothing. The newspapers gave him much-needed diversion. He scanned up and down the inky columns of print for announcements and legal pleadings. He searched for the family name among those listed on the "do not extend credit" list. He found the "Huberts" and the "Gilberts," but not the Guilberts. Safe, for now!

In his momentary relief, Lucien turned his mind to restocking the commissary and obtaining a line of credit. There was a time his plantation-owning neighbors, as spread out as they were, along with struggling piney woods farmers, some Choctaw Indians, some Irish and Germans encamped on riverbanks, and his enslaved laborers, would frequent the commissary to buy goods and rent tools and equipment. He still had rolls of gingham, wool, linen, and a bit of bombazine fabric, hoping wives of Irish ditch and levee workers would buy a few yards. It seemed a string of bad luck hit every other family just as hard as a wave of yellow fever had swept through the parish. No one seemed to have cash, only promissory notes and pride.

He combed through the barkers in print. Even at these good prices, he had to choose between shoes for some of his field hands to get through winter hoeing and replanting, and clothing for all. At least his field hands ate well enough, between their vegetable gardens and time off to fish. Could he afford to give his enslaved laborers that hour to cultivate vegetable gardens and muck up holes for crawdaddies? He needed his slaves fit and robust for work, but no one, particularly Lucien Guilbert, liked to see an idle

Black body when their rest cost him so much.

Lucien moved on to the *Louisiana Democrat*. He studied the legal notices, foreclosures, and sales of once prosperous, enviable plantations. He followed the accounts of poor harvests, disrepair, and plantation mismanagement. *Ah! Better the planter precedes the plantation in death than the reverse,* he thought. For the jaws and lips would jerk and flap to gossip and mourn over the unthinkable: the sale of field hands, house servants, good china, French tea and coffee services, sugarhouse equipment, horses, mules, cattle, pigs. The principal house. The land. Then there were the firsthand accounts of how the planter and mistress stole away in buggy and wagon. The good laughs to be had over those accounts were always mingled with the remembrances of the communion parties, waltzes, weddings, and funeral gatherings at the now foreclosed upon plantations.

Lucien hadn't opened the ledger since Byron had returned to St. James. This task of making entries and recording sales from the commissary now fell to

42

Byron when he was home, and not a moment too soon. Lucien could barely stand the dismal reality of the commissary's income: a cycle of pennies that went from him to his slaves and back to him. The commissary. Yet another business investment that failed to yield a real profit. Some of his slaves were savers, hard to part with a penny. He found this more so with the women, who wore their same dress in the field day in and day out, giving it a washing until threadbare, pushing its wear through another year.

In hard times he was forced to sell his more profitable slaves rather than hire them out. These included a dressmaker who'd made herself profitable by mimicking Parisian styles, and a wood-carving craftsman and son responsible for ornate bedposts, armoires, cabinets, and caskets. The father and son carvers, having learned their craft from their African ancestor, were relatives of his mother's servant, Thisbe, and were meant to be freed when Vié Pè passed on. *(Patience is not required, as that is yet another story.)*

This year's crop promised to rescue Lucien Guilbert from his debts; but these days, Lucien Guilbert, now master for the past thirty-five years, went to bed with worry, and always a flask of bourbon or whiskey.

Things were not yet dire, but everything was tied to a fraught little string. The banks nipped hungrily, and there were property taxes owed. The Guilberts could maintain for another year, but the harvest! The stalks rose and swelled under the sun, their juice threatening to rot if the cutting season was attacked too slowly. And then there was the risk of early frost. He preferred the assurances of his father's gold, buried decades ago, to the long list of hopes he relied upon: He hoped the newspapers would continue to omit from or misspell his name among the list of those denied credit. He hoped his mother would relinquish her hold on the plantation. He hoped she didn't suddenly expire — not until after relinquishing her hold on the plantation and telling him where the gold was located. He hoped to bring his quadroon daughter, Rosalie, home to Le Petit Cottage from the convent where she lived, and to cobble an engagement between her and Laurent Tournier. He further hoped Laurent Tournier would favor him with the use of his planting innovations to ensure an efficient harvest. He hoped women from smaller plantations would flock to the commissary to purchase his fabrics. He hoped to not sell more of the northern field. He hoped Colonel Duhon, under the influence of his sister-in-law, the countess, didn't find a more advantageous engagement for the Duhon girl when all had been arranged with Byron.

He was lucky to engage the boy to a decent family, let alone a well-connected one. As fine a boy as he was, Byron had been a failure in all the ways that would encourage back-slapping closeness between father and son. Lucien believed every man looks for himself in his son, just as every man is excited to also see what great things his son can accomplish. Unlike his own father, Lucien was literate and could navigate the social circles of Louisiana planter society, thanks to his mother. But like Vié Pè, he took to bourbon, cigars, racetracks, and creeping down to the cabins of his favorite Black females. But now, himself a father, Lucien lamented that he wouldn't have fatherly advice for Byron on which Black females to use and which to avoid. Unlike himself, Byron stopped short at one drink and couldn't be persuaded or shamed to drink more. As for taking a lantern to creep down to the quarter, Byron would rather read histories of famous battles. Good son that he was, Byron had pledged to save himself for his wedding night.

Lucien did not dwell on the disaster of the whorehouse in New Orleans some seven years ago. Perhaps the boy was too young — although he himself went about sexing Black females as early as he was able. He had completely put the incident of Byron's child's play with the cook's son near the bayou out of his mind.

Meanwhile, Lily, the cook, who ground corn, baked bread and cobblers, and hacked off antlers with a saw and butchered venison for deer sausage, hadn't forgotten. Even as she peeled, chopped, fried, baked, boiled, and roasted in the hellishly hot cookhouse, Lily hadn't forgotten a damn thing.

III

Madame Sylvie fell asleep in her chair after amusing herself with many games of solitaire. The kings, queens, and jacks were her faithful company. The stories the face cards told of their predicaments, their aspirations for foolish love, their greed, betrayals, and, in more cases than not, their downfalls, never failed to entertain her. Madame's daily visit with her royal courtiers was as important a routine to her as her nightly prayer to the Holy Mother.

Every morning after breakfast was served in Madame's salon, Thisbe would open the drawer where the cards were kept. She'd untie the pink satin ribbon, gently pull the bow loose, and make certain all the cards were accounted for. There was hell to pay if a card, no matter how lowly in rank, was missing from the deck. The task of counting the cards was enormous when Thisbe was six, but she taught herself to compare the cards by their likeness and to always remove the joker from the deck. Over time, Thisbe learned in her own way to count, multiply, subtract, and even to predict probable outcomes by paying close attention while Madame played. Once, the four of spades had gone missing and Thisbe was beaten for it. The card had been found in Madame's drawstring purse. For this reason, Thisbe learned to count the cards before setting them before her mistress, and to always watch Madame Sylvie closely.

Madame now snoring, Thisbe used this time to see to her own needs. She counted the cards and put them away, then tiptoed out of the salon, down the stairs, through the main room and the dining room, then through the pantry and out of the house.

The cookhouse was some forty feet from the back of the house. When Thisbe let herself in, she found the interior of the brick enclosure unbearable as always, its heat from pots boiling in the hearth and sparks crackling beneath a rabbit on a spit. Steam and smoke were everywhere. She had gone from the damnable heat under the sun into hell. Still, there was no other place she'd rather be, besides her family's cabin. Her family, all field hands, ate in the field when they were allowed their break. Eating with her family was out of the question. Thisbe had to remain close to, if not attached to, Madame. Lily, the cook, was forty feet away. Lily became her family.

Lily presided over the boiling and roasting, poker in one hand, ladle in the other. The sun streamed inside from the door opening and closing, but she didn't bother to turn and acknowledge her visitor. She let the sweat from beneath the tignon scarf wrapped around her head drip down her face, neck, and arms as she stirred and poked.

"Miss Lily," Thisbe said, although, at sixteen, she was old enough to speak Lily's name without a title. "I could eat half a hog."

"Dis Be," the cook said, always in that flat way of speaking. "Be glad to get this bacon fat."

To this, or to whatever Lily had to offer, Thisbe said, "Lawd knows I gives him de thanks. Lawd knows I gives it to you too, Miss Lily."

"Hush 'n eat if you hungry, Dis Be."

"Dis Be" ate but couldn't hush. She told Lily about *Mass' Loos'yn vexing Miss Sivee's nerves, digging up Ol' Pap's stone fo' dat gold and Mass' Byr'n as lackadaisical as a lub-sick dawg idling his time underneath that tree.*

"Don't care nothing 'bout no Mass' no Miss, no Byr'n," Lily said. She always said this, but she'd always look to Thisbe for a little more.

Thisbe knew her place with Lily, who was closer to her own mother's age. Thisbe talked her fill, but didn't put any questions to Lily, for the older woman wasn't the talking type. Thisbe, whose life was built around observing, could see there was something between Lily and Lucien Guilbert. But not the business that went on between master and females in the quarter. This was something more. Lily's face, large and seemingly unmovable, changed when Lucien was mentioned.

Thisbe rattled on, partly to exercise her mouth and thoughts in this safe enclosure, and partly to give Lily something different to focus on.

Miss Lily didn't try to be or speak Creole. Thisbe knew not to speak to Miss Lily in Black French Creole, Louisiana French Creole, French, or in white people's proper English. To speak to Miss Lily in those tongues would get her a stone face and a small plate. Le Petit Cottage held bond to many dark-skinned Creoles, but Miss Lily was not among them. Miss Lily was like Thisbe's mother and father and grandparents. Her people had been brought in chains from West Africa to Virginia, and then marched down to Louisiana. She was a Negro, when a polite term was called for. If Miss Lily's blood was mixed, it happened on the continent of her origin, among tribes whose names, enemies, and neighbors were no longer known.

Lily showed Thisbe what love she could. She made a healthy plate of food for the girl. And when Thisbe had to serve herself, Lily showed her which pots to eat out of and which to leave alone. After a while, Thisbe caught on that their food was tastier than the food prepared for the Guilberts.

Lily never said much. Never smiled. It wasn't her way to involve anyone in her thinking. Only Lily knew that, for Thisbe's sake, it was best to eat from the pots and skillets she had been told to eat from and to ask no questions.

Thisbe ate quickly, hugged Miss Lily, and ran back to the salon.

Thisbe, in service to Madame since the age of six, had been taught well how to serve her mistress. Most important, she knew her place — not in the given way between an enslaved person and master, but her peculiar place as Madame's personal servant. She was to stand at Madame's right-hand side, a half step behind wherever her mistress stood or sat so Madame didn't have to see her, but knew she was there. Thisbe, having no room or closet of her own, slept inside Madame's salon, her two dresses, nightgown, knit socks, and sundries in a small chest beneath the low trundle bed with African carvings for legs. She got Madame on and off the chamber pot and wiped her behind in the salon since Madame no longer made the two-hundred-foot walk to the privy. She bathed Madame with a basin and pitcher and dressed Madame. Before Madame slept and when she awoke, Thisbe brushed her hair with the same silver-plated brush Madame used to punish her with. In the mornings she parted Madame's thinning hair down the middle, brushed the hair down the sides of her face and swept it back, knotted, pinned, and netted the hair in the back in the style that Madame had worn for the past ten years. On holidays and for balls, Thisbe fastened hairpieces to make her hair grand. These days she applied white powder to Madame's face and neck and rouge to Madame's cheeks. If visitors were expected, she used a fine brush to

paint coal over Madame's gray, thinning
brows.

IV

Meanwhile, three miles up the river road, at the Lavender Plantation, so named for its rows of French lavender, the postman slouched over his mule with cause to worry. He carried letters from law offices and banks for Madame Chatham. Letters that required an X, although Juliette Chatham always signed her name in a full curvaceous script. Much to his dread, he spied the Chatham girl astride her British charger.

Three hundred feet away, she had him in her sights. The old man was a slow-moving target but a target nonetheless for Jane and her warhorse, Virginia Wilder.

Jane Chatham, clad in her dead father's military jacket and britches, crouched low on her charger. She began with a trot and jumped the marble lovers bench flanked by wisteria. The trot was now a breaking gallop. Girl and horse did as much damage to the grounds as they could, kicking up lavender, crabgrass, and dirt in pursuit of the target. Jane didn't mind the dirt hitting her in the face. She gritted her teeth and gave a yell.

What could he do? He on a mule, she on a hard-charging horse? His mule, frightened and licked, backed up and made an unintelligible sound, a half bray, half choking whinny of a complaint and surrender.

"Now listen here, missy," the man yelled at Jane. The postman meant to stand up to her, but she and her horse corralled him, circling man and mule in a lasso of dust that caused the mule to kick, and the postman to pitch forward and fall to the ground, along with the canvas sack of small parcels and envelopes.

Jane, a self-taught trick rider, jumped off her Virginia Wilder, scooped up the satchel, remounted, and rode back toward the house, ignoring the postman's demands that she and her accomplice return the "dadgummit Post Office Department satchel!" He wasn't about to stand for disrespect from any planter's daughter.

He had had enough. This wasn't the first time she, and barely a she in his opinion, had ridden up on him and his mule. Something must be done. The major offense, the theft of the Post Office Department mail, was serious, punishable by imprisonment. However, it was the act of a female wearing britches and a man's war jacket, and that she straddled the horse, as opposed to riding sidesaddle as a lady would, that outraged him. The very picture of her, down to that strange haircut, was both masculine and indecent. He didn't care that she was a high-toned white Creole planter's daughter. The postman would lodge his complaint with the authorities.

Jane, on the other hand, was satisfied by her morning exercise. She rode Virginia Wilder to the shade of a red gum tree, took the satchel, and sat down. It would be awhile before the postman and his mule caught up to her. And awhile before Madame Chatham would be made aware of Jane's latest episode. Madame Chatham was busy with her morning toilette, a routine Jane couldn't be persuaded to adopt. Pluck. Brush. Apply hair clips, powders, perfumes, and rouges. Jane was concerned with other things. She fished through the canvas bag and removed the envelopes addressed to her mother from the bank, attorneys, and from her sisters, one postmarked from France, the others from South Carolina and Houma. If tearing up the envelopes from the bank and attorneys and letting the wind, scant as it was, carry the pieces to the fields and the river would stop the sale of the Lavender Plantation, Jane would have torn the envelopes. Time wasn't on Jane's side. Nothing could be done about the sale.

She climbed back on her horse, trotted out to the postman, who hadn't moved much beyond the spot where she had left him, and tossed the satchel at the mule's hooves.

The postman cursed and threatened to bring action against her and to have the horse put down. Jane said nothing to the ranting postman. Virginia Wilder, however, gave a few teeth-baring whinnies.

Madame Chatham would learn of her daughter's charge at the postman soon enough.

V

Byron kept the door to the commissary open. His idea of his summer break from West Point, or furlough, didn't include standing behind the counter of his father's store walled in by sacks of goods, equipment for rent or purchase, fabrics, and sundries. What could he do? There was no one else to manage the cashbook and accounts, and lately there was little to manage. He would welcome a customer. Any customer. Even those with promises to pay. For this reason, he was seldom without his books of chemistry, astronomy, and tactics of infantry. He began with astronomy, a science less romantic than he had imagined. He reached a sentence that was too complex to sweep over when he looked away for perspective and caught sight of the postman on his mule, riding slowly toward the small building.

The postman! Byron's spirits rose. He cursed himself for getting his hopes up, yet uttered "Dear God" in spite of himself. Hope created misery, followed by disappointment. He knew he would kick himself for hoping, and then resume hoping the next week, kick himself, and hope again. Still, Byron managed to smile at the sour-faced man when he came into view and slid off the mule.

"Afternoon!" Byron said.

"Let me tell you," the man began without returning a greeting. "Done fought the British. The Seminoles. With the Choctaws. Side by side with and against the Creek Indians. Side by side with some free niggers, even. Yessuh. But it's that dadblamed Chatham gal to drain the life from me."

Byron didn't bother with astonishment. "What has she done now?"

The postman handed him a newspaper and a few envelopes, the topmost envelope addressed to Lucien Guilbert and marked "Urgent Attention." In a quick fanning of the envelopes, Byron saw what he had hoped to see. An Ohio postmark. A particular penmanship.

The postman had been rambling. "I'm not ashamed to admit I'm a lonesome feller. Never met a woman who'd have me. But I wouldn't marry that Chatham gal if she came with a plantation and fifty niggers."

"Nor would I," Byron agreed. "Nor would I, sir."

"You bet you wouldn't," he said. "No man would."

"Had yourself a hard morning over at the Lavender?" Byron asked. "Tell you what. Ride on back to the cookhouse. See what Cook has for you. Tell her Byron says to treat you right."

The postman tipped his hat. "Grateful, Mr. Gilbert. Sure am grateful."

"Byron," the young man insisted, knowing the older man wouldn't overstep. "And take that mule to the stable. Let our boy take care of that old girl."

"Yessuh. Much appreciated, Mr. Gilbert." The postman tipped his hat again and was on his way to the stable.

With the postman sent off for refreshment, Byron beheld his envelope bearing the Ohio postmark. Ohio wasn't the permanent residence of Robinson Pearce, his friend and fellow third-year cadet. Ohio was where Robinson Pearce lodged at the time of the writing. Somewhere upland along the river. He took out his pocketknife, slid the sharp edge into the corner of the envelope, and carefully tore it open to preserve the paper sheath.

B.

Much to share of past and current travels, all dulled by your absence. Will arrive in Baton Rouge by steamer, Monday July 16th. Impatiently.

P.

A handful of words and Byron pushed aside astronomy, chemistry, and tactics of infantry to read and reread the note, giving attention to each phrase.

Lily didn't hide her displeasure when the stringy-haired white man showed up at the door demanding to be fed. In every way she wasn't suited for housework or servitude. But then, the cookhouse was its own place, both hell and sanctuary. Even in the performance of obedience in doing her work, she couldn't feign a docile appearance. Hers was a face that didn't change or animate. If a weary traveler was in need of a cook who fussed, cajoled, and overwhelmed with love, that traveler was better off tapping doors of other plantations along the river road. Lily couldn't be made to smile. She was this way when Lucien accepted her as payment in a card game, and she had little cause to change over twenty years at Le Petit Cottage. She was but ten when her master swore to Lucien, "She'll be a top breeder soon's she gets to bleeding. I solemnly swear on the book of Genesis, God made such a beast to breed mighty giants!" Lucien put her on his wagon and brought her to the plantation, where Hannah, an older woman, took charge of her. Hannah, who had come to the Louisiana shores in chains and leg irons, recognized something in the girl. Hannah, with memory of her original people and their ways intact, recognized what the large, unmoving girl was: *Most*

Desired One. As in, any Akan son's mother would bring the most extravagant gifts with her to knock on the door of the sought-after girl's parents. Bride or queen. Hannah recognized the girl as one who didn't move, but from her throne moved everyone around her. The girl might never have set foot on West African soil, or known about her origins, but Hannah knew. Hannah, childless Hannah, took the girl, not to mother her, but to serve her.

The postman, now in the presence of a "nigger," no matter how big, stood ready to reclaim his trod-upon dignity. His paw-paw had owned a few Black field hands during good times, although he himself wasn't to know those good times as a man. The postman's belly ached, and his pride was in need of uplifting. He might not have owned any Blacks, but he was a white man. That counted for something.

"My refreshments," he told her. "And a cool drink."

She pointed to the outside. "Set out on the step."

He gathered his mouth to object to her

tone. Her words. Her audacity.

She did not seem to care. "Go'n. Set out there."

"When I tells Master Byron and Master Lucien, that'll be yore hide."

She remained unmoved. "Go'n. Set."

He turned, kicked the door, went outside, and dropped on the steps. He'd tell, all right. Might even get the first crack at her big Black self. And he'd whip her from the front where skin was soft and she might could even die. He'd tell.

At thirteen Lily's shoulders were broader than any man's on the plantation. Her legs thick as trunks from thigh to ankle, her arms to match. She had a big face the shape of a three-pound sack of coffee beans. She ate no more than any other field hand, and Hannah defended Lily against anyone who claimed otherwise.

Men in their teens and older wanted Lily, but it was a gentle, older field hand who brought her meat wrapped in cabbage and roughly made cakes he had thrown into a hearth fire himself. He laid her down in the field and entered her as tenderly as he could restrain himself to do. Hannah knew right away Lily was pregnant and rejoiced for this chance to cradle a child.

Typically, a girl around thirteen, fourteen, wondered when Master Lucien would get around to spoiling their chances of saving themselves for their future husbands. But Lucien had plans for Lily, such grand plans that even he wouldn't ruin her product. Imagine, a gal such as she, who could grow big, not by filling her belly with his fish, pork, rice, and vegetables, but because it was as God had intended; she was meant to breed Negroes as large as giants, able to work like machines, impervious to human need and frailty. That's what her former master had promised; that's what Lucien had accepted. Yes! He had shared his plan with Arne Pierpont, across the river on the east side, and they struck a gentleman's agreement. Lucien would get the first offspring and Pierpont would get the next. If twins, which in their thinking was possible, they would each have one. Guilbert and Pierpont often traveled by barge and traded machinery, and rented each other's bulls, stallions, and hogs for stud purposes. They could also conduct a profitable husbandry between their two-legged livestock.

Lily wasn't privy to their gentlemen's agreement, but the master had planned some entertainment and a long-term capital investment for himself and Arne Pierpont, master of the Pierpont Plantation. When he had the overseer gather Lily up one Saturday night, Hannah feared it was to deliver her to a new home, a new plantation. She thought she had seen her queen, her adopted granddaughter, for the last time. Hannah didn't know Lily would be going down the road and on a barge across the river to Pierpont's plantation.

Lily got up on the wagon and hugged her belly.

Lucien had brought two bottles of his best bourbon from his reserve to share with Pierpont. He was excited to deliver the big girl.

Arne Pierpont was astounded when he saw the girl. Astounded that, for a change, Lucien Guilbert hadn't exaggerated the girl's magnificence. Why, she could be rented to a traveling show or circus and make good money, as gawkers wouldn't be able to look away from her unusually large parts. Pierpont turned and patted the backside of his chosen man, impressively tall and broad, of about twenty, and gave him a few words of encouragement. Master Guilbert was immediately taken by the young Black man's size. Both men congratulated each other on the size and overall health of the couple. They further congratulated each other on their anticipated profits and agreed to meet ten months from the date to pair the two for the next litter. The gentlemen smoked their cigars, drank bourbon, and shouted instructions, mainly at the young man to "Go at her again."

When the husbandry was finished, Lily was told to stay on her back with her legs up to keep the investors' seed intact. There was much drunken jubilation between the two planters. They marveled, cackled, poked, and slapped at her as she lay on her back, legs up. When they decided that their investment had been firmly planted in ground, the drunken men, with the help of Pierpont's man, pushed the girl up and onto the wagon. The gentlemen tipped their hats to each other, and then Lucien and the girl, Lily, were on their way.

"Yuh did fine, boy," Master Pierpont told the young man. "Just fine. We'll get some strong *négrillon* out of her for certain."

"I done the bes I can for you, Master," he said. "But she already big."

"Now, now," Master Pierpont said, feeling jovial. "That's no way to talk 'bout the woman done give you your way."

"She give me my way," he said. "But she give someone else their way too. The little feller in her kicked me fierce every time I done my work in her."

Master Pierpont cursed in every ungentlemanly way he could summon. Early, before morning broke, Pierpont arrived at Le Petit Cottage, where he found Lucien among the row of small cabins, and laid his accusations on Lucien. "What are you trying to pull? That cow is already seeded."

Lucien could barely comprehend his

ranting but matched him in his ungentlemanly cursing.

Hannah heard the commotion and appeared from the cabin she shared with Lily. Knowing the girl barely spoke, Hannah spoke up for her. "Master," Hannah said. "I'da told you she big. Hannah never lied to you. Never! You knows better, Master. But hain't no one asked if Lily big. Hain't no one said what you want with her." She purposely spoke like a know-nothing nigger, eyes wide.

It worked.

The two almost fell over each other, laughing. They took turns mocking Hannah, bucking their eyes. "Hain't no one asked," one said. "Hain't no one said what you want with her," the other said. And they'd start it up again. Better the cussing and accusing gave way to laughter than to have gloves slapping faces and pistols drawn at dawn. Lucien said, "What do we gentlemen look like, dueling over a dumb cow? Your man wasn't injured by the loss of an offspring."

"He wasn't injured at all, from the looks of things," Pierpont said. "And the big wench seemed to be agreeable." They went on, congratulating each other in spite of the disappointment.

Hannah had stopped the two planters from killing each other, but she couldn't save Lily from the whip. Hannah had no choice but to take down Lily's top and help her to her knees, while Lily bared her back to the men.

Guilbert extended to Pierpont the courtesy of cracking the whip. Mr. Pierpont was a good aim and lashed his big target six times, good enough to splay open the skin and stream blood down her back and legs, but not so devastating that she couldn't return to the cane field. This made things right between the two men.

Hannah got a mixture of clay and herbs for the gashes on Lily's back, and water and rags to prepare for what must be done for a woman who would soon lose her unborn baby. She would tend to the cleaning, the care of the mother, the gashes the whip left on the mother, and then later, begin the brief funeral song for the spirit of the unnamed baby, and tend to the burial of the baby's body.

It took a gang of women to get Lily up

and to her pallet on her side. Her back was split open, so she had to stay on her side. As soon as the baby was expelled and Hannah was done cleaning and tending to her, she would let Lily lie on her empty belly. But when Hannah examined her, touching her belly and checking her thighs for blood, she said, "Lily. Lily. Got to stay on your side. If the child don't slip out come sundown, the child's here to stay."

Lily opened the door with plate and cup in hand. Not the plate and cup that she or Dis Be ate and drank from, but the tin plate and cup used for anyone not welcome to sit and eat inside the house.

Hunger got the best of the postman. He was grateful to get the fish, biscuits and gravy, and the sweetened mint iced tea to wash it down. He didn't go so far as to thank Lily, but he asked for another plate and wolfed it down as fast as he had eaten the first one.

VI

The dining room was large, mirroring the adjacent main parlor room in size. It was built to Bayard Guilbert's specifications to appease his wife, an ideal room for Sylvie to comfortably entertain a gathering of at least twenty guests. It had been two years since Madame had written invitations to a dinner party, and these days, no one came to call on the Guilberts. In fact, if there was to be a Duhon-Guilbert wedding, it would be hosted at the Duhon Plantation and not at Le Petit Cottage. Without the buzzing and flutter of invited guests for parties and funerals, the dining room, its grand table, and the main parlor all seemed too large for the needs of the Guilberts.

Thisbe seated Madame Sylvie at one end of the table to face her son at the opposite end. She stood to Madame's right. Byron sat between his grandmother and father.

Marie and Louise entered through the pantry carrying platters and a tureen, heavy with hot food. The two were annoyed by Madame's servant and that they must maneuver around the useless standing girl while they served the supper. Thisbe didn't help in any way. She did nothing for Madame but refill her water and wine glasses and pick up whatever Madame dropped to the floor. She stood next to Madame until she was told to move to the corner to pull the punkah back and forth over the table to cool the diners.

"Useless," one whispered to the other in Creole. Theirs was a continuous job of service. Scrubbing, wiping, polishing, dusting, beating dirt in every room of the house except one — the sainted Charlotte Thérèse's room. Charlotte Thérèse, the only daughter of Madame Sylvie to survive birth, had succumbed to yellow fever at almost thirteen, some forty years ago. The twins were forbidden to touch the doorknob, let alone enter the room.

What did they care? They had enough to contend with. Marie and Louise dealt with the surly Black cook, took the backside slaps of the Master, and were grateful those slaps and sometimes pinches were the extent of his attentions. They repaired curtains, bedspreads, and cushions. And here was this girl whose day was spent standing like a young tree with little to do but grow darker.

"Was that the postman with the mail?" Madame asked. Clearly, she knew the answer. Only a rainstorm could keep her away from her outdoor perch.

"Yes, Grandmère."

"What news is there?"

Lucien sang, "The banks want more money. I got no cash! Doodah! Doodah!" That he sang in English an unabashedly American tune of Stephen Foster was meant to raise his mother's ire.

Madame, not taking the bait, waved her hand to dismiss her son. "Let the banks wait for the harvest." She kept her focus on Byron. "And you, Byron. Did you receive any news? Any letters?"

He sighed. That would only make her

press more. "Yes, Grandmère."

"Good!" Madame said. "Read the letter, if you will."

Ordinarily, it would be no issue to read a letter, especially one from Eugénie. Since Byron had been home, he had received letters from his fiancée informing him of the comings and goings of relatives visiting from France. Her father's worsening or improving gout. Her progress in mastering the Viennese composers. These letters, all hand-delivered by a Black boy who was to wait while Byron dashed off a reply, would have been happily shared at the dinner table for his grandmother's and father's amusement.

This time Byron groused at the request.

"Grandmère, you said *if* I will. I won't."

"Oof!" Some rice spat out of Lucien's mouth. Marie stepped forward to wipe up the rice, tucked it in her pocket, and stepped back next to her sister against the wall.

Thisbe could laugh! She didn't. Madame's hairbrush would be waiting for her later, but more to the point, she didn't want to make herself seen. She fought off the impulse to smile or giggle and kept her eyes dull.

Madame pouted. "Why do you deny your grandmother this small thing? A piece of society. What goes on in the world?"

"Byron," his father said dryly, "read it and be done. Tell her about map reading and surveying or Duhon's gout. Fill your grandmother with all the juicy bits of society she craves."

Byron expelled a sharp breath. What more could they want?

"Grandmère, the letter itself is too brief to retrieve for the sole purpose of reading. Instead, let me tell you its contents."

"Tell!" Madame exclaimed.

Another sharp breath. "My classmate Robinson Pearce is finishing his travels and will stop here to visit."

Madame Sylvie wet her lips in anticipation. Byron almost felt sorry for her. But she *was* intruding on his privacy and his reverie.

She tapped her fork tines against the plate to stress an urgency. She needed more information. "Pearce. Pearce. Rob-inson Pearce." She seemed to chew his name in quick bites.

"He recites quite well in French class. You'll like him."

"But that means he isn't French, no?" she asked. "Pearce. Pearce. Is he English? German? No. Scot?" She stopped as if she tasted something unpleasant. *"Amree-cain?"*

"A Yankee!" Lucien chimed in. "Jour-neying down the Mississippi for real hospitality? Let him come."

"Good, Father. He's not been south of Ohio and I'd like to show him our way of life. He'll stay until we return to the Academy. We'll make our journey upriver together."

Lucien's expression changed. "That's" — he calculated — "five weeks. Five weeks of hospitality, pigeons, pork, and wine."

"And a waltz!" Madame exclaimed. "We should host one waltz and fill the room with young people. Give daughters a chance to show themselves to a new suitor."

Byron laughed. "Suitor! Grandmère, my friend will be here for five weeks and for me only."

"Good Lord," Lucien said. "How my pockets bleed cash!"

Byron disregarded his father's complaint and continued his own complaint with his grandmother. "You have him waltzing with every plantation daughter between the Lavender and the Tournier Plantation!"

"No, no," Madame said. "There's but one daughter at the Lavender, and the Tournier daughter is now married two years, although I received no invitation."

Byron threw up his hands.

Sylvie didn't care about Byron's objections. Suddenly, she was lively. Filled with purpose. "Now, tell us, Byron. What about his family? If not French, how do they make their wealth? Leave it to me. I will spread the word in the most discreet but effective way. Mothers will fight for an opportunity for their daughters. No! The Pierpont sisters. I would love to hear Lucille Pierpont thank me. Yes! He is meant for one of them. Neither a beauty, but what a dowry between them!"

"Grandmère. My sweet, insistent *grandmère*. When did my Pearce become yours to trade?"

"Just tell me what I must know so I can go about making preparations. What do they own? How many slaves? Hmm. Yankee. Perhaps just a household staff. A carriage driver. Two groundsmen. A cook. And the rest to do whatever work their business entails. Ten. Would you say Robinson's family owns at least ten Blacks?"

"I can't say."

Madame threw her roll, hitting Byron's cheek. The roll fell to the floor. Louise swept around to Byron, picked up the roll, and slipped it in her apron, a treat for her children. She presented Byron with the dish of rolls, and then returned to her place next to Marie.

"There must be something about him. Why else would you invite him to stay?"

Byron put on a serious face, a sign of mischief, read by Lucien, who smiled. Byron said, "Of all of us third-year cadets, he is thought to be beautiful."

Lucien laughed.

Madame scoffed. "Beautiful. What is that? Even for a girl, 'beautiful' is not enough."

"Now, now, *mô shè* Momanm!" Lucien switched to using the Creole term to further irritate his mother. Momanm was what he called the Black mother of his half brother Henri as the two boys were inseparable as children. Henri and his dark-skinned mother — thorns in Madame's side. Lucien knew where to aim his dart. "Many a planter's daughter has swooned and begged her father to make a match with a beautiful face."

She returned quickly to ignore the wound, "And many a mother has wiped a flood of tears and rushed to the lawyer to protect what's left of the dowry."

Byron rolled his eyes. This was an old squabble that began long before he was born, having to do with his father's youth and the former Juliette Boisvert, now the widow Chatham.

"I've said more than he wrote, Grandmère. I'm thinking of you."

Lucien raised his glass.

"I only wish to spare you the disappointment. And to guard my privacy."

Madame tossed her head. "Hmph. Privacy." She smiled at Byron and clapped her hands in a resolution. It was settled. There would be a waltz in honor of Robinson Pearce, his background and character notwithstanding; her son's ability to feed and entertain the honored guest notwithstanding; her grandson's unwillingness to share his companion of no importance. Her prayers, in part, would be answered. Madame Guilbert was determined to make Le Petit Cottage a satellite of gay society one last time before completely retiring from the public.

It was no longer practical for Thisbe to slip down to the quarter and sleep among her mother, father, and sisters. She was no help to her mother, as she hadn't been taught to do anything but stand next to Madame Sylvie and wipe Madame's behind. Instead, Thisbe slept on the trundle bed at the foot of Madame's four-poster bed. Thisbe learned early she was not to leave Madame's side for any length of time, unlike those who worked the cane, who, by mandate of the church, had Sundays off. If she wasn't in the room when her mistress woke to use the chamber pot, or when Madame needed water or more fanning, the next morning young Byron would, at his grandmother's instruction, give Thisbe two lashes, her clothing removed to spare the linen pinafore she wore as a young girl.

Thisbe undressed Madame at the vanity, helped her into her nightgown, brushed and combed her hair, plaiting it into four braids, and then slipped the muslin bonnet over her head. She steadied Madame up the footstool and into her bed. Once Madame was in bed, Thisbe knelt at the velvet prie-dieu that stood next to the bed, her arms on the padded rests, hands clasped, and head bowed. Madame herself stopped kneeling for prayer the night she took Thisbe from her parents' cabin. Every night since then Thisbe knelt while Madame recited a session of Hail Marys in remembrance of her dead parents and her dead sainted babies. A special prayer was said for her daughter, Charlotte Thérèse, and yet another said for her foster mother, the executed queen of France. (No prayer, however, was said for her girlhood friend Marie-Thérèse Charlotte, who had managed to survive the Revolution and the guillotine but failed to dispatch an army to rescue young Sylvie from her peasant-farmer-abductor husband.) Madame dozed off in the middle of her prayer for Marie Antoinette but was then revived by Thisbe's well-timed cough. She ended her prayer without asking for forgiveness, but instead petitioned for her longevity and for protection while she achieved her earthly purposes — one such purpose, to sit for her portrait. Both Madame and Thisbe said "Amen" when prayer was finished. Thisbe then closed the mosquito netting that hung from an iron ring above the bed and fanned Madame with a funeral fan, a picture of the Holy Mother on one side, the Hail Mary printed on the other side, until Madame snored.

Thisbe undressed. She untied and removed her black leather boots and cursed them, *the tight black jailers.* Then last, she set the basin of Madame's used

water on the floor by her bed and soaked
her feet.

VII

The following late morning, Madame sat in the gallery. She watched Byron leave the garçonnière and was certain he was on his way to the small outbuilding where the Guilberts sold goods, mainly to enslaved people on their plantation, these days.

"Thisbe."

"Yes, Madame Sylvie."

"Go to Byron's room. Open his desk and bring me his letter."

Thisbe hesitated for a number of reasons.

Madame waved her fan at her. "Go. Now."

"Yes, Madame." She left the gallery and salon, went downstairs, and hurried past Marie and Louise, who noted Thisbe's haste. They poked each other as Thisbe skipped by and left the house.

"Galopé, la fille. Va chèché!" Marie said of the girl who was always running off to "go and get" for Madame.

"Non," Louise disagreed. *"Galopé, 'tit chien! Chèché!"* The joke wasn't complete without likening Madame's servant to a dog, running here and there.

Thisbe didn't have to hear them clearly to know they laughed at her. She didn't have to think hard about the differences between herself and the sisters. They were house servants, but Thisbe served Madame Sylvie only, and Marie and Louise served the house. Thisbe, sixteen, had no man or babies. Marie and Louise, eighteen, had married twin brothers and would give birth to a second set of babies, twins for both, in five months' time. Thisbe was unambiguously descended from Africans, while Marie and Louise were Creole mulattoes — their father, a visiting Parisian and associate of Lucien; their mother, unfortunately, a Black Creole woman in that man's sights. In any other Creole household, Marie and Louise would have been playmates and personal servants to the young masters and mistresses. But Madame Sylvie went to lengths to run Le Petit Cottage as she wanted her household to be run. This meant having a household where people of color were not tempted to believe themselves to be white or near white.

Thisbe couldn't think about Marie and Louise. She was sent to do something that could only create trouble for her. She couldn't drag her feet. With Madame watching her from the gallery, Thisbe marched to the garçonnière.

She had never entered the short round tower that rose to a point. There was no reason for her to enter the two-story building, an apartment for boys in their teen years to be apart from their families. It was Marie's and Louise's duty to collect the linens, make the bed, sweep, dust, and empty Byron's *pot de chambre.* Except for Madame's daily practice to look to the tower, as if to will her grandson to show himself, Thisbe wouldn't notice the tower at all.

She entered the open archway of the ground floor, which was more stairwell than room, gathered her skirt and apron, and climbed the spiraling cedar staircase leading to the chamber where Byron slept. She felt herself suddenly in a foreign place, used as she was to perfume, powder, and the scent of freshly cut flowers. The male smell, even with pine scents placed in drawers, was a distinct one. Strong. The room itself called for little housework, without a piece out of place. One might think it was the West Point regimen that made Byron fastidious, but this tidiness had been his habit long before he was accepted into the Academy. All of his items — pitcher, basin, books, pens, inkwell, combs, brushes, scissors, razor, and soap — were displayed on the desk and nightstand as if never used.

Thisbe went to the desk but saw no paper nor envelope to handily snatch and be gone. So now, she must do what she would never do without Madame's orders. She hesitated. The name and pleading face of Joséphine, a former housemaid, came to her mind. Joséphine's crime of opening a drawer and having nothing to put in it, such as laundry, convicted her of stealing and sentenced her to a slap from Madame, five lashes from Lucien Guilbert, and a swift sale to a hardworking farm.

Madame had sent Thisbe and told her to bring the letter. That was true. But there was another concern. Which letter was she to take, and how was she to know Pearce's letter, if asked? Thisbe hadn't been instructed in reading. She had never read a book. But in her service to Madame, she had collected a few words when Madame asked for these labeled items. Even Madame had unwittingly provided a rudimentary education when she asked for her favorite books and had to write the markings — misspelled as they were — for the girl to retrieve them. One day, the markings on the playing cards, *A, K, Q,* and *J,* spoke to her as she stood at Madame's side for hours watching the ace, king, queen, and jack slide from row to row. It was a task to keep her face dumb when noise of markings and eventually words clamored in her ears. She absorbed hungrily.

For now, she opened the drawer. Byron didn't hold on to many treasures, but he did have two stacks of envelopes. Which would she take? Or should she take both? She saw the envelope Madame wanted, on top of the small stack of envelopes, but she couldn't take it. The envelope with the July postmark, this month being Jul, or July. She couldn't let Madame know how well she had taught her to read. She had heard white men at Madame's church say with venom, "A reading slave is a yellow fever, to spread and corrupt the rest."

She decided to take both stacks of envelopes and let Madame choose the right letter.

Perhaps it was the blood pounding in Thisbe's eardrums that made her momentarily deaf. Byron's footsteps were not heavy like his father's. She didn't hear him enter the tower below or climb the stairs. By the time she heard him it was too late.

He rushed at her, grabbed a piece of her blouse, and threw her away from his desk, against the side of the bed to the floor in a single motion, tearing her sleeve. She fell awkwardly on her hip and had snatched the bedding as she tried to break her fall.

"What are you doing?"

Whipped. Sold. Her fate was clear to her.

He raised his hand to slap her. "Tell me! What are you doing here?"

She found her tongue and spoke quickly. "Madame sent me."

"Sent you? To my room? Don't lie to me, girl!"

She looked helplessly around. To herself she thought, *Beg in Creole for mercy, not French. Not too proper.* "The papers, *M'sié* Byron," she began. "Madame told me to bring to her the letters. I don't know one letter from the other, *M'sié.* So I took the papers I see," she said in desperation. *"Pitié, M'sié Guilbert. Pitié!"* She kept her hands close to her face.

"Get out! Get out! And I'll never see you in this room again."

"Yes, *M'sié.* Yes." She picked herself up carefully, feeling the ache of being thrown to the floor. She knew better than to look into his eyes. She clutched her torn blouse and backed out of the room, to the staircase.

■ ■ ■ ■

Lucien happened to ride up from the cane field to the commissary and found it unattended. It didn't matter that no one came to buy coffee beans, thread, or fabric. The boy was supposed to be there to manage the store. Lucien diverted his horse to the garçonnière. It was on the trot to the tower that he saw his mother's servant, fleeing his son's quarters. "Whoa, Zuk," he told his horse. He noted Thisbe's awkward movement and her ripped blouse. He sat on Zuk for a moment. Then he smiled. He had come to scold the boy for leaving the commissary unattended. But what he had seen had changed the substance and delivery of his speech entirely.

This was a cause for celebration. He trotted around to the back of the house and went to the pantry. He went down into the cellar, to his reserve rack, and took a bottle of Armagnac — this bottle not distilled in the States but in France. This very spirit was the drink he planned to toast with Byron on the morning of his son's wedding to Colonel Duhon's daughter. But this joyful occasion! This unexpected occasion put Lucien's creeping concerns away. Now all was right! Lucien exhaled heavily. He had always told himself of his son, "He'll grow into himself." Lucien believed that military school and prostitutes would correct a mistake in nature. Two years away from home proved him right. With the sight of his mother's maidservant, dress ripped and limping, Lucien could scarcely contain his joy.

He climbed the wooden stairs, knocked on his son's door, two cigars in one hand, the reserve bottle in the other.

Byron had just pissed into the pot de chambre and hadn't finished buttoning his trousers when he heard the knock on the door. He was still cross. The nerve of his grandmother, sending her nigger to invade his privacy. He opened the door, surprised to see his father grinning and carrying a bottle and cigars.

"Father?"

Lucien laughed, a big "ha! ha!" laugh, deep and knowing. He marched past his son and swaggered into the room, inspecting the quaint space, noting first the bedding still askew. "My boy! My boy!" he exclaimed.

Lucien broke open the seal on the bottle and offered it to Byron, who didn't accept the drink and was now confused.

"I see she went limping like a lamb gored by a bull."

"Father?" he repeated.

"There's no honor to protect," the older man said. "These things are expected, if not demanded of the planter's son."

He plunked the bottle down hard on the desk and handed Byron a cigar.

"Tell me how you gored her — this not being the first time. Of course not! A bull in the garçonnière! I knew it. I had my doubts, but I knew you had it in you. Your grandfather and I raised our horns in our day. And to think! Before this summer's gone, father and son will go a-wenching in the quarter!" This, he vowed, knowing that the lack of effective cures for his case of unidentified penile ailments rendered his vow hollow.

Byron didn't know what to say.

"We'll keep this from your grand-

mother. Your dear, sweet grandmother."
Byron took that as he meant it. Sarcasm.

Lucien was full of the devil and glee.
This time he laughed at his mother and
her explicit instructions that her maid
was not to be touched. It tickled him so
much that he laughed with all-out hearty
pleasure. "We'll keep this from her until
it can't be kept. Mother's sight is not so
sharp, but even she will see the maid's
belly swelling with her great-grandchild!
Hoo, son! You have no idea what a gift
you give me today. You do me proud."

Byron thought there was nothing he
could do but enjoy his father's gifts and
jubilation. He bit off the end of the cigar
and helped his father fill the room with
smoke.

Madame saw the girl limp across the
lawn. She turned to the door, anticipat-
ing the cache of letters. How she would
enjoy the exchanges between Byron and
his friends, or letters between Byron and
Eugénie, his soon-to-be fiancée. From
what she had observed, theirs was a careful, if not timid, dance of conversation
and romance — and not so much that

their flame would die too soon. While she had been denied the intricate dance of courtship herself, she hoped to experience a bit of that joy through her grandson's courtship and engagement. Heaven only knew her son had denied her that joy at every turn. And of course, her beloved daughter, Charlotte Thérèse, taken from her much too soon.

No. Sylvie couldn't dwell on her losses. Not when she heard the girl padding up the stairs. Her anticipation was so great she could barely hold her urine.

"Come, girl. Let me see!"

Thisbe stood before her, trembling and empty-handed.

"Where are the letters?"

"Madame, Monsieur Byron came back. He took them." She reverted to the French that Madame expected. Demanded.

"And why are your clothes torn?"

"Madame, Monsieur Byron, he tore them."

Thisbe didn't wait for Madame to motion her forward. She stood at Madame's side, extended her hand, and took her thrash on the hand, this time courtesy of Madame's pearl-handled fan. She knew it would come, but she cried out, mainly to satisfy Madame. Madame stopped beating her.

"What else did he do to you?" Madame demanded.

"He pushed me, Madame Sylvie."

"I don't care about that. Did he touch you? Did he put it in you? You cannot enter the room of a saint if you are unclean."

Thisbe shook her head no.

Madame raised her fan.

She spoke up. "No, Madame Sylvie. No. Monsieur Byron did not do that."

"If you are unclean you cannot enter the room of Saint Charlotte Thérèse, clean her statue, or kneel for me before the Holy Mother. Do not lie to me, Thisbe."

"No, Madame Sylvie. I don't lie."

Madame looked at the blouse, the sleeve torn from its bodice. She studied the trembling girl. "You can't stand here looking like a whore. Give that" — she pointed to the blouse — "to Marie and Louise to fix. Now."

Marie and Louise weren't happy to stop their work to repair Thisbe's blouse. This unexpected task only added time to a workday that wouldn't end until the Guilberts were fed and the dishes, glasses, platters, and silverware were washed for the next day. And then, the sisters must tend to their husbands and babies in their own cabin.

No. This disdain for Madame's useless servant only grew.

"Don't be so clumsy," Louise said when she gave Thisbe the blouse. Thisbe took the blouse but didn't thank either sister.

VIII

Lucien and Byron enjoyed the rest of the day shooting ducks that were brought to Lily for that night's supper. The pellets did so much damage to the fowl. Lily managed to pluck the flesh clean, scrape out the birdshot, and butcher what was left of the carcasses.

Father and son were in good moods and proud of their kills when Marie and Louise brought the platter of fricasseed duck meat to the table.

Madame didn't care for Lily's duck but ate it. The duck, like the venison, rabbit, turtle, and eel, was smothered by thick, salty gravy. Madame yearned for the sauces prepared by the old cook. Her valued servant and confidant, now departed from her. The smothered food before her made her feel she had lived too long in a world of limited choices. Chewing the fatty meat and fighting to swallow it only intensified those frustrations.

Yes, Madame thought. *I have lived too long, and when this house is filled with grandchildren and great-grandchildren, they will not know me — the first mistress of Le Petit Cottage. They will not reflect on my sacrifices. My great and many sacrifices.*

But it was also true that Lucille Pierpont had had her portrait painted and hosted a much-talked-about showing at the Pierpont Plantation. Or so Madame had heard. Madame received the invitation but had come down with a sudden illness that day.

Madame pushed her plate forward. She reached for her glass, sipped her wine, and set it down. Then she made a pronouncement. "It is time to hire a painter."

"A painter?" Lucien asked.

"Yes. For my portrait," she said.

"Oh! That kind of painter. But of course. While the plantation sinks to ruin — I agree! It's best to capture the decline in oils on canvas to memorialize our great fall."

"You exaggerate." To Byron, she said, "Had your father not had the plantation, he would have made an exceptional stage actor."

"I think Papa would have preferred the life of a poet," Byron said. "He recited verse after verse of *The Iliad* while we shot ducks."

Madame had already rolled her eyes and waved her hand, no. Her son, however, could not be deterred.

"My friends, be men! Show a strong
    heart!
Have shame before one another in the
    ferocious battle.
Of men with shame, more are saved
    than perish. Of those
who flee, there is no fame, no use."

Madame said, to cut him off, "The bourbon recites *The Iliad.*"

"I might have forgotten a line or two," Lucien said. "But the point is, men cannot be men without a strong heart."

"I second," Byron said, basking in his

father's pride.

Lucien directed himself to his mother. "A painter, Mother? Why would we hire a painter?"

Madame Sylvie found the question itself shocking. "Because it is done. Expected for people of our class."

"A daguerreotype is what's called for. We bring in the artist. He positions the equipment. We stand, sit, arrange ourselves according to his instruction. He pulls the levers and strings, and then develops the plates and we're done with him — less the pork and bourbon."

"Daguerrr-reotype." The corners of Madame's lips pulled down in an unflattering way she wouldn't allow her face to be seen in the company of friends.

Madame put her silverware down and folded her arms. "At my family home we had a sitting before my father went off to battle." Between the wine and candlelight, she drifted into a happiness of memory. "I was six, but I remember so well the sounds of my mother's taffeta gown. That we sat, Mother and I, while my father stood . . . The artist was so taken by my mother's beauty he made a small locket portrait of her for my father and one for me. I managed to save the picture of my mother when your brute of a grandfather threw my belongings to sea. The painting is faint. The family portrait still hangs in La Maison Bernardin de Maret. I'm certain."

Byron felt sorry for his grandmother and was ready to forgive her for sending her maid to take his letter. "A lovely tradition."

"For petty nobles," Lucien countered.

"That you deny your children's children their heritage is an insult to their blood and the blood of my parents. There isn't a home along this River Road without a grand portrait on the walls — including the Pierpont Plantation."

"Then let us be the first to grace our walls with a daguerreotype, Momanm. A photograph. No one sits for portraits in this era."

"They're more in fashion, Grandmère," Byron said. "Every graduating class at the Academy has such a likeness made. Why, they inspire awe in the incoming plebes when they lay their eyes on their betters."

"Listen to the boy. He's been out and has seen all the new things."

New. This word rankled Madame and she shook, as if to shake the word itself off her.

She said to Lucien, "Has your son been to France? To the countryside where the Bernardin de Maret vineyards produce the best wines? No," she answered. "He has seen nothing." She turned to Byron. "Promise me, Byron. You'll take your bride to Paris, and to the Bernardin de Maret family vineyards. You'll breathe in the fertility of the land and your children will be many."

"Of course, Grandmère."

"Of course," Lucien added. He raised his glass to Byron. "To fertility!"

Madame ignored Lucien's toast and continued to press her case. "A sitting is an obligation to the legacy of the family. The painting is an obligation to art. What do you think the walls are for?"

"To shield us, I would guess," Lucien said. "On what do we commission? There's the artist's passage, his supplies. His boarding, and meals. And the tidy

106

business of his fee, Momanm. You don't know what you ask."

"I know exactly what I ask," she snapped.

Lucien looked at his mother. She bore into him, neither jaw nor eyes wavering. He was up against his most tenacious opponent: her will. He relented. "Maybe we can get a painter."

"Get a painter? Get a painter? You sound like you say, 'Maybe we can get a butcher.' This artist can't be found in the *Sugar Planter*!"

"Grandmère," Byron said. "I have a solution."

"Oh?" both father and grandmother asked.

"Colonel Duhon commissioned a portrait of himself — being in failing health. Rather, his sister-in-law in New Orleans, the countess, commissioned the portrait, more as a gift for Eugénie. She dotes on her niece."

Madame Sylvie gasped. Neither her face nor hands knew which emotion to commit to first. Joy that she would sit for the same artist as the countess; derision at the countess's title, paid for by a social-climbing husband, the count.

"Do you hear, Momanm?" Lucien was back to using the Creole term. "A gift from the countess." He made a hand gesture to connote the expense.

Madame ignored the gesture. "Speak up, Byron. Tell us more about the portrait artist of the countess."

"He is French," Byron said.

"Born?"

"Yes."

"And with whom did he study?"

"I doubt Eugénie mentioned that in her letter. I would have to comb through her letters for details, Grandmère. I don't recall his name."

"Foolish boy! Why do you sit there? Bring me the letters!"

"Let him have his pudding," Lucien said. "Those letters can wait for the morning."

In the morning Byron took the stacks of letters from his desk. The smaller stack contained letters from Eugénie addressed to him at Le Petit Cottage, some that he had already shared with his father and grandmother. The letters he sought to appease her wouldn't be found in that bunch, but in the thicker stack, addressed to him at West Point.

He flipped through the envelopes that bore April and May 1860 postmarks and went through them. Before long, he stopped scanning the stationery for the words "painter," "portrait," or "sitting" and was drawn into rereading the letters. He was touched by this "one day" spouse and the care she took to bring him bits of home in each letter. He could hear the lilt of her voice on paper. This Eugénie was not the excitable type and seemed to enjoy the mundanities of plantation life. She didn't coyly try to extract romance from him, and never mentioned the engagement, eventual wedding, or married life. Yes, he thought. One day, Eugénie Duhon would make a good wife to promenade to church on Sundays while parishioners admired their youth and promise.

"Eureka!" He found the two letters that mentioned the painter specifically, including his name, his arrival, how Eugénie and her father dressed up for him, and the sitting. Hours of sitting. Her appraisal of the work was of her father's likeness. She was too modest a creature to regard herself even in a sly way. Yes. This would be enough to satisfy his grandmother. He rushed to her salon with the letters.

Madame's hands shook as she read. "Could it be?"

"What, Grandmère? Are you familiar with this artist?"

"I . . . I . . ."

Madame was seldom speechless. Thisbe fanned her at once.

"Stop!" Madame barked at her. Thisbe stopped fanning.

"Grandmère?"

Madame regained herself. In fact, her neck seemed to inch up from her collar.

"Of course I know the artist, and of course he should seek our patronage. It's only right."

Byron was mildly amused. "How do you know him, Grandmère?"

"Know him? He is Claude Le Brun!"

Byron didn't respond to the name.

Madame made a sound. "Ugh!"

"Grandmère, I don't follow painters," he said.

"If you knew anything of value, you'd know this Claude Le Brun is from the Elisabeth Louise Vigée Le Brun lineage. The portrait artist to the queen!"

To this, Byron made the appropriate look of amazement his grandmother was after.

She went on. "Yes! That is impressive, but the most important thing is Vigée Le Brun painted the queen's daughter and . . ."

"And?" Byron asked. He could see his grandmother enjoyed teasing the information. He wouldn't deprive her of it.

Her neck inched up even more. "And my young self."

"Ah!" Byron said, amazed but not overdoing it. "And you're certain this Claude Le Brun is a relative of the famed painter?"

"Of course! This is how things are

111

done. You are born to a guild class or to artisans and you thrive in what that circle provides for you. And it will be the same for your children. And your children's children for generations to come. This is how the world works!" She was in her glory. Then she wagged her finger at him. "You would know these things if you traveled abroad."

"Grandmère, I hate to see you build your hopes on so slim a coincidence. Why don't I write to Eugénie for confirmation?"

"I need no confirmation," Madame snapped. "No portrait artist would be foolish enough to travel under the Le Brun name, even in this wilderness, with so many Frenchmen. You cannot introduce yourself as a Le Brun and paint like a Le Nobody. You would be blocked from the circles you seek to gain patronage. No! The letter tells me everything: he is a Le Brun from Madame Elisabeth Louise Vigée Le Brun. My nightly prayers to the Holy Mother and the saints have brought him to me."

"Oh, Grandmère. Grandmère, dear."

"There is no time to waste," Madame

said. "Forget the commissary and what-ever your father has asked of you. In-stead, do all you can to locate this Le Brun and propose the sitting for me."

"Le Brun could be busy, Grandmère. From Eugénie's letter, he is in residence in New Orleans for the summer with the countess and will return to France there-after."

"You get word to him . . ." Her thoughts were interrupted by the sound of boots tramping up the steps. She continued, "You let him know that his kinswoman painted my portrait along with the dau-phine when we were girls in Le Petit Tri-anon. That should soften his heart and call upon his sense of loyalty."

At that, Lucien entered the salon. "And when a soft heart and loyalty fail, what sum will you offer to have him pack his brushes and oils and come running to our" — he looked about — "quaint pal-ace?"

"You overheard? Good," Madame said. "Listen carefully. I want Le Brun. And I want you to pay his fee and everything he comes with."

Lucien gave his mother a dispassionate

"With what?"

"With what do you think?" she said. "When I have my sitting with Le Brun and the portrait is complete, the gold is yours, my son."

Lucien was overcome. But she had said it! He had heard it! At last! He had won! He bent down, kissed his mother on both cheeks.

She pushed him back. "Yes, yes. Now you love your mother."

"Mother," he said in French, "my love is constant. But now you let me show it."

IX

Madame, in her gratitude to the holy mother, began each morning with the rosary, while Thisbe knelt in complete supplication. This full circle of a royal treatment, namely the deliverance of the Le Brun portrait painter, was to Sylvie a sign of her righteous struggle and vindication for the life she was owed. At least the final years of her life would give her satisfaction.

That Sunday the Guilberts, along with Thisbe, took the deluxe rockaway carriage to the grand Catholic church in St. James. Thisbe, seated next to Madame, kept her head and eyes lowered. She sought invisibility so closely confined in the cab with the Guilbert men. In Byron, whom she sat directly across from, she saw a guilty charge; in Lucien, a constant

115

smirk. Both men troubled her for different reasons, but at the moment she feared Lucien's knowing look more than Byron's occasional glare of disdain and accusation.

On the few occasions that Thisbe saw her mother and sisters, they would ask the same question: *Master got to you?* They never asked about Byron. She thought, during this ride, that if Mary, this Holy Mother, could grant Madame's wishes, it might be worth a try to ask for protection against the master. And also against the young Master Guilbert. And to have a full Sunday, in the cabin with her mother, father, and sisters. Yes. Pray. *Je vous salue, Marie, pleine de grâce . . .*

Madame went out of her way to catch Lucille Pierpont's eye once the Mass had ended. When she succeeded, and the woman joined her, Madame Sylvie told Lucille about the party she planned to host for Byron and his young friend from West Point.

"Your daughters must come," she said. "He's from the upper states, but from a good family, I'm told."

"Thank you for thinking of us," Lucille

said. "It has been so long since we've been invited to Le Petit Cottage."

"And I so miss invitations to your lovely home. All the grand occasions," Madame fired back. "But let's not dwell on missed invitations, not when this party will be so lively."

Lucien mouthed the word "lively" with disbelief. Byron gave him a good-natured smile, a plea to not ruin his grandmother's fun.

"Oh, yes," Madame continued. "I hope to have an unveiling of my portrait, perhaps at the same affair." Madame purposely rubbed Lucille's nose in it.

"Portrait? It is good you don't feel too old to sit for a portrait."

"Not at all," Madame said swiftly. "This is for our legacy. And I must say, this portrait has the blessing of the Holy Mother."

"Pardon?" Lucille made no attempt to hide her incredulity.

"The Holy Mother blessed me after hearing my prayers each night. If anyone is to paint my portrait, it would be the artist who painted Madame Royale —

the queen's 'Mousseline' — and myself as children." She was sure to use these nicknames of Marie-Thérèse Charlotte's to remind Lucille Pierpont of her closeness to the court. "Since that painter has passed on, who better to do this painting than her descendant? This is why I say the commission has been ordained."

"I see," Lucille said.

"No. I don't think so," Sylvie countered. "But wait for the invitation in four, five weeks, before my grandson and his friend go back to the Academy. You and your daughters must come. Then, you will see."

"I look forward to the invitation," Lucille said.

The two women kissed and parted to greet other acquaintances. Madame, invigorated by the petty skirmish, kept her face intact, even with Lucille's doubt of her divine favor and those pinpricks jabbed at her age. Sylvie understood. Lucille Pierpont, despite her desperation, didn't want to appear too eager when time was running out. The older daughter, twenty-four, was all but given up on. A betrothal to a West Point officer of some means would be better than to be left to wither and rot. The situation wasn't yet bleak for the younger Pierpont daughter. At twenty-one, a year older than Byron, there was concern, but there was still time. It was also true that there were no eligible first, second, or third male cousins on either side of their family. *Oh, yes,* Madame thought. *The Pierpont Plantation is in danger of dying without issue if left to Lucille Pierpont to find matches for her daughters. And Lucille had dared to question Byron's future! Hah! The curse has come back to her!*

Madame had had her fun with Lucille Pierpont and spied her next target among the departing worshippers. The beautiful Juliette Boisvert Chatham. The daughter-in-law she was meant to have.

"Go," she said to Thisbe. "Bring Madame Chatham to me."

Before Thisbe could say her, "Yes, Madame Sylvie," Lucien cut her off. "I will get Juliette."

But Juliette Chatham was already moving through the small crowd toward the Guilberts. Lucien lifted his hat, then took Juliette's hand. "My dear."

"Juliette. My Juliette," Madame said.

The two women kissed cheeks.

"Good afternoon, Madame Chatham," Byron said.

"Byron! At last, a young man," Juliette said, appraising his growth and confident bearing.

Thisbe curtseyed but was not acknowledged.

After pleasantries passed between them, Madame Sylvie said, "At the end of the summer we are having a small affair for Byron and his friend before they return to the Academy. Some dancing. Refreshments. Perhaps you and Jane would like to attend."

The younger woman waved her hand, adorned in a black lace glove, to indicate a resolute no. Widowed for eight months, Madame Chatham still wore all black, and smartly so, from full veil, silk dress with high collar and cuffs, to her parasol. "Nothing would please me more, but I will be gone shortly. I cannot talk now, but, Madame, I wish to speak with you soon. It is important."

"Important!" Madame said. "But of

course! Then please come to tea, as soon as you can."

"Madame Sylvie," Juliette said, her eyes reflecting gratitude. "I have no choice than to visit sooner than you'd like."

"Nonsense," Madame said. "My salon is always open to you."

With that, the younger woman gave her good wishes and was off to her carriage.

The late Mr. Phillip Janeway Chatham, an Englishman, had died after a brief, unexpected illness. Even though he was English, Juliette Chatham, three generations French Creole, saw to it that her deceased husband was funeraled in the highest Creole traditions, with black satin ribbons strewn throughout the house, clocks stopped, the hearse and horses decked in black. Now, only the door to Mr. Chatham's bedroom was decked with a black grosgrain ribbon. Once the house was emptied, the ribbon, along with his personal items, would be given to their daughter, Jane.

With Juliette Boisvert Chatham's sudden and curious need of Madame Sylvie's counsel, Sylvie was now convinced more than ever of the Holy Mother's divine favor. She opened her drawstring purse, took out a coin, and gave it to Thisbe. "Put this in the poor box."

Thisbe took the coin and hurried into the church.

"There goes good cash," Lucien said, watching Thisbe enter the church.

"Quiet," Madame said. "Or you turn our fish into vipers." She crossed herself repeatedly, *Au nom du Père, du Fils et du Saint-Ésprit.*

When the Guilberts returned to Le Petit Cottage, at Byron's insistence, Madame had Thisbe empty her dress pocket and her apron pockets, remove her shoes, and then her clothes, "to be sure the servant hadn't stolen the coin."

X

Madame Sylvie took more time than usual to complete her toilette that morning. She was sponge bathed by Thisbe with the scent of rose petals instead of her daily lye soap and water cleaning. Mother-of-pearl hair combs were arranged on both sides of her crown, in place of simple hairpins. She borrowed a dress from her much younger self, a bright plaid frock. How Madame would relish every minute of this meeting between herself and Juliet Boisvert Chatham.

Thirty years ago, Juliette's father, the Boisvert patriarch, had told Juliette's mother that she could continue her friendship with Sylvie Guilbert, but she couldn't discuss marriage with the Guilbert woman. He felt Sylvie's connection to the throne and that she retained a property in France was good, but her marriage to Bayard Guilbert was not so good. Had only she better aligned herself! When Sylvie pushed, she was told she reached too high on her son's behalf. While Le Petit Cottage was respectable, the line of more qualified suitors for Juliette Boisvert meandered like the Louisiana rivers. It was true that the young couple, Juliette and Lucien, danced the waltz and *cotillon* to the envy of onlookers (Sylvie taking credit for having taught her son to dance like a lord), however, the Boisvert patriarch had seen past their swirling, elegant figures. Like the senior Guilbert, young Lucien's reputation at the racetracks, saloons, and whorehouses traveled upriver from New Orleans to St. James Parish. Madame Sylvie believed the father of Juliette Boisvert was responsible for these rumors.

The widow was prompt to noon tea. She found Sylvie Guilbert in the salon, seated and eager to receive her.

The two greeted each other warmly, and Juliette stooped to kiss the older woman. Madame Sylvie complimented

Juliette on her mourning dress, her hat — a black dainty replica of a man's top hat — and her black lace gloves, different from the ones she wore for Mass.

Madame Sylvie observed that Juliette wasn't as anxious as she had appeared after the Mass. Juliette was a woman of action and didn't seek approval or direction. Sylvie liked these qualities in her and couldn't help but imagine how Lucien would have thrived with a wife like Juliette.

"Juliette, your armoire is stuffed with dresses!" Sylvie exclaimed. "My own Charlotte Thérèse would have dressed as smartly had she not been taken from me."

"I'm sure of it," Juliette said.

"You would be the same age. And great friends."

"Without a doubt." She spoke with neither passion nor malice.

The conversation went on in this way. It was clear to both women they each wanted something of the other; however, both seemed to resist being the first to buckle and speak sincerely.

Marie and Louise served tea, small sandwiches, and sweet biscuits, while Thisbe stood at Madame's side. Marie made sure to step on Thisbe's shoe. The big toe.

Thisbe held her breath and screamed silently to the Holy Mother rather than making an actual sound.

Juliette was diverted by the twins. "How lovely you are," she told them. "It's been years since I've seen you two."

"*Mèsi,* Madame Shat-ham," they said together and dipped in unison.

"They are fine adornments," Juliette said to Madame. "My daughters and I would have enjoyed dressing them for company. They make the house so . . . cheerful."

"Yes," Madame agreed. She made an expression and shooed the two maids.

Madame didn't want to talk about servants. She steered the conversation toward the sale of Juliette's family plantation, hoping this would begin the purpose for the visit.

"Lucien was too slow on his offer,"

Juliette said. "And I must sell, not give away."

"True," Madame conceded with no injury or pride. To put up a fight would have been ridiculous. She couldn't help herself and added, "I'm sure my son has many regrets."

"We all have regrets," the other responded. But this was out of kindness only. Sylvie could see that, but relished the little morsel, nonetheless.

"Now, my dear child," Madame said. "Tell me your troubles."

"I have no troubles," Juliette said. "But one." Now the calm exterior began to crack. It was obvious she was in distress and ready to tell it all. "Jane. What can I do with her?"

"Has she taken ill? Is this the reason she didn't attend the Mass with you?"

"Illness would be so simple. Easier to explain," the younger woman said. "The truth is, my Jane isn't fit to be seen."

"How do you mean that?" Sylvie asked. All the while, Madame congratulated herself on putting on her unaware face. Unaware enough to coax Juliette to speak freely. In reality she had heard of Jane, accompanying her father and men on hunting trips, galloping on her horse, her hair cut to her ears like an adolescent farm boy.

"Surely you've heard from others," Juliette said. She searched Madame's face, but Madame wouldn't crack.

"I am shut off, in the wilderness. What can I hear?"

"It's my fault," Juliette said.

"Let me be your priest. Confess."

This was good! Delicious, even. Everything was turning around. The very girl who had refused her son now sat before her, seeking compassion. Madame had heard about the wild daughter of Juliette and the Englishman, but she enjoyed even more hearing the full account from the mouth of Juliette Boisvert Chatham.

Juliette's forthright confession didn't disappoint Madame. She took it all in. How the Englishman wanted a male heir after three daughters. Juliette's prayers to grant her the legitimate male heir to please her husband. That her husband was desperate for a white male son and had taken up with the wife of a German ditchdigger working on the levee. This dalliance produced another female child. Once Juliette had received the news, she poured her energy into her health and into becoming pregnant for the last time. She meditated on a male child. Prayed for a male child. Consulted Marie Laveau, the famed Vodou priestess. Instructed the knitters to prepare a bassinette for the nursery of a male child. Made generous donations to the church in exchange for blessings on her womb. When the child, born robust, with thick tufts of red hair — the picture of Phillip Janeway Chatham, her husband — had been pronounced female, Juliette didn't believe it and checked between the baby's legs to be sure. Months of darkness followed Juliette. She had done all she could think of for a blessing. Instead she had been cursed.

"Nonsense. Nonsense. You take too much on," her confessor said.

"What else am I to think? My daughter is cursed."

"No!" Madame said in a way to get more out of Juliette.

"Days ago the postman hired an attorney to bring suit of indecency and criminal injury against Jane. I paid the attorney to settle the matter and to keep the complaint out of the public pleadings. You have no idea."

"I am a mother," Madame said with sympathy. "I can imagine."

"It isn't the money but the name. There is no hope of a man's family to have her, no matter the dowry."

"You speak too harshly. This postman. This nobody. Who is he to bring suit against the Boisvert-Chathams?"

The younger woman laughed. "Here, the nobodies can cause trouble."

"True, so true," Madame said.

"Be honest with me, Sylvie. Would you let your son or grandson enter into a contract with a girl described as I've described Jane?"

"Don't be too quick. I have a son in need of a wife," Sylvie said, the irony not lost on either woman.

"Sylvie, I can't joke about this. I must face Jane's future, but I must also protect the good names of her sisters and their husbands."

"You've done well for your daughters," Madame said. "All three married. One husband, a sugar planter in Houma. Eighteen hundred acres? The other, a rice planter in South Carolina. The third husband with the ministry of finance in France? You are to be congratulated on these matches."

Madame turned slightly to her right-hand side. "Take the tea service away. We'll have our cordials."

"Yes, Madame Sylvie."

Thisbe removed the plates and tea service, placing them on the sideboard. She disappeared out of the salon and returned with two glasses and a decanter of a cordial that had been made earlier with rum and crushed persimmon.

Thisbe poured modest amounts of the cordial for both women, and then returned to Madame's side. Her job, now, was to watch the glasses and to refill each before Madame or her guest looked up for service. She could do this and bring to mind the feel of her father's rough hand cupping the top of her then six-year-old head, or her mother taking a wet

131

rag to wash behind her ears, or her sisters making cane dolls, or . . .

"I can't enjoy those kind words until my Jane is settled. You see, she is beyond schooling. No school will have her. She defies the purpose of a girl's education: to cultivate the art and practice of young womanhood, to enter society, to flourish as a wife. Manage a household. Prolong her husband's name through children."

"As we have," Sylvie said.

Juliette raised her hands in helplessness and disdain. "I would rejoice if she excelled in any one of those. What would the world be if women didn't further their education? Their responsibilities?"

"Chaos in the streets," Madame said. "As bloody as any revolution."

"Yes," the other wearily replied. "The unraveling of a necessary tapestry."

The two women drank a toast to "a necessary tapestry." Thisbe left her reverie to refill their glasses. She watched — even with eyes downcast — as they drank mostly to the virtues of the plantation mistress. Then to the wedding and the successful marriage, and last to the du-

132

ties of the plantation mistress. For no one was more celebrated than the plantation mistress, but on the plantation, no one worked harder. Without these fond memories of being brought into society, the plantation wife would simply be broken, a workhorse whose value was estimated just above the worth of a slave.

Thisbe watched, listened, and took care not to make a sound, specifically a snort.

"As I recall," Sylvie said, "it was three years past Lucien complimented your Jane on her riding and shooting. How did he say it? 'Oh, if only Byron took to these great pastimes like the young Chatham girl.'"

"Yes," Juliette said. "But Jane was to outgrow those preoccupations. She is fifteen and refuses dancing lessons! I'm afraid it's my fault. I let Phillip ruin her with his own favorite pastimes. But what could I do? He was so pleased to have Jane, his constant companion."

"English," Madame said. "I don't understand the English. God rest your husband's soul."

Juliette ignored the slight against her husband. She had her own motives and continued on. "But now, what am I to do?" she repeated. "I've sold the plantation and Phillip's will can be fully executed. My daughters' husbands are to receive their shares of the sale. My half brothers will get the sawmill and live on six hundred acres. And I will take my nephew and join my youngest's household in Paris."

Half brothers. Thisbe knew of the Boisvert colored men through Marie's and Louise's gossip. Both sons of the personal maid of Madame Chatham's mother.

Madame listened with relish. "Ah! Such news! I can scarcely take it all in. I am too isolated."

"I wish that these details were as new to you as you say. You must know how wild Jane is. I threatened to forbid her from coming out in society. Do you know her reply?"

"I can't imagine it."

"She said, as sober as a nun, she had no intention of coming out in society. That she only cared to ride her horse."

Madame gasped.

"You've not heard the worst of it,"

Juliette said, waving her finger, left, then right.

"There can't be more," Madame said. "Impossible."

"I had her nanny lay out a dress for her and burn the pants of my dead husband. Do you know what Jane did? She ran outside in a shirt, riding boots, and nothing else. Imagine! I screamed at the wretched beast to get inside."

"No! She wouldn't! How terrible!" Madame fanned herself with her hand.

Thisbe attended to Madame with the funeral fan, all the while keeping her face lowered and expressionless. The hairbrush to her hand, she could endure. But a guest was present. A plantation mistress of higher social rank, wealthier than her own mistress. Madame would have no choice but to make the best show of punishing her before Madame Chatham, should she give in to any outward sign of her inner thoughts of the indecent Chatham girl.

Thisbe continued to fan.

"The men covered their eyes lest they feel the whip. My wenches were fast on their feet. They caught her and threw a bedsheet from the wash over her. They scolded her well and marched her into the house."

To picture it! Still, Thisbe didn't want a beating. She bit her cheek flesh, hard.

Madame tried not to laugh but couldn't overcome it.

"I can't blame you," Juliette said. "If it weren't my daughter, I would laugh too. But tell me, Madame Sylvie. What am I to do with Jane? The new owners will take hold of the property and we must be gone."

"It is this savage land," Madame said. "Bayous. Swamps. Alligators. Sad birds singing sad songs. You must take her to France, where she will bloom into young womanhood." She added, "Every young person born to these plantations should see where their roots spring from. And it will be good for her. The right air. Exposure to the right culture."

"Oh, Madame. You're too optimistic. It's far more grave than that, for Jane . . ." Madame Chatham stopped herself, looked soberly at the older woman, and completed her thought. "Jane threatened to throw herself into the Atlantic if she were separated from her horse."

"My God," Sylvie said right away. "These threats cannot be tolerated. You must not give in to her threats."

By now, Juliette was sniffling into her black handkerchief. "I can't sleep at night. I close my eyes and see her jumping into the ocean. I hear the plunge. I see her swallowed up." Sniffling now turned to sobs.

"There, there," Madame said. "It is good that you unburden yourself of these horrors. This situation."

"You don't understand, Madame. Her sisters won't take her. Jane's behavior would only bring scandal to their homes. You see, Madame, I am without options."

"Perhaps my son and I can be of help." Sylvie made sure to stress "my son." The man who was not good enough thirty years ago. Sylvie couldn't help but relish the idea that the Guilberts would come to the Boisvert-Chathams' aid.

"I don't see how," Juliette said, still sniffling.

Madame Sylvie, on the other hand, was

certain Juliette hoped this part of their dance would arrive all along. Madame didn't doubt she was listening to a well-practiced delivery. It didn't matter. Madame went along with the performance.

"No, no, dear. Your prayers have been answered."

The other woman began to make protesting gestures, but Madame dismissed them all. "Retire to Paris in peace, dear Juliette. Stay with your daughter and her husband. We are practically family. Jane will be a guest in our home. We'll board her horse in our stable. All is solved."

"Oh, Madame, you are my prayers answered. But I must be forthright. My daughter isn't civil in the ways of a young lady. Even the way she speaks and understands what you say is a bit unusual. And I must warn you, Jane does not have a delicate appetite. She eats like a man. I don't know how much you, Lucien, or Byron can tolerate. Believe me, about Jane, I don't exaggerate."

Triumphant, drunkenly, Madame waved her hand to dismiss Juliette's concerns. "You will see," Sylvie told

Juliette. "Under my tutelage, she will change. Blossom, even."

"Blossom. Hah! Impossible," the younger said, her sniffles now stopped.

"I will exhaust my training on her and within the year she will come out in society. Lucien and I will act as her godparents."

"No, no, Madame. This is too much to hope for. But if I can make arrangements for a room, meals, a bed, and space for the horse."

"I don't accept your request," Madame said, "unless you agree that I am to usher your child into womanhood. You see, this is our pleasure. Lucien and I. You are almost a daughter to me. Let me help to further Jane's feminine development. I have no daughter or granddaughter to pass on my benefit of having grown up under the queen's eye."

"You are too generous," Juliette conceded. "Or perhaps too drunk."

The women laughed.

"Perhaps," Madame Sylvie said.

"I will meet with Lucien to discuss fees."

"Fees?"

"I am well prepared. You don't know what I'm asking of you. But if Jane wears a dress, any dress, in polite society, I would be contented beyond my ability to repay you both."

"You aim too low, my dear girl," Madame said tipsily. "When I write to you, it will be with news of Mademoiselle Jane at the waltzes, laughing at a gentleman's wit, dancing the quadrille."

"When you write to me, it will be as a writer of grand romances. But that's all right. I like fairy tales. Romances. Stories of imagination."

Madame laughed. "I'm so glad to lift you from the dark cloud. So glad, my dear. If it makes you feel better to make arrangements with Lucien, I can't stop you. Go, then. Humiliate our hospitality."

Not too soon after, Madame's head dropped, her chin against her chest. Madame Chatham removed herself from the salon to let the older woman sleep. She went to the little cottage that was Lucien's office. He rose to his feet upon seeing her. Without saying a word, they seemed to drink in each other.

Lucien didn't bother to tell her how beautiful she was, or any of those compliments made for a time like this. He simply said, "Look at us. Two widows in the world."

"But for Jane, my work is done. I have quit the plantation. And this life."

"What can be done to dissuade you, Madame?"

"No, no," she said. "We are old friends and too old to play with each other. You and I know this life. How hard it is. What it demands to keep everything running."

"Ah, but it is a life without equal, worth every sorrow," Lucien said. "Still, I agree, dear Juliette. No one knows hardship like a planter."

The two conducted their business. Lucien didn't balk at the sum of three thousand dollars, to be drawn from the Bank of New Orleans, to board one unusual girl of fifteen, and one horse, for a year.

XI

By week's end Madame Chatham arrived once again at Le Petit Cottage, this time with an air of spectacle. The carriage was followed by a four-teamed horse and wagon carrying trunks and household treasures. The carriage and wagon were trailed by a colored boy (and Boisvert relative) in his teens riding a magnificent black charger. It was a sight, especially to a group of Black children picking berries for Lily to make the Guilberts' desserts. The children stopped to wave to the parade.

Madame observed the procession from her gallery. She made no motion to get up from her chair. Instead, she sent Thisbe to let Lucien and Byron know the Chathams were arriving.

Thisbe dispatched quickly, but with

dread of confronting either of the Guilbert men. Since Monsieur Lucien's office was closer than the commissary, she thought to find him first. Once outside, Thisbe found she didn't have to make the journey in either direction. Both father and son had exited their buildings and were walking toward each other to greet the visitors. Relieved to avoid the two men, Thisbe returned to Madame Sylvie.

Marie and Louise peeked from the window. They shook their heads. "Why do they come today?" Marie asked. "Why not Saturday?"

"Vendredi treize," Louise said of the unluckiest Friday. "Not good."

Byron and Lucien met each other and strode to the carriage. Lucien opened the low passenger door and held out his arm to Madame Chatham, who gathered her skirt before taking his arm and stepping down onto the dirt-way.

"My dears, my dears. Welcome. Welcome to your home."

"Good morning, Lucien," Madame Chatham said. "Good morning, Byron.

So pleased that you welcome us."

Juliette turned to her daughter, still seated, chest stiff, eyes unblinking. "Come, Jane."

Byron stepped forward and extended his hand.

Jane lifted herself, refused Byron's hand, and jumped out of the coach, landing so her feet were wide apart.

"Welcome, Jane." Byron looked her over in a glance but didn't react to Jane's dismount or appearance, her haircut both severe and lopsided.

Jane didn't reply.

Her mother looked over her shoulder. "Jane."

The girl didn't answer. Instead, she called to the mulatto boy still mounted on her horse.

"Georgie, get off her! Now," she told him.

The curly-haired boy, Georgie, laughed unabashedly. "Yass, Cousin Jane. I'm off her." At closer examination, Georgie greatly resembled Jane's mother, his aunt. It was obvious he enjoyed teasing

Jane and was slow to dismount.

Jane's mother wanted to believe her daughter's meanness to her cousin had everything to do with him accompanying her to France and leaving Jane behind. But Juliette Chatham knew better. Her daughter cared that her cousin rode her horse, and nothing more.

Byron found the row between cousins amusing but came quickly to Jane's aid.

"Boy, get off that horse."

Georgie jumped off at once. *"Oui, M'sié."*

"Now walk him to the stable," Byron said, nudging the boy in the direction of his chin.

"Virginia Wilder," Jane said.

"Virginia Wilder?" Byron asked.

"My horse is a she," Jane stated. "Virginia Wilder."

"Interesting name." He smiled at her the way adults smiled at children. There were only five years between them.

Jane refused to answer, to make pleasantries, or to move.

Her mother, taking note of the scene,

excused herself from Lucien and crossed over to the motionless, foot-planted girl. Juliette smiled at Byron, who understood the plea in the smile and stepped away to give them privacy.

Her mother spoke English through gritted teeth. "Jane. Remember what I said."

Jane only looked to the stable, where her horse had been led.

"You let Cousin Georgie ride my horse," Jane said to her mother.

"It was the best way to deliver it."

"Her."

Juliette huffed through her nostrils. "This is your best and only chance," she said firmly, her voice low. "I've told them what they can do to the animal if you become unmanageable." She looked at Lucien, turned her head so that her mouth couldn't be seen or her words heard. "You are a boarder here, not a beloved child. Don't trust their smiles. They will shoot that animal." She pulled Jane's chin close so that they faced each other squarely, eye to eye.

Jane blinked, which was rare. Ordinarily, Juliette would have been satisfied with this small capitulation. But Juliette Chatham had a long road ahead of her. She loved her daughter and needed to know that Jane had a chance under this arrangement.

"Do you understand, Jane? Do you?"

Jane exhaled hard, also a short huff through her nostrils.

"What are you to do while you're here?"

Jane said nothing.

"Jane. Speak. Speak now and let me know you understand, or I'll have that horse put down before I leave."

"Have lessons and tea with Madame Guilbert every day."

"What else?"

"Speak French. Wear a skirt. A dress."

"And?"

"No pants. Leave my hair to grow."

"Good girl." She kissed her daughter's forehead, turned on her heel, and walked toward Lucien with a gracious smile and an overflow of apologies.

Byron held out his arm to Jane, but she refused to complete the image of a pair of cakewalkers fancy-stepping on a late Friday morning. She did follow him into the house.

The coachman and Georgie together carried the trunk that belonged to Jane into the house and up to the room where Jane would stay. "Touch nothing," Marie and Louise said in Creole and English, speaking mainly to Georgie. The boy made sure to touch everything in Jane's new room.

Downstairs, Madame Chatham explained that she couldn't stay for the afternoon meal. She was expected at her daughter's home in Houma some forty miles east, before leaving the country for good. When it was time for Madame Chatham to leave, she pulled Jane close and stroked her hair, as short as it was. Juliette hoped for some signs of emotional erosion from the girl. Some sniffling. Tears. Even a plea to take her with her. It wasn't too late. Instead she received the stiff standoff she had grown accustomed to.

"Your sister will have you and your horse if you behave," Juliette whispered in her ear.

"Virginia Wilder," Jane answered.

This answer told Juliette what she knew. Jane couldn't be made to behave as a young lady should. Madame Sylvie was deluding herself. Still, she knew Sylvie would put forth an effort, and that Lucien wasn't averse to receiving money for Jane's care.

She held her daughter close, most probably for the last time. "Behave and be well, my Jane." Juliette Chatham, Georgie, the coachman, and the wagon team were gone.

At last there was a fourth at the table. Someone to sit opposite Byron. Madame appreciated the balance.

She couldn't help but stare at the youngest daughter of Juliette Chatham. It was inconceivable that this girl was born from the same parents who produced the other successful, elegant daughters. Inconceivable.

Juliette Chatham didn't exaggerate about the girl's appetite. Jane didn't seem to notice the staring if there was food before her. She ate more than her portion, and almost single-handedly finished the berry cobbler that was made to welcome her.

Marie and Louise flashed looks while the cobbler disappeared. There would be no berry cobbler to bring to their husbands and teething babies.

Madame told the girl, "It is natural to excuse yourself for a cry in your room. But it also shows good training on your mother's part that you don't. You see, I was once a child alone in the world. Mother, father, dead. Grandfather, dead. Siblings, none. But as I'm sure your mother has told you, I was taken in by the Royal Family as a favor to my father, Captain Dacier, who served King Louis XV well in battle."

Jane spoke plainly. "No, Madame Guilbert. My mother didn't tell me about you."

"Ho!" Lucien exclaimed. "How is it possible you've not heard the fairy tale that we've sprung from? Momanm," he said to his mother, "I'm sure we're owed penny royalties from all the mammies telling the story to their young masters and mistresses."

"I don't care for fairy tales," Jane said,

unaware of the bemused looks of the two men.

"All girls like fairy tales," Byron said.

"Do you like fairy tales?" Jane asked.

"Dear Jane," Byron said drolly, "I'm not a girl."

"Of course, Byron's not a — what a silly thing!" Madame Sylvie said. "And we stray from our polite conversation. Dear, I only meant to comfort you. To encourage you and to say, even I know separation. Separation from my family and from the Royal Family. But you see? My life didn't become a tragedy. You too, Jane, will rise above your situation."

Jane asked, "What is my situation?"

The Guilberts passed looks among one another. Looks that acknowledged what slowly became clear. Their guest lacked that mask of protection, as pliable as deft speech, or as featherweight and transient as a smile. This Jane lacked a social manner.

Even with sufficient warning about Jane, Madame didn't anticipate having to explain the simplest things to a daughter raised by a woman as artful as Juliette

Boisvert Chatham. She accepted the challenge and spoke gently. "Your father is dead. You may never see your mother again. Your married sisters cannot take you in. This would make any girl all alone want to cry."

"Grandmère!" Byron objected. "You'll make her cry."

"I don't want to cry," Jane said. "I want to ride my Virginia Wilder."

Jane didn't cry that night. But she was angry. And bereft. Why did it all go away? The father who indulged her with the things she loved; hunting, swimming, fishing; the hardworking but happy farm; her nanny, now employed in Shreveport with relatives who took the bulk of field hands and house servants but would not take her and her Virginia Wilder. Her nanny she loved. Her father she loved. Her Virginia Wilder she loved.

She opened her trunk.

Her mother meant to leave the oil painting of her father behind. Nanny made sure to roll it up and put it in Jane's trunk, along with his sword and his war jacket.

She was glad to have the portrait of her
father in full military dress uniform. The
look of him, Major Phillip Janeway
Chatham. Upright and fearless. She loved
how his red beard clung to his chin and
face and how his thick red brows jutted
over his eyes. It didn't occur to her to
seek his likeness and qualities in other
men. To want to one day marry a man
like her father. What Jane wanted was her
father's life. She accompanied him on
hunting trips and saw herself as one of
the hunters. Being a deadeye shot, Jane
held her own in duck hunting, wild boar
and deer kills — although her father
wouldn't allow her to squat and shit or
piss among the men. There, the former
Major Chatham had drawn the line.

XII

The next morning, Jane put on the blouse and stepped into the skirt, attaching the hooks and eyes of the waistband. She tugged the ankle socks over her feet only because they were knit by her former nanny. She slid her feet into her shoes and kicked the toe against the bedpost. She walked to the vanity, with its modest but unavoidable mirror, but didn't sit down on the brocade settee. She did, however, notice that her personal items — a toothbrush, hair comb, and brush — had been laid out on the vanity along with her father's razor, soap cup, lather brush, and mustache comb. She picked up the small comb, sniffed it, then placed it down.

She did what her mother told her to do. She left her hair alone. She put on a skirt and blouse, but left the petticoat in the armoire. The petticoat wasn't on her mother's list. For that matter, neither were the blouse collar, corset, bindings, and other items that had been packed in her trunk. She was not told to pluck her eyebrows or to apply powder, rouge, or toilette water.

She would have lessons with Madame, then tea. Say *Oui, Madame Guilbert* to everything. Then ride her horse.

This morning wasn't the first time Madame Sylvie had seen the girl, but when Jane stood at the entrance to her salon, the very look of the girl was astonishing to Madame. While the girl had her mother's height, she was her father in bearing and thickness. Where Juliette Chatham and the three elder daughters were expressive, Jane was plain-faced. Where her mother and sisters were appropriately slope-shouldered, with stately and elegant décolletage, Jane was broad-shouldered and rectangular in frame. And the hair, so unusually cut. She was her father in a white blouse, skirt, and large women's shoes.

Madame wouldn't hold these failings against the girl and welcomed her inside her salon. "Come, Jane. Come, dear girl."

"Good day, Madame Guilbert." Jane spoke with effort, as if to remind herself how to address her tutor.

Madame gave her student a welcoming, encouraging smile.

Jane made no address to Thisbe, nor did Thisbe give one. The rule was, Thisbe was to pay the proper respect due a white person of any age or status. However, when she stood at Madame's right hand, it was understood that she was an extension of Madame, and not her own person. In keeping with the rule, Thisbe kept her eyes downcast.

"Your hair," Madame said. "I don't loan my maid. She is for me alone, but she will comb your hair if you like."

Again, Thisbe made no acknowledgment of acquiescence. However, Jane spoke quickly. "No. I don't like. And I don't like her touching my things."

Madame turned her head to Thisbe and then to Jane. "Did she break something? Steal from you?"

Thisbe did the thing she wasn't to do. She lifted her head and looked directly at the white girl. If she was to suffer the girl's lie, then a whipping or worse would be hers to bear anyway. The broad white girl would have to lie to her eyes.

"Nothing is broken. Nothing stolen," Jane said. "I entered the room yesterday and found my things put away in the armoire and on the vanity."

Madame laughed.

Thisbe exhaled, her eyes lowered to their usual resting place.

"But this is what a servant does," Madame said, still laughing. "She puts things away. You can't unpack yourself, dear. We have so much to learn."

"Yes, Madame Guilbert."

"Mademoiselle! You stand before me like a gentleman. We are ladies. Sit, Mademoiselle Jane. We will need all of our time together."

Jane sat in the very chair her mother sat in nearly a week before. Her simple motion shocked Madame.

Madame said gently, "Please stand, Mademoiselle. Stand and try again."

"Pardon?" the girl asked.

"Please," Madame Guilbert said firmly. "Stand, Mademoiselle."

"But I'm already seated. I did what you asked."

"That is true, Jane. But there is a way a lady enters a room and takes her seat."

Jane was sincerely perplexed.

"Please, dear. Please stand. Thisbe will show you the proper movement." Madame turned to her maid. "Thisbe. Sit."

"Yes, Madame Sylvie," Thisbe answered, and walked over to the chair.

Jane stepped aside and watched as Thisbe placed her hands on both sides of her skirt, gathered fabric in both hands, lifted while bending, and then sat, back straight. Placed her hands in her lap. She then rose from the seat, repeating the same movements, and stepped away from the chair.

"Now try," Madame told her student.

"I don't understand," Jane said.

"I promised your mother to improve upon you, but you must try or there is no point to the arrangement."

Madame was smiling when she said this. The smile Jane's mother warned her of. While the sitting and standing lesson perplexed Jane, the "point to the arrangement" became clear. Her horse. Her Virginia Wilder.

Jane took her place in front of the chair but didn't move beyond that.

"Remember, Jane," Madame said. "Lower yourself without sticking out your behind. And float to the seat, as Thisbe did. Don't drop your weight on the chair like sacks on a wagon. No one should know what it takes to carry you."

"Virginia Wilder knows."

"Virginia Wilder?"

"My horse."

"Yes, dear. But you can't marry your horse."

"I won't marry anyone," Jane said.

"Now, now," Madame said. "There is hope yet. But we must start at the beginning. You must sit like a lady."

"I'm not a lady," Jane said.

"True," Madame said. "True. We have much work before us. But now we start.

159

Try, Jane. Sit."

Confused, Jane stood for what seemed a long time. She snorted. Then she lowered herself, spine straight, hands taking swatches of fabric on both sides of her skirt. She did plunk a bit into the seat cushion, but she didn't drop herself as she had before. In other words, she tried. That was the victory Madame claimed.

"The cards, Thisbe," Madame said.

Thisbe retreated to the partitioned quarter of the room that served as Madame's bedroom. She returned, setting the deck facedown before Madame.

"Fine, then. Let us begin our lessons."

The work would be great, Madame thought. Greater than anticipated. In her opinion, Jane had been mismanaged from the start. Madame was challenged but hopeful. She couldn't reach into the girl's troubled mind and untwist what was incorrect, but she could teach Jane to make an appropriate presentation of herself to society.

"Let's start with understanding the

most important protection to women and their value: marriage."

Jane's expression didn't break. But she was puzzled nonetheless. "I will take the lessons," Jane said, "but I won't be wed."

"Now, now, my sweet. Don't be so hard on yourself," Madame said. She searched the girl, starting with the bushy red coils. "Yes, somewhere in you," she said, waving her hand to convey a vast uncertainty, "is enough to entice a young man's family to inquire into your holdings."

Jane replied in earnest, "Madame Guilbert, I won't be wed. I will refuse all callers."

Madame chuckled. She thought this Jane remarkable and had never known a female like her. "It won't come to that, my dear. There is too much work to do on you. Who would call?"

Thisbe found herself challenged to not laugh.

"Are you familiar with playing cards?" Madame asked, fanning and displaying the cards to Jane.

"Poker, euchre, Nap," she answered.

"Nap," Madame said, voicing her disdain for Napoleon, for whom the game was named. "Men's games, dear. What games have you played with your sisters? Your mother's circle of acquaintances?"

"Poker, euchre, and Nap. With my father."

"I see," Madame said. "There are more than saloon games. It wasn't until I played Triomphe with my husband and another couple that I saw how clever he was. And now your lessons begin."

"Yes, Madame Guilbert." Clearly, she spoke as she was obliged to do and for no other reason.

"Before you know it, you'll learn to play among women, and in couples. This is how you know if you can respect your gentleman caller. You'll see if he knows how to silently conspire with you to upend everyone else's chances of winning. How your friends will envy you."

"My father said I didn't have to receive gentlemen callers."

"My poor girl. Your father was being realistic about your future and intended to care for you for all his days . . ." Madame knew to stop herself from saying something cruel.

She tried again. "I was like you. An orphan . . ."

Thisbe knew this story well. How Madame had been taken in by the Royal Family, who would make a match for her and protect her family's property. The wealthy planter who rescued Madame, and how they fled the Terror in France, then the revolution in Saint-Domingue. And on and on. The fairy tale.

The girl, in Thisbe's estimation, didn't seem moved by the story, but she did seem pensive. Madame noticed Jane's intensity. This wasn't the reaction of awe and sympathy she expected.

"What is it, Jane?" she asked. "What are you thinking?"

"You made your match without your parents. That's unwise."

Madame's face turned red. She had been caught in her words.

Madame recovered. "Yes. This is true, Jane. So true. And this is the lesson for today. No young woman or girl should be forced to make her match and decide her future in times of peace. But in times of revolution and war, we must play our cards laid before us. We must play the hand dealt us."

Thisbe put the playing cards away.

■ ■ ■ ■

BOOK II

■ ■ ■ ■

Book II

I

The day had come at last. Much to his father's objections, Byron closed the commissary that Monday and had the stable boy couple the buggy with a well-rested and well-fed horse. There was no need for the carriage and coachman. Byron took the reins and was off on his seven-mile journey down to the port.

The horse clipped along at a springy jaunt down the river road. A pride awakened in Byron as he passed by plantation after plantation. Now that he had traveled north, he knew there was no other region in this union of states as inviting and lush as this, St. James Parish, with all that it provided. He smiled. His grandmother wanted desperately for him to travel, to experience both the Parisian countryside and society. His father had traveled as far as India and had seen many wonders, but mainly relayed details about the females of India when he spoke of those travels. But as Byron rode upright and proud, filling his lungs with the morning air, fragrant with almond verbena, magnolia, and sweet olive trees, he knew he could feel a greater love for no other place than the land of his birth. When seemingly little else besides blood and name bound him to his father and grandfather, it was because of his love of land that he found his place among the Guilbert men. He wanted nothing more than to show his friend what he loved best. While Byron was sure that he himself would travel and see the curiosities in the world, he looked forward to one day taking the reins as master of Le Petit Cottage.

Byron cracked the whip to pick up the pace. In his mind's eye, the image of his most cherished mate, Robinson Pearce, urged him on. Where Byron, from his youth to of late, had heard himself called good-looking — his blond curls and blue eyes gifts from his deceased mother — Robinson Pearce was a stunning young man, in the likeness of the famed West Point graduate Pierre Gustave Toutant Beauregard. There was no relationship between his friend and the fox-featured legend, but a group of instructors, upon seeing Pearce when he first entered the garrison, drilled him thoroughly about his background. His fastidiously trimmed winged mustache was shaved on the spot and he was ordered to part his hair down the middle for the duration of his enrollment. Unbeknownst to Pearce, the instructors, former classmates of Beauregard, harbored many resentments from yesteryear that were renewed upon seeing Pearce. New candidates or "plebes," being the natural subject of all indignities, anticipated such pranks and didn't take the hazing rituals personally. They simply bore them. Pearce seemed to like the attention, and overall found amusement in adversities, large and small. In that, he was Byron's opposite.

First, Byron would have to adjust to seeing Pearce out of the gray fitted uniform, a look that showed his excellent and efficient form. How he missed the look of him. The dark waves and locks that crowned Pearce's warm complexion falling naturally with no middle part. Where the famed Beauregard was said to have small steely eyes, Pearce's eyes were dark-brown jewels. His perfectly thin, tapered mustache a gateway to his thin rose lips. Other men made note of him right off, and women found him distracting. Pearce was kind and sweet to the ladies, where Byron was gentlemanly but detached. Pearce danced with the instructors' daughters at the balls, even the wallflowers, and they all swooned and giggled at his flirtations. Byron danced with them to perfection, as a gentlemanly duty, always holding the debutantes at a respectable waltzing distance as he whirled them around the ballroom.

Byron and Pearce knew each other in class and at camp, but it was on the dance floor, while both whirling beautiful young ladies in their arms, when they turned and locked eyes, Pearce's richly dark eyes into Byron's pale-blue ones, that the spark had been lit between them, without setting off the awareness of their respective partners. Pearce always found ways to engineer his movement with his partner so that the two cadets would find themselves eye to eye. Pearce set his snare on Byron. The unmistakable pull of object to magnet, once caught, held Byron at ransom. That the attraction should happen so quickly, so strongly, swept through Byron with delirium and great apprehension. The only question between them, unspoken but apparent, was, *When?*

That was the only question Byron could ask himself since, and throughout what promised to be a dismal summer without Pearce.

Byron hoped to see the riverboat pulsing down the Mississippi and sidling up to the port. He hoped to take in Pearce's arrival among the disembarking handkerchief wavers. However, the riverboat had docked long before his arrival, and the thought of catching that first glimpse of Pearce as he stepped onto parish land was to be that. A thought.

He searched the bustle and busyness of the Port of South Louisiana until he spotted his mate. Pearce wore a camel-colored hat, a matching waist jacket, and gray trousers. At his side stood a Black boy in brown short pants, a cotton shirt, and wool cap, eager to be of service and earn a silver three-cent piece.

The two embraced warmly, Pearce pecking Byron's cheek, and Byron slapping him on the back. The boy holding Pearce's bag, who'd been taught not to stare into the faces of white people, didn't stop his open gawking. The men chattered on, neither paying attention to the boy. Byron took Pearce's travel bag and dismissed the boy with the silver coin, which he snatched up gladly and ran off.

"More to follow," Byron said of their greeting. "We'll have some pints and a Louisiana treat. Something to welcome you to this parish. Then home."

"Lead on," Pearce said.

The saloon was raucous and full of traffic when Byron and Pearce entered and found a table. Byron ordered boiled crawdaddies, pickles, and two pints of beer. Pearce was reticent, but Byron showed him the proper way to attack the shellfish, how to snap the body, extract the meat from the head and tail, and then suck out the juice from the head. Pearce caught on quickly.

They were soon joined by a large and drunken sailor, American, by his accent. He, most likely on leave from a docked ship, seemed lost from his group. He pounded his fist on their table. "What have we here?" The man was teetering.

"Seaman," Byron said, "can we buy you a beer?" He hoped to quiet the man with the friendly offer and send him on his way.

"I don't —" He wobbled some. "I don't drink with the likes of you." He spoke loud and gruff, a Northeast coast accent.

Heads turned toward their table, in a place already boisterous with activity. The sailor thrust his fat pointer finger in Byron's chest.

Byron slapped his hand down. "Squid, West Point won't drink with you."

With Byron's insult plain, Pearce looked about the saloon for more sailors. There were none. Only the lone American sailor.

"Wess point. Wess point. Whassa wess point?"

A certain arrogance said to be cultivated at the Academy rose up in both
Byron and Pearce as the two cadets eyed
the interloper. The sailor's uniform —
tam askew, navy pants loose, navy shirt
loose about the belly and arms, its collar
wide and the tie looped in a slovenly way
around his collar — was the antithesis of
the West Point uniform.

The large, teetering man reared back
with much of his drunken might, signal-
ing Byron his intent to strike. By the time
the sailor's knuckles, arm, and elbow followed through, Byron had leaned his
head and torso swiftly to the right. The
seaman pushed himself forward over the
table, his own force the culprit. Craw-
daddy heads and shells scattered on the
floor.

Pearce, waving two quarters, called to
the waiter, "Let this settle us." The waiter
took the quarters, dropping one in his
apron pocket.

Byron and Pearce walked hastily to the
buggy, paid for the horse's oats and
water. Laughed as they made their escape, glad that the man had been separated from his fellow seamen.

"You could have thrown a punch," Pearce said.

"Why fire at a target so poorly armed? Best to save it for a real cause," Byron said. "Besides, the navy attracts a certain class. All comers."

"Imagine if we had been outfitted in gray."

"In parade dress."

"With plumage on our caps and gold buttons across our chests."

"He might not have missed his target."

Byron and Pearce rode away, entertained by their escape.

Within each plebe or cadet at the Academy is the fear of being "found." Even among the best is the preoccupation, the dread of being found lacking. It is a necessary dread that keeps the cadets on their toes. The Academy prides itself on finding that cadet and expelling the unfortunate soul so that no future soldier is placed in jeopardy by another's lacking.

On the ferry across the Hudson, and on the lonesome journey home, the "found" one wonders, when did they single him out? At what point did they know? Having once been among the murmurers, he imagines his fellow cadets saying, "There goes failed Candidate X, or failed Cadet Y; he has reached as high as he could and must now be shunned from this great brotherhood."

It is a terrible thing to know that despite the candle that burns through the night in the barracks with books open, no matter the hours of drill, and weeks at camp, the unfortunate one is found lacking, and publicly so. It is a terrible thing to know that, try as one might, the outcome cannot be changed. The expelled cannot march among or rise above. To be so fixed. So defined! It's a terrible, terrible thing for a young man to know of himself.

In the highest spirits from besting the navy man with little effort, Byron and Pearce put aside these normal anxieties of being found lacking. They sang furlough songs and reveled in the arduous but worthwhile hardships of cadet life.

The gallop of their escape eventually

became a trot. Byron showed Pearce his country with pride. Quaint in its Creole cottages and transplanted banana trees, and superior in its elegant manor homes with Grecian columns and formidable live oak trees. He even pointed out humble wooden shacks along the banks with a pride in their addition to the character of the parish. After Byron called to Pearce's attention yet another sugarhouse smokestack or plantation manor house, peppering in tidbits about the families and their scandals, Pearce's eyelids, heavy with what Byron supposed was the beer and a long journey, began to close. It was when Pearce placed his gloved hands on Byron's knee, and then thigh, that Byron's incessant talking came to an abrupt end. The carriage stopped on the quiet dirt road, the sun at its late-afternoon peak. As the roof of the buggy offered them very little cover, Byron had the presence of mind to say, "We can wait. We've waited more than a month."

Pearce disagreed. They had waited long enough. Pearce leaned slightly, and took Byron by the face with both hands, opened his mouth, and kissed him as deeply as he could. Both collided with each other's teeth, and then laughed, and stopped laughing, and kissed fully and slowly, savoring lips and tongues. A moment to gasp for air and to begin again. Pearce reached down in Byron's trousers, fumbled through his drawers to find what he wanted.

"Not here," Byron said. "Not yet."

"Words from your mouth," Pearce whispered. "Your member dissents."

Byron removed Pearce's hand with care and straightened himself. "We're soon there."

With their longing expressed between them, they looked forward to their privacy even more. Pearce buttoned Byron's trousers and fixed his shirt collar beneath his jacket. Byron pulled the rein for a gentle clip-clop pace of hooves against dirt and pebbles.

"From here we must be careful . . ."

Pearce refused to fall into Byron's melancholy. "We should be awarded stripes for our great care. We are the corporals of care."

"I only mean to protect us. We've

already taken a chance in the open."

"The kiss couldn't wait. Tell me you agree." His friend was being his joking self.

"I agree, I agree," Byron said. "Just be patient. We'll be left to ourselves in our separate living space. I can declare my body yours."

"Oh, we've made a few declarations," Pearce said. "If I were the delicate sort, I'd take umbrage at your declaration of body only, but having reacquainted myself with a certain girth" — he made the gesture of penis pulling — "I forgive you."

Byron was exasperated. "I want to laugh."

"Then do. Laugh."

"But I can't. Don't you see? I must care for your safety. Our safety."

To this Pearce gave the sigh Byron was used to hearing. The "there he goes again" sigh.

"All right, then," Byron said. "Tell me you took the steamer downriver to fuck."

"I hope not once, but again and again."

179

"And that's all?"

"My fellow, my friend," Pearce said. "I care for your company. I do. I don't know what else to say, other than I've traveled the river, endured other inconveniences, to spend the remaining weeks of furlough with you."

"Yes. And we must take care."

Pearce hated to see his friend in his thoughtful mood. It wasn't his own way to deeply ruminate, but to do and to be. He didn't think too long on the matter, tapped the side of his nose with his forefinger, and said, "We'll have a game, you and I, and only we know we are the engaged players. But they will help us play along."

"Come again?" Byron asked.

"We will have a word," Pearce said. "A secret word. That when said by those in the household, will remind the other of his deep affection."

"Beyond marvelous," Byron said. "I couldn't think of anything so clever."

"So now that we are agreed and lifted in spirit, and, I add, in flesh, so to speak."

"Agreed."

"What do you propose our word be? Think now. It can't be so common in use that its mention will produce no spark, or we will weary from its utterance."

"True, true," Byron said. "And it can't be a word so esoteric that there is no hope of its utterance."

"For surely you would die." And then he regretted the reminder of the chasm between his lover's sentiment and his own. "And that wouldn't do."

"Agreed. Death by moroseness won't do."

"But it should be a word of equal probability: to be said or not to be said!"

"Then I have it," Byron said. "Our word for our special purpose is 'cane.'"

Byron let Pearce sleep for the remainder of the ride. It wasn't to be a long sleep or ride. The sound of oncoming hooves awakened him from his nap. Byron was already aware of the charging horse and was firm on the reins to steady the horse as it reared up on its hind legs, giving the buggy a bounce on its wooden wheels. Byron called "Easy, easy" to his horse, but kept a tight rein all the same until the whinnying calmed.

Byron and Pearce looked at the on-comer, the flag of dark-green silk, its rider low against the neck of the horse, clods of dirt flying. She circled around them to startle their horse even more.

Pearce was thoroughly entertained. "Take my pocket watch, highwayman!" He leaned forward to feign a harder look.

"Highway lass. Forgive me."

"Jane," Byron stated.

She gave Pearce a good look. "Who is this?" She spoke English.

"No introduction for you," Byron said, also in English, mainly for his friend's sake, although French was the rule at Le Petit Cottage. "But for the benefit of my associate, to whom I am ashamed to make your acquaintance known, this is my fellow cadet."

"Associate?" Pearce spoke up. "I hold your life in my hands on the battlefield. *Associate* won't do. Mademoiselle Jane, is it? I am Robinson Pearce. Forgive me, but my heart still pounds from your advance."

"Robinson Pearce," Jane said. "My father says your academy is where you parade in costume and play war tactics."

Pearce fell back hard against the seat, clutching his heart. "I am hit."

"Said," Byron corrected Jane, dismissing Pearce's theatrics. "Her father is deceased. He *said,* Jane. He *says* no more."

"My extended sorrow, Mademoiselle

183

Jane," Pearce said and bowed his head slightly.

"No extended sorrow," Jane answered. "You didn't know him or cause his death. Sorrow is enough."

"That was almost pleasant," Byron said. "Good to see your lessons with Grandmère are progressing."

"Lessons?" Pearce asked, although it was apparent, in his eyes and half grin, he thought it amusing.

"Jane is like a family member. We played together as children. Rather, she ran after me. Grandmère is giving her special instructions."

"I take the lessons to ride my Virginia Wilder."

Pearce was taken aback by her candor and expression.

"Madame Guilbert talks about matchmaking, marriage, and cards while I sit in this frock. Then I ride my horse."

"Naturally," Pearce said.

"Jane is quite the fisherman and huntress."

"Hunter," Jane corrected. "I don't

know what a huntress is."

Pearce couldn't contain himself and laughed full out and heartily.

"I don't like making your acquaintance," Jane told Pearce. "I won't like being in your company."

"Mademoiselle Jane —"

"My mother is French Creole. My father is English. I prefer Jane and English. I hope to not see you, but if I do, I am Jane."

"I will make note," Pearce said.

"I am to say, 'It was a pleasure to meet you, Monsieur Pearce Robinson,' but I won't say any of it to you. I just have to know what I must say. Now, I have until dusk to ride my Virginia Wilder. I am gone."

Jane and her horse galloped away.

"Creature!" Pearce said.

"Creature. Indeed."

The two men laughed together and didn't stop until they reached the house. The boy, Henri's grandson, was there to lead and uncouple the horse from the buggy. Byron took Pearce's bag and they started to the garçonnière. He stopped his friend from climbing up the steps with him.

"Grandmère is watching. She always watches. If we go up to the room, I doubt we'll leave, and she'll send her maid for us. Forgive my grandmother. She's hungry for visitors. Better you stay down here."

"Fine," Pearce said.

Byron ran up the stairs with the bag and was back to the ground floor with his friend.

"I've told you," Byron said, "my father speaks English, Creole, and French, but he will speak English. My grandmother speaks English, but I recommend standing on her good side and speaking some French."

"Good to know," Pearce said in French, for practice.

Byron made a face. "She won't like your French, but life here is easier if you make the effort."

"Also good to know."

"Now, my father might burst into poetry, *The Iliad,* any poems by Lord Byron

— hence my name — or he might try to regale you with tales from India and her mystical treasures. It does us no good to keep him from his outbursts. Laugh politely — less the sulking, which leads to melancholy and cane rum."

"Melancholy! Sounds familiar," Pearce said. "Byron, at ease. Let me discover them as they are. All the more for my enjoyment." He looked over at his love. "How else will I know you, if I don't know them?"

III

Jane, fresh from riding, entered the dining room. The men stood. She marched to her chair, carrying and releasing an unescapable musky horse scent with her. Her hair and face were sopped with sweat.

"Jane," Madame Sylvie said quickly and flatly. "No need to rush to the table on our behalf after your ride. We will wait for you." Madame made a fluttering, shooing motion with her hands to direct Jane to the stairs.

Jane was dumbfounded by the hand gestures that had not been included in her lessons.

This put Madame on the spot. "Gentlemen are expected to wait for ladies while they . . ." She looked to her maid in the corner pulling the punkah. "Thisbe."

Thisbe went swiftly to her mistress and bent low to receive her instruction. Madame whispered, and Thisbe nodded once. "Thisbe will attend to you."

Jane only stared at the lamb chop, still hot and smothered in lemon and parsley sauce. She didn't understand that she was being rescued or the pains that Madame went through to delicately rescue her. "But I need no —"

"Mademoiselle Jane." Madame's tone was no longer delicate. "Follow Thisbe. Now."

Jane eyed the platter of meat. Then Pearce. "The biggest chop is mine," she told him and then followed Thisbe out of the room.

The men couldn't contain themselves, although Pearce tried to keep his merriment to titters for the sake of his impression on Madame Guilbert. He left it up to Byron and Monsieur Guilbert to laugh as hard as saloon men.

"A handsome young lady," Pearce offered.

"And fragrant," Byron added, waving his napkin.

"Now, now." Lucien regained some decorum. It was Juliette Chatham's money for boarding the girl and her horse that kept the creditors somewhat at bay and kept his name out of the latest legal pleadings. If the girl took to writing letters to her mother, Lucien had to emerge as Jane's protector. "Poor Jane. She doesn't know any better."

"Be kind," Madame added. "She was raised to be wild and is now alone in the world."

"Momanm," Lucien said. "Jane's father doted on her and taught her many . . . useful things."

"That is what I said," Madame snapped. "Raised wild in the hands of the Englishman. That is why the confusion."

Madame looked at Pearce. Byron saw this look, this scrutiny in his grandmother's eyes, and sighed heavily.

"You are not English, are you?"

Byron was set for objections, but Pearce, happy to oblige, said, "Madame Guilbert" — and he used the French pronunciation, with a soft *G* and an unarticulated *t* and not "Gilbert" with its hard *G* and spoken *t* as Byron answered to when called by corporals and lieutenants alike during drill or inspection. "We are originally from Massachusetts, but my living situation is in Yorktown Heights, New York."

"No, no, Monsieur Pearce. No one is truly from these . . . wild states. These territories. I look at you and I don't see in you strong bloodlines. Where is your family from?"

"Grandmère!"

Pearce had the confidence of one who chose to amuse himself by observing the particulars of others rather than attack them. He couldn't help but be amused and charmed by the older woman; her heavily potted-rouged cheeks, her hair parted, slightly poufed, and netted for his benefit.

"I'm told my father's grandfather settled in Massachusetts from Wales. His wife, my great-grandmother, I cannot say. Only that she didn't come with him from Wales. My grandmother might have been German. Or Dutch. I don't know my family. Only that they were originally printers who fell on hard times. To ensure I would have an education, I was given to a childless couple of means when I was ten. They campaigned for my military career."

Each word of fact spoken by Pearce, Madame found more shocking than the ones before. In her mind she was having dinner with one of the ditchdiggers that encamped along the levee or a descendant of a family that had arrived in the States as convicts.

Marie saw the color drain from Madame's face and all motion of talking and breathing cease. She rushed to Madame to pat her on the back. Madame pushed Marie away, and the servant returned to her station and stood with her sister.

Lucien, however, enjoyed the fruits of Pearce's revelation. He noted how his mother's chest seemed to collapse, and how her hard, uplifted cheeks were now sunken in and made more pathetic by their highlighted color. Lucien tilted his glass to her and smiled. He read her concerns: *How am I to ride to church on Sunday and rescind the invitations to the Pierpont daughters? How am I to face*

Lucille Pierpont? Lucien smiled and tipped his glass her way, and then sipped. *Yes, Momanm,* he seemed to say with his smile. *You have stuck out your neck to impress your friends and rivals with a proud American descended from he knows not where.*

"What are you doing?" Jane asked the girl who was unbuttoning her blouse.

"Undressing Mademoiselle," Thisbe said softly in French. Jane pushed Thisbe's hand away. She was hungry and wanted to eat.

"Madame says I must clean you before you return to the dining room."

"English," Jane said. "Speak English."

Thisbe paused. She chose the English she was expected to speak. "Yes'm, Miss Jane. Madame say I have to wash some dat sweat off ya fo' yuh kin sit with de mens."

"I'm hungry," Jane said again.

"Ya gwine t'eat, Miss Jane."

"Jane."

"Yes'm, Miss Jane. And den I tend to

193

yo hair."

Thisbe spoke while peeling away the stinking blouse from Jane's arms and body. As she suspected from the ripe smells, Jane, the daughter of wealthy planters, wore no underskirt, bindings, petticoat, or bloomers. Her odor was overpowering.

Thisbe went about her work quickly. She didn't know how long the girl would sit and be washed, but she feared Madame's retribution should she fail to return this Jane, this large, white, freckled, fleshy girl, to the dining room clean enough to be seated at the table.

Thisbe poured water from the pitcher into the basin and wetted a small huckaback towel in it. She dabbed the towel around Jane's eyes and mouth and about her face, neck, and ears, as she did for Madame each morning. The same cloth, she wetted generously and ran through the thick crop of red hair on the girl's head. Even short as it was, Jane's hair was not without knots and tangles, some of her locks fusing together. Next, Thisbe took the comb from the vanity and attempted to pull it through Jane's short but tangled hair. Jane slapped Thisbe, but Thisbe was not deterred. "Beg pardon, Miss Jane. Beg pardon. I'm only try'n ta make you decent."

Jane settled down, somewhat. There wasn't much that could be done as hastily as Thisbe's efforts called for. She needed more time to comb through the neglect and tangles of Jane's hair. But more to the point, dinner was being held for Jane. Thisbe knew Madame would not let the men eat until Jane was seated. While Jane might be the cause for the delay, it rested upon Thisbe to move quickly.

Thisbe took the larger cotton cloth, soaked it in the basin, and washed Jane's neck, arms, and breasts, while Jane sat. Thisbe was used to lifting up her own breasts as well as Madame's to wash, but there was no fullness to lift on the girl, so she washed across her chest. She wetted the cloth and continued to wash Jane's belly, her back, her thighs, inner and outer, and down to her legs. She scrubbed hard. The girl was strongly built and needed a good cleaning. On the last dip of water, she scrubbed the patches of thick red hair under the girl's arms and the coils that guarded her sex.

"My nanny used to wash me," Jane said.

"Where she gone?" Thisbe asked.

"Shreveport. Mother sold her."

The moist evening heat dried the girl quickly. Thisbe searched the vanity for powder. There was none. Only the shaving things of Jane's father's. Men's things. Thisbe went quickly to Madame's room, brought the powder ground from talc and dried honeysuckle, and dabbed some on the girl's body.

And now to dress her. She took the bloomers and corset from the mahogany armoire.

"No," Jane said. "I won't wear them."

"*S'il vous plaît,* Mademoiselle Jane."

"English. And no."

Thisbe brought out a plain black dress from the armoire that she had put away. It was a mourning dress for church. It would have to do.

Jane breathed heavily. A horse snort. But she didn't fight Thisbe and stepped into the dress while Thisbe carefully but quickly pulled up the skirt and the dress bodice, and then helped the girl's arms through. What lack of foundation worn underneath the dress was no gentleman's concern. Thisbe fastened the hooks in the back. The girl was freshened, she carried on her a more suitable fragrance of honeysuckle and talc, and her hair — well . . . what could be done?

Jane returned to the dining room, Thisbe trailing her. The men stood.

Madame said, "May I present to you, my close family friend, Mademoiselle Jane Chatham, daughter of Juliette Boisvert Chatham, family from France, the Rouen region." She turned to Jane, who was fixed on the platters. "Jane, this is Monsieur Robinson Pearce, friend of Byron, student at the military academy."

"My pleasure to meet you, Mademoiselle Jane." Pearce bowed.

Jane had the look of intensity. A look that Madame was afraid denoted thinking on Jane's part. Madame's first instinct was to interrupt Jane's thinking.

"Well —" she began.

But Jane spoke up. "We have met,

Madame Guilbert. And I told Pearce it was not a pleasure to meet him, as you've shown me. I couldn't lie." Then Jane focused on what she was to do next. Lower herself into the chair, spine straight but leaning slightly forward, and to not stick out her backside, her hands in her lap. She had done so.

The men sat as well.

"Mademoiselle, I am still most charmed," Pearce said.

"I am not charmed," Jane replied. "I am hungry."

"Jane is correct," Madame said quickly. "The formal introduction was to be made here."

"A lover's row," Lucien said. "You work quickly, Mr. Robinson Pearce."

Pearce gave a fencing sign, *touché*, although he was amused and certainly not injured.

Jane didn't wait for the servants to bring the platter to her. Her chop was on the platter. She stabbed the thickly smothered meat, laying claim. She didn't care about their fun at her expense. She would make short work of the chop and then have another.

Madame counted her small achievements with her pupil. The girl spoke well to her grandson's friend. She seated herself somewhat properly. And if the girl's mother had been diligent in one area of the girl's development, Jane seemed to have some dining room decorum. Jane could manage a knife and fork in concert, her drinking glass, napkin, and finger bowl competently — perhaps not with ladylike grace, but with military precision.

"We must cancel the waltz," Madame said soberly.

"Speak up, Mé." Lucien used this local term in mixed company to add to his mother's injury. "What you say?"

"I said, there is no point to host a waltz."

Pearce looked to Byron. Byron waved his hand as a promise to explain later.

Lucien had decided he liked this new houseguest. He liked Pearce's youth and unabashed pride in all the things that caused his mother discomfort. There was no attempt, other than his French, to impress or to make himself more than he was. Lucien pressed the young man for more.

"So tell us of your adventures, Mr. Robinson Pearce."

"Monsieur Guilbert, I answer to Pearce, if you don't mind."

"Pearce it is. Tell us of your travels during your furlough. To be a young man on his own!"

Byron rolled his eyes. He dreaded tales of the women of India or a full canto of *The Iliad.*

Madame made a face. She and Byron caught eyes and sighed.

"I'm not quite unencumbered, sir," Pearce said.

"You see, Mé, there is something to this Pearce after all. A fiancée? Perhaps a lover?"

"Lucien!" Madame scolded. "And you, Monsieur Pearce. We are a Catholic home."

"Yes, yes, Madame Guilbert. Let me clarify immediately. I have the responsibilities of my adoptive parents' business affairs. Papers to sign. The properties are in Boston, Ohio, and Illinois. For my widowed mother, furlough couldn't have come at a better time."

Madame's neck seemed to grow an inch. Her face warmed with color. She made no gasps of joy or relief, but only she knew how rapidly her heart beat in her chest. She didn't bother to repay her son with a look of satisfaction. She didn't glance Lucien's way. Instead, she said to Pearce, "You are a good son to your adoptive parents."

In the meanwhile, she plotted. The waltz was on. If there were businesses to manage in places as diverse as the three he mentioned, as well as the family's holdings in Yorktown Heights — whatever they might be — then the stock of this one-day military officer, now an heir, was on the rise.

The family retired to the west parlor room, except for Jane, who wanted no more of Robinson Pearce. Madame renewed a spat with Byron.

"But do spend your days here in the house," Madame said. "Read the books in our library. Send the servants to the cook for what you like. Recline in the parlor rooms. Do you play the piano, Robinson?"

"Pearce," he said. "Please. And, I don't."

"Lies," Byron said. "He plays beautifully."

"Please!" Madame said. "Please play for us. Bizet, I'm sure, is too complex for your talent, but play us something from Brahms. Or any of the German or Viennese compositions. But no Stephen Foster in this house. No. I don't allow it."

"Grandmère," Byron said. "What will Pearce think of us? We insult his talent, then demand that he play for us. Have mercy on my friend."

"Madame Guilbert, I humbly and graciously accept your hospitality, but I'm afraid my piano playing is limited to Beethoven, and not his superior movements."

"Don't listen to him, Grandmère. He can be coaxed to play Chopin."

"Not for an audience, Madame. But I will make the effort."

"Then you must practice here!" Her

cheeks were rosy again. "But don't hide yourself from us, with your card games, drinking, and boyish preoccupations. For your school days at the Academy will soon end and you must become the men of our society."

"For once, my mother, I agree completely," Lucien said. "Rise early, men. For tomorrow we go among the cane."

Madame's letter writing couldn't wait for the morning. It didn't matter that Juliette Chatham and the letter would find each other across the Atlantic in a month's time. Madame Sylvie dipped her nib into the inkwell while the latest developments bubbled within her.

Thisbe couldn't make out all the words, or Madame's writing. The letters in Madame's handwriting were not like the letters on a book cover, fully round or straight. But also, the letters of the alphabet in English were easier to piece together to form words. The French language on paper, from what Thisbe could glean, was trickier. But as Madame wrote, Thisbe put together three words. Jane. Pirs. Byron. Byron's name she had seen many times before.

Thisbe looked on anyway with carefully hooded eyes.

July 16, 1860

My Dear Juliette,

I hope by the time you receive this, you are settled in your daughter and her husband's home.

I write with good news. The Holy Mother has heard our prayers and has responded in the most favorable way. Already Jane is getting the practice a young lady needs to enter society. She is now acquainted with Byron's friend, M. Robinson Pirs, a wealthy young man and soon military officer. If you could have seen how the sparks ignited between the two. They are in the testy part of their acquaintance, but I am not worried. This Robinson Pirs is already giving Jane practice in the art of turning away a suitor. You would be proud.

Don't be concerned that Jane and this Pirs sleep under the same roof. Lucien and I insisted the young officer stay in the garçonnière with Byron for the sake of Jane's honor. He is quite the gentleman. He might have some French blood, although I cannot say for sure. More to come on these developments.

I hope to put your mind at ease and to send you to your knees in prayers of gratitude.

Your truest friend,
Madame Sylvie Bernardin
de Maret Dacier Guilbert
Le Petit Cottage, St. James Parish,
la Louisiane

IV

That night, after a long-awaited union of kissing and urgent coupling, Byron and Pearce lay together, exhausted, legs entangled. They listened to the sounds of the dark as a stream of moonlight crept into their room through slightly parted curtains.

Byron was still breathless when he said, "Jesse was like a brother. We were" — he exhaled deeply — "as close as one body. Shortly after he ran away, my father took me on a trip to New Orleans for business. After that we went to the racetracks. I looked forward to that."

"I've enjoyed a horse race or two," Pearce said.

"And then to Madame Suzette's Tea Service."

"Tea?"

"A euphemism."

"I see."

"We went to Madame Suzette's on Basin Street at number forty-four for afternoon tea, my father and I."

"And were there varieties of tea?"

"You could say. While my father was being served in one room, I was in the adjoining room with two" — he paused — "hostesses. One, a quadroon, the other, white. They almost looked identical. What I remember is both wore bows in their hair, like bows on a child's smock. Long tendrils hung down from their crowns, I suppose to make them look childlike. Their curls, perfect. Not a rogue strand on either head. I thought, How do they make their curls so round and perfect?

"And then they began to tickle me and stick feathers in my ears, beneath my chin, around my neck. And there was ice cream. They spoon-fed me ice cream."

"Torture."

"Laugh if you will, but I was a boy. For me, yes, torture. Then I heard moans in the next room. Terrible moans. The

207

quadroon said, 'You na hear dat sweet pain 'fore, *chère*?' The girls laughed.

" 'They're hurting my father,' I said.

"The girls caressed my face to tease me, not to calm me. The other girl said, 'Chère, they nat hurting M'syoo. He is hurting the m'mzelle. Nicely so.'

"I tried to get up to save my father, but the two sat on me. I was no match for the two girls working in tandem. I, a boy of twelve. They had to be fifteen. Sixteen."

"Amazons," Pearce said.

"The quadroon said there would be hell to pay if M'syoo didn't finish his business. She said, 'Look. Your ice cream melt,' and shoved the spoon in my mouth. They took turns licking the running cream from my neck and face."

"Sweet torture," Pearce said. "What did you do?"

"I tried to make myself small. Squirm. Tighten my shoulders to evade their tongue bath. Later my father emerged from the other room with boots in hand, his clothes sloppily more off than on.

"The white girl said to my father, 'We

would like new feathers. Two bits more.'

"My father was in a good mood and peeled off a note. Then he looked at me and saw that I'd been crying. His mood changed. He yelled at the two girls, and the white girl pulled a velvet rope that hung from the wall. No doubt the bell. The madame of the teahouse and her strongman appeared shortly. The yelling. I remember that clearly. Finally, the madame asked the girls why they didn't give what was paid for. The girls said, 'We tried to tease him in every way, but he cried, so we fed him ice cream to make the little boy happy.'

" 'Little boy? *Little boy?*' My father took offense, but I assure you, even down here where the sun ripens one fast, a twelve-year-old is a boy. 'Madame,' my father bellowed, 'I've paid for services not rendered.'

" 'But, monsieur,' the madame said, 'you cannot make the horse drink if he isn't ready. Or thirsty for the water.'

" 'I won't hear it,' my father said. 'I've paid well. I demand satisfaction.'

"Madame said, 'I will give you a free half hour.' She and the strongman left.

" 'If it is instruction the boy needs, there is no better tutor than his father!' he said."

Pearce stroked Byron's face. "I shudder to think."

"Don't stop me now," Byron said. "I've never spoken of this nightmare. Let this be my first and only admission of the ordeal.

"My father said, 'I will show you, boy, what you are to do.' He looked at the two girls, grabbed the quadroon girl, ordered her onto the settee, and opened her legs. She wore open pantaloons. All the while he is rocking side to side, like a bull ox getting his horns up. I truly feared for the girl, and with cause. He ripped the lace pantaloons and she cried for the expense of her garment, as flimsy as it was. 'Boy. Here!' he commanded. I didn't want to get up from the chair where the two had held me hostage, but I feared my father and got myself up and took only one or two steps forward. My father said, 'Ah! Boy! Look on it: the gateway to manhood.' Believe me, it wasn't anything I wanted to see. My father began my education, saying, 'For the sake of the wife you'll take, you must learn this.' He squeezed the seated girl's nipples until she made sounds, then fingered around her belly, round, circular. I hoped that was the end of the education, but she heaved and opened her legs more so. If I didn't want to see it before, I prayed for instant blindness. My education was only beginning. Her sex was unsightly, as it was peach colored, shaven, and swollen. But he had to make sure I knew what I saw, so he splayed open the swollen flesh and said, 'This is the gate we storm.'

"While this was happening before my eyes, the other girl stuck her hand down my pants and found my member. She pulled on it — which I might have liked if I was, perhaps, blindfolded to the chicken innards that gaped before me. My father ordered the girl to be quick about pulling my pants down and exposing me. I can still hear him shouting at her, 'Don't let him spend yet!' But she pulled and squeezed, looked at my father, and said, 'No gun for the soldier to shoot, M'syoo.'

"I will shorten this sad tale and spare you my father's profane spew. He told me, 'Watch how it's done. This will clear all confusion.' He added that, if my pistol gained courage, he would stand back while I 'waged war.' "

"And?"

"He went into her."

"And?"

"I fainted."

"Dear, dear boy."

"Don't pity me. No, no. Please don't do that."

They lay in the moonlight for a time.

Byron held his breath. He turned over, perhaps to sleep it away.

"Byron."

"What?"

"Are you sorry you told me?"

Byron didn't answer.

"Can I ask you a question?"

Byron still didn't answer.

"So, you've never entered the holy, or shall I say, unholy canal?"

Byron shook his head no. His back was still to Pearce.

"And you are engaged."

212

"Yes."

"And, can you?"

"I have to produce an heir," Byron said.

"Suppose you can't. Or, suppose you don't produce this heir."

"Then everything dies with me."

"Mr. Melancholy. Prince of Solemn-choly."

"Maybe this was a mistake," Byron said.

"Which? Me being here, or that you told me?"

Byron kept his back to Pearce and said nothing.

"Dear Byron. Dear friend. Silence won't do. Be sorry and melancholy if you like, but I'm here and we've shot off our rockets on this glorious star-spangled night. O'er the ramparts, if you will."

Byron said nothing.

"Army mule! You want to laugh. I know you, beneath the melancholy and doom. What can I do to make you happy? Something not so strenuous, please. I am spent."

Byron finally turned around so that

they lay together, breath to breath. "Tell me something. Tell me about you."

Pearce sighed heavily. He sat up. Something in his face changed, which, for the affable Pearce, was significant. "Can I put my confidence in you?"

"I've put mine and more in you."

"Serves me right," Pearce said. "I resolve to bare my soul and you throw the obvious jab."

Byron almost smiled. "It was there to be thrown."

"Good, then," Pearce said. "And now I'll tell you what I didn't tell your grandmother at the earlier inquisition — heaven forbid! I'll tell you what I've told no one."

Now Byron sat up.

"You asked me why I removed the Stewart name from my person and reverted to my family name, Pearce. Here it is," he began. "My first years with the Stewarts were more than a boy in my circumstance could hope for. I was well fed. Wore the best clothes. Attended school and church. I was given their name, introduced as their son, and not made to feel like the charity case that I was. I was twelve when my duties changed."

"How so?" Byron, who had turned inward, was now attentive. He yearned to know Pearce beyond being drawn to him. And now he would.

Pearce exhaled.

"I'm not the tender sort. I don't take too much to heart. I think you know that."

"Regretfully, true," Byron said.

"Well, now, in the name of tenderness I ask for a kindness."

"Which is?"

"To let me finish a tale I thought I would never recite — as it were." Pearce and Byron understood the word as it applied to West Point. To *recite,* at the Academy, was to stand and be tested before everyone.

"I won't stop you," Byron said. "Recite."

"At the time that I was welcomed into the Stewart home, I was told my adoptive father wasn't a well man. That he needed care and that I would attend to him. I bathed Mr. Stewart. Dressed him. Groomed him. He'd stroke my hair in the evening and say, 'Come, sweet boy. Give us a kiss. One here' — he'd point to his cheek — 'and one here' — to his knob. 'Now, now. 'Tis nothing. Don't be shy,' he'd say. Then I was asked to play with it and to finish him off. It was always so polite — as if I had a choice. For an orphan, there was no choice. It wasn't long before Mrs. Stewart joined in and told me I was becoming a young man and that I would have to do what Mr. Stewart could no longer do. On further reflection, I'm certain Mr. Stewart never performed that husbandly task on his wife. Not only did I learn to serve at Mrs. Stewart's pleasure, I became expert in withholding mine. In the meanwhile, we sat in the front-most pews, straight and proud as the minister preached on filth, fornications, and sodomites. It only heightened my adoptive parents' zeal.

"Then one night after supper we had plums. Plums stewed in brandy and tree sap. The tastes and texture stay with me although I've not had that dish since. 'Eat your fill, Master Robinson,' Mrs. Stewart said. 'Eat.' And Mr. Stewart sang the rhyme, 'Little Jack Horner sat in the corner. He put in his thumb and pulled out a plum and said, "What a good boy am I." '

"I should have known. They'd given me every hint. But I was a boy of thirteen. I went to my room thinking I was off from service that night. I put on my nightshirt and went to bed, but before I could fall into a good sleep, the Stewarts entered my room carrying a lit candle. From his positioning on my bed, it was clear what I was to do. Mind you, I had washed his ass not an hour ago, and now I was to unlock the door and enter him, without an ounce of lard. Just my own spit. I hadn't done that or had it done to me. Imagine. Thirteen! I was frightened and overcome. Exhilarated and disgusted. Something in me was both broken but had also unbuckled. And while I still serviced Mrs. Stewart, it was with Mr. Stewart that I . . . found myself. The only thing, whilst I fucked him, the merry couple sang 'Little Jack Horner,' and other nursery rhymes."

"Pearce . . . ," Byron said. He kissed Pearce's ear and cheek. Pearce leaned away.

"Don't pity me," Pearce said. "No pity kisses. For, I wonder, how would I know to unlock that door?"

"I think we know. Eventually."

Pearce did not reply.

Byron wanted to console, but he waited for his friend to come back to him. He waited for Pearce's consent. He could see Pearce wasn't done talking, so he waited for him to begin again.

"And then the tide turned against the Stewarts," Pearce said, his voice picking up pride. "And as I grew older, it was understood between us that I was privy to what the Stewarts kept from their society. I benefited from my education. Mr. and Mrs. Stewart needed me more than I needed them. For my silence, they took care of me with an annual income, the introduction to our congressman, and letters of reference from the pious members of the church so I could interview at West Point. It was really quite sad. Mr. Stewart died. And Mrs. Stewart made me heir and executor of their holdings,

218

fearing the unpredictability of what a new husband would bring. Since she cannot own property and businesses, everything was put in my name, which was reverted to my original, Pearce. I ended my service to Mrs. Stewart, but I remain decent to her. I do care for her and maintain the properties and her Yorktown Heights home so that she wants for nothing. I've profited greatly, but this is not a story I'll again repeat."

"Dearest, believe me. I won't ask you."

V

The garçonnière was never an undertaking to clean, or a noteworthy task. The fastidious Byron's habits were such that he gave the servants little to do in his private room. Marie and Louise entered the tall round building daily and climbed the steps loudly enough to be heard, often singing, in case the young maître was sleeping. Now, there was a reason to enter with caution or to save this room for last, after the young maître and his friend were out engaged with their day.

They remembered the talk years ago about Maître Byron, when they were young. The talk about Maître Byron and Lily's boy. The dead boy. The night before, Marie and Louise remembered the boy as they watched the two, Maître Byron and his Pearce, while they served the meal.

The sisters climbed the stairs singing in their usual way. This time when they entered, they found the room in disarray, clothing strewn about, and the bed lumpy beneath the light cotton sheets and quilt. Marie pulled back the quilt to strip the sheets. She stopped cold. "Weesa! Look!"

Louise had already picked up the clothing and began dusting. She looked at her sister. It was Marie's nose that she saw first, scrunched in the revulsion reserved for the contents of Lucien's pot de chambre.

Marie pointed at the sheet. "You see?"

The copious stains needed no name, just an acknowledgment between the sisters.

When they brought the underclothes, shirts, and sheets of the men outside to the metal tubs to be washed, Marie spoke low so her voice wouldn't carry.

"We scrub hard, Weesa," Marie said. "We say nothing about this."

Louise laughed.

"You like gossip. I like gossip. But think, sister. If we talk among us, with our husbands, our mother, the words spread like cane fire. If we look them in the eye, they know we know. What happens to us?"

"Everyone already say things about young maître."

"That's talk," Marie said of the name, "little girl-boy," that Byron had secretly been called in the quarter. "But we know. That's different. When those words rise up from the quarter, whose tongue gets cut? Who will be sold? Think, Weesa. We have our men. Our children. We lose everything. We scrub hard. Hang the wash. Don't point eyes at no one. We say nothing."

VI

With each passing day, as the house brimmed with conversation and activities, Madame grew to forgive Robinson Pearce for his flaw of being American. While his French didn't improve, his piano playing gave Madame hope. She saw this as a selling point and imagined evenings of courtship between the American and a Pierpont daughter, sitting two by two on the piano bench playing Viennese compositions. These thoughts of romance made her think about her son's happiness and what it could mean for the future of the family.

"You must remarry, Lucien. The house is in ruins."

This was far from the truth, but Lucien let his mother have her way.

"No woman in her right mind would

test her luck."

"Nonsense," Madame said, although she could think of no eligible woman so despised by her family or acquaintances that they would allow her to enter a union with Lucien Guilbert. Still, she said cheerfully, "A widow would jump at the opportunity. It has been six years."

"And six brides."

Madame stopped to count. "I don't recall them all. Three dead. Two ran off. One, I can't place. Still, son. The house needs a mistress. A strong one."

Madame had long quit the rigorous work of the mistress. Following the death of her husband and the excursion of her son, she had become both master and mistress. She managed the household budget and ran the household staff; planned the menus, the social gatherings, the dressing of the rooms; chastised one cook for overseasoning the dishes and chastised another for underseasoning the dishes. Her domain extended well beyond the house. She tended to the sick among her enslaved people when there was no doctor or dentist and negotiated shrewdly with vendors to provide clothing and shoes for the enslaved as well.

Women had been taken from cane production to launder and scrub in the house, but Lucien would get them big with child and Madame would insist he sell the babies to places far flung from Le Petit Cottage. Never to friends or to just a ways up or down the river, but cheaply to poor subsistence farmers who couldn't use house servants but needed field hands to toil and bleed in cotton fields, or to rice plantations in South Carolina. Rice farming was hard, soul-killing farming. What doesn't break a back in rice-planting country would feast on blood and bring on yellow fever. "Keep them far from me" was Madame's demand. "Keep them out of my house." Unlike most plantation mistresses, Madame Sylvie wouldn't tolerate certain aspects of the Creole life, mainly the mixing of blood. Seeing her likeness in brown skin, with wide noses and tough hair. As long as she held on to the location of the gold, she wouldn't tolerate what plantation mistresses turned a blind eye to.

"I'm afraid we must wait for Eugénie

to take the reins," Lucien said.

"Ack! But a girl," Madame lamented.

"As were you, Mother, when you married Father."

"You forget, my son. I was forced into service."

"With a marriage contract."

"If I was not smart enough to insist on a marriage contract, we would not be here," Madame said. "The right situation can still happen for you, son. The older Pierpont daughter, perhaps. Lucille will insist on a contract that keeps everything on the Pierpont side, but we can abide by that."

"Mère," he said. "There will not be another Madame Lucien Guilbert. I am resigned."

"I think you mean it," Madame said, alluding to his use of the proper French.

"I believe I do."

Lucien did fondly regard at least three of his six wives. His society was sympathetic to the deaths of his wives. But no one would apply enough sympathy to inflict the gentleman planter on a daughter, an aging sister, or a widowed mother. Certainly not after rumors had traveled to St. James that he had been barred from Madame Suzette's or any other such establishment. (Traveled? Truthfully, dear reader, the rumor had been planted by his whoring cohort, Arne Pierpont, who held a grudge from their failed business.) While it wasn't uncommon for the master to make concubines of enslaved women or to break into the chastity of adolescent girls, or to take a woman in her cabin while her husband and children were sent outside or away, Lucien, given his confirmed case of syphilis and the difficulty it presented as he aged, had relinquished those rights and privileges as master. It was also said that he had been chased with broom and hoe by Black women when he last came creeping to the quarter with his lantern. True, a bondswoman had no rights to herself or her children or husband. But talk of the master among the women, and what they had known about the master's condition, made the women strong when he had come for one of the young girls. "Sell us. Beat us. Hang us from a tree until we dead. We won't give the child over." This was their stance as they circled the girl, brooms, hoes, and cane knives in hand.

He had laughed it off, as if he had been on a drunken tear, and then he staggered his way back to the house. The women waited for retribution to come in the morning. For a posse of white men to come to seek justice for the spurned plantation master. No sounds of horses' hooves stirred dust on their land, nor did howling dogs rupture the morning air. No one had come. The work bell rang at five thirty, and the women, along with the men and children, went out to the cane and cotton fields and worked as they had any morning. It had been six years since the master had come down to the quarter with his lantern.

Following that time, Lucien had proposed to a woman of thirty-two who had never married. Her family had only the never-married woman to offer — and they had done so gladly, as her chances had all but come and gone. But on the bridal night, this final Madame Guilbert fled in horror at the sight of the oozing pusses and poxes on her bridegroom's misshapen penis and committed herself to the convent.

Lucien Guilbert managed to galvanize the field women to risk their lives to save a young girl and had inspired a hopeless spinster to claim chastity with fervor. That was the extent of his recent success with women.

Failed at being attractive husband material, Lucien had one warm spot in his heart for a member of the female sex, and it was for his daughter Rosalie, whom he would not allow his mother to sell away. He could see promise in her as a little girl, holding on to her mother's skirt in the cane field. He hadn't seen a girl Black or white or Spanish or Choctaw as beautiful as Rosalie. Even after he had slapped her hard enough to kill her, the swelling and color went away, and he could see more and more his Rosalie, his Rosalie. In her he knew he had made one near perfect thing.

"We have someone capable of running the household until Eugénie is Byron's wife."

"Who is that?" Madame asked.

"My daughter," Lucien said. "I am going to inquire into the portrait painter, and then I'll go to the school to retrieve my Rosalie."

Madame's appled cheeks fell, flattening her face. "What is that to me?" she snapped. "Don't say it. Don't say what you're thinking, if you have any feeling for your mother."

"Mère," Lucien coaxed. He wouldn't put on too much. "If you do this one thing. This one thing."

Ordinarily, Madame would savor the small victory of his weakened voice. But what he asked for was too much.

"We have more than enough rooms. Let Rosalie maintain the house. By the time my plans come into effect, Eugénie will be Byron's wife and she'll take over."

Mother looked at her son. "How can you ask this of me? How?"

"You make me out to be a brute, when all I ask is to bring my daughter into the house and help you manage it."

"Out of the question. No." She removed the hurt from her face and made herself what she'd had to be since death blackened her childhood: impenetrable in spirit. "And you think you can distract me with the portrait artist? That I will forget that you spilled hundreds of years of Bernardin de Maret blood of my family on animals? You, who traveled across the ocean to bring me a whore bride to mix with my grandfather's blood? Now, you ask me to welcome into my home, near my sainted daughter's room, your dirt?"

"She belongs in Charlotte Thérèse's room. She is your blood. Every time I see her, I see what my sister —"

Madame howled. Like an animal. A howl so disturbing it brought the two housemaids rushing, hands soapy and wet. Thisbe tried to attend to Madame, but Madame pushed her aside.

The two screamed at Thisbe, "*Vini édé* Madanm! Help her!"

Thisbe spoke to the twins with a glare: *This is a thing between white people. Go about your washing.*

Marie and Louise saw that they were not needed and left the maître to his mother and the useless standing girl.

Lucien knelt at his mother's side. This

was now beyond a game of blink between mother and son. He had gone too far — his dead sister a subject implicitly understood as out-of-bounds. "All right, Mère. All right," he conceded, while the Black girl cleaned his mother's face with a cloth from her apron.

Still he said gently, soberly, "I hoped you would let her move to the house, but I was prepared for your reaction. Rosalie might not enter this house, but she will be here in the overseer's cottage. I will have Rosalie here, Mother. I have plans for her."

Madame made no sound other than sniffling. Lucien kissed her hand and left the house.

"Fix my face," Madame told Thisbe. "Before Jane comes for her lesson."

"Yes, Madame Sylvie."

"And attend to Charlotte Thérèse's room. And wear your gloves. Always wear your gloves."

"Yes, Madame Sylvie."

Charlotte Thérèse had been born on a Tuesday and died on a Tuesday before her thirteenth birthday. This became the day of observance at Le Petit Cottage for the child, now Saint Charlotte Thérèse, in Madame's eyes. Madame wore black on Tuesdays while she sat at her perch on the gallery to watch as Thisbe marched to the Guilbert statues with brush, water, a spray of field flowers, and a washrag. Madame's eyes always followed the girl past the big obelisk erected for Bayard, and over to the statue of his only white daughter — as far as it was known. Madame had spent a good deal of her husband's gold on a statue in the likeness of the girl in white Italian marble. The obelisk made for her husband, however, was molded in cheap cement. It was Thisbe's duty to clean the statue of bird droppings, wash the face of the girl first, remove last week's flowers, and place daffodils, honeysuckle, or lily of the valley in the holder, but never the mature flowers that carried a heavier scent. Never dusky magnolias or sensual roses, but tea roses were allowed when they were in bloom.

This task let Thisbe's hands be useful. To be out from the close proximity of Madame. To act as opposed to standing motionless. Although the mistress watched carefully, Thisbe found the outdoor air and the distance from Madame a solace of the week.

When this act of observance was finished, Thisbe hurried to Charlotte Thérèse's room and turned the doorknob, decked with a white satin rosette, her hands still gloved. She dusted the furniture and books with a full feather duster, one kept in the room and not used by the house servants. Next she used a cloth, also proprietary to the room, to clean the mirror. The mosquito netting was taken down and out to the gallery, shaken, and then rehung. Last, without handling these items, the comb, brush, curio jar, and doll face were dusted with a small duster made from hummingbird feathers. She was not to disturb the girl's hairs still caught between the teeth and bristles of the comb and brush. Madame would not bring herself to enter the sacred room. But she stood in the doorframe and watched that all was done as she had instructed.

VII

*Patience. All entanglements require pa-
tience.*

The story of Rosalie, Lucien's daughter,
cannot be told without the story of Jack
and Selma, field hands at Le Petit Cottage, bound to each other as husband
and wife, as properly and respectfully as
any enslaved couple's union without
clergy or a certificate. The pairing was
documented in the Master's ledger, and
the couple rewarded him with eight
offspring, all healthy and dark-skinned,
adding to the prosperity of the plantation. While it can't be said that they were
happy, the bond between Selma and Jack
allowed each day to rise bringing them
crumbs of humanity, and they learned to
make a meal from those crumbs.

After nearly fourteen years of union

and eight offspring, Selma had stopped producing babies. It had been three years since she came up big, or what the Master called "profitable." Lucien Guilbert, who had counted on her productivity and profitability, had taken notice.

Around the same time, John, a favorite field hand, and also Jack's younger brother, had come to Master with a plea. Master Lucien's mind turned quickly on the gears of opportunity. Little John, as he was called, swung his cane knife in the cane field like a machine. "If I could have ten Little Johns," Master would say, "I'd have no worries." Little John proved himself trustworthy to Master Guilbert. He was sent across the river often to the Pierpont Plantation, to bring goods or bourbon to Master Pierpont. It was at the Pierpont Plantation where he fell in love with a house servant. A girl his mother and grandmother warned him to set neither his eyes nor heart on; "keep on and you'll lose your soul." He and his siblings were field hands of untampered-with blood, while she was Black and the product of some French white man's meddling. She, Camille, always had orange water or lemonade and hearth biscuits for Little John. A piece of salt pork or fish. And always a smile. When he came back to Le Petit Cottage with the Master's business complete, his heart light, his soul and loins full of wanting, Little John decided he must have Camille as his wife, his own. No matter the constant warnings from his mother and grandmother.

Never let it be said that Lucien Guilbert was not a fool for love. It was past time that Little John stop withholding his seed from his master and produce some strong, work-all-day bucks and wenches. He slapped his young buck on the backside and thought up an agreement binding Little John to pay for the woman on the Pierpont Plantation. Master made up some papers that Little John couldn't read to begin with and showed him where to put his *LJ* for Little John. No *X*s for them! Lucien had Little John dip the pen nib in black ink and guided him, hand on hand, to scrawl out an *L* and a *J*.

Lucien then struck an arrangement with Monsieur Pierpont over bourbon and hand-rolled cigars. Instead of purchasing the woman for his field hand, he made a trade. The morning that Little John was to bring home his bride from the Pierpont Plantation, Lucien had told Little John's older brother, Jack, to say his farewells to his family; he was going to be placed at the Pierpont Plantation on the east bank. Imagine the scene. The sudden disruption. The wailing of wife, children, parents, and grandparents. While the two brothers rode in the wagon and then in a ferry across the river, imagine the sentiment between them. Jack, not yet thirty, was traded to get children into Pierpont's Black females of childbearing age. It seemed that Pierpont's buck of remarkable size and health had unexpectedly succumbed to a heart attack. Jack was to be his replacement and would be allowed to visit his family at Le Petit Cottage on Sundays.

Before the exchange was official, Guilbert demanded an inspection on the spot to ensure Camille was healthy. He did what had been done at slave auctions. With her betrothed looking on, Lucien put his hands under Camille's skirt to feel her calves, thighs, sex, buttocks, and hips. He opened her mouth, ran his fingers along her teeth and gums last so she was made to taste herself. He slapped her buttocks, then gave her to his favorite field hand. "Go on, Little John. Take your wife."

Little John couldn't look at her or his brother, who had witnessed the scene.

The exchange completed, they ferried back across the river to the west bank and returned to Le Petit Cottage. Little John brought Camille to the cabin he shared with his mother and grandmother. Sooner or later, everyone would know the cost of his prize. They, husband and wife, didn't speak to each other. The sun rose and set six times before she opened her mouth to call him for supper and he answered. Another six days came and went before he touched her. There was no justice to seek. They did as other families had done — rose with the work bell, worked the cane until the bell rang, ate, tended their cabin and garden, and slept. Camille, no longer a house servant, learned quickly to pick up the hoe, swing a blade, and drive a mule and plow. The

Black women never missed the opportunity to make the joke of "the mule (or mulatto) driving the mule." No one forgave Little John or his mulatto wife for breaking up Jack and Selma's family and leaving their eight children without a father. In time, the new young couple found their way to each other and in the community of bondsmen and women. They had children. Two sons. The woman's fairer complexion had no hand in determining the future of their children. They were Black children, destined for the cane field, although Camille hoped to have a daughter to pass down yarn-spinning and sock-knitting. She picked up the hoe and cane knife, and during grinding season, she ministered over boiling kettles of cane syrup along with the other women. Eventually, the memories and opinions held by some of the women would lose their sharpness, and Little John and Camille were accepted. Selma, however, had to be reconciled with the loss of her Jack, who, over time, became agreeable with his new situation across the river on the east bank.

Master Guilbert, a recent widower,

took note of how fast Little John's wife had adjusted to work in the cane field and in the sugarhouse. He kept his eye on her as he rode his white horse behind the slave driver who pressed the work gang down the rows of cane. He didn't want to stop her in the stride of her work: the arms that raised the cane knife and chopped; the full breasts that rose along with her arm movement; the hips, now widened after childbirth; the bending as she stripped away cane stalk. Lucien Guilbert rode up to the slave driver and spoke briefly. The slave driver, as Black as any field hand, then cracked his whip at the family, the father and two boys, but not at the woman. The driver yelled, "Get along, get along! Git!" Little John had already been hacking and stripping and moving at a fierce pace, but now he obeyed the whip, and the children didn't lag behind their father. But Little John turned his head to see about his wife, and the whip answered him. He continued to do the whip's bidding, hacking, hacking, tearing those stalks. The cane knife in his hand now, in his mind, a weapon. The power of it, the intent in his swing, in his eyes. The driver didn't see what burned in his eyes but saw how wildly he swung the cane knife. The slave driver knew the field hand swung with a killing mind, and snapped the whip, giving Little John one clean taste across his back and neck, and said, "Nigger, I'll kill you." The oldest boy called out, "Mama!" but Little John swatted him on the back and said, "You keep on. Don't you look back." Better he swatted his son with his hand, for the driver's whip would kill a child. The boy, also named John, choked on his sobs and the father patted his child's back, this time to console him, until the boy breathed again. Little John pushed his son forward. Neither he nor the boy looked back.

Wringing basketfuls of wet cotton shirts and pants until damp had made Camille's grip strong. She clutched the cane knife's haft. The smell of dirt-clay, freshly cut cane, and cane juice thick in the air. She was going to die that dry fall day during cane-cutting season. There was no way she could live after swinging a blade or a fist at the Master. She was going to die. Widow Little John. Orphan her sons. But first she was going to kill.

Camille meant to strike first and kill, and she meant to accept the death they would give her, for who had heard of such a thing? What planter would stand for property fighting its owner?

She gripped the haft tighter as he pinned her to the clay soil and worked to get his pants down. "Lie still. Don't you move," he told her. When he pulled up her skirt, Camille raised the hand, the haft, the blade, not two inches off the ground. No sooner had she raised it, she felt the hot sear across her hand before she heard the leather snap. Blood seeped and gushed from her palm and bloodied knuckles.

The slave driver had ridden back a few paces, undoubtedly to watch. If not for his want of entertainment, Camille might have succeeded in killing Lucien.

The Master was not deterred by her attempt to kill him or the driver's whip striking and missing him. He had his pants down, and then used his weight to smother her efforts to defend and resist. With one hand over her mouth, he shoved himself inside her.

She bit at his hand but didn't call out. Didn't scream.

Scream, and her husband would come running. Come running and her husband would be hung from the live oak. Scream, and her son would be haunted day and night.

She didn't scream. She didn't need to know her husband wouldn't come running. She didn't need further proof or sign he had no rights to her.

She failed. She lived.

When the Master finished, he wiped himself on her skirt, got up on his horse, and continued surveying the work gang.

The following day, the slave driver came for Camille and had her remove her apron and dress to get what was coming to her. He whipped her until she passed out.

At his mother's urging, Little John waited for one month to pass before touching his wife. No menstrual blood came. He waited for another month. The same. Camille knew, but Little John had no choice but to wait for what the coming months would bring. It was plantation life. Their family rose with the work bell and worked the cane field. Camille grew big and delivered the girl, pink and stringy-haired, in July, the season when the cane crop thrived on its own and the field hands were diverted to the smaller cotton field and ditchdigging.

The cook, Marcelle, brought Madame Sylvie's consommé to her salon, an excuse to share gossip, that a Guilbert baby had been dropped in the cane field. "Pinker than peonies." Madame generally didn't care to hear these things but listened to the old cook, who had her network of gossipers that extended from the cookhouse to the vegetable gardens to the cabins and fields. Madame had a genuine affection for the mulatto cook, a gift from her late husband. Marcelle made the treats of her youth spent in the queen's hamlet. Delightful candies and pastries that always put Madame in a good mood. Marcelle had made these jolly treats for her Charlotte Thérèse before she succumbed to yellow fever. She remembered the child fondly, even though Madame's daughter had passed more than forty years ago. She couldn't resist spoiling the girl even when Madame threatened to sell the cook. Marcelle would say, "But let Charlotte Thérèse taste this pudding before you ship me downriver to the Saint Louis Hotel" — a known location of slave auctions. How Madame favored this half-Black woman who understood the French cuisine.

And one day, Marcelle rushed to tell Madame that the girl, Rosalie, was no longer a pink bundle. She had her own little face, which Marcelle had seen firsthand. The cook happily reported, "Ah! Madame Sylvie! She has the face of Charlotte Thérèse, our angel."

Surely Marcelle had hoped to lift Madame's spirits, who was never her gay self once her daughter died a horrible death, and the door to Charlotte Thérèse's room was ordered closed and a white ribbon was hung from the doorknob.

Instead of going to the quarter to see the child, Madame walled herself away from Marcelle, who could no longer serve her or see her in her salon. Or share her gossip. Just cook. Not too long afterward, Marcelle died in the cookhouse while making the Easter lamb. How she had loved and missed Madame.

Hannah had informed Lucien of the addition. He recorded the child named Rosalie into the ledger on the page set aside for his issue outside of wedlock. He refused to sell Rosalie, as his mother demanded. Even when Madame threatened to cut him off entirely. He wouldn't pluck her from her mother, although her stepfather, who now only went by John, would not have objected.

Madame told Lucien to keep the girl from her sight. Keep her away or she would be sold. And having the power of the gold, Madame was sovereign in most things. She had her way. The child was kept in the field and in the cabin, out of Madame's sight. John would have liked to issue the same demand to the girl's mother. "Keep yo' white trash from my sight, or else." But what good was this threat without power? However begotten, the girl was the Master's daughter, and had the Master's protection.

Madame couldn't understand why she

was made to suffer so. Why it had taken fourteen years for her to deliver a healthy daughter, only to see her blossom, and then die in the most horrific way. Now it is true that Blacks and mixed bloods also succumbed to yellow fever. That those mothers picked up their hoe and broke the unsympathetic ground and cried for their losses, but what were those losses to Madame but notations in the ledger? What were the mournful wails and moans of the field that, even when they carried across hundreds of cane acres, were no more to Madame than the howls of animals?

And now her son schemed to put her in her grave prematurely. This is exactly what Lucien would achieve by bringing this girl, this Rosalie, to Le Petit Cottage. Madame Sylvie didn't care to see a colored version of herself or her bloodline. This injustice she refused to suffer.

VIII

Lucien had done all he could with what he had. Why couldn't his mother see that? The harvest would be a little better than fair. He took every precaution, every measure. He made sure the crop had been planted close together but without choking one stalk with another. He made sure the stalks would shoot up high and not be stunted. The almanac predicted frost; he packed a good portion of the field tightly to hedge his gamble. Many was the farmer who kicked himself in October during cane-cutting season for what he didn't know in January, planting season. He had paid his male hands fifty cents each over a few days to build sluices to drain water overflow. The larger farms had more field hands and the best in machinery. With full night and day shifts, those large farms could press cane and stir the boiling, thickened juice without breaking for rest. The sweat of the field hands, the constant snap of the whip, and for some, a few coins, was the best Lucien could do to guarantee the harvest.

Now, his good friend Alphonse Tournier, at La Fleur Blanche Plantation, had a fine colored son with his banker's daughter. Laurent was the young man's name, as perfectly made as God could fashion a body possessing one-half Black Creole blood. Not only was Laurent tall and filled out, with good teeth and a well-shaped head, but he showed himself early to be a quick learner — his mother, one of the *gens de couleur libres,* having taught him prayer, reading, and arithmetic, and having encouraged him to draw mechanical instruments. The master sent Laurent and his mother to France, where he was educated in engineering, sciences, and French culture. When the boy returned to St. James in the spring, it was well publicized in the *Sugar Planter* that the colored lad held many patents in farming innovations.

Lucien had always hoped to advantageously marry Rosalie to a free land-owning man of color. There were many who owned a plantation and enslaved people. But for Lucien, an engagement to young Laurent Tournier would be the best possible outcome. This colored boy, now twenty-one, with vast knowledge of agriculture and machinery, would surely rescue his father-in-law's farm. Lucien's mind reeled with the possibilities of what the boy knew and could do for Le Petit Cottage.

Lucien was now excited to see his daughter. He had poured so much into the girl, for reasons that gradually revealed themselves to him.

From the time he'd seen her pulling at her mother's skirt in the field, and when he'd sit her on Zuk, he had seen something in Rosalie. Her birth was recorded in the ledger, under property and the slave roll, but also on the Guilbert page, two spaces under Byron's name, with a little c for colored and Camille's name next to hers. She was the only one of his colored children so noted. This coincided with the time his mother, Madame Guilbert, retired from recording births, deaths, and the status of enslaved people or property in the ledger.

Lucien spoke to Rosalie in French and Creole, although the girl's half siblings and stepfather spoke English. He had her mother make her a wide-brimmed hat of sweetgrass to keep the sun from browning her face.

On Sundays, the day of rest and worship, he took her to the church where the free people of color celebrated Mass and took communion, while her siblings and parents gathered to shout, sing, and worship down by the river.

And when she was eleven, Lucien sent her to live in a school, mainly for colored children of white men. With money from Jane Chatham's room and board, he paid the school that had housed Rosalie what was owed to them. Now, it was time to collect his daughter.

IX

Rosalie knew her time at the Sisters of Mercy School for Girls had come to an end. At seventeen, she was to decide on either a path of devotion and charity, or to leave the school that was mostly attended by orphans and children of inconvenience. Some girls dreamed of being cared for by a well-to-do businessman or planter, but that dream was a fairy tale. The other choices for aging girls were to be a wife in a prearranged marriage, a domestic servant, a factory worker, or a prostitute on Basin Street.

The Reverend Mother wasn't in a hurry to show Rosalie the door. Because most of the girls were expected to take up the needle in a clothing factory, the nuns taught the girls how to cut patterns and fabric, and how to sew a variety of stitches. Rosalie took to the hours of cutting and sewing. She was trusted with the Singer machine, and before long, she designed and sewed the students' shirts and pinafores. And then a gown for a patron. And another. The nuns of Les Soeurs de la Pitié profited by Rosalie's talents.

The Reverend Mother was disappointed to read in the letter addressed to Rosalie that her father would come to collect her on the twentieth of July. Since M. Lucien Guilbert would arrive shortly, and his outstanding bill had been paid, the Reverend Mother had no choice but to give the letter to Rosalie.

Over the years, Rosalie's only caller had been her father. No matter how infrequently he saw her, she was envied, for he, the white planter, finely dressed and bearing gifts, created the picture of a dream come true. Many were the girls who went to bed dreaming of the father who would come to see them. Maybe take them away.

Rosalie packed her few belongings after reading the letter. She continued to sew but waited for the day that her father would come. Before she left, she found Sister Jean David to return the last pages of *The Hunchback of Notre-Dame.* The young nun possessed a voracious literary hunger and a few books, but had no one to discuss them with. While Sister Jean David could read as she pleased in her room, she was forbidden to add to the enlightenment of the daughters of pity. At great risk, Sister Jean David devised a means of sharing books by the gathered and folded section with Rosalie, a quick reader. Sister Jean David had someone with whom to discuss the enjoyable Austen, the darkly daring Mary Shelley, and the compassionate Victor Hugo. Thanks to Sister Jean David, over the years of reading, Rosalie gained a slightly larger view of the world beyond Les Soeurs de la Pitié and Le Petit Cottage.

The Reverend Mother returned to her the doll her father had given her for comfort during the first year of her enrollment. Unbeknownst to his mother, Lucien had taken it from his dead sister's room. For six years the doll lay somewhere without a child's admiring gaze or loving hands. What a comfort it would have been to talk to her pretty dolly. Upon seeing it, Rosalie bowed and said, "*Merci,* Reverend Mother," although she no longer wanted or needed the doll.

Rosalie was dressed like a laundry matron, plain, with a simple bonnet. Her hair was pulled tightly to her head. She had but one tapestry bag to hold her undergarments, an extra skirt and blouse, her missal, rosary beads, and two books by Saint Thomas Aquinas.

She stood in the courtyard alone until her father arrived, making it a point to turn and wave, in case one of the girls stood at the window above watching her. She remembered her time in the window, watching and waving as girls left the school.

Her father strode toward her in jaunty but sober steps, she noted with quiet relief. His hair was losing its fullness; his face was tanned by days in the cane field. *We are all aging,* she thought.

Lucien's broad smile gave her confidence.

"Rosalie, my Rosalie," he said, kissing her several times. "Let me look at you."

"Mon Pè," she said. Rosalie, cautious by nature, couldn't repress her smile. This moment made the day real. Her father had come for her.

"This prison rag won't do," her father said, frowning at her outfit.

His words surprised her. She looked down at her skirt.

"It's fine for a girl's school," Lucien said. "But you are graduating on to bigger things. You must dress accordingly." He held out his arm, and she took it. They strolled away from the school, father and daughter. Rather than think the worst, that she was envied, Rosalie chose to believe their scene in the courtyard gave an onlooker hope.

After a meal, Lucien took his daughter to the dressmaker on Dauphine Street. Rosalie was more interested in the Singer machine, the dress form, the array of scissors, and items in the shop. Lucien conducted the business with the dressmaker. "She will need a dress for everyday wear, and a ballroom gown to outshine all the ballroom gowns."

Rosalie caught the last bit of that. "Father?"

He waved his hand at her, a "don't concern yourself" wave.

The dressmaker showed Rosalie and Lucien a wardrobe of outfits that had been ordered for a honeymoon trip. The wedding had been canceled, and the customer refused to pay. The dressmaker assured Lucien that there was nothing wrong with the apparel, and was too happy to recoup the loss, even after Lucien had worked the price down to the barest margins of profit for the dressmaker.

Rosalie tried on the plainest dress. Clearly, she and the jilted bride were two different sizes. This she attributed to her steady diet of broth and bread. Fortunately, she and the original customer were close enough in height. She admired not herself in the dress or the dress itself, but what the dress could become.

"I will alter these to my liking when we are home," Rosalie told her father.

"Is this where my money went? To learn darning and sewing?"

"Father, it gives me great satisfaction to make garments," she said.

"Then you'll employ those talents to

sew for your children."

"Father?" *Children?*

Lucien didn't answer. He took her in. His daughter was lovelier than when he had last seen her. She was no longer the coltish girl in the wide-brimmed hat, the child he'd sweep up from the ground to lift onto Zuk. She was aware of herself in the way that young women are, she, a young woman of seventeen. It was in the way she kept a careful guard on every movement, while managing an air of delight. He watched and appraised her as she gathered her skirt with one hand and used the other to step up and into the carriage to be seated. At the very least, his daughter ran a full racetrack lap ahead of Juliette Chatham's hapless Jane. With the right coaching, his daughter could move in circles as a respectable lady.

"Mon Pè," she said, "how are my brothers?"

"Fine, my girl. Fine, fine. Byron's home from West Point. Quite the manly soldier. You'll see. Your youngest brother chops cane like a machine. Got a woman on the Pierpont Plantation. Just had a boy.

Long's he chops my cane, I'll share him for now. John-John got a woman, two boys. Both going to grow big. Strong. Chop cane like machines."

"And Mama?"

"She's getting on."

Rosalie wanted to hear more than three words about her mother, but she didn't press. Theirs had not been a coupling made of love. Her father couldn't tell her anything about her mother: her life, how she felt. She would see her mother and brothers for herself, soon enough. And her stepfather.

"I have plans for you," Lucien told her softly. "And you must do everything I say."

Although Rosalie had been removed from the plantation, plantation life hadn't been removed entirely from her. Her father, a white man, asking for her obedience, and not demanding it, rang strangely in her ear and made her quiet.

"Yes, Mon Pè."

"I have plans to marry you to Laurent."

The shock of it was overwhelming. She knew Laurent and his white sisters. They played together after the Sunday Mass, although Laurent was older than she was. It was a fallacy to believe mixed-race children had an instant fellowship. As the saying goes, "When mulattoes get to fighting, one mother is more at fault." And so it was between the pale young Rosalie and the high yellow Laurent. She had her own Black brothers to thank for her well-honed practice at calling the Dozens. Her brothers bested her every time. But come Sunday after Mass, when Laurent said, "My mother is free, your mother drives a plow," Rosalie would shoot back, "My mother drives the plow, but your mother is the mule." She'd answer out of the earshot of her father, who proclaimed her sweet, smart, and "virtuous despite her hue."

"Laurent, Mon Pè. Did his father ask you for me?"

"Don't worry none about that. It is business between his father and I."

"Yes, Mon Pè."

"You're not a little girl. He will see."

"But, Mon Pè, do you think Laurent . . . do you think . . ."

Lucien laughed. "Oh, ho! Rosalie, you

want to hear how beautiful you are? Have you learned nothing, all this time with the nuns? Leave fishing to the Acadians in the bayou. My girl, it flatters you none." Rosalie smiled to go along with her father's teasing. Her beauty wasn't the question, but the *quality* of her looks. And even so, dressed like a scullery maid, she imagined the worst: her childhood tormentor seeing her so plainly clad. Because his mother was a shade or two darker than her mother, it was important to him to remind her that his mother was free. That he was so many steps better than she. She wondered if such ideas fell away with childhood teasing or gathered strength with manhood. She would like to think Laurent a gentleman. She had been the target of his nastiest jabs.

"Mon Pè."

"Speak, Rosalie."

"Are there others? Other suitors?"

"Why would we need others? You played as children. There is perhaps one more beautiful than you among the mesdemoiselles of color in St. James."

"Please, Mon Pè. Are there others who will speak to you about me?"

Lucien altogether dismissed the notion. "There is no better placement than in his household as his wife."

Her father's appraisal gave her confidence. But she had to say, "Our lives at the school were very strict, Father. I will be a fool in a silk gown, standing and not dancing."

"Is this your concern? What have I spent my money on? Don't know the dances?" He shook his head.

"Reverend Mother said, 'Surely a foot shall slide to hell should it glide across the ballroom floor or stamp a beat.' "

"Byron will show you the latest quadrilles and waltzes. You'll dance like a debutante in no time."

This almost put a smile on her face. Her white half brother treated her more or less as her Black half brothers did. They all treated her as an annoyance. A younger sister.

"Mon Pè. Would you give me to a man who would beat me every day? For I fear Laurent —"

"Dear girl, every wife must learn obedience. This is why I sent you to this school. Don't worry about these things," he said, equally dismissive and light-hearted. "The Reverend Mother kept me apprised of your progress," he said with pride. "Your arithmetic has always been good. Measuring, percentages, fractions, and the like."

"Yes, Mon Pè."

"Tomorrow you'll take over the work in the commissary from Byron. You'll fill the orders, what few there are. You'll keep the books. Watch the inventory. Now," he said, giving her a purposeful, stern look, his tone changing, "you must be mean, dear girl."

"Mean?"

"Oh, yes. No cutting excess inches here and there. No fattened bags of rice, flour, beans, or coffee. Them niggers will wear you down with their big eyes and aching bellies. To give them these excesses is to steal from me. No tobacco or candy to the po' Irish ditchdigging, big-bellied women and their filthy ragamuffins. They call you a nigger, you pull out the drawer pistol and tell them to git. Now, I know you've been in this school, doing works of charity, but, girl, it will be worse for you if you give away my goods. Don't steal from me, girl."

"Yes, Mon Pè."

He breathed. His tone changed again. "This is temporary work, child," he said. "You'll serve me even better by getting into that Tournier household. I aim to gain by what your husband can do for a farm like ours . . ."

She shuddered at the thought of Laurent Tournier as a husband. Her husband.

But now they were nearing the plantation. This ease between father and daughter would change. She hadn't been gone so long that she had forgotten she was property. A slave.

"When you step off this carriage, every Jasper will smell your scent and come sniffing. Don't give nary a one the time to splay a fish. Nary a one. No use getting set on one, no matter how many stalks he can strip and hack down. If you're violated or come up big, I divorce you from anything you have coming to you as my daughter. You might as well hide in your mammy's cabin out of my sight. Disobey me, girl, and you'll grow

Black and old under the sun with a hoe in your hands. Obey me, and you'll be the mistress of a great plantation."

"Mon Pè, you'll see my obedience."

"Words are cheap when Jasper comes doing his buck-and-wing dance toting a bucket of cool water. You say these words now, but temptation is true to the snare it sets for you when they come courting you with scraps of gingham. Don't be fooled. Don't trade two thousand acres for a handful of field flowers lying on your back. When them Jaspers call you, say, 'Master says I'm not for you.' And you send them to me."

"Yes, Mon Pè," she said, although she knew she would turn no such man over to her father.

As the carriage jostled and hummed over twigs and pebbles along the dirt road, a strangeness of heart-leaping and melancholy ran through Rosalie. Love of the familiar, but also the pain of the familiar. Of belonging and not. The nuns taught Rosalie how to be insignificant. To not lavish thought on herself but to give those moments of contemplation to vigilant prayer. She could soothe the feelings of loneliness in the incessant mumble of rosary recitation. She could let those intonations overtake the petty concerns of her own being. But now, as she and her father rode and he told her his plans for her life, there was no greater subject of her thoughts than herself. The closer they were to the place she called home, the more real and sharp her feelings. The Lavender Plantation. The steeple of the church that allowed free people of color, and the steeple of the church that did not. The smell of cane and honeysuckle. The evening sound of the *zozo monpè,* a black-and-white bird said to resemble a priest, pronouncing his sad song and warning from tree to tree. All these things said she was nearing home. All these things, these familiar things, stirred her heart and cast over her a veil of melancholy.

Lucien had been watching her while she drifted in thought. "What is it, Rosalie?" he asked. "Speak."

She couldn't hide her reticence, her clear voice now timid. "Madame Guilbert. Will she see me?" She was careful to not call her father's mother her grand-mother, in French, Creole, or English. Her own mother's constant scolding and warnings put this firmly in her head: *Watch what you say. Watch who you call what.*

Her father said nothing for a long while. She waited. It was clear he wouldn't answer. That was her answer.

Rosalie had never seen the color of her grandmother's eyes, but she had seen her grandmother with her little Negro maid from a distance. She remembered the maid, a Black girl of about eight, forever close to her grandmother's side like a favorite pet, while she had been told, "Hide yourself, girl, or the maîtresse will sell you away."

Her father was master of the planta-tion, but even she knew it was Madame Guilbert, her grandmother, who ruled the plantation. The extent of the hold Madame Guilbert had over her father, Rosalie couldn't imagine. She knew bet-ter than to ask.

She looked up toward the big house. *Le Petit Cottage.* She thought, *One day, old woman. One day before you close your eyes for good, I will see you and you will see me.*

The carriage didn't make its way to the quarter often, so when the rockaway was spotted, activity ceased in the vegetable gardens and word spread quickly that Master was coming that way in his carriage. Mainly, the women and children stopped to see. In the meantime, Camille, Rosalie's mother, stayed in her husband's cabin and hovered over the pot of beans in the hearth for his supper.

The children Lily kept busy in the vegetable garden chased the carriage. Rosalie gave into the happiness of being home and waved to them. She expected the carriage to slow as they neared the third cabin among twelve ramshackle single-porched cabins, the place she called home. Instead of stopping at her mother and stepfather's cabin, the horse came to a halt at the last cabin. The overseer's cottage. Both the exterior and its cypress fence had been newly white-washed, setting itself apart from the twelve cabins that housed the field hands and the house servants.

X

Rosalie didn't change her skirt and blouse. She raced down to her step-father's cabin. It had been six years since she had been inside the one-room cabin and sat on the crocheted rug before the hearth, where her mother combed and braided her hair. There, before the warming fire, her mother's patient fingers combed through her knots, to show her what love she could without John raising too much of a fuss. That was what she remembered: scraps of love in small, secretive amounts, and then yanked away when the giant of a man appeared. As a girl she could only feel the pain of it, the puzzling nature of her mother's love. As a seventeen-year-old woman, she saw what she couldn't see as a little girl.

There was no need to knock. The door

was wide open on that moist July night. Her stepfather might have seen her coming down to the cabin. He stood in the doorway. John was not as tall as she remembered him, but he was tall enough, big enough to be unwelcoming. He took the smile right off her.

"Thought the Lawd took ye." He ground his teeth even with his jaw clenched. A stream of brown saliva ran down his mouth. Tobacco. "What ye want heah?" Now that she was no longer a child, he spoke plainly.

It was still there between them as thick as ever. The accusation and unwelcome. Except she didn't go running and crying to hide in the folds of her mother's skirt. That was what she remembered. She'd cry to her mother, who took his side or her brothers' side. *Stop crying, girl. You'll kill your father and brothers with them tears.* Even if John raised his hands to her or her brothers pulled her hair, it was she who could get them killed. It was wrong when she was a girl, and wrong now. But at seventeen, she understood.

"Evening, Mr. John. Been missing Mama all these years." She was careful to say *Mama* and not the French Creole terms for mother. She had learned early to keep that dialect between herself, her mother, and her natural father. "Miss her so, suh."

"John! You let her in!"

Her mother's voice leaped out like a deer. Rosalie put her hands to her own face and bounced on her heels.

"Let her in!" her mother said, but Rosalie stayed on the porch.

John wouldn't move. Camille couldn't be deterred. Her hands reached through the spaces around him, and then her small body found its way through, wrapping her arms around Rosalie. Warm arms and hands, the color of wet beach sand, held her face and then wrapped around her body. Rosalie nuzzled her head against her mother's face and tignon, glorying in the smell of her mother's hair, where her mother's locks fell out from under the headscarf. Her hair was always tucked and hidden under the tignon like an apology.

Camille pried herself from Rosalie. "Look at you, my child. A woman now! But four twigs!" She took Rosalie by the hand and led her inside the cabin, passing her husband. "Get in here. Get you fed right," her mother fussed.

Her older brother stood and came to her. He was now taller and bigger than John.

"John-John!" Rosalie screamed. "John-John!" He picked her up with no effort.

"Gave you up for dead, girl!" he said. Her brother had what her stepfather once had. An easygoing, joking way about him.

"Shoulda stayed dead," John said loud. "Don't know what you want heah." No one, especially Camille, looked his way.

Rosalie, in the sweep of joy, pieced things together quickly. John-John, big and strong, was her mother's protector. She didn't ask about her brothers' great-grandmother, who was absent from the pallet occupied by their grandmother. The death of the older woman meant one fewer voice to criticize her mother's gombo.

John-John spoke over his father. "This here Telma." He gestured to the woman nursing his child.

"We not strangers," Rosalie said, grinning broadly. She remembered Telma from childhood, and grinned because she could have predicted Telma had staked her claim on John-John in the cane. And vice versa.

"Welcome home, Rosalie," Telma said.

"Glad to be here," Rosalie said.

John-John said, "You won't be without a man and some babies before long." Telma agreed.

Rosalie opened her mouth to speak but closed it. The old rules fell back into place. *Don't speak Lucien Guilbert's name. Ever.* She kept Master Guilbert's plans to herself and said, "Lawd willing." For the same reason she asked, "Where's James?" although her father had told her about James. She let her brother and mother tell her all about her younger brother and his wife and children on the east side.

She sat down with the family at the hearth and ate a small portion of beans and fish and savored every bit of the meal and the reunion. John sat out on the porch with his chewing tobacco and his bottle of fermented cane juice. She had seen in his eyes that he could only despise her. And now that she was older and had some understanding of their small world, she regretted that he would never know that she wasn't at fault. Her mother wasn't at fault. He wasn't at fault. Only her father. Lucien Guilbert. She took in all the scraps of what she used to call home. Rosalie knew she had stepped inside her stepfather's cabin for the last time.

When Lucien had entered his mother's salon, he found her still dressed for the day at the vanity while her servant brushed her hair. He took his mother's state of dress as a sign that she waited to hear from him before she prepared for bed.

He bowed to kiss her on the cheek. "Mother," he said. "It's only best that I tell you."

"So you've come home."

"Yes, Mother. I am home. Rosalie is home."

"How is that my concern?" she snapped.

Lucien sighed. "Mother, I don't want

to hurt you."

"Show me evidence of that. You do the very thing to quicken me into the ground. Perhaps that is your plan. To destroy me. Well, your father was a brute, but he is dead. I can walk on his grave if I like."

"Why say things that will keep you at the confessional? Your knees can't take it." Lucien had so wanted to keep the tone of their talk gentle. With sympathy. He could see that she wouldn't let him be gentle, and he prepared for the parry and stabs of their usual conversations.

Madame said, "I would say, don't worry about my bones, but why bother? You don't care for your mother. You care for the gold. And that girl of your making."

"My daughter. Rosalie."

"So, you don't object about the gold? Only to what I call that girl." She sighed, but more for effect. "I despise liars, so I can't entirely despise you, my son."

"Nor I you, my dear." He matched her dispassion.

They could go for hours at each other, but there was a purpose to his late-night

277

visit. He would not let her derail that purpose.

"I only thought to tell you, to spare you. Prepare you. I have plans for Rosalie. Plans that affect you and me."

Madame laughed a one-note high hiccup. "That's not possible. I don't even speak the girl's name. How can she affect me?"

"Tell me the location of the gold, Mother. Tell me, and Rosalie will no longer be part of the plan. I won't be desperate to marry her to the Tournier heir. I won't need the assistance of Laurent Tournier."

"Tournier? Who is that to me?" Madame said. "We have our arrangement. My sitting, and then the gold."

"But my way, we both get what we want."

"My way I get what I want."

"Foolish woman! Don't you see? To plan for the future of this estate is to plan for you, my son, and his heir should he summon the drive to produce one. What we need is an agreeable and binding alliance with the Tourniers: the marriage between Rosalie and Laurent Tournier."

Thisbe brushed her Madame's hair softly, as if deaf to their argument. She couldn't help but marvel at the idea that the futures of her white owners lay in the fortune of a colored girl. While the two went on, Thisbe imagined herself among her mother and sisters, sewing and laughing about the antics of white folk. Except, she didn't sew. Her mother and sisters didn't sit around laughing and sewing. And more to the point, she wasn't let off on Sundays like all enslaved men, women, and children. Nor was she paid for the "overtime," as she might have been on a different plantation. But she could imagine it. She could imagine it all. And want it.

Madame grabbed the brush and struck Thisbe with it. The girl, for some reason, had brushed too hard. Thisbe took back the brush, then continued softly.

"What have I to do with that?" Madame asked.

"Everything, Mother. Everything."

Madame turned her head left and then right to mimic searching. "Where did the foolish woman run off to? She was just here."

"Mother. My mother. Don't you see? I've done what I could to prepare Rosalie for this role. She can read the Bible and behave like a lady. But what is needed to set her apart from the others is a certain education in the art of being a lady in planter society. She needs an air of nobility, yet humility. What she needs is the benefit of your years at court. Not merely a game of solitaire and a reminder to wash herself, but the intricacies, the subtleties, the arts of womanhood."

"Ah! Ah! Now, it is of value!" Madame flapped her hands so wildly that Thisbe stopped brushing. "Now all that I know and all that I come from is of importance. Not the joke you make it to be."

"Yes, Mother. You win. Do you hear? You win. I can humiliate myself because our future depends on what I ask of you."

Madame didn't drag it out, as he anticipated. She didn't let him linger and further humiliate himself. She snapped quickly and decisively: "No."

Thisbe continued to brush, but she closed her eyes, the natural response to lightning flashing before the boom of God's cannon. Thisbe guessed right.

Lucien pounded his fist down on the vanity. He knocked the jar of powder off the vanity, dispersing and spilling white dust on Madame's dress and the rug.

He spoke calmly. "Avoid the parlor with the view of the commissary. That is where she'll work. Furthermore, Rosalie will be about the grounds, doing as I need her to do. Perhaps you'll want to stay in, dear lady. Perhaps you want to shield your eyes."

He left her.

XI

*Shouldn't mother and father solely deter-
mine sister and brother? If that were so,
there would be no need to ask for patience.
But alas, I once more implore your patience.*

Byron and Rosalie's story as brother and
sister cannot be told without Lily's story.
Lily's story cannot be told without Marcelle's story — or without the story of
Byron's mother, for that matter.

During those times when France and
the American colonies grappled with
independence and upheaval, Marcelle
traveled often between France and New
Orleans with her white half sister, both
the daughters of a French diplomat. In
the company of the American president,
Marcelle became a favorite of the president's favorite, a Miss Sally Hemmings.

In this way, she became a favorite of the president because she entertained sixteen-year-old Miss Hemmings.

Marcelle and her own half sister grew up together, Marcelle as her sister's playmate, then personal maid, and later as her cook when her half sister married. Marcelle studied French cuisine in palaces throughout France and made sure her sister hosted the most talked-about soirees in Baton Rouge with her gourmet dishes. When Marcelle's half sister died young, her husband's new bride came with her own household staff and had no need for her predecessor's cook. This husband, having no blood relationship to Marcelle, who hadn't been freed by her sister or father, had planned to sell her.

At that time, Bayard Guilbert conducted business with the remarried widower. His own wife had delivered stillborn twin sons and sank into profound darkness. Bayard had sympathy for his wife, for she had conceived and carried his children only to bury them, except for one son, Lucien. This refined cook would make a wonderful gift to his stricken wife. He bundled the grateful cook with her belongings, and he brought Marcelle to Le Petit Cottage.

In the meanwhile, Bayard's grief-stricken wife lay in a puff of black fabrics on her chaise. Sylvie had lost so much weight, the dress seemed to cloak and bury her. Bayard rarely entered Madame's salon but to seed her. This time he himself took the tray of consommé and bread, prepared by the new cook, and brought it up to her. The very idea of him serving her should have stirred her, but she didn't blink or turn her head when she heard his boots ascend the stairs. She lay as wan as a hooked fish on a dock without the will to flop its tail. But then, she lifted her head and turned. It wasn't her husband's rare appearance that stirred her, but the aroma that accompanied him. The saucy piquant smell arising from the shallow bowl made her nose sniff and her head turn. It was the aroma of a plain dish that had warmed her belly as a child. Bayard fed the first spoonful to her mouth and wiped her lips with the linen napkin. The act of care and intimacy didn't bother her husband, but young Madame Sylvie's color began to return. She blushed.

Charlotte Thérèse was born the following year.

During their nearly forty years together, Madame had overlooked Marcelle's color and grew close to her cook, whose French was impeccable. Marcelle brought Sylvie stories of high society and the Bonapartes in France and in Maryland — having accompanied her sister and father to their palatial estates. She was a consummate partner of the quadrille dance between the legitimate white relations and the common law colored relations, always knowing her privilege and her place. But as time went on, Marcelle relaxed in this small estate home. She relaxed in the comfort of an old friendship and made the mistake of endeavoring to push Madame to accept her colored granddaughter and to go and see her. Hold her. If this wasn't enough, Marcelle added more to Sylvie's anguish by insisting the colored girl was the image of Charlotte Thérèse, come back to life. The cook had overstepped her bounds and was barred from Madame's company and sight.

Le Petit Cottage aspired to modesty compared to the palatial estates Marcelle had known. She was moved from the dormer in the main house to a cabin in the quarter with a family she didn't know. She continued to prepare the meals in the cookhouse, but never again entered Madame's salon, or the house. Marcelle was said to have laughed wildly one night for no reason the family could discern, and from then on, she spoke no more. It was spring, the eve before Easter Sunday. Marcelle returned to the cookhouse to prepare the lamb. She sat alone before the lamb, stared off, and died, having no one to tell. No one to understand. It wasn't Madame Sylvie who condescended to accept Marcelle's friendship, but Marcelle who reached down to bring society to the poor isolated woman. Marcelle, an enslaved woman. Daughter of a French diplomat.

Lily's boys were growing fast. Soon, her days as wet nurse to the Master's son would end and she would return to the cane field, her son at her ankles. She sat out on the back porch nursing the boy, Byron, on a warm spring morning. Lily wasn't the type to enjoy the natural things around her: the chirping of birds, the determination of crocuses to push up out of the earth. But that morning, something she had taken for granted made her take notice and listen. The sudden absence of familiar sounds alerted the young mother that something wasn't right in the cookhouse. Lily had been accustomed to a clattering of busy that seeped out onto the back porch daily in sounds and smells, through the one small window of the cookhouse. Dishes. Hacking. Chopping. Crackling. Even the shuffle of age as the fancy French cook went from counter to pot racks to hearth.

Lily pulled the white child off one nipple, and instead of picking up her crying child to take his turn, she set both toddling boys in the basket, then went to see about the absence of smell and sound. It was just as her mind had supposed. Only death would keep the fancy French cook from trying to win back the favor of her maîtresse. Sure enough, Gabriel had sounded his trumpet and summoned her up before she could spear the leg of lamb to roast on the spit.

Lily moved the body out of her way. It didn't take much. The woman had withered to bones. Later, it was believed that the fancy French cook had stopped eating. She had starved herself to death. Lily didn't take part in the speculation. That wasn't her way or her concern. She simply stepped in and became the cook and continued to nurse both boys. She withstood the oppression of the small area. Flames jumping from pots. The oven. She made the bread, butchered the pig roughly until she could butcher it lean, always throwing the pigs' ears to her son and the Master's son, Byron, to chew and grind the incoming teeth that she would reckon with when both boys cried for her milk, although at two years old, both boys were to be weaned.

Lily took no particular love in what she

did in the cookhouse. This became clear to Madame, who was not up to missing her friend, but was vocal about missing her fine French cuisine — her few comforts of being held captive in the wilderness. With this new cook, there would be no French pastries, rich sauces craftily made from wines, butters, capers, and herbs. There would be no childhood memories pricking her senses when Madame placed her fork or spoon in her mouth. No. This new cook applied little if any seasonings or gravies to indicate an appreciation for taste. When Madame complained and demanded a French cook, her son said he could purchase one at auction at the St. Louis Hotel, if she told him where the gold was buried. As always, Madame didn't blink. She turned on her heel and entered the cookhouse and told the girl to season the meat with these seasonings. To make a sauce with this wine — and how much to pour. To make a sponge cake, a pudding with brandied peaches. She said, "Most important: make the food with love." Lily didn't understand her and asked, "Where's dat kep, ma'am?" Two things about the girl's inquiry astounded Madame. Taking care of the most pressing matter first, she corrected Lily by saying, *"Madame."* Madame Sylvie didn't cotton to "ma'am." The big girl, the one who nursed her grandchild, said, "Yes, mah damn."

Lucien had been told by the physician to refrain from relations with his wife for yet another month after the birth of his son. That her constitution was in a delicate state after she had lost a significant amount of blood, and that she should refrain from her wifely duties until the coloring fully returned to her hands and face.

"Nonsense," Lucien told himself. "Nonsense." He'd specifically picked this young woman, the daughter of a poor sugar planter, a girl with rosy cheeks and wide hips beneath her unhooped skirt, to produce heirs. Six, he thought she was good for. Six children to fill his house with. He looked forward to hearing their noise about the dining room table, and then eventually shunting the male children off to the garçonnière when they reached their teen years. These would be his heirs. They would take over Le Petit Cottage in his dotage.

His young wife fooled him. Her wide frame and rosy countenance, both deceptions. She carried and delivered his boy child but was too weak to nurse him, even if she wanted to. She hadn't regained her health and rosiness.

Lucien had a good mind to sue her father, whom he had bailed out from his troubles. He bought his notes with his harvest money. Took his father-in-law's old equipment and Negroes off his hands, allowing his wife's father to retire to a townhouse in Baton Rouge free from worry about his crop, feeding his field hands, and having creditors nipping at his heels. In the bargain, the girl's health and virginity was all that he required. He gloried in his wife's ample body, because the sight of her filled his tiny mother with disgust. His mother wasn't pleased with this large-proportioned addition to the household. But at the very least, her daughter-in-law was born of French Creoles with families in Bordeaux and Lyon. How quickly Madame's requirements had dwindled after so many poor matches. But seeing as how anyone could marry into old French families, Madame Sylvie had to be satisfied with the girl's French stock. She didn't press for details of the lineage, to avoid disappointment.

It was a shock to Lucien that his healthy young bride succumbed to death two months after the birth of their son. Lucien's father-in-law's grief at the unexpected passing of his only child and daughter compelled Lucien to not sue the old man. Also, the family physician threatened to testify that he had vehemently advised Msr. Guilbert to abstain from relations with his wife. The physician pleaded with Lucien to drop the suit, as he liked Madame Sylvie and didn't want to testify that the fifth Madame Lucien Guilbert died from complications of infections to her unhealed birthing area, the responsible party being her husband. Lucien dropped the suit.

The boy, Byron, was left in the care of the girl who had also just given birth. The same girl who had cost him a business opportunity with Arne Pierpont. At the very least, her milk would be useful, and as the boys grew, Byron and the cook's son, Jesse, became inseparable.

Over the years, Rosalie grew jealous of their closeness, and angry about her exclusion from their romps. One day she followed the boys and watched as they lay near the bayou, touching each other. She would make sure her father put an end to their wicked play, and that he would love and favor her more than he did his filthy white son.

When she told him, her father didn't reward her with anything she had expected. But he did rush to the place Rosalie said they were, found them, and told his son to get up. "Git! And don't look back." His pants barely fastened, Byron ran to the house, like his father told him. Ran as fast as he could and didn't look back.

The boys' closeness, their years of nursing and slumber together, didn't matter to Lucien when he murdered Lily's son with his own hands. Murdered the boy who had ruined his son with his vile act. Lucien took Jesse's breath and life in seconds.

Even with his hands acting as the

instrument of the boy's death, Lucien couldn't name the dis-ease he felt in the presence of the cook. He couldn't name it, but he felt it as sure as house ghosts breathed on him. Anyone might hastily characterize this dis-ease as guilt, but the guilty must know a wrong had been committed to acknowledge their guilt. Lucien knew no such wrong. This notion, guilt, no matter how fleeting, wouldn't occur to the Master. His was the act of a master pruning the vine that would kill the harvest. He did what a farmer must: rid the virulent worm that would contaminate the vineyard and cause it to bear no fruit. Lucien possessed reason, and a right for his defense if one had been asked of him. As swiftly and soundly as he had slapped his daughter, knocked her off her feet as instantaneously as he had struck her, he had gripped the boy's neck in picking him up, squeezed and choked him, and threw his body on Zuk's rump. Master Lucien took Jesse's body down to the bayou where alligators were known to breed, and he took the not-yet-stiff body of the cook's son, the boy who she saved her sweetness for and had named

Jesse, and dropped him into the murky feasting ground.

Rosalie pretended to let that day cloud in her mind, disappear, even, especially when her father looked into her eyes. She had forgotten the boy's name, and then it came back to her, like something that refused to be thrown away. Jesse. She did remember clearly that she was not allowed near the big house where they played because of the old lady, and how Byron and Jesse kept her away from their games when they played in the quarter. She remembered one Sunday afternoon, a day of rest for field hands and near rest for house servants, that she followed the two boys, to show them she was not to be excluded from their play. She moved like a woodland creature, focused and stalking, careful not to disturb the crispy oak leaves on the ground as she crept. It was a long journey to the marshy bayou where the grass grew tall, but she stopped walking when they stopped. She thought the two would go for a swim in the brisk fall. She had decided she didn't want to be part of their wet, cold games. She had a mind to turn and walk back to the quarter. She remained hidden, and with each passing moment she told herself, "Now, I'll go." Her curiosity kept her still. She watched the two boys. They didn't remove all their clothes for a swim. But Byron unfastened his buttons and Jesse loosened the drawstrings to his trousers and they let their pants fall. She watched the two, Byron and Jesse, lie down on their backs, side by side. She couldn't see clearly what they were doing, but she told herself it was wicked.

Rosalie watched. She had discovered their secret play and why she was not invited to join in. She didn't want to take part in their wickedness and left as quietly as she had come. She missed a turn and found herself near the forbidden part of the plantation. The door to the privy swung open and she froze for fear that her grandmother would step out and see her, and then she would be sold. (This is what her mother warned her each day: "Keep from the house and from the maîtresse!") It wasn't Madame Guilbert who came out of the privy, but her father. Upon seeing him, Rosalie was filled with her whiteness and she ran to him, completely forgetting she was on forbidden ground. She ran to him and told him what she'd seen near the bayou. The words hadn't left her mouth but a second, and Lucien struck her across the face. Struck her so hard he had knocked her down on her backside. "You keep your lying mouth shut!" he said. Then he went to the secret place.

"Hush, don't cry, girl," her mother told her when she found her way to the cabin. "Just hush."

Rosalie cried and howled until John raised his hand. She stopped.

When Camille tried to comfort her and find out the matter, John-John said, "Master struck her down, that's what! That teach huh tuh play white." John-John and James had no mercy on their sister. "Look at you, Rosalie. You white, Black, and red!"

No one from the quarter knew the details, but the pale gal's fall went neither unnoticed nor unmocked, especially with the Master's handprint smacked into half her face. While Rosalie worked in the cane among her family, she couldn't escape the saying "The high horse is good until the horse starts to buck," or simply "High horse, big fall" in pidgin and in Black Creole. No one in the cane would let her forget it.

No matter how much they teased and prodded, she kept her mouth shut. She had seen the devil in her father's eyes. Something she couldn't name but knew enough to fear. Within the week Rosalie had been sent away to Les Soeurs de Pitié, the school for poor and colored girls.

Lily combed through the grounds calling for her son. Jesse. The sound of her call, so disturbing in its shouts, shrieks, and moans, was said to have made the dead get up to seek new resting places. The Master had told Lily that Jesse had run away and that they'd send the dogs to find him. A runaway slave got their hamstring cut, to make any other attempts at freedom impossible. Lily would have gladly taken her Jesse, cut and barely able to walk, just to have him.

Jesse was never captured by the runaway patrollers.

Lucien never put the dogs on the boy's scent.

XII

Rosalie knew the way to the commissary, although she had never walked to the little building or been inside. John-John and James had always been allowed to dash off to buy flour, salt, or an egg. She was to stay clear of the buildings near the house.

She entered, grateful for the shade. The sun hadn't reached its full height or power. Hopefully, an afternoon rain would follow.

"Rosalie! Sister." He reached for her hand and held it between both of his.

Did she dare call him brother?

"Monsieur Byron, it is so good to see you."

His laughter was muffled. "Monsieur Byron? Is this what you've learned at school? To be a stranger to your own

300

brother?"

Her skin warmed. "Are you teasing me, sir?"

Now he laughed outright. "Sir? *Sir?* This won't do, Rosalie. I won't have it. My sister cannot go about calling me 'sir' and 'monsieur.'"

"Hello, Byron," she said. "My brother."

"That's better," he said. "Now tell me about life at school."

How changed his voice was. Strong. And yet kind. And he laughed! Can six years change one so? Still, each time he spoke her name she heard those other names he had taunted her with. *Darkielee. Niggerlee.*

"I learned all they had to teach. I was either to become a novice and devote my life to charity. And sewing," she added. "Or I was to leave. Monsieur Guilbert had plans for me and came to retrieve me."

Byron laughed, this time small, still muffled. "Monsieur Guilbert!" Then he stopped himself but kept some amusement in his eyes. "I won't laugh at you, Rosalie. Time has improved you greatly.

You're such a lady."

"Thank you, Monsieur . . ."

"What's that?" he asked.

She relented. "Byron."

She managed to smile but remained guarded. Now that they stood near level and saw into each other's eyes, she couldn't help but think, *Surely you remember, brother. Surely you remember about Jesse.*

His eyes, his easiness, his demeanor, didn't betray any part of their darker past. "How can I keep my word to not laugh at you if you continue to tempt me?"

"I'm sorry," she said.

"Don't be sorry," he said. "You know, it isn't often that Father's plans are good ones. But I agree with this one."

"You do?" She thought she had spoken too quickly or had cut him off. A thing she mustn't do. She waited to be put in her place.

"Of course I do," Byron said. "You will be a good clerk in the commissary. Father says your arithmetic is excellent. The measuring, meting out, and recording in the ledger should come easily to you. I'll show you everything, although truthfully, your most constant task is to pray for customers. Real customers with more than a penny for flour."

There were the times that Lucien would pull her up onto Zuk, behind Byron, while her brothers John-John and James looked up at the pink soles of her feet. There were times when Rosalie was reminded to watch her mouth, especially her tongue that grew increasingly sharp and fast. But always, there was the reminder of place. That her brother, Byron, was also her master.

"I see," she said. Her father had already warned her.

" 'I see,' " he mimicked. "Just look at you. All grown up. How I've missed you."

"I've missed you, as well," she said.

He stared at her hard. "I can barely stand it. Where is my combatant nigger sister? What have the nuns done to you?"

And there it was. A touch of the familiar. She responded without missing a beat. "It's like you say, Byron. I'm growing up."

"Well. I'm glad you're home. I'm glad you'll be here in the commissary. I won't be home for long," he said. "And Father will need you."

"The Academy!" Rosalie said. "Monsieur . . . Father says you are in the finest military institution."

"You must see me in my uniform once before I leave."

"If you say so, then I agree. I must see you in your uniform."

"That time will come soon enough," Byron said. "Let's go over everything. First, don't let anyone fool you. We don't give change, only store credit. And this is how we record it." He opened the ledger.

"Father spoke plainly about payment for goods. That I am not to let anyone cheat or think they can cheat. Don't fall for a hard luck story or big sad eyes. I believe him when he says it would be worse for me if I do."

Byron chuckled. "To hear you talk like a learned pupil! My, you've changed!"

"And you, Byron. You're a soldier. I

304

think you will do well commanding soldiers."

Byron's chuckle was now hearty. "Listen to us! Who would have thought a few years would make lords and ladies of us with cordial conversation? Do you remember our teasing and playing?"

"We were happy children." She lied easily.

"Yes, we were! Very happy."

At this point Pearce entered the little store. He put on a show of being pleasantly surprised to see the young lady and bowed.

"Robinson Pearce, at your service, mademoiselle."

"A pleasure to make your acquaintance, monsieur." She detected right away he wasn't Creole and didn't speak French as his first language.

"No 'monsieur,' " he said, "though it sounds lovely from you, mademoiselle. Please. Call me Pearce. It's all I respond to." Then he stopped. Fixed his face, looking at Byron and then Rosalie, doing this several times before Byron said, "Yes. This is my sister, Rosalie."

"Rosalie Guilbert," he said, still studying both. And then, "I must speak the truth, mademoiselle. Your brother is a beautiful man —"

"Thank you." Byron bowed.

"But you are . . . you are beyond mere beauty."

"Don't be fooled, Rosalie," Byron said. "Pearce has quite a reputation. He's spooney with the ladies."

"Spooney?"

"Our slang at the Academy."

"Slang?" she asked.

"Hmm . . . I can't say for certain, but think of it as a secret language," Pearce said. "Slang. And we say 'spooney' to mean . . ."

"Sweet," Byron finished. "Pearce is said to be sweet to the ladies."

"Not *all* the ladies," Pearce said.

"No wonder you're changed and gay in spirit," Rosalie said, smiling at her brother. "You have a comrade. And a devilishly clever one, if I might add."

"You may!" Pearce insisted.

Byron looked at Pearce, exhaled, then

looked at Rosalie. "Truthfully, sister. I could have no closer comrade in arms."

"Hear, hear!" Pearce cheered. "We, on this hot day and no pints of beer. What can be done to address this matter? I know. We'll go for a swim."

XIII

On undoubtedly the hottest day of mid-summer no one could blame two cadets on furlough for stripping down for a swim in the cool pond. The pond had been dug out by enslaved men and filled with catfish and bass for subsistence and sport for Bayard Guilbert and his son. But on this bright hot day, the sole purpose of the pond was to refresh the cadets as they swam and pleasured each other under the cover of the water, while Madame watched their dolphin maneuvers from eight hundred feet away. This was part of Byron and Pearce's fun. To entertain their unwitting spectator. The secret word that they would listen for during dining room conversation would be "swim," although they agreed to also accept "swimming," "swimmer," "swam," and "frolic." They enjoyed themselves fully, and now swam leisurely.

Byron was the first to hear horse hooves pounding. He called to Pearce. It was Jane riding toward the pond.

The men treaded water, looking to each other to gauge how they should receive the interloper. Pearce smirked, and Byron shook his head, a terse "no" to disabuse his smirking friend of the notion of meddling with Jane. Pearce, the happy instigator, spat out water and called to her, "Join us, Mademoiselle Jane! The water is cool and inviting."

To their surprise, Jane dismounted Virginia Wilder and unbuttoned her blouse.

Byron panicked. He swam toward her but stopped. He dared not wade farther and expose himself to her. "Jane," he said soberly. "Dear Jane, stop." There was no right way about this, and nothing he could do to stop the girl from disrobing.

Jane had tossed her blouse to the grass. She wore no chemise underneath, exposing her chest. "It's hot," she said. She unhooked her skirt and was removing it.

Byron, despite his nudity, rose, covering his penis with his hands. "NO, Jane! NO!"

Jane wasn't shocked, or ashamed — or spritely or lustful. She was, however, dumbfounded by Byron's command. *Why couldn't she enter the water?*

Pearce laughed and shouted, "YES, Jane! YES!"

Jane sat on the grass and unlaced her shoes. With shoes off, Madame's pupil was now completely nude. She stepped down into the water without a sense of impropriety and swam out to the center of the pond, where she dived downward, bottom up!

Madame screamed. When she finished screaming, she shouted at Thisbe. "Save her, Thisbe! Go save her!"

Thisbe didn't know what she would or could do, but her orders were clear. She was to save the girl from herself.

Jane came up and spat water. She shook her head, wiped her face, and continued to swim with gusto, her arms slicing stroke after stroke, proving their strength against the water.

Pearce cheered her on with applause.

Jane ignored Pearce. She focused on only the water and slicing through it.

Byron called to Pearce, "Let's vacate. With haste!" He dragged himself out of the pond and scrambled for clothing. "Dress now!"

Pearce was slow to follow.

"Remember, my grandmother is watching. In full hysteria. Trousers, man! Trousers, now!"

The two hopped and ran, half dressed, Pearce laughing all the way to the commissary. Rosalie was immediately taken aback by the sight of the two men. Both shirtless and completely soaked — one's pants inside out. Their other articles — shirts, shoes, half socks, drawers — spilling out of their arms. She stood agog, then turned away, not knowing what to make of the mad scene.

"Rosalie. Go to the pond with cloth to cover Jane."

"Monsieur?"

"You heard me well, girl. Jane

Chatham. She's in the pond. In her . . . altogether. I need you to go and cover her before she is seen."

"Monsieur Byron, your father said —"

"I am telling you to get to the pond to cover the young lady. Now."

It was at the "young lady" that Pearce laughed. Byron, who understood the gravity of it all, shot Pearce his most severe look of reproof.

"Forgive me," Pearce said, but his eyes glistened with mirth.

"Please, Monsieur Byron," Rosalie begged. "Please stand watch while I go."

He waved his arm. "Go. Just go."

There were bolts of gingham and cheap calico, but Rosalie grabbed a rough woolen horse blanket. She didn't stop to marvel at how quickly she had gone from sister to slave. She took the horse blanket and made her way to the pond. If she had a worry, it was that she had just stolen from her father.

Madame Guilbert's servant was at the pond's grassy edge, calling out to the girl in the pond. Rosalie remembered seeing the girl from a distance and that she spent every day and night at her grand-mother's side. In the grand house.

"Miss Jane! Miss Jane!" Thisbe called. "Madame say come out dat water!"

Rosalie hated her voice. She couldn't help herself as she stood a few feet behind the girl. She couldn't help but ask, How could Grandmother prefer this Black girl to her?

Despite Thisbe's shouts, Jane continued to swim and not look toward the girl.

Rosalie approached Thisbe. She barely regarded Thisbe but joined in calling out. *"Mademoiselle Jane! Mademoiselle Jane! Venez ici! Venez ici!"*

"Elle ne parle pas Français. Seulement Anglais," Thisbe said.

"Oh," Rosalie said.

The two girls looked at each other.

"La fille du Harriet et Daniel?" Rosalie said.

"Oui, mademoiselle. Madame Sylvie m'appelle 'Thisbe.'" She hadn't heard her parents' names spoken in years.

"Je m'appelle Rosalie."

"Oui, Mademoiselle Rosalie."

Thisbe knew who she was. The daughter of Master Lucien. The one Madame said was made in the dirt. Now that Thisbe had seen her, the resemblance to Madame was remarkable. But that wasn't for Thisbe to say.

They turned their attention back to the white girl who had completely submerged, down into the water.

Thisbe began to call again to Jane. She couldn't be seen conversing with the Rosalie girl, and not doing her duty.

"Miss Jane, please come out dat water. Please come out 'fore I come get you!"

Rosalie called out in English. "Please come, Miss Jane! Please come!"

The two girls looked at the water, the still pond. They waited. Nothing.

Thisbe, wincing, removed her shoes — they were so tight. She hobbled and then waded into the pond, lifting her skirt. She heard Rosalie say, *"Prends soin!"* and in English, "Take care," as she waded farther into the pond. She wasn't particularly tall and was submerged to her neck. Suddenly, there was no ground beneath her feet. Thisbe screamed. And then was under the water.

"Help! Help! Come! Please come!" Rosalie called out in English. Then French. She stepped up to the edge to see where the girl, Thisbe, had gone. Rosalie herself was afraid of falling into the pond.

In a rush of water, Jane broke through the surface, headfirst and chest up. She saw the girl pointing and screaming, "Tisbe! Tisbe! Get her! Get her!"

Jane submerged herself.

Rosalie clutched the blanket and prayed and waited.

A few seconds later Jane reemerged with Thisbe in her arms. She pulled Thisbe up and out of the water and Rosalie ran to help drag her to the ground. The naked Jane rolled Thisbe over and hit her on the back until the girl coughed up water.

Rosalie didn't know what to make of the strangely fantastic scene. She didn't know what to make of the white girl. And when she heard voices, other voices, Rosalie regained her senses and covered the white girl's broad body with the horse blanket. She hurried about, grabbing

Jane's clothing and the shoes, but Jane was now standing, with Thisbe slung over her shoulder. The blanket, meant to uphold Jane's modesty, fell to the ground.

It was a sight to behold from any distance. From atop the gallery, where Madame was now in danger of falling off her perch. From outside the stable, where the stable boy gaped, taking it in. From the grounds, where the gardener, who had been attentive to gathering Spanish moss, was frozen until he thought better of being a Black man staring at a naked white woman, and then he turned away.

The bare white girl carried the Black servant girl, limp as a lamb, possibly lifeless. Both drenched. Rosalie endeavored to wrap and keep a blanket around the white girl's body, while holding on to shoes, skirt, and blouse; she made a crazy addition to the parade. The big white girl's bottom was all Rosalie could manage to cover, as the girl strode in the wide steps of a hunter returning triumphantly from a good kill. She took a few steps and the blanket would fall. Each time, Rosalie stooped, caught the blanket, and pulled it up and around the girl while the girl, Jane, marched onward. The horse she called Virginia Wilder trotted behind them to complete the spectacle of the parade.

"Merci, merci, mademoiselle. Let me cover you," Rosalie pleaded. "Merci, mademoiselle. Perhaps put the girl on the horse."

"That is my Virginia Wilder," the girl answered in English.

Rosalie didn't know what to make of her answer, but she continued to follow, holding up the blanket like a bridesmaid holding up a wedding train.

The broad white girl continued to stride, shifting the unconscious Black girl in her arms to the other shoulder. The horse, perhaps eager for water and mash, trotted ahead to the stables.

Rosalie was now aware of where she was. She wasn't *near* the forbidden grounds but was *on* those grounds. The very grounds her mother warned her to stay clear of. She could see the doors. She was only feet away from where her half brother took his meals and where those with the Guilbert surname lived. Where rooms lay vacant, that she should occupy. Rosalie couldn't resist the urge to look up toward the gallery.

Madame could be heard shrieking. Shrieking at Jane and at Rosalie. "Go away, nigger! Filth! Indecent!"

Rosalie assembled the skirt, blouse, and one shoe at the door. She ran back and found the other shoe, which had been dropped during an attempt to wrap the blanket around the moving girl. She placed the shoe with its mate and fled.

When Jane entered the house with Thisbe, Madame was there, on the main floor, screaming at Jane. "Drop her! Cover yourself! Hide yourself! Shame! You will never marry. No family will have you. Shame! Clothes! Put on clothes!" She shouted all these things with equal shock and fervor.

Jane seemed to hear one thing only. She laid Thisbe down on the sofa and didn't seem aware of her own nudity or the shame of it. Jane said calmly, even with the two housemaids frozen in the distance, hands covering their open mouths, "She couldn't swim. I think she is alive."

"Of course she is alive," Madame

scoffed and then coughed up saliva from her tirade. "Get to your room and clothe yourself. Then I will see you. I will see you then."

Jane went up the stairs in no hurry. Marie and Louise couldn't look away. Nor could they stifle their giggles.

"Marie. Louise."

The girls appeared before Madame holding each other's hands.

"Yes, Madame Sylvie."

"If this goes to the quarter, I will ship you both to Cuba. Do you understand?"

Cuba. Known for unspeakable atrocities in the cane fields and sugarhouses. Better to die than be sent to Cuba, the supposed fate of Henri, the colored son of Vié Pè, who had gone missing in the 1830s, as the rumor went.

"Oui, Madame Sylvie." They understood Madame's threat.

"Get her to the quarter. See that she is all right."

"Yes, Madame Sylvie."

Marie and Louise called the gardener to bring Thisbe back to where Madame had gotten her from ten years ago.

XIV

Patience. Even the least of us has a story of how we came to be.

On Madame Sylvie's seventieth birthday, she felt it was time to make a change. She wished to entirely shed the "new" and be once more "old." She couldn't return to France. Her son had so scandalized her by taking up with the cabaret performer. Her childhood friend, "Madame Royale," had passed away, failing to reclaim the throne. She couldn't return. Still, Madame decided to play the final cards life dealt her. She would live her final years in a particular style and comfort to remind herself of the life she was owed. She would retire from the demands that the role of mistress required. She would never have to stretch a dollar, stare down the open mouths of

320

tooth- and gum-infected Negroes in the absence of a dentist, or be subject to any man, including her son. Her last efforts would be spent on her grandchildren, should they come before she expired. She proclaimed her retirement and planned to devote herself to reflection and prayer.

In lieu of a soiree — since the cook couldn't prepare the treats the predecessor, Marcelle, would have created — Madame took it on herself to pick out her own birthday and retirement gift. She left the house from the pantry, then passed the vegetable garden, passed the outer buildings, the Blacks waving and calling out, "*Bonswa,* Madame Sylvie." Passed the smokehouse, the *pigeonnier,* and the privy, and went down to the quarter.

They all rushed out, glad to see her. The little pale girl was pulled into the third cabin by her mother, while her brothers stood outside waving to the Madame.

She went from cabin to cabin, finding Negroes in whatever state of being at home. The end-of-work bell had sounded long before she came down to the quarter. The enslaved families weren't used to seeing Madame Sylvie unless someone was sick. Although the children were jubilant, the adults worried (all the while bidding her well). Madame down in the quarter. It couldn't be good news. Families huddled and shivered and waited for the worst.

And then she stopped inside the seventh cabin, the home of Harriet, Daniel, Harriet's sisters, and their three children. Harriet and Daniel tried to make polite conversation, but the dowager mistress was fixed on their children. There was one with bright eyes. Smart, bright eyes that brought to Madame's mind the faithful dog of Marie Antoinette. Thisbe.

"This is my gift," she told herself aloud. Then she turned to Harriet and Daniel. "Is it a boy or a girl?"

Harriet's voice quaked. "Girl, ma'am."

"Madame."

"Girl, Madame," Harriet said. "Her name is —"

"Thisbe," Madame said. "She'll be called Thisbe." Madame patted her skirt, as if coaxing a dog. "Come, come. Come, Thisbe."

XV

Madame calmed herself. She had no time for the waves of hysteria that momentarily seized her. She had much to put in order. First, Jane. Juliette Chatham didn't lie when she warned her daughter was "too much." Madame would have to either correct Jane or stand by helpless as this girl brought down what vestiges of respect the Guilberts managed to uphold. This girl defied civility. And what would she write to Juliette, after Lucien had taken a hefty sum to house the girl?

Madame looked at the crucifix that hung over her bed. Then at the painting of the Holy Mother. Even with these images to draw strength from, she felt an absence of her own power. As though it had been taken from her. Perhaps it was the exhaustion. The tax levied against her nerves, seeing the girl waltzing as naked as a sow, the other girl daring to enter her house.

She took a deep breath.

She herself was something of a living saint. She submitted to her husband's brutality, and yet the many children he got onto her didn't kill her. She kept the plantation running and profitable when she had been deserted in death by her husband and then deserted by her pleasure-seeking son. She had survived two blood-filled revolutions. She could direct this Jane Chatham to a proper womanhood. She could survive this girl.

There was no need for delay. Madame went to the girl and found her in her room, dry, skirt and blouse on. Her hair damp.

"Jane," Madame spoke, not knowing what to say next. The girl waited.

"Jane."

Jane didn't blink. The girl didn't seem to understand the rudeness of staring.

"Jane. Do you know what you did?"

"Yes, Madame Guilbert."

"French, if you please."

"But I don't please," she said in English. She spoke swiftly and without spite.

"This time," Madame relented in English. "This time, because what I say, you must understand."

"I understand English," Jane said.

"No, no," Madame said. "You understand French. You speak French. You prefer English. See the difference?"

Jane said, "You understand English. You speak English. You prefer French."

The girl spoke without expression.

"Jane. Now, I ask you. Do you know what you did? Today. The pond?"

"I went for a swim, Madame Guilbert."

"Jane. You take off your clothes. In view of men."

"To swim, Madame Guilbert. It was hot. I rode my horse until I was covered in sweat. Byron's Robinson Pearce said to join us. I joined them."

"This is not a thing to laugh at, Jane."

"I'm not laughing, Madame Guilbert."

"Jane, a lady doesn't jump into the pond. She strolls to the pond or along the riverbank, wades with a bathing skirt.

Lets the water cool her ankles. But disrobe in public before men? Before Negroes? Jane, this is . . . is scandal! No family will have you."

Jane seemed confused. "But, Madame Guilbert, I won't be had. My father is dead. My nanny is sold. My mother is gone. I only have my Virginia Wilder."

Madame noted that her father and nanny were dearest to her. Mother next. Sisters not mentioned. Her horse was her consolation.

"Promise me, Jane. Promise me that you won't remove your clothes in public. That you won't expose yourself. When you expose yourself, you expose your family to ridicule and reproach. You expose this family to worse. Promise me you understand."

"I can't promise you my understanding. I don't understand. I don't."

Madame thought for a moment. This girl was not so complicated, she told herself. She could find the words to trap her. Then they came to her, as if the Holy Mother whispered the words of English so she might repeat them: "You don't understand, Jane. Good. But you can promise to not show your naked body in public."

"Yes, Madame Guilbert," Jane said.

"Now, let us pray together to the Holy Mother."

Madame told Marie and Louise to serve Mademoiselle Jane in her room. Jane would not dare to take dinner with the men.

Still, Jane came downstairs and seated herself as she had learned in her lessons with Madame. She couldn't be moved or made to understand the relationship between shame and taking her meal in the dining room. She didn't feel shame. She felt an insatiable hunger that the meal brought to her by Madame's servants could not appease.

"Mademoiselle Jane," Lucien said, full of impishness and a few glasses of claret, "I hear you are quite the swimmer."

"I am," she said quickly.

Pearce's eyes showed their usual brightness. He did all he could to contain himself. He kicked Byron. *Swimmer,* but received no help or corroboration from

Byron. Byron found none of it amusing.

Jane said, "My father and I went fishing and swimming. He said swimming was useful for a body to know and do."

There was more under-the-table foot kicking.

"A wise man, your father was," Lucien said. "Wise man."

"If not for Jane's strength and swimming, I hear we would have lost Thisbe," Pearce said.

"We couldn't have that, could we?" Lucien asked. He winked at both Pearce and Byron without discretion.

Byron looked down to avoid his father's winks. Lucien would not be satisfied until Byron, in some form, acknowledged his supposed relations with his grandmother's maid. He nodded to his father. Lucien raised his glass and sipped.

Madame, who knew otherwise, rolled her eyes. "If not for these two," Madame said of Byron and Pearce, "my maid would be at my side."

"Grandmère," Byron said, "you sent Thisbe to save Jane. We sent Rosalie to save Jane's dignity, and it's Jane who saves Thisbe from drowning. Mind you, with no regard for the very thing we moved heaven and earth to protect."

"She couldn't swim," Jane said.

"Yes," Pearce said. "However, Jane had dominion of the water like the Lady of the Lake, that heroine out of *Le Morte d'Arthur!*" He smiled at Jane, but Byron kicked him, for reasons unknown to him.

Madame hissed.

Jane would not return Pearce's smile.

"Is there no woman you don't flatter?" Byron asked.

"A man's man," Lucien said, winking at Byron.

"I state the obvious," Pearce said. "Jane is brave. Why, she's the sort that wouldn't falter upon the order to charge."

"You can't do that," Byron objected. "You can't equate Jane tearing off her clothes and jumping into the pond with frontline heroism."

Lucien, full of claret, said, "I can see the battle scene now!" He pushed himself up from his chair with his wineglass in hand.

"Cannon to right of them,
Cannon to left of them,
Cannon in front of them
Volleyed and thundered;
Stormed at with shot and shell,
Boldly they rode and well,
Into the jaws of Death,
Into the mouth of hell
Rode the six hundred."

Pearce applauded. Byron kicked Pearce. Lucien bowed his head and took his seat.

"See what you've done," Byron said to Pearce. "At least he doesn't know *Le Morte d'Arthur.*"

"I'll see your challenge," Lucien said, rising once more. " 'What damosel is that?' said Arthur. 'That is the Lady of the Lake,' said Merlin . . ."

XVI

Thisbe heard voices fading in and out. Humming. Singing. She felt the shadows of light and movement around and over her. The crackle of wood popping and burning from the hearth. The smell of herbs burning. And other smells of wood, walls. She didn't want to open her eyes. But her eyelids flickered, and this produced more sounds from above her. She was being watched. By her mother. Aunts. And sisters.

And then she felt her mother's hands on her face. Warmth spread throughout her body. The thing that she missed most, the embrace of family, mother, father, aunties, sisters, overwhelmed her like the water she nearly drowned in. Then her father. Her father laughing and crying. And now there was praising, hopping, clapping, like the ring shouts by the river where she and her family gathered when she was five. There was this great joy spinning around her.

She couldn't move. She had been wrapped in blankets. All that they had.

"The Lawd brung her back!" her mother said. "The Lawd brung her back to me." Her father put his arms around her mother.

"We fitting to lay you out," her older sister said. "Start letting folk come by and see you in the body one last time. But sho' glad you got yourself up."

Thisbe missed her sisters. Her oldest sister was a grown woman of nineteen with a baby and a husband. The sister directly above her in age, seventeen, had a full face and a warm smile. Her sisters. Holding her hands, brushing her face and hair with hands rough from sugarcane that felt good and comforting.

How could they be so far away and close at the same time?

From the back porch of the Guilbert house, she saw nothing but cane, swaying in the distance, as far as could be. But she couldn't see the people in the cane, hoeing and slashing at the stalks. Still, when she stood on the porch, she imagined. Mama out there. Papa out there. Aunties out there. Sister out there. Sister out there. In the cane, cane, cane, cane, in the cane, cane, cane. This was the song the wind played in her mind, as she stood on the back porch. This was the comfort of knowing that Mother, Father, aunties, sisters were there. And one day she would be with them.

XVII

Madame had a word with Byron privately while Lucien strained to recall passages about the Lady of the Lake from *Le Morte d'Arthur* for his audience of one, Pearce, who egged him on. Madame put an end to her son's performance.

"That's enough," Madame said. "Byron, early in the morning," she said.

"Yes, Grandmère," he said, taking Pearce with him.

And now she was left with Lucien. She started as soon as they had left.

"I've given Byron the signet ring." She waited for a reaction from Lucien. There was none. "We have to make sure Eugénie will wait for Byron."

"And the pinkie ring will accomplish what?"

"Pinkie ring. That is no pinkie ring, but

my family's fortune."

Lucien was becoming less clouded by alcohol. He fumed. "That ring."

It was clear to Madame that her son remembered the ring. Whose fat finger he had placed it on. And why she had been forced to take action against her own son in his youth. This memory only made Madame stronger in her stance.

"Do you think the colonel will give us his daughter now? Do you think he will join with this family of lunatics and scandal? The family that houses a young lady charging on a horse like a man in battle? Then jumping naked into the pond for all to see?"

Lucien was drowsy at this point, but he heard his mother. "If the girl feels no shame, why should we?"

Madame said, "So cavalier. Say your poetry. Make fun. Will you think it's nothing when the colonel dissolves the engagement?"

"It won't come to that," Lucien said, finding his sobriety.

Madame hushed her voice and spoke mostly through her teeth. "Don't take this lightly, son. A broken engagement invites ridicule. Gossip. And then what family of any importance will attach themselves to the Guilberts at Le Petit Cottage?"

The two cadets retired to the garçonnière. Pearce lay in the small bed and sang furlough and drinking songs, certain that one voice would soon be two. Byron wasn't in the mood for singing. Pearce reminded Byron that he was owed much fun and lovemaking, as their word was spoken once, twice, and three times by others in the dining room. Byron said a cold "Not tonight" and added, "I will be gone for most of tomorrow. But do stop by and see Grandmère in her salon. First thing in the morning."

Rosalie had eaten very little that night. Her neighbors gave her a cabbage and an onion to make a soup. She couldn't put her mind on food or the garden she would have to cultivate for herself. She could only hear her grandmother screaming at her from the gallery. She could only fear her father would beat her or worse, for she hadn't followed his instructions at all.

There was a rap at the door. A tremor ran through her. She both feared the knock and expected it. It was him. Her father. She readied herself, come what may, and opened the door.

"*Bonsoir,* Mon Pè," she said.

Lucien stepped inside, the smell of wine oozing through his pores. He circled about the room, looking at everything, how the cottage was furnished. He nodded.

She asked, "Yes, Mon Pè, what can I do?"

"Who have you talked to?" he asked. "Who have you told about the girl? Jane."

"No one, Mon Pè."

He lifted her chin using his thumb and looked in her eyes.

"No one, Mon Pè," she repeated. "I swear on the crucifixion."

The two seconds of his review passed more like ten seconds. Finally, he released her face. "Say nothing about the white girl." He spoke in Creole and not French.

"Yes, Mon Pè."

"Nothing to no one. Not your mother. Your brothers. Their women. Don't make buzzing bees out of this."

"Yes, Mon Pè."

"Why did you not cover her body?"

"I tried," Rosalie said. "She would not hold still to tie the blanket. I ran, holding up the blanket to keep it from falling. Madame Guilbert screamed for me to go away. I ran from her sight."

"Yes, yes, my pet. Stay from your grandmother's sight for now," Lucien told her. "There is a room for you in the house. And if not, there is your own salon at La Fleur Blanche Plantation. The time will come."

"Yes, Mon Pè."

In the meanwhile, Marie and Louise had their own families to care for but were told to stay with Madame after they served the family, cleared the dining room, and washed the dishes. They brought Madame to her salon. Undressed her. Removed her jewelry. Brushed her hair. The sisters were rougher with Madame than Thisbe was when they wiped her and cleaned her. Marie and Louise were used to the rigors of housework and scrubbing, working their hands until raw. No amount of raps from Madame's fan could make them work with the gentle touch that Madame had come to know.

They couldn't both kneel at the prie-dieu, so they knelt on the rug and prayed in Thisbe's stead. When Madame was ready to sleep, they draped the mosquito netting around her bed. Together, they slept in Thisbe's trundle bed at the foot of Madame's bed, holding each other like they had when they were girls and couldn't bear separation.

XVIII

Pearce awakened in the morning and found himself alone in the garçonnière. He put aside his feelings of abandonment and readied himself for his appointment with Madame Guilbert. He found her in her salon, seated on her rose throne, ready to receive him. It was obvious to him that she had been expecting him for some time. Without Byron, he was a bit apprehensive about being with the Guilberts on his own, but he entered with cheer and apologies nonetheless.

He bowed low. "Bonjour, Madame Guilbert. Please forgive me if I am late." He straightened.

"Bonjour, Monsieur Pearce," she said. "I gave no hour of the day. Only that you must see me."

"Then I am at your service," he said.

"But, Madame. I'm so used to seeing your servant. It is odd that she's not standing there at your side as she does."

"And here you stand before me without Byron. We are both without the ones we are closest to."

"Yes, Madame. I suppose we are."

Madame didn't speak right away. She didn't invite him to sit. There was an iciness in her air. It made Pearce uncomfortable.

"Thisbe, is it? A curious name."

Madame knew she made the young man nervous. She waited a few seconds just to enjoy that feeling of putting someone on edge. At last, she broke. "It's a pity they don't teach French history at the Academy. You would know the loyal figures of the court."

"A loyal figure?" he asked.

"Of course! There was none more loyal. Bright. Comforting. To the end, none more loyal to the queen than her dog."

He paused. Her answer was unexpected. "Dog," he said. "She is named for a dog?"

"Not any dog. The queen's loyal dog,"

she answered.

"I'll not forget that piece of history," Pearce said.

"I played with Madame's dog. The royal children and I."

"You, Madame Guilbert? Madame preserves well." Pearce was careful to not go too far.

"Monsieur Pearce. A gentleman and a liar! You flatter. That is good! Useful, but wasted on me. I am immune to those charms."

"In that case, please forgive me, Madame Guilbert," he said.

"No," she said straightaway. "I don't. In fact, it is this quality I call upon."

Pearce was puzzled and intrigued. If Madame meant to throw him off balance, she had succeeded.

"Do sit down, young Pearce."

Pearce sat, relieved for this extended invitation, but didn't relax his guard entirely. He noticed that she offered no refreshment. No tea.

"If I can truly be of service, Madame Guilbert, I am only too happy to oblige."

She got to the point. "Monsieur Robinson Pearce," she said, her French accent thick, "I believe you owe the family of Boisvert Chatham a debt."

He was taken aback, but after a swallow, kept his composure. "Madame Guilbert?"

"We are a distinct society, Monsieur Robinson Pearce."

"Pearce, please, Madame Guilbert."

"We maintain tradition. We uphold the values of our society."

He waited.

"You don't understand our traditions. How could you? You come from no traditions."

"Well, Madame —"

She lifted her hand. "If this were true, you would not have allowed Jane to compromise her fortune."

"Madame?"

"We are alone, Monsieur Robinson Pearce," she said. "So we will speak truthfully. I saw my grandson get up to flee the pond as soon as the girl began to disrobe, while you lingered."

He closed his eyes. Guilty. He couldn't deny it.

"Yes. From the distance I saw everything. Byron sought to defend Jane's fortune, but I believe you found Jane's actions and Byron's attempts to save her fortune amusing."

His face reddened. If Byron had been there to see it, he might have enjoyed this rare moment of inquisition and conviction. Pearce was hard to put at unease.

"Madame Guilbert, I throw myself on your mercy for your forgiveness. I meant no harm to the young lady. The truth is, I've never met anyone as, as, unique as Jane. She doesn't ruffle."

"I don't know your ruffle," Madame said, "but I know your meaning. I am glad you find her unique, but the Boisvert-Chatham family is injured."

"But how?" Pearce asked.

Madame shook her head. "This comes with the risk of welcoming outsiders. They don't understand how society is made. How it must work to maintain order. I speak plainly. No man will have Jane if it's known that another man has enjoyed her in ways that only her husband should. Clearly, you see that."

"I promise you, Madame Guilbert. On my honor as a cadet, that I didn't touch Jane."

"Of course not," Madame said matter-of-factly. "Of course you didn't touch her. But you see, touching isn't the only injury to her family and her future husband. Think of it, Monsieur Pearce. How will you mix in social circles with a smirk on your face because you have seen her? Her husband will be humiliated, should she find a man to marry her. Here, Monsieur Pearce, the spread of gossip burns a family's prospects to the ground."

"Madame Guilbert," Pearce spoke sincerely, "dear Madame Guilbert, I would never speak a word about Mademoiselle Jane and the pond, and I will do all that I can to make amends."

"That is expected," Madame said in the same matter-of-fact tone.

"Tell me what I must do," he begged.

The sound of his remorse and begging pleased Madame greatly. She felt vital.

345

"Jane, as you have noticed, is a special, unusual girl," Madame said. "The influence of her English father has quite confused her. As a friend of her mother, I am helping to clear some of this confusion. What I need from you is to pay some attention to her. Give her the practice of social intercourse with a man."

"I blush, Madame Guilbert."

"You don't," she said. "You have traveled. You have access to your family income. You have seen and experienced the world." She presented her list as if she had been preparing it for some time. "Don't romance her. That would be cruel. But show her the attention a gentleman would show an eligible young lady. Give her practice to behave in society as a lady."

"Why would you entrust this young lady to me when it seems that I have wronged her and her family?"

"Monsieur Pearce! Isn't it obvious? For that reason you owe the family a debt, and I know you are honorable enough to repay it. If you weren't honorable, my grandson would have nothing to do with you. You would be — as you say — found out."

He lifted his brow in admiration and wonder. "That was one straight to the heart," he commended her. "The foil well placed. *Touché,* Madame Guilbert."

■ ■ ■ ■ ■

BOOK III

■ ■ ■ ■

Book III

I

Patience. At the root of something great lies something terribly small.

Although small and not particularly ornate, the Bernardin de Maret signet ring has its place in all of this. If Bayard Guilbert and Lucien Guilbert had their way, the little ring would be lost to all but fishy creatures on the ocean's floor. The father had sought to shed all reminders of class, but the son had his own reason for despising the ring.

Lucien Guilbert was Sylvie's jewel and justification for a life of suffering. Her son would not be penalized for the fault in his bloodline. She educated him. Taught him to dance like a courtier. Prepared him to enter society as a gentleman planter. She had coached him in wooing Juliette Boisvert while she worked

351

on Juliette's mother. At every social event, cotillon, and waltz, Sylvie was strict with Lucien: "Don't touch her." This was especially difficult as Lucien, skilled in the art of blowing into the ears and on the neck of dancing maidens, had felt Juliette ripening as he romanced her on the ballroom dance floor. Unfortunately, both mother and son were dealt equal blows when Juliette's parents announced her engagement to the Englishman, Phillip Janeway Chatham.

Sylvie was moved that her son's heart could be broken. She arranged that young Lucien would travel to France and be introduced to the respectable circle of society that she had maintained a sliver of connection to. Once received, Lucien would be introduced to eligible daughters for intentions of marriage. For the trip he packed a few volumes of poetry and was given letters of introduction, money, and most important, the signet ring that belonged to his maternal great-grandfather, along with instructions to claim the vineyard. Above all, he was scolded to speak only French and to not let a word of the Louisiana Creole language roll off his tongue.

Once on the open seas, Lucien, a young man of twenty-one, felt an unknown freedom and desire to see more of the world. He drank cane rum and read volumes of poetry to soothe his broken heart. When the ship arrived at the South of France, he learned of another ship bound for India. This appealed to his curiosity and he boarded that ship and continued east. This left the welcoming party of the family that was dispatched to receive him and collect his steamer trunk to send the unhappy letter to his mother that her son was lost.

In the meanwhile, Lucien Guilbert's broken heart was on the mend. Once docked in India, he pursued every aspect of his curiosity. Beasts he'd never seen, tastes that set his tongue and senses dancing, and at times, his bowels churning. And music he couldn't comprehend, and women, exotic to his mind. He was smart enough to hire a guide to explain customs and to — unbeknownst to him, on many occasions — keep him from harm. This guide directed him away from what was sacred and led him to the pleasures he sought. Mainly, brothels. "Best you live long, young sir."

India! Fragrant. Intoxicating. Metaphysical. Abundant. How could he return to the world he knew?

Luckily, Lucien ran out of money and had enough self-control to cut his losses and keep the signet ring on his person. He couldn't return to St. James without the signet ring. He had no choice; he put his father's gold pocket watch in his guide's hands, and in exchange, the guide secured him cheap passage to France on a freighter carrying never-seen-before animals, such as camels, to the French zoo. When he arrived, he made his sincerest apologies to the host family in Paris and was charming and contrite for a week. He remained ingratiating and penitent, attending Mass daily and the confessional every Saturday. The family, forgiving and glad that he was alive, planned to host a soiree to introduce him to a particular young lady who might find the offer of a country life in Louisiana appealing.

But they were in the heart of Paris! A city of marvelous distractions. One such distraction, Le Théâtre Latin, attached its irresistible pull on Lucien's soul. A cabaret of magic, theatrics, and champagne. Never shy, Lucien would stand before the patrons and recite Molière and Voltaire for drinks. On a Saturday that Lucien was to go to confession, Lucien found himself at Le Théâtre Latin, in the thrall of a cabaret singer. A blonde who couldn't reach her higher notes without flashing her meaty ankles and calves clad in silk stockings. He bought her champagne just to hear her joyful laugh. He was smitten. In a short time he brought her to the house of his hosts and introduced her as his bride, showing the signet ring he was to offer as a promise to the girl that he was supposed to meet. The family asked to see the certificate of marriage. When he couldn't produce it, they offered separate lodgings for his "bride" and sat a servant outside her bedroom door.

The new "M. and Mme Lucien Guilbert" were fast on a ship bound for America, and then on to Lake Erie, the Ohio River, and at last, the wide Mississippi, to ferry them to St. James Parish.

It wasn't the steamboat he had hoped to impress her with. But the new — if not legitimate — "Madame Guilbert" was agreeable, and the couple made their way on a flatboat hauling fruit and vegetables en route to Baton Rouge. Lucien was happy with the prospect of seeing his mother. He had something much better to give her than the letters he had never written. He returned to Le Petit Cottage with the woman he would call Madame Lucien Guilbert.

His mother didn't speak of those times that followed the death of her husband and the launch of her son into French society.

Only the Holy Mother knew the relief that Madame felt from the deathly release of her husband. Only the Holy Mother knew that Madame hadn't known the ecstasy of marital union, but only cruel coupling, often followed by the death of a child. Madame felt she had been for-given for her sigh of relief, her exclama-tions of thanks and praise, when after thirty-three years of marriage, her body was bound to her, and her, alone. She had envisioned a future for herself and had set it in motion.

When she had sent her son to France to mend his broken heart, it was with an enormous chip on her shoulder. She intended he return with a fiancée of old, old blood, fine French breeding, and a chaperone. And if the young lady was fair, well! All the more to rub her neighbors' noses in it! Then she would surrender the reins of Le Petit Cottage to her son, and they would overwhelm St. James planter society with their charm and style. In Madame Sylvie's mind, she saw the two Mrs. Guilberts sharing stories while going through the younger's trousseau. And in this way, her heart would be eased from the pain of losing her own daughter so many years ago. When a female child was born to her son and wife, she would take over the education of her granddaughter to steer her into society. This was far from the life she was born to, far from the circumstance that brought her into Marie Antoinette's generosity, but to see her son take the reins of Le Petit Cottage, prosper, take a wife of a fine family, and have holdings in France, Madame Sylvie could find contentment in the story of her life. The one she would recast and tell her granddaughter.

Unfortunately for Madame, those dreams faded into fear, sorrow, and then utter humiliation as, after some time, word reached her that the young Guilbert hadn't been received by the host family. His trunk arrived but not he. The letter sent was short on details and strove to make one point: Lucien Guilbert was gone.

Madame was unable to go on with the operations of the plantation. Hers was a familiar grief. Dark. Pervasive. Enormous enough to pin her down to her bed for days, if not weeks. Marcelle made broths for the weakest stomach, but Sylvie would not lift her head. She was bone and muscle as it was. Now, her muscle was softening and falling away.

Word from the house reached the field. For a short while the field hands took holiday early. Work slowed. Then work stopped altogether. The overseer spent more time whipping, but to no avail. After having had some rest, the women began to talk among themselves. Nearby laboring plantation owners would see these idle slaves as an omen of things to come. If some can be idle, why can't all be idle? The other planters might force Madame to sell the plantation to a harder, crueler master. Now, Madame had done her hard driving when she took the reins in the absence of her husband and son, but the enslaved women knew this devil and her whip. The murmurs began to spread about workdays on other plantations, brutal enough to make a ghost moan for the living. Bit by bit, "Christmas in March" was voluntarily ended, and steady production was reinstated.

Madame had lifted herself from her bed but hadn't ventured outside to survey the rows of cane. She began to take food in small amounts. It was a humid Wednesday afternoon, while Marcelle coaxed a little food into her, that the postman trotted to the house on his mule with a letter bearing a French postmark. It was a brief letter addressed to Madame S. Guilbert, stating that the young man, Monsieur

L. Guilbert, had found his way to the family's care, penitent and none the worse for his ordeals. Madame and Marcelle hugged, and then Madame got on the floor and cried and walked on her knees with hands clasped to show the Holy Mother she knew a mother's tears and a mother's rejoicing.

Madame and Marcelle waited for her son to return with a fiancée and two chaperones. Yes, she told Marcelle. "Two chaperones shows a good family." Together they prepared the rooms warmly in a plain decor so the new bride could add a few of her own touches. The two women began to plan the menu for the first week of dining as well as arrangements for a reception. Madame even managed a kind thought of gratitude toward her dead husband for having brought to her home Marcelle, who would reassure the bride and her chaperones through familiar French cuisine served at Le Petit Cottage.

Three months later, Lucien swaggered into Madame's house with a woman in a cheap silk dress he introduced as his wife.

The signet ring, the symbol of three

hundred years of family blood, jammed on a swollen pinkie finger. A ring that had been smuggled, that safeguarded proof of an inheritance. Proof of her own life and true place, on the hand of a cheap cabaret girl. Madame sized up the situation in one blink and didn't bother to ask where her family was from. It didn't matter. The harsh street life. The makeup applied theatrically couldn't hide the woman's life story: one no doubt begun in squalor, fighting for morsels, selling flowers, and stealing off carts. This woman didn't have sense enough to hold on to most of her front teeth. Her hair was piles of curls, locks dangling over her eyes. Her wide hips told Madame she had carried not one but at least three babies in her womb in spite of her corset, children more than likely squeezed out like feces and left at the very orphanage she had no doubt come out of. Madame asked for no details of the woman's life. She smiled politely. Made sure her "daughter-in-law" had been fed. Slyly ascertained that there was no marriage contract or certificate registered. She listened to the woman tell stories of singing in the gayest houses for emperors and generals alike. With every word the "daughter-in-law" spoke, Sylvie, who didn't believe in the legitimacy of the marriage, was careful to not address the woman by name, while she contemplated an end to this so-called union.

Madame Sylvie interrupted a story of the new Madame Guilbert about how she entertained the regiments with her singing and her costumes. It was all the woman could talk about. Singing. Costumes. How the patrons loved her. Madame Sylvie didn't bother to tell her son the obvious. That this "wife" was not long for the life of a plantation mistress. And give up a life of drunken warbling and kicking up her legs?

In the meanwhile, she canceled the reception. "Marcelle. Bring the food for the soiree to the quarter. Let the Negroes enjoy the feast."

Madame went to church alone that Sunday. "Enjoy your bride at home," she told her son. "You are still unsettled from a long trip. Rest on this holy day. I will petition the Holy Mother on your behalf."

■ ■ ■ ■

Later, when she returned, she had a moment of clarity. She had been so overwhelmed with joy to receive her son, and then overwhelmed with shock by the reality of the situation, that she had forgotten to ask the important questions. She began at supper.

"Son, tell me about the vineyard."

In spite of everything, Madame's face was filled with the coloring of her youth. The vineyard at least salvaged the ordeal. That, and that her son, alive, had returned to her. The woman was set aside in her mind.

"What vineyard is this, husband?" the wife asked. The manner of speech rough and hungry in Madame's ears.

"The vineyard. Oh. Yes! The vineyard," Lucien drawled.

The realization came faster to Madame than she wanted to receive it, and the truth of it almost knocked her down.

"Lucien. You didn't go to the convent or the vineyard to make the claim? They have been waiting for you. This is your inheritance. My life. The family blood."

"You see?" he said to his bride. "I told you about my mother."

Her earlier tears of joy be damned. Madame could have murdered her own son. She was speechless for the rest of the meal. This was no matter to the couple. Msr. Guilbert recited poetry while his wife whistled through her near toothless mouth.

Sylvie watched the pair. First with a simmering disgust, and then with a resolve. He was a fool, and she possessed an unabashed need for an audience. Sylvie made the Guilberts an offer.

"Son. Bring your bride to New Orleans. Show her some culture."

The ordeal brought forth her cunning nature. Her focus and ferocity. She bided her time, never betraying her intentions. Madame proposed that her son, with a bit of money, show his bride what the lower country had to offer before she settled into the life of a plantation mistress. After the filthy passage on the flat boat, they would take the riverboat down to New Orleans in grand style. Before they took their leave, Madame said, "That little ring won't do, Madame Guilbert" — the first and only time Madame Sylvie called her so. "It is choking your finger." She brought out a box of jewelry her husband had gifted her with, after his trips to cotton and cane exchanges followed by drunken jaunts. The other Madame Guilbert gasped at the baubles — all cheap in the first Madame Guilbert's estimation. "Please," Madame said, pushing the box to her. "Choose as you like."

The woman popped her finger into her mouth, sucked hard, and then worked to pull the signet ring bearing the Bernardin de Maret crest off the reddened pinkie, and handed it to her mother-in-law. It took all of Madame's calm to maintain her face. Her legacy had been returned to her. Without being told, Marcelle took the signet ring and boiled it to remove the stench of the woman.

The happy couple went off on their honeymoon. It had worked as Madame Sylvie had calculated. They enjoyed nights of gambling and the gay life. This was the life for the new wife, who loved the frivolity of the steamboat. However, as much as she was enamored of the luxurious steamboat, she was completely absorbed by the carnival of Mardi Gras. Gamblers fought over her. It was a flashy gambler who bought her a satin dress with new boots who won her. Lucien Guilbert spent the first night in New Orleans looking for his bride.

When Lucien returned to Le Petit Cottage quiet, surly, and most important, alone, Madame Guilbert didn't raise a question of his bride's whereabouts. In fact, she didn't mention the woman. It wasn't necessary to sweeten the triumph. The win was enough.

The image Madame nursed all the while waiting for her son to return to her from France was replaced with cold reality. A reality she dared not deny: her son couldn't be trusted with her legacy or her life. She blamed the morals of the young country. This idea that only the new is of value and the bones on which society is built are meaningless. This idea that lineage could be broken, scattered. The rejoicing that white skin made everyone from the postman to the Texan to mongrel Yankees equal to her. These ideas of liberty for all whites permeated the air and had corrupted her son.

No. Sylvie couldn't put her life and the future of his legitimate offspring in Lucien's hands alone. Nor would she petition to transfer the late M. Guilbert's property to herself, although she was well within her common sense and rights to do so. No. To petition the court was to name her son a mismanager and circumvent any hope of arranging a match with a good family. She had thought it out carefully. During the time that she'd sent Lucien and his bride downriver, she moved to take complete control of the plantation. She summoned his half brother, who was of no blood to her, and had him accompany her to a place undisclosed. She sat upon a horse and watched him dig up the earth and bury the satchel of gold coins. She had already taken what she felt she needed. Then the half brother, a man of twenty-four, with a wife and children, accompanied her to the harbor. They were met by men who took him captive, in a boat bound for Cuba, a sugar-producing island that would continue to take in the enslaved long after the European and American territories outlawed the import of this human cargo. She took no money for him. What were a few hundred dollars compared to the actual control of her fate? And now she and only she would know the location of the gold. Moreover, she would not miss this reminder of her former husband, who carried Vié Pè's features truer than her own Lucien.

She would continue to run the plantation in terms of having the final say, until her son proved himself ready to take control of a life she was forced to take pride in.

II

Eugénie Duhon had two aunts, and the Guilberts reckoned with each in one way or another. Both aunts were childless and focused their maternal energy on Eugénie. One aunt couldn't be confused with the other. Eugénie's deceased mother's sister, a countess by marriage, lived a countess's life in New Orleans. This aunt had suitors lined up from wealthy, well-connected families on both sides of the Atlantic for Eugénie's societal debut. However, at the tearful behest of her niece, the countess was forced to desist from her networking efforts, although she was equipped to present her niece in grand style.

The older aunt, Eugénie's father's aunt and Eugénie's grandaunt, had been watching over her niece from her early

369

childhood. Aunt Agnes kept the younger, wealthier aunt at bay, and provided Eugénie's moral and religious education. The grandaunt was devoted to her niece's chastity and hoped to direct her toward the convent.

Byron intended to do as his grandmother advised. As the engagement was negotiated and understood, it lacked the token to make it official: there was no engagement ring. The token he planned to give Eugénie was not an engagement ring, but it would bespeak the intention of marriage, children, and property. His grandmother had given him instruction on how he was to bestow the ring and the story of the ring's journey. This would hold Eugénie Duhon's attention during the two years of Byron's absence. How could she not want to take her place in the history and triumph of the Bernardin de Maret Dacier Guilbert lineage?

When Byron appeared at the Duhon home without an invitation, Grandaunt Agnes did all she could to turn him away. If not for a house servant, Eugénie would have been unaware of Byron's arrival at the home. Eugénie rushed to Byron's aid, much to her aunt's objections, and took a stroll on the grounds with him. While the young couple strolled, Agnes kept four paces behind, muttering the rosary and issuing warnings, periodically reminding them to keep a cordial distance; "flesh rots to dust; the soul is eternal."

It wasn't a good day for a walk, the grounds damp from an earlier rain. Eugénie was likely to ruin the hem of her dress with mud. She didn't want to stay indoors. She did what she could to cheer up the home, but her father's health was poor. His doctor said he had a few years to look forward to in his condition, but Agnes prepared the home for what she deemed the somber end.

"Your friend sounds like an interesting fellow," Eugénie said after hearing stories about Cadet Pearce of Yorktown Heights.

"He isn't my friend, but my dearest, closest mate. We've learned to rely on each other at the Academy," Byron said. "My letters do the rigors of West Point no justice. I won't bore you with it, but it's impossible to succeed at the Academy without true camaraderie."

"I see."

"Do you, Eugénie? One day I might put my life in my friend's hands," Byron said. "Or any cadet I train with."

"Then I am indebted to him and will keep him and all of the cadets in my prayers," she said cheerfully, a contrast to Byron's serious tone. "I should be indebted to your Pearce. One day the life he protects will be mine."

Byron stopped his stride. "What an admirable way of seeing things," he told her, thoroughly moved. "You are so pleasantly calm, and make barely a fuss. Dutiful to your father. Sweet to your aunt. I can't think of a more giving soul, Eugénie."

At that, the cheerful Eugénie demurred, looking away from him. That made him smile.

"Your grandmother," she said. "I believe no one can equal Madame Sylvie in your eyes."

"That's not a fair comparison," Byron said. "Grandmère is eighty — and she is all fuss! But she has lived long and has endured so much."

"You see!" Eugénie said. "You don't

deny you hold her in a higher esteem. But I can't fault you. How can I?"

He smiled at that. Her complete acquiescence. "She speaks of you with great fondness. You have no idea the remedy you provide us with."

"I? What remedy, when I haven't lifted a finger?"

"Your letters," he said. "Grandmère seeks to engage a portrait artist. If not for your letter, I wouldn't have been able to suggest Monsieur Claude Le Brun."

"Yes! Monsieur Le Brun. A true artiste! A modern fellow," she added. "You must see the likeness of Père before you go. You know, Le Brun is with my aunt for the summer. Let me do what I can to arrange the sitting for your grandmother."

"I would kiss you, but I fear Aunt Agnes."

"With good reason," Eugénie said.

The two laughed, and Agnes remained behind them, chanting, *"Le corps, la poussière, la mort éternelle,"* or flesh, dust, eternal death.

"I have two more years at the Academy," he said, his tone a shift from jovial to steady.

"I don't mind the long engagement," Eugénie said. "I will have time to organize my father's house."

"Your father is fortunate to have you." They walked along. "How is the colonel? Do you think Aunt Agnes will let me see him before I go?"

"I'm sure he expects to see you before you leave. It isn't fun for him, having no male company to rail against the governor or the election. He tries to shield me from these great matters, but he does worry what will become of the farm. A Northern president can't be good for the Southern planter."

"Your father is right to not bother you with those matters. I'll be sure to sit with him before I take my leave. I doubt the country will elect an abolitionist president. If they do, and Lincoln pushes the planters to the brink, I fear the worst will come."

"The worst? What do you mean, Byron?"

"I fear there will be war. And I'll go to defend our interest."

374

"Oh. Byron."

"I will defend our land and your honor to the utmost, Eugénie. You are meant to be served and provided for all your days."

Byron stopped and took her lace-gloved hands in his hands.

Aunt Agnes cried out in French, "Don't take his hand! Don't take his hand."

Eugénie smiled sweetly to calm her aunt. "It's all right, Aunt Agnes. It's all right." She and Byron, both embarrassed, smiled at each other, then walked on.

Byron's mood turned as they walked. He had been determined to be pleasant and lighthearted, but couldn't help himself. "Eugénie, I should give you the opportunity to refuse me," he said plainly. "I'm bound to fight, if it comes to it."

She had not expected his pronouncement. "Will it come to that?"

"No, beloved. Not if every planter votes for the good of their farms."

"I can't imagine one who would not."

"The large planters, undoubtedly. The poor fellows scraping by with sons and daughters for field hands, I'm not so certain," he said thoughtfully. "In the meantime, I must be prepared. Most important, you must be prepared."

"Me? Prepared? What are you saying, Byron?"

"If war is declared, I'll fight, without question. But, dear Eugénie, many things can happen. I could be crippled. Blinded. Or killed. Would that be fair to you? To keep a promise to half a man, or a dead man?"

She tried to laugh it off. "Why, Byron Guilbert, you say the most unpleasant things! Is this a warning of what's to come in our lives together? Unpleasant dinner conversation? Doleful strolls in the garden?"

He remained serious. "I can only be fair to you, Eugénie. Here, between us. Without your father. My grandmother. My father."

"Don't forget Aunt Agnes," Eugénie said.

Aunt Agnes grunted. The two noted she was catching on to English.

"I think we are well matched," Byron said. "But your aunt behind us and the countess in New Orleans would choose a different future for you."

"I've spent time with my aunt in New Orleans, and I find I like a quieter life. One much like the one I've known with my father."

"What?" Byron said, finding his sense of humor. "No fancy balls? No emerald and ruby earrings, or pearls from constant suitors? No trips to France — or where is your aunt's husband from? Rome?" Byron gave her a knowing look. "We won't be impoverished at Le Petit Cottage, but I'll say it: it won't be an improvement on how you live now. How your father agreed to bind you to us under those terms is a mystery. The Duhons and the Guilberts live a similar life."

"Precisely."

"And this is fine with you? Do be honest, Eugénie. I'll hold nothing against you."

"Byron Guilbert, I think you wouldn't. Would you?"

"I wouldn't."

"Or are you trying to break the engagement? Are you not a man of your word, and you seek the coward's acquittal?"

"Eugénie. My Eugénie. To break our engagement isn't my intention. Knowing what's possible for a soldier if war between the States breaks out, I only seek to give you a choice: betrothal to a man marked for dismemberment or death, or disengagement to allow the countess to better align you for your own good."

"No, you coward!" Eugénie was only half joking. "I don't accept the choice, as you put it. Not in this matter. You will declare yourself as my betrothed, or I will understand that you are not a man of your word and that you scheme to have me do your work for you."

Byron was a bit surprised by this small outburst from his otherwise demure betrothed. But if this was the extent of her outburst, then it would not change his opinion of her. "Dear Eugénie, even when you are cross, there is a sweetness about you," he said. "All right, then." He admired her as he might admire a pair of shiny cuff links. A thing that is beautiful, but apart from himself. "On my word and my honor to our families, as a gentleman, as a cadet, I pledge to you my troth."

"And your chastity."

"And my chastity," he vowed without hesitation but kept the signet ring in his jacket pocket.

Byron spent an hour with Colonel Duhon, admiring his portrait, discussing politics and his own progress at West Point. He declined to join the family for supper and made his apologies for his uninvited visit and its abrupt end. Only Aunt Agnes was pleased to see him go.

His ride back to Le Petit Cottage gave him much to contemplate. His grandmother was wise to send him to the Duhon plantation. He had an agreeable situation. While Eugénie Duhon didn't set a fire within him, he could envision her as one day being his wife. He could see Eugénie as one to manage the household, scold and punish the servants, and perform acts of charity for the poor. Most important, she would bear an heir. He smiled, thinking about his grandmother. His wise grandmother. How did she know that the even-keeled and good-natured daughter of Colonel Duhon would be the perfect wife for him?

But first, he had to make amends with his friend.

"I won't have you guess my whereabouts," Byron said to Pearce when he found him in the garçonnière.

"I didn't put the question to you," Pearce said.

"Then why bother you with it, if you don't wish to know."

"I'm sure it's none of my concern."

"Put that way, you're correct. It doesn't concern you. It's family business."

"Then by all means, carry on. Do what a good son does. Take care of the family business."

Byron broke down first.

"Grandmère urged me to pay my respects to Colonel Duhon, and to court Eugénie. My fiancée."

"How goes the courtship? You must make me familiar with the rituals. I'm sure there are customs specific to your marvelous St. James country."

"Parish."

"Two shits for St. James *Parish.*"

The two didn't speak until it was time for supper.

Byron said, "I hope you like her."

"I will. I'm sure."

"Are you?"

Pearce breathed heavily. "You hope I'll like your fiancée. I assure you I will. And yet, you furrow your brow."

Byron didn't know how to respond. "Are you being sincere with me? I can't always tell."

"Byron, what am I to say? I won't like your fiancée? Why would I say such a thing?"

The silence between them reasserted itself. Byron didn't have an answer and Pearce knew it.

"If you agree to marry her, I'm sure there is something altogether agreeable about her or the situation. Why would I have quarrel with that?"

"Because it sounds like we're quarreling."

Pearce sat up. "I have no quarrel with your fiancée. I'm sure she's perfect. An excellent example of Louisiana woman-hood. I have a quarrel with you, Byron. Only with you."

The very thing Eugénie couldn't do for Byron, Pearce did. He stood up to go to Pearce. But Pearce put his hand up.

"No."

"You can't mean it."

"I do. No."

III

Thisbe's family's one-room cabin was small and poorly lit, with sixteen feet by sixteen feet to step on or sweep around. Still, it was a house full of her people and Thisbe didn't want to leave. But Marie and Louise had come to check on her progress and found her fit to return to the house. Thisbe gloried in the embrace of her mother and father one last time, for as long as she could, the smell of her mother's hair and skin, these treasured amulets tucked in her memory. She pushed her feet into the tight black shoes and made the walk to the big house, but not without taking breakfast in the cookhouse.

"Didn't spec you back," Lily said. "Spec you passed on."

Thisbe was supposed to laugh or answer. Instead she considered Lily's words before speaking.

"I want to stay with Mama, Miss Lily. Mama and Papa and my sisters. My aunties. Just want to be with them."

"Shucks, girl. You don't want to be in that cane. Your back broke. That whip crack 'cause you stop to breathe. Lawd knows, I done cut my hand more on them stalks than chopping onions in the devil's boiling house with these knives."

"I miss Mama and Papa, Miss Lily. My heart's sore from missing."

"I know about missing," Lily said. "I do, girl."

This was enough to release Thisbe from her spell of grief. She knew Miss Lily spoke about missing her son, whereas she would see her family, perhaps not soon or for long. But she would see them.

Lily pointed her head at the plate teeming with gravy, oysters, and bacon that sat before the grieving girl. "Sop that up with that biscuit. Eat while you can."

■ ■ ■ ■

Thisbe woke Madame to sit her over the chamber pot. She held Madame's hand as she always did when Madame relieved herself, then wiped Madame and prepared to clean and dress her. No words were spoken about Thisbe's health or absence.

It was rare that Madame took her first meal in the dining room and not in her salon. Thisbe seated her at the table with her son, grandson, his friend, and Jane. Madame was in high spirits, anxious to hear about Byron's visit to the Duhon home.

"Well? Tell us, Byron. Was there weeping? Much joy?"

"Weeping, Grandmère?"

"When you presented the ring."

"Ring," Lucien said.

His mother ignored him.

"That blessed ring," Lucien said.

The tension became obvious to Pearce. His eyes darted from Lucien to Madame, waiting. Jane ate her egg.

"Yes. The ring," Madame said. "My grandfather's ring."

Lucien pushed himself back against the chair. He muttered something. Only his mother understood the source and depths of his anger.

"Grandmère, please forgive me . . . ," Byron began.

"You didn't give Eugénie the ring? This was the purpose for the visit. To give her the ring."

"I know, Grandmère. I had every intention of giving it to her, but the time wasn't right."

"What do you mean? That was the time. That was the time!"

Seeing his mother thwarted and peeved turned Lucien's mood around. "It is no use," Lucien told Byron sympathetically. "Your grandmother doesn't understand about romance. What sends a young lady's heart to soar within her breast."

"Watch your mouth at the Lord's table," Madame said. "What you talk about, romance, is for poetry, not life. It is meaningless without a future."

"The future is here in St. James," Lucien said.

"But Byron and Eugénie's legacy is in France with my grandfather's vineyard."

"Then go, Momanm. Go claim your grandfather's vineyard."

"You know better than anyone I cannot return."

"That's right!" Lucien exclaimed. "Napoleon III is after you. The royalist offshoots, don't they look for you too?" He wiped his hands with his napkin and dropped it over his plate. "Mother, I have it on good authority, no one knows you."

"Father! Grandmère. Stop. Please," Byron said. "Just stop before you say something to hurt each other."

Lucien looked at his mother. Madame looked at her son. They laughed, perhaps for the same reason. Hurting each other was what they did.

Byron seized upon the broken tension to change the subject. "Good news, Grandmère. Good news."

"What is it?"

"Claude Le Brun is still in New Orleans

with the countess. Eugénie has sent for and expects to hear from her any day. If the countess dotes on her niece, as I suspect, I am certain your Le Brun will stop at Le Petit Cottage for your sitting before he returns to France."

Madame clasped her hands, delighted with the news.

"As long as it is safe for him to return to France, of course," Lucien said.

Madame no longer cared about that subject or her son's petty retort. She looked forward to her sitting.

"Grandmère, you won't be disappointed. I've seen the work of this Le Brun. The portrait of Colonel Duhon is a masterpiece."

"This Claude Le Brun is descended from Elisabeth Louise Vigée Le Brun. Of course it is a masterpiece!" Madame said. "But this is not the only portrait he painted. Did you also see the portrait of your future bride?"

"No, Grandmère." Byron paused. Everyone seemed aware of his hesitation except for Jane. "The portrait of Eugénie is —"

"Is what, Byron? Speak up," Madame demanded. "What of Eugénie's portrait?"

"The portrait of Eugénie is in her bedroom."

"Ho, ho!" Lucien laughed. "Excellent restraint, my son. Excellent. You will see her bedroom soon enough."

"Filth. Filth," Madame said. "You desecrate the table and curse our blessing."

Byron and Pearce excused themselves from the dining room table and left the house.

"This could go on between them for half the day."

"I'm glad to make the escape, but poor Jane," Pearce said.

"We could go back. Effect a rescue maneuver on her behalf."

"I am happy with effecting our own escape maneuver."

"Agreed," Byron said. "Let's choose some rifles. Take in some duck hunting."

"Let's," Pearce said, the cloud between them now removed by distraction. As they walked to the garçonnière, he asked,

"Byron?"

"Yes?"

"Why didn't you give her the ring?"

Byron didn't answer right away. "I did want to, for my family's honor and sake. But —"

"You couldn't."

"I wasn't ready. The time wasn't right."

They left it at that.

IV

The family, along with Pearce and Jane, met the carriage to receive Eugénie. Byron helped Eugénie out of the carriage, while everyone welcomed her warmly. Madame, however, couldn't hide her surprise to learn Eugénie rode unescorted, but for the coachman.

"Your chaperone!" Madame said. "Where is she?"

"The modern young lady doesn't ride with these appendages," Lucien said.

"My aunt wanted to come, but she won't leave my father's side," Eugénie said.

"Perhaps he is too ill for you to leave him," Madame said.

Eugénie laughed. "Madame Guilbert, my father pushed me out the door. He complains I'm more mother hen than daughter."

"You are so welcome, Eugénie," Byron said. "And long awaited." He turned to Pearce. "May I introduce my closest friend, and classmate, Mr. Robinson Pearce of Yorktown Heights in New York."

Pearce bowed his head. "My pleasure, mademoiselle."

Eugénie seemed to take him in head to toe. "Mr. Pearce. I didn't think you were real. Byron talks of you like one talks about mythic heroes."

"I mean you no insult," Pearce said, "but that can't be true. He mistreats me like a brother. But we can't take Byron's word for anything. He said you were beautiful and he, a lucky man. Both vast understatements!"

"I'm outdone," Byron said. "You see what I mean?"

"May I ride my horse now?" Jane asked amid the welcoming.

"No, Jane. You've ridden for today," Madame said.

"Ah! And one more member of the welcoming party to make your acquaintance," Byron said. "Eugénie, this is our family friend, Jane Chatham of the Lavender Plantation."

"The Lavender Plantation!" Eugénie said. "I'm pleased to meet you, Jane. I was invited to your home for your sister Phillipa's party. I don't know how I missed you."

"I went hunting with my father," Jane said. "I'm pleased to meet you, Eugénie." The latter was said as part of her more recent lesson in social conversation.

It had been years since the dinner table had seated so many. Madame delighted in having this gathering of young people, conversing, laughing, and in Jane's case, eating. This was how Madame saw the future of the home: a lively place of good company, discussion, and entertainment. Madame thought, later tonight, while Thisbe knelt at the prie-dieu, she would give thanks for her longevity and petition for ten more years, to live long enough to educate the next generation of Guilberts.

Lucien played the part of father and host. To see his son act the part of solicitous suitor toward Eugénie gave him pride and further put to rest his concerns about his son's interests. He would, however, remind his mother later that the table was missing one Guilbert. His daughter.

"We furlough men are highly envied," Pearce said. "You'll not find a greater assembly of camaraderie and honor than among us at the Academy. But wave a weekend or holiday pass before a first classman, ready to graduate, and he can't help but look forward to it."

"Is the Academy life as difficult as that?" Eugénie asked. "Byron's letters are so cheerful." She turned to him. He returned a sheepish smile.

Madame wasn't at all pleased with the conversation. "It's a cruel thing to share the miseries and trials of the Academy when all it does is create despair. Byron! Think of your poor fiancée."

"My letters are cheerful because there's much to take pride in, and I do take great pride in the routine," Byron said.

"Yes!" Pearce said. "The singing. The marching from pub to pub. I'll have you know Byron is the champion pugilist of our class."

Only Lucien seemed familiar with the

term "pugilist." His face enlivened. "You don't say!"

"I do, sir! Byron has the reputation for avoiding the jabs. He bounces like a crafty kangaroo in the ring." Pearce put up his boxing hands to illustrate. "But heaven help the opponent who receives his blows. Honestly, I don't think it gives him great joy to cut them low, and he would avoid it every time. But when he puts glove to the foe, he is unequal in power."

"This isn't pleasant. Not at all," Madame protested.

"I agree, Madame Guilbert," Eugénie said.

"Yes, but it's manly," Lucien said. "The art and science of the pugilist. Hear, hear!"

Pearce joined Lucien in a round of cheers. "Hear, hear!" He saw that Madame was not at all pleased. He cleared his throat. "And did you also know that Byron is quite the man about the hop?"

"Hear, hear, for the hop!" Lucien said.

"Op?" Madame asked, "What is *op*?"

"What you call a waltz."

Eugénie smiled broadly. "Byron! You didn't tell me about the waltzes!" She scolded him, but with a good-natured tone.

Byron flushed. "Eugénie, how would it sound if I wrote about the waltzes? As if I were having a good time while you waited for me."

"Yes, son. Patch up that quilt," Lucien said. He set a more serious eye on Pearce, but it was clear that nothing serious would follow. "Pearce. I'll speak to you sooner than later."

"Perhaps I gave the wrong impression," Pearce said, not sure how to take Lucien's mock anger. "Mademoiselle Eugénie, let me render the picture as it is."

"I'm waiting," Eugénie said.

"It's the duty of the cadet to rescue the instructors' daughters from the wall. It's frowned upon if too many young ladies stand around the floor hoping to be asked to dance. And while it is known that he is spoken for" — he said this for her benefit — "Byron, in that gallant manner of his, kindly offers his hand to the plainest of the plain."

"Of course, Byron is gallant," Madame

said. "It's in his blood."

"You exaggerate my dancing skill," Byron said to Pearce.

Pearce would have none of it. "Eugénie, your betrothed is so skilled a dancer he is charged with the duty of correcting the plebes who are fortunate enough to get a dance with the ladies. Plebes must attend waltzes, but the ladies prefer to not dance with the lowly beast."

Eugénie looked at her fiancé. "I wish you had written to me about dancing and not about geology, inspections, and camp."

Pearce said, "Why not see for yourself?"

"Yes!" Lucien said. "Let us see the couple dance. A prelude to what is to come."

Eugénie flushed even more than before. "Please. I can't be put on the spot. And no music? Mademoiselle Jane, you're brave. Please dance in my stead."

"I am brave," Jane agreed, "but I won't dance."

"You will, my dear," Madame said quickly. "In short time you will dance the cotillon like a courtier."

Jane ate.

"Byron," Eugénie said. "Are there other studies at the Academy that you purposely keep from me, besides dance instruction?"

Byron couldn't tell if she was genuinely disappointed with him or if she only played at being disappointed. In either case, he didn't answer.

"Dance instruction. What has the military come to?" Lucien asked.

"Mademoiselle Jane," Pearce said.

"Miss," Jane said. "English."

He bowed his head. "Miss Jane, I would be most delighted to dance with you."

Madame clapped her hands like an expectant child before a choice of puddings. Oh, the letters she would write to Madame Chatham! She could hear Juliette praising her name from over the Atlantic.

Jane said with food in her mouth, "Monsieur Pearce, I would not be happy to dance with you. Thank you, no."

"Jane!" Madame snapped.

Jane wiped her mouth with her napkin.

"If you please, no thank you, Monsieur Pearce."

"Much improved, Jane," Lucien said, raising his glass. "Good for you, clever girl."

"Merci, Monsieur Guilbert," Jane said.

Madame seemed pleased with this driblet of French and flattened attempt at civility even in the swirl of Jane's insult to Pearce.

Jane nodded and continued to eat.

"The military takes its grooming of officers seriously. Why, a cadet could earn demerits for a sluggish performance in the ballroom, just as he might earn demerits for a less than sharp performance in drill," Byron said. "Dance. March. Either case, excellence is expected."

"Why lecture your beloved when we can demonstrate the military form," Pearce suggested.

Pearce already stood, his hand extended to Byron.

Even Thisbe, Marie, and Louise watched as the two men met each other face-to-face at the cleared-out area. "But you will take my lead," Byron insisted, and with a snap of his boots at the heel, Pearce complied and took the follower position.

In lieu of music, Lucien alternately struck his water glass and plate with his fork, while counting, "One, two, three, one, two, three . . ."

Byron bowed to his partner. Pearce curtseyed. The room fell into giggles. This didn't deter the two dancers or encourage either to give in to the laughter by exaggerating their steps and making clownish expressions. Byron took Pearce's hand in his, the other hand on his shoulder. With elbows high, Byron led his partner in light but commanding steps, heel, toe, toe, heel, toe, toe, in a gliding box formation. Both men danced, their heads up, backs straight, chests open. To finish, Byron guided Pearce to a turn, and then continued the gliding box step so that their two figures whirled elegantly in the small space.

After the exhibition, Lucien set down his instrument and clapped and shouted, "Bravo!" Eugénie patted her hands together. Madame made a smiling expression with eyebrows raised. Jane heaped another chop on her plate. Marie hurried to the table to ladle gravy over the meat.

"My son, my son! A leader of men on the ballroom dance floor and in the battlefield."

"Thank you, Father."

"I would make a great leader of men on the battlefield," Jane announced.

"What strange ambition," Eugénie said.

"Our Jane is full of, of . . ."

"Surprises," Lucien completed for his mother. "She entertains us all."

"I don't mean to entertain," Jane said.

"Of course you don't, Jane," Madame said. "We shouldn't tease the girl."

Lucien raised his glass. "To leadership on the ballroom floor and leadership on the battlefield!"

"To the battlefield and war," Jane said.

"Jane, Jane," Madame said. "We women don't speak of war, let alone encourage it."

"But should it happen, we women protect the home and the family while the men are away," Eugénie said. She looked at Jane and smiled. "Like my mother did when my father went to war."

"If it's any comfort to you, Jane," Pearce said, "you would make a fine protector of the home."

Eugénie smiled, noting this compliment from Pearce to Jane. Byron noted Eugénie noting Pearce and Jane.

"Now, we must have the ladies dance with the men. A quadrille or a cotillon between the two couples," Lucien said.

"If Jane won't do me the honor, I will be forced to grab your servant girl in the corner," Pearce said of Thisbe, who did nothing to indicate that she had been listening, especially not show her teeth. As sure as Madame's eyes darted to her, she felt the raps against her bones.

"You won't," Madame snapped. "She is for me, and me alone."

"Well, then, Madame Guilbert. I beg a dance of you."

In the meantime, Lucien had poked his son in the ribs, leaned in, and spoke in a low hush. "Check your mate before he runs off with your wench."

"Father," Byron said sternly.

Lucien, observing Eugénie nearby, corrected himself. "Yes, yes. The lady is present."

Byron walked to Eugénie and held out his hand. "Eugénie?" he asked.

"Byron, I am much too shy. It was all I could do to endure being put on parade by my aunt in New Orleans."

"The countess!" Madame exclaimed. "I'm sure she hosts many fine affairs at the palace."

"Oh! Madame! It is a townhouse," Eugénie said. "Not a palace."

Madame, who was not used to being contradicted or corrected, would not let Eugénie's correction lie. "With two grand ballrooms and five carriages? I am no stranger to palace life, as you well know."

"We know, Mother dear."

Later, the young men bade the ladies a good night, walked to the garçonnière, and climbed up the steps to the bedroom.

"We've done the incredible. The unfathomable."

"We danced, two men in step . . ."

"Two men in lust . . ."

"Before my grandmother. My father."

"And your *fiancée*," Pearce said, with what Byron could only discern as relish. "The only thing missing was a stroll along Flirtation Walk."

"And a kiss witnessed only by the moon."

"Poetic, Byron. You *are* your father's son."

"Did you like that?"

"I did," he said, unbuttoning his lover's trousers.

"We had no word for the day."

"This time our word comes after the fact."

They laughed and both said, "Waltz."

V

A room had been prepared for Eugénie and her aunt, but Eugénie wouldn't hear of it. She missed the company of others, especially those closer to her in age, and she moved her things in with Jane. The two girls sat on Jane's bed.

"You are strange, Jane," Eugénie said. "But I do like you."

"I do like you, Eugénie," Jane said.

Eugénie laughed at Jane's dispassionate response. "Oh, no, Jane. You don't have to say you like me if you don't. It's what I like most about you. Your honesty. I could never say the things you say."

"I just say them," Jane said.

"Precisely."

Jane genuinely liked Eugénie and opened her steamer trunk to show Eugénie her treasures. She took out a thick canvas and unrolled it to reveal a portrait in oil paints. "This is my father."

Eugénie gazed at the portrait of the stoic man, his thick red beard and bushy red curls, and then looked at Jane. She nodded, having concluded the obvious about father and daughter. "You must frame it and hang it on your wall."

"It's not my wall or my room. My room is at the Lavender Plantation."

Eugénie didn't know what to say to comfort Jane, or if Jane needed comforting. She spoke so plainly.

Jane continued to show Eugénie her treasures. "This is his saber and pistol. His war jacket. They made my nanny burn his trousers." Jane took these things out, one by one.

"I have all of my mother's hair combs," Eugénie said. "Some of her jewelry. Her handkerchiefs, gloves, shoes. Her toilette water. I never use it. I keep it to smell it."

"I have my Virginia Wilder."

"Virginia Wilder?"

"My horse. She's an English charger.

My father gave her to me."

"Your dear departed father," Eugénie said. "You must have been your father's favorite."

Jane thought about it. Then she agreed. "Yes. I was his favorite."

"Is she named for anyone? Your horse?" Eugénie asked.

"Yes," Jane said. "She is named for herself."

Eugénie laughed because she couldn't help it. She said right away, "My horse is Peppermint. She's both friendly and spirited, I think, like me!"

"Peppermint." That seemed to strike Jane as a strange name for a horse. "Do you ride her every day?"

"Not every day. I have much to do at home. But our boy, Jacques, takes good care of her and the other horses. He spoils her with apples and cane sugar. He thinks I don't know."

"I ride Virginia Wilder every day," Jane said. "I take my lessons with Madame Guilbert and then I'm allowed to ride Virginia Wilder."

"Lessons?" Eugénie asked. "Madame

Guilbert is your tutor?"

"My mother said I must take the lessons or they will shoot my Virginia Wilder."

Eugénie gasped, her hands to her mouth. "How awful," she said. "That can't be true. Can it?"

"They will shoot her, my mother told me. I take the lessons with Madame Guilbert, wear a skirt, and let my hair grow to keep my Virginia Wilder alive."

"Oh, dear Jane."

"I ride her every day. She's not one for trotting. She was made to charge."

"That must make you happy. Riding the horse your father gave you."

Jane wasn't sure if what she felt was happiness. But she did feel driven to mount and charge her horse. She couldn't bear the thought of not having her horse and not being able to ride her. "Yes," she answered. "That makes me happy."

Eugénie took Jane's hand, which startled Jane somewhat. Eugénie, older by a year, sought to soothe Jane and stroked her hand. "Thank you for sharing your bed with me. I sleep alone at home. My own sisters are out of the house, busy with their families."

"I have three sisters."

"I know," Eugénie said. "Remember? I went to one of your sisters' parties."

Eugénie's things had been put away in a drawer. She took out her nightgown and bonnet. She blew out the candle on the nightstand.

Jane prepared for bed as she had done always. She removed her clothes completely.

Eugénie undressed and put on her nightgown.

Even in the dark, Eugénie could see that Jane wore no nightgown. "Jane," Eugénie said. "Where is your nightdress? I'm sure you have one in your trunk."

"I don't wear it."

Eugénie could barely face her. Jane eyed Eugénie blankly, unaware of her new friend's discomfort.

"Can you wear it for me?" Eugénie asked.

"I can't sleep with it on," Jane said.

"Can you not wear your nightdress for me?"

Eugénie was at a stalemate. But then answered, "Dear Jane, I cannot."

"Can you take off your bonnet?" Jane asked.

This surprised Eugénie. "My bonnet?"

"I used to smell my nanny's hair," Jane said. "But she was taken from me and works on my mother's cousin's plantation."

"And your mother?"

"She's in France with Genevieve, my other sister, and my cousin Georgie."

"Wouldn't you rather stay with your other sisters?" Eugénie asked.

"I am not suited for their homes."

"Jane, dear Jane, that's not true. It can't be."

"My mother told me. My sisters' husbands won't have me there. Or my Virginia Wilder."

"My sweet, homesick friend," Eugénie said. "No wonder you are as you are." She untied the ribbon to her bonnet and cast it aside. "You can smell and pet my hair if you like."

"Yes," Jane said. "I would like."

As uncomfortable as Eugénie was, she overlooked Jane's naked body and climbed into bed with her, her hair a free spray of golden-brown against the pillow. She neither combed nor brushed her hair and dreaded the price she would pay in the morning at the vanity table.

Jane didn't like the feel of Eugénie's muslin nightgown against her skin in the moist heat. But once the two were lying in the bed, the smaller Eugénie nestled in the arms of the bigger girl, the softness of Eugénie's neck and the honey-and-lilac smell of her hair calmed Jane enormously. She entwined her fingers and nuzzled her face in Eugénie's locks, and inhaled deeply, the two settling into their friendship.

VI

Madame was pleased that Eugénie had taken Jane in as a friend. In fact, she saw no reason for Jane's morning lesson. There could be no better lesson than actual social interaction with a proper young lady, although Madame kept an eye on Jane while the two young ladies joined her in her salon for breakfast. The young men, she explained, always slept late. "They are storing sleep for school. The cadets sleep so little." This quip served Madame's need to excuse Byron and Pearce more than to meet the girls' desire for an explanation. Eugénie and Jane didn't miss the men's company in the morning and busily chatted away about horse riding.

Eugénie said, "Jane, you can't go riding in your skirt and dresses. They are much too nice. You need a riding suit."

To this Madame perked up, a smile on her face. "Yes, yes!"

"I would send you mine, but we are . . ." Eugénie, searching for words, hesitated to speak.

Jane finished Eugénie's thoughts for her. "We are different sizes. I am a robust size," she said with pride. "My father told me that."

"And you are," Madame said. "This calls for your own riding suit."

"I can wear my father's uniform," Jane offered.

"No, no!" Madame cried. "A woman does not wear men's clothing. No, no, no!"

"I'm not a lady," Jane said factually.

"Not yet," Madame said. "Not yet."

"Jane," Eugénie said. "You would like a riding suit. I don't ride Peppermint without it. The outfit makes me a better rider. I believe my riding suit gives me confidence."

Madame was amused that Jane didn't speak right away. Madame concluded that either Jane had no answer or Jane was considering Eugénie's suggestion in the odd way that the girl considered all that puzzled her. It didn't matter which was the case. Madame was pleased by Eugénie's influence on Jane.

"You must go to New Orleans to the finest dressmaker."

Perhaps Lucien had been planted on the periphery listening. It was at the mention of fine dressmaking and the implied expense that he made his presence known.

"Dressmaker? Ferry upriver to see a dressmaker? And bonjour, mesdemoiselles. Bonjour, Mother." He nodded to the ladies and kissed his mother's cheeks.

"Monsieur Guilbert," Eugénie said. "Bonjour!"

Madame gave Jane a stern look, and Jane followed with her greeting, "Bonjour, Monsieur Guilbert."

"Bonjour, *mon fils,*" Madame said.

"What is this about a dressmaker in New Orleans?" Lucien asked.

"Jane needs a riding dress," Madame said.

"Riding suit," Jane corrected. "To ride better."

"Mademoiselle Jane," Lucien said, "I've seen you mount, gallop, and charge well enough to lead six hundred soldiers to their deaths. There is nothing a bolt of fabric can teach you about riding."

"Lucien!" Madame snapped. "You are throwing water on the good fire we've started. Madame Chatham would love to hear her Jane was fitted for a lady's riding dress." She looked to Jane and added "suit" before Jane could open her mouth. "Think of the joy it would give her mother. Why would you deprive Juliette Boisvert of that?"

"Chatham," Jane corrected.

"All right," Lucien said. "Let it not be said that Lucien Guilbert denied Madame Boisvert Chatham a pinch of joy. Jane shall have her bolt of cloth. We have plenty in the commissary."

Madame scoffed at the suggestion. "That might be so, Lucien, but the dressmakers are all in New Orleans."

"The suit makers," Jane said. "For a riding suit."

"And we have a fine dressmaker here at Le Petit Cottage. A maker of suits, if you like," he said to Jane.

"Son, you are mistaken," Madame said. "We have mothers who patch holes, stitch up sack dresses and cottonade pants. There is no seamstress among them. What this calls for is fashion!"

"I tell you, we have fashion." He turned to Eugénie and said, "My daughter, Rosalie, is an excellent dressmaker. I'll send for her."

"You will when I'm cold and dead. Not before," Madame said.

Eugénie, now uncomfortable, squeezed Jane's hand.

Madame caught Eugénie's look of discomfort in one glance. She quickly ceded that she had lost the skirmish and relented. "You might be right, son. Jane and Eugénie will go see the fabric. It might work better. More selections."

"Thank you, Momanm, my love. Thank you for seeing that," Lucien said. "After all, that is where the dressmaker is."

"Suit maker," Jane said. "I want a riding suit. With military buttons."

"Yes!" Eugénie said. "Mine has my father's buttons."

"Yes!" Jane said. "Mine will have my father's buttons."

"It is settled," Lucien said. "And see how happy the mesdemoiselles are," he told his mother. "Write that in your next letter to Juliette. How happy her Jane is." Satisfied with having created both an annoyance and a solution, Lucien tipped his hat and exited.

When Jane and Eugénie left to meet the dressmaker, Madame told Thisbe, "Go with them. Listen to every word said in the commissary, then tell me what they say. But you don't mix in. Don't muddy the water. You have nothing to say."

"Yes, Madame Sylvie."

Rosalie was enormously surprised to see the two young white women enter the commissary. The taller of them, the Jane that she had been sent to rescue, stared ahead. The other young woman, perhaps eighteen by Rosalie's estimation, and a contrast to Jane in every visible way, looked about the store, taking in the roomful of tools, barrels, sacks of dried goods, stocked shelves, bolts of fabric, and the counter where Rosalie measured and cut cloth and took money.

Rosalie nodded immediately, spoke French. "Ladies, how can I serve you?"

Jane spoke up. "You can serve me by sewing me a riding suit. And speak English."

"Of course, miss," Rosalie said. They didn't introduce themselves, but "white" was all Rosalie needed to know.

By this time Thisbe had entered the commissary but was careful to not stand too close to Jane or Eugénie. Rosalie made note of Thisbe's presence but kept her attention on the two women.

"A riding suit?" Rosalie asked.

"Miss Jane would like to have a woman's riding outfit, for her daily ride," Eugénie said. She stared intensely at Rosalie.

Rosalie went on, asking for specifics about the garment as if she hadn't noticed the smaller one's stare, although it was evident. Rosalie was used to the examination. She surmised this person was seeing the Guilbert resemblance in her, or more to the point, the Bernardin de Maret Dacier traits. It couldn't be denied that Rosalie carried these features more so than Byron, who resembled his deceased mother.

"Make it like my father's war jacket in the regiments."

"Yes," Eugénie said. "But you will fashion it for a woman." By this time Eugénie had learned to refer to Jane as a woman and not a lady.

Rosalie seemed slow to answer the white females. She had her father's instructions.

"She doesn't speak," Jane said.

"Are you dumb?" Eugénie asked. "Speak up."

"Pardon me," Rosalie said. "Please, I beg your pardon. I can sew the proper riding outfit. Before I cut cloth, mesdemoiselles, my master asks for payment."

"Master Guilbert recommended you for the job. He sent us here." Indignation drove Eugénie's impatience. She stamped her heels over to the bolts of fabrics and after a brief survey, swept her hand across the indigo material. "There is little here, but this dark bombazine will do. Don't stand there. Measure Miss Jane and start cutting."

"I beg mercy, mademoiselle, but Master Guilbert was severe with me on how I'm to dispense his goods. I am so willing, but if I could have his guarantee to cut the cloth, then I can do better than be willing."

"Madame wants the dress for Miss Jane," Thisbe spoke up, although no one spoke to her.

Eugénie and Rosalie turned to Thisbe. Jane didn't.

"Riding suit," was Jane's only response.

Rosalie said, "If only Madame would write the order for me on paper. I can give it to Master Lucien. Please forgive me. But I will pay with my hide and more if I disobey the Master."

Eugénie huffed, then said to Thisbe, "Go, girl. Go quickly to Madame Sylvie and ask her to write the order. Then run back with no delay."

"Yes, Mademoiselle Eugénie." Thisbe dipped, turned, and was off. She delivered the message to Madame, who was instantly enraged.

"Oh, she is his piece of dirt," she said of Rosalie. "She is everything he is." Thisbe stood quietly while Madame wrote the words "Make it" and other letters Thisbe couldn't discern. She looked on as Madame signed *Mme* and a big *S*.

Thisbe returned and gave the paper to Eugénie.

Rosalie was already engaged in measuring Jane. Jane stood stiff and proud, as if being measured for battle clothes.

"The pants should look like my father's military pants," Jane said.

"The pantaloons, mademoiselle? Miss?" Rosalie said.

Eugénie stepped in. "Do what you can to make it for a woman but to command —"

"Command an army," Jane finished.

Rosalie looked to Eugénie.

Eugénie said, "In a way fitting for a lady."

"I'm not a lady."

"That's all right, Jane," Eugénie said. "I'm describing the outfit so she understands how to sew it."

"Thank you, mademoiselle," Rosalie said to Eugénie.

"Eugénie Duhon. Fiancée to Master Byron Guilbert."

"Thank you, Mademoiselle Duhon," Rosalie said. Rosalie knew the air of a girl destined to take the reins of the plantation as the mistress. If all didn't come to pass as her father schemed, the girl would one day be her mistress, half brother or no. Hers would be a life of currying favor to live with whatever advantages were due her, if any. With her future flashing before her, a life with Laurent Tournier began to look attractive.

Rosalie glared at Thisbe.

Thisbe said nothing. Thisbe knew the quadroon resented not being handed the note directly. But she was not about to receive the white girl's scorn because the corn-silk-colored girl was disconcerted. Thisbe remained cloaked in feigned unawareness, but she knew.

Eugénie read Madame's words aloud. *"Make it. Cut the fabric. Sew the riding dress, you impiden cur. Mme S. Bernardin de Maret Dacier Guilbert.*"

"Thank you for reading it to me, Mademoiselle Duhon," Rosalie said, all the while thinking, *You see, servant. I can do what you do. I can wear my mask too.* "I have the measurements and will begin cutting right away."

"Yes," Eugénie said. "You see to it."

"See to it that you make a riding suit, not a riding dress," Jane said.

"Come, Jane," Eugénie said. "Why don't you show me your horse."

"Virginia Wilder."

"Yes, of course," Eugénie said, taking Jane's arm. "Virginia Wilder."

Pearce and Byron lay in bed, Byron snoring, his arms forming a pillow, while Pearce's left leg draped over him. Laughter from the outside cut into their otherwise quiet morning. Pearce was now awake. He propped himself on his hands, lifted himself up to look outside the window. What he saw made him smile. Eugénie and Jane arm in arm, crossing the property to the stable.

He lowered himself back down onto the

bed and kissed Byron's nape, shoulder, and then collarbone until Byron stirred, but turned away.

"I spy a happy twosome," Pearce sang.

Byron mumbled an assent.

"Not us, you beast." Beast, a designate to all Academy plebes, was now an occasional endearment between them. "The handsome Jane and your betrothed."

Byron snored on.

VII

Lucien dusted off the coachman's hat and jacket before the coachman took his seat. They rode back to Rosalie's cottage in the carriage his mother preferred for church and town. He helped Rosalie into the carriage without a greeting or flattering word about her appearance.

She looked at her father when he climbed up in the carriage and sat across from her. While it was her father's habit to start his mornings with whiskey in his boiled chicory, Rosalie only smelled chicory on his breath, and bay rum, no doubt slapped on his face. She didn't smell whiskey. She read her father's mood and didn't ask any of the questions on her mind about her grandmother or the Tourniers. His mood told her what she needed to know about the exchange between her father and grandmother. She only greeted him, "*Bonjou,* Mon Pè," sweetly, curtly, with no expectation of a reply.

As they passed the big house, Rosalie was tempted to cock her head toward the upper porch, although she was certain her grandmother sat in the wicker chair, watching. She thought better of it.

They rode for some time. What could have been a light and pleasant outing was sure to be about business. Now was a good time to tell him about the fabric. He couldn't slap her and expect her to put forth a pleasing impression for the Tourniers. She took a breath and began.

"Mon Pè, I had to cut the bombazine fabric for Mademoiselle Chatham," she said. "Mademoiselle Duhon wouldn't hear of the cheaper fabric."

"Fine, fine," Lucien said, to Rosalie's surprise. "She's to be your brother's wife. We'll keep her happy."

"Yes, Mon Pè."

"Construct this dress well. I've spoken for your abilities without having any evidence. Don't make me answer to your grandmother for having done so."

"No, Mon Pè."

"Yes, Father. No, Father," he sang with contempt. "You must be more clever than that with Tournier," he said. "He must find you beautiful, for sure. But you must hold his fascination."

"His fascination?" she asked.

"Despite his color, he has a great and profitable mind. A mind I'm sure is filled with books. What books have you read that you can discuss?"

"Books . . ."

"Girl, don't echo. Laurent will think you a block of wood and this endeavor will be a failure before its start."

"In our education the only books we were allowed were the Old and New Testament, a booklet of prayer and meditation, and the writings of Saint Thomas Aquinas." She didn't mention the younger Sister Jean David, who lent her *Pride and Prejudice, Frankenstein,* and *The Hunchback of Notre-Dame* — all that had taken Rosalie years to read. All carefully slipped to her in folded sections, and read in secret away from the other

427

girls, who might tell on her out of jealousy. The young nun had done a good thing for Rosalie. A good thing that carried grave consequences for Sister Jean David if she had been caught sharing the stories. Realizing the risk and privilege, Rosalie devoured the lessons of society and manners, the human monster, and the fleeting and subjective quality of beauty. The best way to repay Sister Jean David was to put what she had read to some use.

"The Bible? Saint Thomas Aquinas? No, no. These won't do for conversation with Master Tournier. What have I paid my money for?"

"I've learned a lot, Mon Pè," she said.

"Yes. To thread a needle and to cut chintz." He rolled his eyes. "Rosalie. You must be agreeable," he told his daughter. "But not too eager."

"Yes, Mon Pè."

"Your hair is too plain."

Rosalie touched her hair, parted in the middle, pulled back into a tucked-under bun. She placed her hand back in her lap.

"It has grown full. You'll take it down

for Tournier on your wedding night."

Rosalie felt her face warm.

"Good!" Lucien said. "Manage to blush the color of roses at the right moment."

She didn't dare contradict her father and explain that she had no power to blush at will.

"Now!" he said. "Imagine that Laurent has said something amusing. Let me hear you laugh at this amusing remark."

"Laugh?"

"Yes. He will try to charm and impress you. Well, let's hear it."

Rosalie didn't want to anger her father. She wasn't given to laughter, but she complied with an inaudible titter that was more smile than laughter.

"No, no, no!" Lucien said. "More like, 'Ho, ho, Monsieur Laurent. So clever!' " he said in a higher pitch. That gave her a horrified start. And then she laughed aloud.

"No! Too common! Too common. He can hear braying like that in his cane field or from a donkey. Come now, Rosalie. Like a lady. 'Ho, ho, Monsieur Laurent.

So clever!' "

She raised her hand to her mouth, the way she imagined Jane Austen's silliest sisters in the Bennet household would. "Ho, ho, Monsieur Laurent. So clever!"

"Again, girl! Again! As if our lives depend upon it."

At last, she seemed to please her father with her attempts at laughing to flatter Laurent Tournier's wit. They were nearing La Fleur Blanche. Rosalie felt she must take advantage of her peculiar position with her father to ask the question that weighed on her the more she imagined herself as the wife of her former tormentor.

"Mon Pè," she began. "Do you believe Laurent will be happy to marry . . ."

Lucien made a circling hand gesture to get on with it.

". . . a slave?"

He said nothing.

In that silence she thought to speak quickly. "Wouldn't Monsieur Tournier publish the banns and the announcement in the newspaper?"

Lucien only nodded thoughtfully but

didn't reply.

She had asked her question and didn't press further.

The two men greeted them. The two, mirror images, one older, white, the other bronze. Rosalie found Laurent Tournier an older, taller version of his younger self. His confidence showed in his straightforwardness. How he looked directly at her father and her. How he stood and held his head while listening, as if calculating every word spoken and deducing the answer. She was attractive enough; he was a man of breeding and privilege. This was surely a Creole planter's match! This mulatto son and quadroon daughter of planters. He, fair, but considerably darker than she.

Rosalie was aware that she was being studied but made no air about it. She complimented the home but didn't gush over the grandeur or the decor. She kept her gaze discreet and was careful to not survey the interior. Standing in the home of mahogany, cedar, and marble made her painfully aware of her lack of basis for a comparison. She had spent the last six years in the Spartan surroundings of a boarding school and had yet to place her feet on the floors in her grandmother's house. Rosalie purposely avoided looking up at that great eye-catcher, the chandelier in the main salon, but even without looking up, she couldn't deny its brilliance. She couldn't imagine herself at home in this splendor, but she would do her best for now, to not betray her humble circumstance while in the opulent Tournier home.

"My sister sends her apologies," Laurent said. "She is unable to join us for lunch. She and her husband are needed elsewhere."

"That is kind of her to think of us," Rosalie said. "Please convey our sentiments."

"Which are?" Laurent asked. He sought to put her off balance and make her feel vapid, but she spoke quickly.

"A bit crestfallen to be deprived of her company, but I do appreciate her commitments. You must understand, Laurent, it has been years since I've last seen her." While she spoke, she hoped her father would say nothing or wink at her in approval. The slightly surprised Laurent spoke first.

"I do understand, Rosalie. I'll do my best to fill in for her."

"Well, let's to the dining room," the older Tournier said, extending his arm to lead the way.

Lucien wanted to talk about innovations and to see the sugarhouse. Everything that Laurent said fascinated him. Rosalie could feel it. Her father hadn't only settled on Laurent Tournier as her sole suitor, he seemed to play his hand openly, dreaming of it. Yet while Mr. Bennet's problems in Miss Austen's book would be solved by the advantageous marriages of his daughters, she noted that Mr. Bennett had no urgent desire to part with a single daughter, namely his favorite.

Rosalie felt Laurent's eyes on her while she ate but refused to let him unnerve her. She was certain he waited for her etiquette to reveal her to be nothing more than a field hand in a proper dress. To thwart his expectations, Rosalie used each knife, fork, and spoon on her place setting with simple grace throughout the meal.

Her father said, "Now that Laurent has returned with all of his know-how, I am eager for harvest, to see these great wonders in action."

Alphonse Tournier said, "Then come during the height of things, if you can get away. I'm as anxious as you to see the cutting blades rove across a row of cane."

Lucien's eyes lit up. The imagining of it! He sipped from his water glass but hadn't yet touched the wine at his place setting. He laughed and said, "If Laurent keeps designing these wondrous tools, I might not mourn so the deaths of my best field hands."

"Or the loss of the election to Mr. Lincoln?" Alphonse asked, half in jest, and, perhaps, half not.

"Let's not go too far," Laurent said.

At that the men laughed. Rosalie gave a weak smile, rather than try the response her father coached her to say. *Oh, ho, ho! How clever!* When the subject was the election, she was not invited to or expected to respond.

"No, suh!" Lucien cried. "Should that sad day come to pass, I will curse and spit on it."

Laurent scanned Rosalie and noted that she blushed. "A lady is present."

"Yes, yes," Alphonse said, suddenly regarding her. "This can't be any fun for these young people. Elections. Cane cutting. Laurent, show the young lady the grounds."

Laurent stood. "Mademoiselle, my sister cultivated the garden. May I show it to you?"

Rosalie looked to her father. He nodded, although what other response could there be? They were two masked dancers at a ball, bowing and playing their parts.

Laurent took Rosalie to the garden, a garden that conspired to promote romance, the air heavy with its roses, camellias, and honeysuckles. He talked about the maze and the geometric shapes of the shrubbery incorporated within the design and that it had been a miniature replica of his sister's favorite garden at their family's French castle. "I hope you

435

aren't too crestfallen," he said, purposely using her word. "My sister would have been a better guide."

She sensed a part of him was making fun of her. She smiled. "I've enjoyed seeing the garden. I have no complaints. No disappointments."

"Rosalie, you've improved in every way," Laurent said.

"Thank you, Laurent," she said. "You would know."

They came to an iron bench in the center of the maze and sat. "We both understand the purpose for this visit," Laurent began. "As you point out, we've known each other since we were children, so let me be frank, Rosalie."

"Of course, Laurent," she said.

"Just as you've improved, so must I improve."

"How admirable," Rosalie said. "By my father's word, you have improved beyond all measure."

He looked at her. There was no shine in his eye, only seriousness, but without the air of confidence and superiority. "Through no fault of yours, Mademoi-

selle Guilbert, we cannot be matched."
He turned away from her and then faced
her again. "Together, we would produce . . . we would produce . . ." He said
nothing, but then added, "Do you understand what I am saying?"

She smiled graciously. It was evident
with his hand near hers. *Color.* "My dear
childhood friend, I do understand. Tonight, my father will cry, but I will rejoice
in your future happiness and that you
should have it."

She took him completely by surprise.
He had strolled with her to the garden to
give the appearance of courtship, but also
to give the child he remembered the
chance to stamp her feet and weep bit-
terly. This was the scene he had anticipated of the Rosalie he had once known.
He hadn't counted on this relief from
her. This gratitude for having been released from this proposed match.

While he was still in shock, she added,
"I ask a favor of you, good Laurent."

"Good Laurent? Oh, Rosalie. You
shame me."

"It's not my intention. Believe me."

He could barely smile but found it

within him to do so. "Then how can I ease your suffering?"

She wanted to say, "Laurent, you clod. You wish I were suffering," and relish it. Instead, she said, "It isn't my suffering, Laurent, but my father's disappointment. Please let me tell him when we are far enough off the grounds of La Fleur Blanche. You understand. He will take it hard."

"Rosalie, I don't know what to say."

She was all smiles, which perplexed Laurent even more. Not a wide jackass smile that would let him dismiss her as uncouth, but a small amused smile that could only bother him at night and cause him to wonder about her thoughts.

"Please say yes, for my father's sake."

He looked at her in astonishment, but she cut his amazement short. She said with a hint of cheer, "Shall we join our fathers? We'll remain pleasant, so they feel pleased with themselves."

When Lucien and Rosalie boarded the carriage, Laurent followed on foot for a while waving to them. Rosalie didn't turn back to wave.

"Rosalie! Rosalie!" Lucien said. "Wave your handkerchief."

"I won't, Mon Pè," she said, even at great risk.

"You will —" He raised his hand and she, in anticipation, raised hers to shield her face.

"Pè. Mon Pè. Laurent declined to court me. This was why he was eager to take me to the garden."

"What did you do?"

Her hands still covered her face.

"It wasn't I, Mon Pè. Laurent will only marry a white woman. Not one with colored blood."

Lucien was apoplectic. It took seconds for his face to achieve full boil. He couldn't speak.

It was safe, Rosalie thought, to lower her hands.

"He will only accept a white woman."

"Bastard!" Lucien cursed and then damned Laurent and his future wife and offspring to all levels of hell, that is, if he weren't first strung from a sturdy live oak for daring to take a white wife, no matter how low-born.

When they returned to Le Petit Cottage, she said, "Laurent took me outside to tell me he wanted a white wife. But, Mon Pè, it was he who followed the carriage and stood and waved until we were gone. I didn't wave, but I could see from the glass."

Lucien was quiet. He asked, "What does this mean?"

"It means, Mon Pè," she said with confidence, "Laurent Tournier and his father will come to call."

VIII

The next day Madame ate with her family and guests, and then returned upstairs to her gallery. She once again suspended Jane's lessons in favor of Jane spending time with Eugénie, whose influence was having an encouraging effect. The two, although oddly matched, were inseparable.

Madame took in the scenery of her garden from the gallery and enjoyed the songs of the happier birds roosting on the live oak instead of the mournful song of the nocturnal zozo monpè. The warm air, refreshed by her servant's constant fan, cooled Madame, as the design of a splendidly woven tapestry of her life's purpose came together in her mind's eye. There was no better match for her grandson than Eugénie Duhon. In her mind, the Guilberts were saved; the legacy and blood of the Bernardin de Maret Daciers were saved.

This was a peace short-lived. Madame's satisfaction and reverie were interrupted by the approach of a carriage nearing the house with urgency. First, she thought, *Could Le Brun be early?* And then, *How dare he catch us off guard!*

"Get Monsieur Lucien and Byron! Go! Go!"

Thisbe dropped the fan and hurried away, first to Lucien's office, and next to the garçonnière. There was no need to alert Byron, however. He and Pearce had obviously heard the carriage from the tower and came down to meet it. Thisbe returned to the house to help Madame, who was already on the main floor.

Eugénie, with Jane, rushed down to Madame Sylvie.

"Oh, Madame Guilbert! Madame!" Eugénie cried tearfully. "They have sent my carriage. Oh! I shudder to face the news!"

"I'll meet it with you," Jane said.

"Now, now," Madame said. "We are

with you should you faint from the news."

This only made Eugénie moan with pain. Jane did her best to console her.

"Don't cry," Madame said. "I'll send for Byron."

Thisbe said, "Yes, Madame," before being told what to do, and went outside to Byron. She excused herself before the four men: Lucien, Byron, Pearce, and the Duhons' coachman.

She spoke in French. "Monsieur Byron, Madame Sylvie asks that you come to give comfort to Mademoiselle Eugénie."

"Ho, ho!" Lucien found that amusing. Pearce went along, giving a chuckle.

"What has happened to Eugénie?" Byron asked.

"The mademoiselle is afraid to receive bad news that comes with the carriage." Each word spoken by Thisbe, a luxury.

Byron smiled. "Tell her to not worry. Go."

"Monsieur Byron," Thisbe said. "Madame Sylvie sent me to get you."

"It seems you are desired by all three women," Pearce said. "The grandmother, the fiancée, and the holy servant."

"Who can deny this summit of the female trinity?" Lucien said.

Thisbe followed Byron back to the house.

When Eugénie saw Byron's face, his gentle smile, she relaxed. Jane still held close to her.

"Well, Byron? What is it?" Madame asked.

"I think Eugénie would prefer to hear this in privacy, but it would kill you, Grandmère, to not know, so I'll tell you the matter." He paused only to annoy his grandmother.

"Speak!" Madame snapped.

"Your father and aunt are at each other's throats with their constant quarrels. I'm afraid the colonel hasn't had a moment's peace since your absence."

First, Eugénie laughed. Jane laughed also, only to mimic her friend's laughter.

"Oh, Madame Guilbert. I've worried you needlessly."

"No, no. I would worry if you didn't worry for your father."

"You are too kind, after this disruption," Eugénie said. "I hoped to stay the night to introduce you to Monsieur Le Brun tomorrow, but I must go to my father and rescue him from my aunt."

"But of course," Madame said. "And you will return for the little party we will have in nine days' time. You, your father, your chaperone. You must come."

"Madame, I am so happy to be here at Le Petit Cottage. I think this name is clever, for this home is grand in its warmth. I will make sure to tell my father and aunt how much I enjoyed my brief visit. And of course, we will all come to the party."

"I'll have Marie and Louise pack your things. The cook will make a lunch for your travels."

"Madame, please. You go to too much trouble."

"My pet, it is not nearly enough," Madame said.

Jane watched as the servants folded Eugénie's things. She stroked the nightgown before Louise pried it away from her.

"Come, Jane," Eugénie said. "Walk with me to the carriage."

The two girls walked arm in arm. Jane, who was reluctant to part with her friend, tamed her usual marching pace to a slower gait.

"Jane, my friend Jane," Eugénie said.

"Yes, my friend Eugénie."

This just made Eugénie weep and throw her arms around Jane. "Oh, Jane, I hate to leave you alone, but my father is calling me home."

"Go to your father," Jane said. "I can't go to mine."

"Yes," Eugénie said, wiping her eyes with her handkerchief. "I didn't mean to remind you of your father."

"It's all right, Eugénie. My father is dead."

That only prompted Eugénie to throw her arms around Jane once more. "But I will be back to help you with your riding outfit. And when I return, I'll bring mine and we can ride together. Will you like that?"

"Yes, Eugénie. I would like that. And

Virginia Wilder too. She would like that."

"Oh! We'll have lovely rides together in our riding outfits."

She kissed Jane on both cheeks, and Jane smiled like a child, and this made Eugénie weep even more.

"Come, Jane," Lucien told the girl, leading her a few steps away. "Let Byron and Eugénie say their farewells."

Byron said, "Your stay with us was too brief. I hoped you'd stay longer."

"My father can't do without me. Of all people, you understand."

"Of course," Byron said. "Perhaps I should ride along. Check on the colonel. I've seen your aunt in action."

"Oh, no. You can't desert Mr. Pearce."

"Charming Pearce can fend for himself."

"Byron," she said, her tone serious. "I'm concerned about Jane. I think you tease her too much. You and your Mr. Pearce. He takes a certain pleasure in it."

Byron chuckled to lift her spirits. "He likes Jane. You can see that."

"He likes to tease her," Eugénie said.

"But Jane, even without knowing, seems to win the matches between them. 'If you please, I don't dance.' She is dear and brave and honest."

"I hope you have kind words for me."

"I have cross words for you."

"Cross? Are you to tell me I've earned marks in your book of delinquencies?"

"Yes, Byron Guilbert. If you were as honest as Jane, you would have written to me about your dances at the Academy. Now I think you to be a dishonest fellow. Secretive, even."

"What can I do to earn your trust, dear Eugénie?"

She smiled. "I like you this way. Contrite. I hope when we are wed, you'll always care what I think of you. I believe your high regard for me will fade when our marriage begins and our courtship is over."

"Eugénie, you must know how highly I regard you."

"Then confess your sins before you take communion. Confess your sins in earnest and fully. Do your penance."

"Is that all you ask?"

"No, Byron. No. I ask that you take care of Jane. I want to think of you as a gentleman."

"Ah!" he said. "When you say think, do you mean dream?"

Eugénie's face reddened. But instead of retreating into the feelings that made her blush, she collected herself and found her strength. "Byron, when my father told me you and your family would come to call frequently, I had to grow used to the idea. The inevitable idea. And then I saw how shy you were that first visit. That you could barely look at me. I began to consider the possibility. I could see how gentle you were and hoped you would grow to be a patient, gentle man."

"I am as you saw me, Eugénie."

"Oh, no, Byron. You left St. James a shy boy and returned —"

"I promise you, Eugénie. With me, you will have the life you seek. One of comfort, gentility. Honor."

Byron kissed Eugénie's gloved hand twice, knowing Pearce watched from the garçonnière.

"Confession, Byron," Eugénie said

before the carriage left. "Go to confession."

IX

Madame made certain both she and the house were ready to receive Claude Le Brun in the morning when he arrived with his supplies. He was most gracious, but also firm about his schedule. A buggy would come to take him to port in eight days. He warned her that the painting would not be dry, but it would be finished. Most important, he impressed upon her that he couldn't be deterred from his schedule.

Madame, in kind, tried to be gracious at the morning meal, to make Le Brun feel welcome, but she couldn't help herself and started on him no sooner than he had sat down to eat.

"I don't understand, Monsieur Le Brun. Why must you rush away? We are not the count and countess, but you'll find our small home pleasant, the views picturesque, and our hospitality, although simple, to your liking."

"I do appreciate your hospitality, Madame Guilbert."

"Sylvie, if you please."

"Well, now!" Lucien was amused.

"Madame Sylvie," Le Brun said, not at all at ease with addressing a woman of her years informally. "It isn't that I wish to leave you, but that I'm anxious to join my retreat in Maine."

Madame looked about. "Maine? Where is this Maine?"

"Grandmère, it's the northernmost of the eastern states," Byron said. "We have a cadet from Maine."

"Retreat?" She pursed her lips.

"It's a group of artists, Madame Sylvie," Le Brun said. "We gather to paint. To try new styles. New ideas."

Madame huffed through her nostrils at the sound of a familiar enemy. *New.*

"Monsieur Le Brun. I don't understand," Madame began.

"Claude, Mademoiselle Sylvie. Claude."

"Claude," she said, "you are related to the finest mistress of portraiture. These friends of yours should sit at your feet to learn the artisan tradition. Why would you cast aside all that you know?"

"Now, Mother," Lucien said. "Monsieur Le Brun cannot be blamed for wanting to further his artistic abilities."

"New ideas!" Pearce said enthusiastically. "I know nothing about art or painting. What sort of ideas?"

"New ideas," Madame said, almost spitting.

"Oh," Le Brun said, in a way of gauging whether Pearce was truly interested. "Simple approaches, Mister Pearce —"

"Pearce," he said. "Just Pearce."

Le Brun nodded and continued. "Different ways of seeing the subject. Perhaps not so exact. Perhaps feeling the brushstroke in a different way."

Pearce kicked Byron under the table upon the pronouncement of "stroke."

"This is not the daguerreotype, Monsieur Le Brun?" Madame asked.

"No, no, Madame Sylvie. In fact, it is

453

the opposite of that final, firm picture. The photograph."

"You see," Madame said to Lucien and Byron. "You see! Le Brun does not approve of the daguerreotype."

"Madame Sylvie," Le Brun said, "at the risk of contradicting you, I don't disapprove of cameras or daguerreotypes — the latter process moving fast out of style. It's just, the photograph is not what I do. It does not interest me."

His statements only bolstered Madame's righteousness. "They are the same: Disapprove. No interest." She turned to Lucien and then to Byron. "You see? I am wise to not listen to either of you. Daguerreotype."

Le Brun's silence was clear. He would say nothing further to contradict his patroness.

"But you paint portraits, no?" Madame asked.

"Yes, Madame Sylvie. I paint portraits, as do a few of us at the retreat, and I assure you, I am here to paint your portrait. But I find my interest in subject matter changing. There is . . . restlessness in the air. I suppose that's why we gather to share what we're learning. Our experiments."

"What sort of new subjects interest you?" Pearce asked.

Byron eyed Pearce.

"Horses interest me," Jane said.

"Very good, Jane," Madame said. "Very good."

Le Brun smiled kindly at Jane, who went back to chewing forkfuls of duck sausage. "Some of us will focus more on the ordinary."

"How awful," Madame said.

"Oh, it isn't so awful, Grandmère," Byron said to cheer his grandmother and bring levity among them.

"Ordinary," Lucien began, obviously amused. "What do we consider ordinary? Like pigs in the pen? Or pigeons roosting? Or perhaps Jane's horse? That sort of ordinary?"

Le Brun wiped his mouth and took a sip from his cup of chichory coffee with bourbon. "For example," he said. "Here, you have the endless cane field. And

Blacks at work in those fields." Thisbe's eyes shot to Le Brun ever so quickly, and in that flicker, she ceased to pull the punkah back. She resumed before it was noticed.

"What about the slaves?" Byron asked.

"The Black man, woman, and child might make an interesting study in the cane. I should like to wander and see these bodies at work."

Lucien laughed aloud. Madame was speechless. She stopped chewing, and possibly breathing, for a moment.

Le Brun sought to explain himself. "You see, the drawings in France of your Blacks and Indians are not as they are. The drawings are ideals of these persons in high dress. The Frenchman or -woman gazing at one such portrait sees a French ideal of a Black man or Indian," he said. "If I find the time I would study expression. Posture. Emotion. Color. Material. The fabric of work and the material of crop. Mood."

Lucien laughed. "Mood of the cane cutter! Do tell, Le Brun! Forgive me, monsieur! I am entertained!"

"Father. So rude to Le Brun, here on

his first day," Byron said. "At least wait until he is unpacked and comfortable."

In spite of Byron's rebuke to his father, it was Le Brun who apologized. "I am sorry if what I said was wrong."

"Not wrong," Madame snapped. "Ridiculous."

"Ridiculous." He seemed to weigh her word. "I'm not certain of that. In fact" — he turned so that he faced Thisbe directly — "this young lady in the corner providing us with the fan."

Thisbe did what she had learned to do. She stood erect in both back and shoulders, and stared into nothingness — a balance of dignity and unawareness — while the white people talked about her. She pulled the punkah, easing it slowly back, then forward, without a change to the motion. In the meanwhile, she had heard him correctly. *Lady.*

"She makes a strong subject," Le Brun said.

At this, the table erupted in laughter. Except for Jane.

"Virginia Wilder would make a strong subject," Jane offered.

"Yes, Jane. I agree," Madame said. "A better subject for art than the Negroes. Monsieur Le Brun, we don't pay for painting the field hands and servants. What would Madame Elisabeth Louise Vigée Le Brun say to this?"

"Should she still live today, you would be surprised," Le Brun said.

"Don't surprise me," Madame scolded. "Don't make me new. Don't try these new ideas on me, Monsieur Le Brun. I don't want to be new. Tradition is why you are here. To uphold traditions of a certain class. That is what a sitting is for."

"Of course, Madame Sylvie," he said.

"Guilbert. I am Madame Bernardin de Maret Dacier Guilbert."

X

Lucien, Byron, and Pearce went their separate ways, and left Madame in the west parlor with the painter. Except for wishing Lucien a good day, Byron and Pearce didn't speak to each other. It was when they took to the stairs of their domicile that Byron said, "Is there no one who doesn't pique your interest?"

Pearce grinned at this sign of Byron's jealousy. He savored it. "I have many interests."

Byron laughed. "And just a day ago you pouted because I was attentive to Eugénie."

"Pout? I, pout? I didn't pout. I was kind and solicitous to your bride-to-be. And by the way, did you give her the ring?"

"You sound like Grandmère."

"Did you?"

"Not yet. I will."

"I see," Pearce said. "And I would like to learn more about Le Brun's brushstrokes."

Marie and Louise were washing the laundry, which left Thisbe to pour claret for Madame and Claude Le Brun in the west parlor. Monsieur Claude Le Brun, Thisbe observed, was a different kind of white man. He was careful with how he spoke to Madame, but he didn't smile and try to charm her. He spoke directly, with only the purpose of making himself clear. Thisbe listened as he said again that he would finish the portrait, but he must leave when his carriage arrived. He wanted to talk about the work and what was needed. Madame Sylvie, on the other hand, wanted social engagement. To talk.

"Madame Guilbert," he said, "I must ask, that the first day of the sitting, you sit. Find the pose most natural to you. And don't move."

Madame was put off by what she read as either an attack on her age, or an accusation of her ignorance of portrait sitting. "Oh, Monsieur Le Brun, I am no stranger to sitting," she said right away. "I've had sittings at my family home and at the queen's hamlet. I was a child at the time, but these things are not foreign to me."

"Perfect, Madame," he said.

"You must know that I had the honor of sitting for Madame Elisabeth Louise Vigée Le Brun herself."

"The countess mentioned this," he said without expression.

"But of course, I am a woman now. And I've learned much from being in the queen's sphere. I feel I carry a piece of her in my marrow."

"What a sentiment," Le Brun said.

Thisbe made a point to recall his expression later, when she had a moment to herself. These moments were few, but she wanted to enjoy what she saw and knew: this French white man, Madame's countryman, had contempt for Madame.

"Like the queen, I have been tested in horrible, unspeakable ways." Yet Madame went on to speak of them at length: Fleeing from one revolution to another. Losing child after child after child. And then learning in the cruelest manner that, in his youth, her husband had sought to marry her own mother, and that she was a mere consolation. "But when I was told, I did not flinch or raise a brow," she said with pride. "Don't you see? It was the lessons I had learned from the Royal Family that saved my dignity."

Le Brun thought perhaps he had missed something in her telling and asked, "Madame Guilbert, pardon me, but what lesson was that?"

Madame made a sound of mock exasperation. "What lesson? What lesson? Monsieur Le Brun! I learned the art of defense, dignity, and how to laugh through it all. I have seen how enemies tried to slander and destroy the queen. Yet she maintained her dignity, stepping over insults that should not dare to touch her feet. Did she weep, kick, faint, or curse at the guillotine? No! The queen bore the suffering, the jeering, the humiliation, with such dignity. Simplicity.

"It is said — and I believe it so — that three weeks after the unspeakable crime, the queen's faithful companion, her dog, returned to the bloodied site and howled and cried for her mistress. Ah! Her comfort. Her beloved Thisbe."

At this moment, as she heard from Madame's mouth that she had been named for a dog, Thisbe felt the painter's eyes on her. She didn't react. She didn't blink. For three, maybe five, seconds, she didn't breathe. But only she knew her breath was trapped within her. The moment that she would steal later, for herself, for her soul, her outrage, would be for her alone.

Madame, unaware of any turn in mood, made her point: "So you see, Monsieur Le Brun, if the queen, Marie Antoinette, could bear so much humiliation without blinking, I can sit without moving for an occasion as happy as enduring this gift of immortality for my future generations."

Against Madame's objections, Le Brun insisted on a small room on the main floor. He explained that he rose before the moon disappeared and didn't want to disturb anyone on the upper floor. And then to Madame's further objections, he helped Thisbe carry his things downstairs to the smaller room.

463

"Marie and Louise will bring you coffee, bread, and ham in the mornings," Thisbe said. "Madame and the family take supper at four."

"Do you take supper with the family?"

Thisbe was surprised by the question. "Monsieur?"

He put his hand up. "Don't answer," he said. "I am only curious to see how the Guilberts live. Who they are — if I am to paint the portrait."

Was he talking to her or to himself, the way Madame did when she needed to hear her thoughts? Thisbe was unsure. She answered him anyway. "Yes, monsieur."

"And what are you called?" he asked.

This man, Le Brun, was older than her oldest sister. Twenty-five? His eyes so directly bore into her eyes. She wasn't used to being regarded like this. To being seen.

"Is this what your parents named you?"

"I am called Thisbe, Monsieur Le Brun." She returned the stare. And then regretted it.

He cocked his head dubiously. "Thisbe?

This is your name?"

"Madame gave me this name, Monsieur Le Brun."

He nodded but kept his thoughts to himself.

It had been Thisbe's training to take her leave when a white person told her to do so. She seemed trapped by Le Brun's silence and stare. She didn't want to just leave but to be invisible.

And then her rescuer came, from the upper floor, shrill and insistent. "THISBEEE! THISBEEE!"

Thisbe bowed quickly. "Pardon, Monsieur Le Brun." She ran to Madame's salon.

Madame sat on her throne, ready to play solitaire. She was able to retrieve the cards from her drawer, but this was Thisbe's job.

"Yes, Madame Sylvie. I am here."

"What were you saying, Thisbe? What were you saying to Le Brun?" She patted the little table, to indicate that she wanted her cards.

Thisbe hurried to the drawer and

brought the cards to Madame.

"He asked my name, Madame Sylvie. I said to him, Thisbe."

"And what else did he say?"

"I ran to you when you called."

Madame steamed for a while. She began to shuffle the cards, and then deal.

"You are not a child, Thisbe. Don't let him flatter you with his talk. You are nothing to study. Should this man touch you, I have no use for you. You are here to serve me."

"Yes, Madame Sylvie."

"You have no idea what I save you from."

"Yes, Madame Sylvie."

XI

Le Brun cornered Lucien in his office at the first opportunity before supper, and away from the others in the household.

"There is another matter to settle before we begin," he said.

"Speak freely, Le Brun."

"I am without my assistant and will need hands to complete this work as quickly as it must be done."

"Hire who you like," Lucien said.

"For eight days' work I need two dollars per day and lodging for an assistant."

"Why did I follow my father into planting? I could have made my fortune assisting portrait painters."

"Monsieur Guilbert, what you pay me is not worth who I am. I paint as a favor to the countess, who dotes on your daughter-in-law."

"See here, Le Brun," Lucien said. "Surely we can come to some arrangement."

Le Brun spoke up, as someone who had already considered the matter. "I can employ someone already in your service. Someone who can follow instructions and who will be attentive to task."

"Have your pick." Lucien was indifferent and on the verge of intolerance.

"I'll take the servant, Thisbe."

In that instant, Lucien's mood reversed. "Thisbe." A happy repetition more than an inquiry.

"Is there an objection?"

Lucien was filled with good humor. "Not from me, my friend. Not at all." He took a savoring moment before he said, "Come. Let us explain the terms to my mother."

Le Brun was not blind to family bickering. The ability to discern motives and emotions within families came with the business between artist and patrons. The tension between Lucien and his mother was obvious. Le Brun didn't need the commission and was prepared to leave the Guilberts without a painting. No work had been done for the family. He'd suffer no loss. But if he was to work at all, it would be on his terms.

In his glee, Lucien sang, "Allow me to tell her," when Madame looked up from her spread of solitaire to see the two men in her salon.

Thisbe didn't mean to lock eyes with Le Brun, but she did, and then quickly looked back down to the kings on the tableau in need of their own space.

"Mother, my dear," Lucien said, a buoyancy in his delivery.

Madame cut a glare at her son, immediately suspicious. "Two gentlemen. To what do I owe this visit?"

"For your sake, my dear mother, this cannot wait. I have been talking to your portrait painter, and he tells me, to better render you, he requires an assistant."

Madame went back to her cards. "What is that to me? See to it."

Lucien smiled, enjoying what was to follow. He couldn't help himself. "These things cost, and I won't discuss the affairs of our household in front of our guest. You've taught me that much."

She breathed hard and then gave him a look. *Go on.*

"I am at my limit for what we can offer, but there is a solution," Lucien said.

Le Brun now grew impatient. He said, "I am willing to take on your servant, Thisbe, as my assistant."

It couldn't be helped. Thisbe gasped. Looked up. Then looked down. Then looked at Le Brun, and then back at the cards.

Madame placed the ace of clubs on its space. "I am sorry, Monsieur Le Brun," she said calmly. Courteously, even. "There is a misunderstanding. My maid is for my use only." Madame's calm deprived her son of the reaction he came for.

"I see," Le Brun said. He then turned to Lucien.

"Consider my daughter, Rosalie," Lucien said happily. "She can read, write, perform arithmetic. I'm sure she can follow the instructions you require far quicker than this one you ask for. Why, I can have her moved into the house to begin right away. But understand, my good friend, she is an engaged woman."

"No! I won't have it!" Madame threw her card down. "No!"

"No, you say?" Lucien was enjoying himself.

Le Brun summed up the family. Their messiness. He said to Lucien, "Guilbert, it is too late for a livery to town, but if I could be brought to the train station in the morning? As you say in America, no harm committed."

"We are not *Amreecains,*" Madame said.

Lucien spoke over her. "The steamer upriver would get you to Ohio with haste, and from there you can travel farther north and east. It's a lovely ride."

"As long as I can leave early," Le Brun said.

"Ah!" Madame snapped. "I see the conspiracy. I see the two of you at work. My son and my countryman."

"Or . . ." Lucien intoned with undeniable relish. "We *could* unearth what is

471

needed to hire the assistant. And that would take what, Le Brun? Two days to summon the assistant? Which would rush the masterpiece, wouldn't it?"

Le Brun made a "more or less" hand gesture. He didn't need coaching in this maneuver. He seemed to know his part.

Madame gave a noise somewhere between a growl and a cry, much to her son's delight.

"Fine."

"Fine, Rosalie?" Lucien asked. "Or fine, Thisbe?"

"Only Thisbe," Madame said, refusing to speak her granddaughter's name.

"Ah!" Lucien said. He tipped his hat to his mother. "Le Brun, here is where we make our exit."

"No, no. *You* are invited to leave," Madame told her son, who took his invitation and left.

Madame picked up her card. "Monsieur Le Brun, I must speak to you."

Claude Le Brun had the look of someone who had been snared. He cleared his throat. "Yes, Madame."

"Well! I expect as much from him, but I expect loyalty from one who understands place. Society. Especially given our connection."

There was no point to rubbing salt in an obvious wound. He said nothing and let the wronged woman continue.

"Thisbe is more than a servant. Thisbe is what I am owed for my suffering. For all that I've sacrificed. In these years, I shouldn't lift a hand, not even in my own cause. She is my hands. My legs. My feet. She is meant to serve me and me alone. But you and my son. You've taken that."

"Madame Sylvie —"

"No, no. It is done," she said, putting up her hand. "When I put Lucien's father in the ground, I thought I would never utter the words of suffering again. But once more, I say with grace, I will draw from my strength and bear the sacrifice. I submit to the pain. I play the hand I am dealt." She inhaled, but was not finished. She said, "And now you must meet my terms."

"If possible, yes, Madame Sylvie."

"I should not feel the difference. I

expect Thisbe at my side when I rise, and at my prie-dieu when I lay down to sleep."

He nodded as respectfully as he could.

"You are to show her what you require. Show her but don't exchange with her or be conversant. Don't impregnate my servant with ideas. She will understand you perfectly, but she has only one role: servant. And she serves you only as an extension of serving me. She is not for you in any other way. Hear me when I say, do not impregnate my servant with ideas. Possibilities. Imaginings. Her response, if there is one, will be, 'Yes, Monsieur Le Brun' — and there should be no occasion when she answers, 'No, Monsieur Le Brun.' "

Le Brun nodded.

"You must return her each day as I loan her. It will be on your hands, Monsieur Le Brun. If you ruin her in any way so that she forgets herself and tries to engage me in conversation while attending to me, then I will have to undo your meddling. It has been a while since I've whipped Thisbe, but I've not had the strength lately." She drifted for a second, then revived. "But to save her, I will whip her vigorously."

Throughout these instructions, these declarations, Thisbe made no expression. No movement. No tremor. She simply stood.

"I accept your terms," Le Brun said. "There is much to be done, Madame, in a short time. I will need Thisbe at five o'clock every morning in the studio."

"Good day, Monsieur Le Brun. You keep me from my game too long."

XII

Madame remained sullen for the day. She kept Jane barely an hour to practice appropriate responses when engaged in conversation and then dismissed the girl to ride her horse, reminding Jane to wash herself well after riding. "And don't eat more than the men." Those were Madame's last words for their lesson.

Those last words had no effect on Jane later at the dining room table. Marie and Louise already knew to put extra meat on her plate. Even so, Jane turned to seek out the two servants after she devoured those extra pieces. Marie took the dish of potatoes and placed a large potato on her plate and said to the girl in Creole, her voice low, "I give you more meat when everyone is full."

Ordinarily, the servants wouldn't speak

to, let alone issue a directive at, a dinner guest, but with more people in the house, Marie had been keeping watch over the table to be certain everyone was fed. Madame nodded her approval.

"If it is hunting you like," Lucien said to Le Brun, "I'm afraid we'll disappoint you in these parts. The last chance for such sport was a sighting of a rare baboon from the wilds of Kentucky."

Byron's chuckle, and Lucien's delivery, signaled Pearce that amusement was in the air.

Le Brun, a quick study of facial expression, played along. "I see . . ."

"I saw him with my own eyes." By now, Lucien stood to better physically reenact all that he described. "Grunting and gesticulating. Nostrils flared. Stovepipe hat askew! What a sight, making its way on a barge down the wide Mississippi! The creature came to these parts but narrowly escaped, never to travel these southernmost banks again!"

The three men laughed with gusto, Byron and Pearce catching on to the joke. Le Brun gave an obligatory chuckle.

Jane didn't care. Madame was humiliated.

"Please," Madame said. It was too raucous for her and thwarted whatever good impression she could make on the guest. While she didn't appreciate Le Brun's demands, she worried about what he would relay to his patroness, the countess. "Please, gentlemen."

"You're right, Momanm," Lucien conceded. "I'm just saying, in my way, the planter must vote his interest."

"Is it so clear a choice, Father?" Byron asked. "The government understands the plight of the farmer. Don't you agree?"

"I have no quarrel with the federal government," Lucien said. "They laid handsome tariffs on our Cuban competitors. Gave aid for the levees. But that is the federal government. This baboon flinging his pucky, however . . ."

Le Brun caught on. "Ah! Your Abraham Lincoln."

"Monsieur! Take that back. He isn't my anything. Perhaps my eternal shame and thorn."

"I must admit," Pearce said, "the debates are thrilling. I've stood in the gallery while Lincoln and Douglas went at it. I'm not yet one and twenty, but if I could cast a vote this year, it would be . . ."

Pearce stopped cold. Byron kicked him hard under the table. There could be no good answer. And he was right.

"Bowel gas expelling into the air," Lucien said. "Forgive me, Momanm."

"Decency!" Madame cried. "Decency, please."

"We know where Lincoln stands on our livelihood. And this Douglas. A Northern Democrat? A farce," Lucien said. "Only a planter knows the life of a planter. The hardship. The sacrifice."

"If I may, sir," Pearce said, "Lincoln doesn't want to end slavery. He only seeks to contain it."

Lucien gave Pearce a wry smile. "Naive boy. Get back to West Point and let them finish making a man of you. Only a boy would listen to politicians and believe them. 'Contain it,' " he mocked.

Byron tapped Pearce's shoe, a consoling gesture.

"Why not end it?" Le Brun asked.

The quiet was a riot of noise unto itself. Even Madame put her hand to her mouth.

Lucien set down his glass of brandy. "You go too far, Le Brun!"

Byron stepped in. "Père, he doesn't understand." To Le Brun, Byron said, "This is the best life for the Negroes. Surely, you see that."

"In France we have done away with the trade. Liberty for one is liberty for all."

Only Thisbe seem to notice Madame's swoon.

Lucien felt he had been tolerant and civil. It was time to pin the young man in a corner. "And has France liberated its colonies?" Lucien began. "French Afrique? French Martinique? Have you given up your taste for sugar? Need for cotton? Love of tobacco? Long-grain rice?"

Madame had enough and tapped her water glass until all looked her way. "We spent the enjoyable hour of the afternoon talking about Negroes and baboons."

"I won't be judged in my home," Lucien said, indignant.

Byron sought to change the tension in the room. "Le Brun, if only you were here for Christmas."

"Yes!" Madame exclaimed, encouraging Byron's attempt at generating a lighter conversation. "Christmastime!"

"I can't describe a happier time," Byron said. "The bonfires along the river. Negroes in the boiling house making molasses — some that will make pies, cookies, puddings for the holidays."

"Tell him, son," Lucien said. "Negroes in the boiling house."

"The cane has been cut and loaded and brought to the sugarhouse. On our small plantation there is a parade of gaiety. The négrillon squeal in delight, for they know they'll have candy. The work gang throws their might into pressing and grinding. It's true that the heat in the sugarhouse is without mercy, but how the Negroes take to it with a frenzy is not to be believed! The boiling and stirring the kettles without a second's rest to scratch their noses. You've not seen a marvel like the concert of limbs and sinew stirring and grinding."

"Indecent!" Madame said of the mention of moving body parts at the table. "Jane, cover your ears."

"But I can't cover my ears and eat," Jane said.

"The boy speaks well," Lucien said with predrunken pride. His eyes teared. "The Negroes take to it, as the Father ordains it. We all have our purpose. Don't you see how we provide for them?"

Le Brun was speechless as he took in his hosts' righteous passion.

"You misjudge us," Lucien said, "because you come at the wrong time. If this were boiling time! If this were boiling time, you would see how the Negroes dance. They toil to a frenzy and then they dance. And, Le Brun, they dance harder than they work! Why, we stock red fabric for the wenches, who buy the scraps to wave while they dance in the sugarhouse. And the men dance around them. Why, by next harvest, the same dancing wenches, with a hoe or cane knife in one hand, will drop brown bundles in the cane field to keep it all going."

Madame set down her fork. "Monsieur Le Brun, don't hear this indecency." To

Lucien she said, "You paint the picture of demons cavorting in hell, and we, full of sin and depravity. Le Brun, it is not so. It is not so."

Le Brun didn't seem to know what to do. He said, "Of course, Madame."

"This season, Mother is correct," Lucien said. "For we have plans to bring innovation to the sugarhouse, so all of that stirring and sweating, and bodies writhing in the boiling hot —"

Madame screamed.

"— will go by way of the dinosaur. Is that right, Mother?"

Thisbe secured the punkah and came to Madame's aid. She helped Madame up.

"Mark my words," Madame said. "You laugh, but less work and the niggers will have no purpose. They will demand freedom and plot to kill us. Go ahead. Laugh. Smirk. Your father made the same mistake in Saint-Domingue and woke up with the niggers screaming for our blood."

The men stood up.

"Don't bother," Madame said.

Thisbe helped her away.

XIII

Thisbe woke in the dark without disturbing Madame. She washed herself, got into her dress, breathed in deeply, pushed her feet inside the black shoes, and then crept down the stairs and stood in the doorway of the west parlor, the space set aside for Monsieur Le Brun's studio. She didn't expect him to be there before five a.m., but he knelt on the floor, on a paint-splattered cloth the size of a bedsheet, and hovered over the large, flat white surface she imagined would eventually become Madame's portrait. He wore a loose-fitting shirt speckled in the same paints as the drop cloth. His movement looked like scrubbing to Thisbe, but she thought his hands worked too gently to scrub the way Marie and Louise scrubbed pots and floors.

He looked up at her. "Bonjour. Come." He motioned.

"Bonjour, Monsieur Le Brun." She entered, her steps timid.

"Come," he repeated firmly. He gave her a pointed, direct look, one that made her uneasy. While that was obvious, he didn't seem to care. "What does your mother call you?"

"Pardon, Monsieur Le Brun?"

He stopped scrubbing and was annoyed. "I am here but a short time. I expect my questions answered. What does your mother call you?"

Her voice cracked. Still, what came out was above a whisper. "Gal."

"Gal? Is that your name?"

She looked to the open doorway she had entered through.

"Don't be afraid," he said. "I asked your name."

"Thisbe, Monsieur Le Brun."

He grunted. "Thisbe. Do you want me to call you this? Thisbe? A dog's name?"

"Thisbe, Monsieur Le Brun."

He made a motion for her to squat.

"You can't do this from there, standing."

She was too slow to move.

"You stand all day. I would think you would like to work sitting. Or am I wrong?"

She moved beside him and dropped to her knees.

"We are doing the invisible part," he said. "The part unseen. That is not entirely true; the eye *does* see this part. It isn't aware it sees. Still, the eye sees."

"Yes, Monsieur Le Brun."

He continued. "We see the picture. We're able to see the picture because the preliminary work has been done. If it's not done to prepare the canvas, the eye sees something else."

His words rushed at her, as did his nearness. It was clear she was as uneasy in proximity to this man, this white man, this French white man, speaking directly to her, not ordering her, but telling her things that she must know, and she was overwhelmed by it all. It was clear she grasped little, but listened. It was clear to him, the teacher, and to her, the learner, that he was doing the thing Madame had told him to not do. Le Brun was filling her with ideas.

"The canvas must be treated, so we start with the primer. Yes. This mix," he said, pointing to a bowl of thick white roux, but smoother, like a cream. He pointed to each item he named. Canvas. The thick white substance — the primer. The broad brush. The sandpaper. "When that is dry, we sand the surface. This is what I'm doing now. What you'll do. And then we repeat, until the canvas is ready to receive the next layer. And with this sanded and dry, *you* will apply the last coat of the primer. The gesso. Say it."

"Gesso." She hesitated. "I will do this?"

"Why else are you here?" he asked flatly. "Now, touch the surface," he said in the voice that was more suitable for teaching. "Run your fingers gently from end to end. This is the texture. The smooth feel. Perfect. That is what you'll work for. Smooth, perfect canvas. Since I must rush the work, I must spend more time with the canvas before we actually paint."

"We?" she asked.

Le Brun didn't clarify. He gave her a

sweeping glance and shook his head disapprovingly. "You cannot wear your dress to mix the primer. Those clothes are not right for this work," he said. "Wear something plain."

Thisbe looked down at her clothing. "This is my dress, Monsieur Le Brun. I have one other to wear when I go with Madame to church." She spoke Madame's French and not the Creole spoken by Marie and Louise and, at times, Master Lucien. She looked to the door again, afraid to be overheard speaking proper French.

He unbuttoned his overshirt, what he called a smock, and removed it. "In the meantime," he said, "put this on." He handed her the large cotton shirt.

She took it and rubbed paint that had been dried on the shirt.

"We have work to do. Put it on."

"Yes, Monsieur Le Brun." When he saw her steady herself on her hands to rise, he gathered, to change into the shirt, he said, "Over your clothes."

She smiled a small, embarrassed smile, and then put her hands and arms through the sleeves of the paint-speckled garment. The smock seemed to swallow her up.

"There is much to learn . . . ," he said. She uttered "learn," but he didn't hear her. ". . . Much to do in too little time. But if you can do these rudimentary steps, then I can focus on the greater task before me."

"Yes, Monsieur Le Brun."

"We are almost finished building up the canvas," he said. "But now I will show you how to apply the last coat. How to apply the stroke. Up and across. And here, up and across. At angles. When it dries, you will learn the proper way to sand the canvas."

His words gave her too much to consider, and he spoke fast. She watched him with the hope that the words would match the actions.

"There are so many opportunities to ruin the canvas before a drop of color touches the surface of the portrait. You must be steady. Mindful. We want no globs here. Everything even. Even strokes. See?"

"Yes, Monsieur Le Brun."

He paused for a moment. "Do you understand, or do you just say, *Yes, Monsieur Le Brun?*"

She looked to the open doorway, for assurance that they were alone.

"I understand, mostly, Monsieur Le Brun."

He gave a dubious grin. "Oh?"

"Yes, Monsieur Le Brun."

To her shock, he handed her the brush. She held it for the longest time. Before he spoke, and she was certain he would, she dipped the tip of the brush into the thick white solution and made the smallest effort onto the canvas. He gripped the hand that held the brush, pushing it down into the bin of white glue, then stroked the brush decisively against the canvas. "North, south," he said. "East, west." And then he let go of her hand.

"Dis Be. Fry you some eggs if you go'n get them."

Lily didn't have to repeat herself. Thisbe preferred the smaller pigeon eggs to those found in the henhouse. She took the straw basket and climbed the ladder inside the wooden silo. She was grateful the pigeonnier was out of sight from the river-facing view of the gallery. She would pay with a beating by brush or fan if Madame should see her entering the pigeonnier to get eggs for Lily. She quickly filled the basket with the small pigeon eggs, climbed down the ladder, and ran to the cookhouse with her breakfast. She had minutes to eat and to then be at Madame's bedside.

The skillet was already hot and greased with lard. Thisbe's eggs had been scooped up onto her plate almost as fast as Lily cracked them into the hot pan and gave them a quick stir.

"You fittin' to burn your tongue."

"Gotta eat fast, Miss Lily." Thisbe blew on the eggs, chewed, and talked. "Ma'am's picture painter here. I help him mix his paint and such."

"Hmph. What you know about paint?"

Thisbe shrugged. "I do what he tells me."

"Be careful doing what he tells you. You no little girl, Dis Be."

"Just hungry," Thisbe said, lapping up

492

the last bit of egg before running out of the cookhouse to the main house. She didn't have to be told she wasn't a little girl. It wasn't lost on her, however, that two women had pointed that fact out, both for her benefit. One told her last night. The other just after daybreak.

XIV

Thisbe hurried with much dread and entered the salon prepared to face an ill-tempered mistress now that Madame was forced to share her. To her relief, she found the room quiet.

Madame hadn't yet awakened, but when she did, she rose happily, stretching her back, arms, and legs like a marmalade cat. She had Thisbe pull out everything she asked for, from brooch and earrings to undergarments, dress, and gloves. Madame didn't want to eat too much and took lemon mint tea and ate half of a light doughy roll in her salon instead of joining her family and guests for breakfast in the dining room. When she was ready to do her toilette and then dress, she sent Thisbe to call Jane in for her lesson.

Jane, puzzled by Madame's appearance, stood in the doorway, but didn't enter the salon. Madame was always dressed when she received people in her salon. She never received Jane in her silk robe.

"Come. Come, Jane," Madame said upon seeing her. "Do come."

"Bonjour, Madame Guilbert." Jane gave a small nod instead of a curtsey. She refused to curtsey, preferring to nod or bow. Madame accepted the nod and discouraged the bowing.

"Bonjour, Jane," she said. "Today, you will watch how a lady prepares for a sitting."

"You are already sitting," Jane said.

"That is correct, Jane. I am sitting," Madame said tightly, but with patience. "But I am preparing to sit for my portrait. You see the difference? It's good that you watch me, because we do the same things to prepare for an important event or a party."

Jane didn't speak. This told Madame she must clear up a confusion in Jane's thinking.

"What don't you understand?" she asked.

"Is a party important?" Jane's sincerity was matched by the bewilderment on her face.

Madame threw her head back, her hands up, bringing them down to both cheeks, and back to her lap. "Is a party important? Is a party important? Everything happens at a party. It's the most important gathering, besides a wedding, which takes place because of the party that took place the year before! Come, sit," she said, and then told Thisbe, "Put a chair here."

Thisbe picked up a chair and brought it to the vanity. Jane sat next to Madame.

"Good. Good," Madame said. "Now, I will explain everything. How to present yourself. Dressing the face with makeup. Jeweled pieces. Your hair. You see, a portrait is for eternity." Madame preened before the mirror, pointing to the features she spoke of.

Jane furrowed her thick brows.

This didn't escape Madame's notice. She frowned at those brows. The brows of the Englishman. "What is it, Jane?" Madame asked.

"To prepare for a portrait sitting is the same as to prepare for a party," she stated with a question or follow-up implied.

"Yes! Yes! You do listen," Madame said.

"A portrait is for eternity."

"Yes."

"So, a party is for eternity?"

Madame gasped, which startled Jane. "A party is not for eternity, but what happens at the party can last a lifetime, for the lifetime of the children and grandchildren to come."

Jane relaxed. She would have no children or grandchildren. She asked no more questions, but listened, said, "Yes, Madame Guilbert," and looked forward to riding Virginia Wilder.

Thisbe carried the rose-colored chair down the stairs and brought it to the west parlor where Madame would have her sitting. She moved the chair several times for Le Brun and then moved the curtains each time she moved the chair. He made a face and said, "We'll see," before he sent her upstairs to escort Madame for her sitting.

"I don't see why I can't have my sitting in my salon," Madame complained to Le Brun.

"I work on the portrait even when you are not sitting, Madame Guilbert. You would have no peace. And the oil paints. You don't wish to smell them when you sleep."

"I am still put out," Madame said.

"Please, Madame, don't pout. I might find that face interesting, and then you won't be pleased with what I do with it," Le Brun said. He turned to Thisbe.

"I need graphite. A pencil. Where can I get this?" He asked Thisbe, but Madame spoke.

"My grandson will give you some. He is in the garçonnière. Or about the grounds with his friend, Pearce."

"I need two, three pieces. I use them quickly," Le Brun said. "Do you sell it in the little store I saw?"

Madame didn't answer right away.

"I cannot take your grandson's last

pencil. I need several. I need these now."

Madame exhaled. "Thisbe. Go to the commissary. Get these pencils. Say they're for me. Get them."

Thisbe made the mistake of turning to Le Brun. Madame screamed, "Now, you see? Confusion! You have already ruined her, and we have not begun."

Le Brun said to Thisbe. "Go."

Thisbe hurried to the commissary. If she got the graphite and returned quickly, Madame might forget about the punishment she was sure to give her for hesitating to obey her. As it was, she expected to hold out her hand to be struck with the hairbrush that night.

She had neither coins nor a written note to pay for the graphite. But she greeted Rosalie and then asked for the graphite.

"Madame sent me."

To her surprise, Rosalie asked nothing further. She opened a drawer and placed two wood-cased graphite sticks, or pencils, on the counter.

"Merci, mademoiselle," Thisbe said and

turned to leave.

"Wait," Rosalie said, "I need a message sent to Madame Guilbert."

"Yes?" Thisbe had no time to stand around listening.

"The girl, Jane. Her riding suit is ready for a fitting. Ask her when I can come with the outfit."

"I'll tell Miss Jane to come," Thisbe said.

"No," Rosalie said. "I must come to her room to try it on her."

Thisbe's eyes widened. She shook her head no. "Write it and tell Madame," she said.

"You can tell her. You see her every day."

Thisbe was still shaking her head no. She said, "I'll carry the hornet's nest, but I am not the hornet. Please. Write it."

They stood eye to eye, Thisbe impatient, Rosalie resentful. The staring lasted six seconds, a long time to not speak. It was the things between them that spoke loudest. They were both listed in the ledger as Guilbert property. Thisbe was in the constant company of Madame, and Rosalie had yet to look into the eyes of her grandmother.

"I'll tell her myself," Rosalie snapped. "You have your pencils. Go."

Thisbe was already out the door, rushing to the parlor.

XV

Le Brun paced from one side of the west parlor to the other, studying Madame. It wasn't a sunny day. But the overcast sky suited Madame. Too sunny, too bright, and the contrast with Madame's complexion would be too striking. The viewer would dwell on her age and not much else, although Madame kept herself well.

"Thisbe," Le Brun said. "Stand here."

He anticipated that she would look to Madame for permission or to apologize. Madame, annoyed, said, "Go."

Thisbe crossed quickly to his side of the parlor. "Yes, Monsieur Le Brun."

"Look." He pushed his chin toward Madame.

Thisbe trembled. "Monsieur?"

"Take note of everything. How she is

seated. Lift of the head. Direction of the eyes. The cameo. Crucifix. Earrings. Hair. The lace. Position of the hands. Do you see everything?"

Thisbe could barely lift her eyes to look at Madame, for Madame looked back. Still, she said, "Yes, monsieur."

"Stand here. Look until you have her perfect. When Madame sits, she is to look like this. Everything perfect."

"Of course, perfect," Madame said.

"Yes, Madame. Yes, Monsieur Le Brun."

Thisbe looked again to Madame. But not in her face. She tried to look but couldn't. She washed Madame's face. Combed her hair. Wiped and washed her ass. Dressed her. Put food in her mouth. Washed her hands. Threaded the earrings' gold wire through her ears. Fastened her jewelry. But this thing Le Brun asked of her: to look openly at Madame as though Madame were a teapot on a tray. She couldn't do it.

Madame was not pleased with Thisbe, her servant, staring so directly at her. The tension was clear to Le Brun.

"Madame Guilbert, have you returned to France?"

Instantly, she was diverted and flushed with color.

"I can't return to France. I cannot."

"But you must," he said.

"No, no. Too unstable. And I have ties with the Family."

Le Brun said with great care, when he could have laughed, "As you must know, my kinswoman took her daughter and fled the guillotine, but she returned to Paris. Like you, she was connected to the Family."

"It was a bloody time," Madame said.

"But it has changed. You must see France as a woman to appreciate the changes."

"Never! I sent my son to Paris. Through him, I saw enough. The Bonapartes and the peasants trample on everything."

"A matter of opinion," Le Brun said. "But how would you know? You left France so very young."

"I didn't just leave. I was kidnapped," she snapped. "I had no choices. I had to marry Bayard Guilbert or face the mobs. Your own kinswoman saved her neck."

"Yes. She fled with her daughter, but she returned. And flourished."

"She had a network of friends. I was left at the convent. I waited for the Family to come back for me, but the only one who came for me was Guilbert. I was alone. Orphaned by my family. Orphaned by the Royal Family. I did the best I could to stay alive. To keep my family vineyard alive for my children. Not that my own son appreciates the sacrifice.

"From one ordeal to the next, I endured the voyage to the island hell. A place so hot I couldn't keep a child inside my body. My husband made me wear a pauper's dress. When they first saw me, the Black wenches of Saint-Domingue, the ones he used, they laughed at me and played with my hair. For ten years I endured what I won't describe. Brutality. Tragedy. An infant son I still remember who lived no longer than I could hold him. Each night I prayed to the Holy Mother for rescue or death. Either one I would take to escape that hell. Saint-Domingue. There is no saint."

"They say *Ayiti*," Le Brun told her.

"Ayiti," she repeated. More or less spat.

Le Brun studied her while she talked as if to take some detail of her to later render it on the canvas.

Thisbe saw no person on the canvas. No face. No body. No Madame. No start of a person. Only bursts and patches of dirty green, gray-blue, and some yellow underneath.

"What have I done? What hell have I entered? His brown children run through the house while my children die year after year.

"One night, we have not long buried another son, named Bayard. We are asleep. But my eyes open." Madame seemed to leave Le Brun and Thisbe as she spoke. Her eyes drifted and glazed, as though she could not only see what she described but could also touch and smell her recollections. "I think I am being visited by ghosts. It's dark, but I feel their eyes before I see them. We are surrounded by his brown sons. Their eyes afire, noses big like his. Faces long like his. Their mother holds a candle in one hand. The flame is bright and calm. I am

506

sure they are there to murder us.

"When Bayard opens his eyes, she laughs. This Black one. Then she looks to the window and says, her eyes sparked by the candlelight, 'Run!'

"I am screaming. Her sons bleat like goats, 'Papa, Papa.' The Black wench is shrieking. I see the blur of Bayard spring from bed. Gathering things. Yelling at me to come. Come! I reach for the pauper's dress. My mother's picture and my grandfather's ring sewn in the hem. There is no time to put it on. I grab it. I can barely move, but I run.

"When I look out of the shutters, in the distance, in the hills, there are lights. More than a hundred balls of light. Torches. They are coming. Bayard grabs his satchel. A goat hide full of gold pieces. 'Come!' he shouts. I scream, but he slaps me. I am sore from birthing. He puts me on a horse with the satchel. In the night. He ran on foot. For miles. To the shore. We are not alone. Many planters fled that night, carrying their lives. For one moment I am glad my child was taken from me. That he was buried with his brothers. I am grateful Bayard took the dead boy from my arms after one day and had him buried with the others.

"Napoleon's brother-in-law sent troops, but what troop can defeat these devils? The English gave them guns. God does not mean for white men to be among the devils."

"What an ordeal," Le Brun said.

"No, no, Le Brun," Madame said. "My ordeal is only begun. We reach the port, where the soldiers are. We, like the other planters, give what we can to get a place on the boats leaving the island for this Louisiana."

"The journey was rough, Madame Guilbert?"

She laughed. "The journey was calm. The ocean was calm. That should have warned me. Better a storm than to sail calmly into a place of horror.

"We reached the gulf, then the port, and changed to another ferry. A long, flat boat. We floated before the sunrise. How I wished we ferried through the night. Better to not see."

"Madame?"

"The water covered with green marsh.

508

The gray trees, trunks and limbs twisted in unnatural shapes, reaching out of the murk like dead things not told they are dead. Everywhere, moss hanging, alligators, and long-legged birds — neither graceful nor beautiful, but shrieking and screaming. When at last we saw humans, hope was again taken from me. Brown people. White people made brown by the murk and sun. Women and children barely clad. Shanties that seemed to float on the edges of the marsh. How it stunk worse than the sewers of France. The people, hiding, but you could catch a glimpse. And the Natives. Natives everywhere. The different people all seemed to live among one another. At last, we saw Germans and other people. My husband called out to them, and they waved and called out in a French . . . Northern, with some corruption. I tried to speak to one of the women, but I couldn't take the stench of her. We had no choice but to smile and eat what they offered. "Acadians," my husband said. "Trappers." He was able to understand them, and they, him. My husband couldn't read, but he could make his way around most people.

"We found some civilization. He knew people from having done business. And he left me with the Rochets, wealthy people involved with the French government. He promised to come back for me when our house was complete. But if he returned and found me gone, he wouldn't look for me."

"So you had opportunity to escape your ordeal," Le Brun said.

"Yes," she said, weary from her own story. "Madame Rochet, I believe, would have brought me into her circles. She would have enjoyed dressing and presenting me — even after she had revealed to me the reason my husband sought me out to be his wife. But what was I to do? After ten years, I was the wife of Bayard Guilbert. Mother to his dead children. When Bayard returned, I left Madame Rochet's hospitality and went with my husband to our home. Le Petit Cottage."

▪ ▪▪▪

BOOK IV

▪ ▪▪▪

Book IV

I

Rosalie stamped her feet on the cedar-plank floor. She stamped, then kicked the wall too hard. She refused to cry out or curse at her self-inflicted hurt. It was one small hurt heaped atop bigger wounds. That her grandmother's servant delivered the wound gave the small hurt the power of a vicious slap. One day, Rosalie thought, the Black girl who had taken her place would pour her a cup of tea in her grandmother's salon.

Lucien would come soon to inspect the cashbook and to count the money. Whatever slight and indignation she felt at the hands of Thisbe and her grandmother had to be set aside. She couldn't make the mistake of expending any of that on her father. Though she thought herself better than her grandmother's servant, she would not forget herself around her father. She had only a few coins in the way of sales to show him, and on top of that, she had used six dollars in silk thread and four yards of bombazine fabric to sew Jane's outfit.

Rosalie set the few coins on the counter.

After they greeted each other, Rosalie said, "The riding suit is ready for Mademoiselle Jane to try on before I make it final."

"What is that to me?" Lucien asked.

"I have no place to fit her," Rosalie said while he flipped through the cashbook. "Negroes and others come in and out of the commissary . . ."

"And don't buy."

"I would fit the riding suit on her in my cottage, if she would consent. But for her privacy, she might prefer to be fitted in her room."

"When things change, you will have a room in my house. A room that has been closed thirty, forty years. A ghost can't use a room," Lucien said. "Don't worry about this fitting business. Leave that to me." The coins scraped against the counter when he swept them up and dropped them in his pocket.

Madame happily and busily dipped her pen in ink and wrote her invitations at her desk. She worded the invitations succinctly and, in her mind, with gaiety to bring young people to Le Petit Cottage to bid bon voyage to Byron and his handsome friend, to make known the implied engagement between Byron and Eugénie, and to view her portrait, painted by an artist of one of the oldest artisan clans in France. Madame didn't have a sweet voice for singing, but that didn't deter her from humming and singing as she wrote. Occasionally, there was a lull from moments of reflection. How she missed having a daughter to plan affairs with. To fuss over the refreshments to be served. To choose the floral arrangements. She had been cheated out of her own chance to show off her daughter at palatial ballrooms where debutantes assembled like white bouquets on parade while their parents sat above in box seats watching the progress of their daughters as the eligible young men circulated. Sadly, she wasn't to know that joy. But this little party would have to do, and it would be good for the house to be filled with young people. She thought of how the party would give Jane practice for behaving in public, and the letter of progress and triumph she would write to her dearest friend, Juliette Chatham. Those thoughts made Madame once again giddy. She sang and wrote.

Thisbe said nothing as Madame sang, wrote, set her pen down, rubbed her fingers, and wrote. Her eyes followed Madame's penmanship. She wondered what it was to hold a pen or graphite, to scratch out words on linen paper. She didn't have a minute to scratch in the earth with a sweet gum twig, but she occupied herself imagining what might come of it if she did. Madame's penmanship was tiny and made it difficult to discern one letter from another. But a few words were clear to her: "Invite," "Mademoiselle," "Monsieur," "Soiree," "Danse," "Bon Voyage."

Thisbe heard his boots. She deadened her eyes and became invisible.

Madame stopped singing and writing.

Lucien dispensed with pleasantries and got straight to the point. "Momanm, Rosalie must see the girl in her room to fit her for the dress."

"This is your doing. You plan to kill me before my grandson is married."

"Momanm, you try my soul. My essence of being. I won't deny it! But kill you? What, then, would I live for in your absence?"

"I tell you what you live for. To turn this house into your father's house, with brown faces in every corner. You don't know our lives before, in the little hell. That Saint-Domingue."

Brown faces. In that instance, Lucien saw his own half brother's sun-bronzed face. *Henri.* He hadn't forgiven Henri for leaving him. For running away.

"You don't know," Madame went on, "what I've lost . . ."

"Nor do you know what I've lost . . . ," Lucien began.

Thisbe listened to them argue, glad she hadn't brought Rosalie's hornets' nest to Madame. She stood at Madame's side, unmoved, eyes downcast while they continued.

"I know your wicked plotting," Madame said.

"Momanm, I don't plot to fill the house with niggers. I only ask to bring my daughter here to do one fitting."

"You ask to kill me." She collected herself. "And should she work on this outfit on a holy day, I don't want that on my soul."

Lucien sighed heavily. "Rosalie will come to Jane. Jane will try on the dress. Rosalie will then make the notations. Take the dress and leave. On those insults to hard labor, I absolve your soul."

Lucien's attention fell upon the envelopes and letters. He picked one up, swiping it with flair in his movement, before Madame could protest. "What have we?"

"Invitations to the soiree."

"Ah! A soiree! Of course. Why not have a dinner dance?"

Madame ignored his sarcasm. "This is not news. I said we would have a party when Byron announced his friend would come. It's time for the boys to return to school and time for Byron to dance with Eugénie before he hops with all the instructors' daughters."

"I agree," Lucien said too easily.

Madame eyed Lucien suspiciously, but continued. "And, it will be a perfect time to show the portrait. The painting will be wet, yes," she said, "but I'm thinking of you, son. We will kill two birds at once."

"Yes, Momanm. We will kill more than birds, I'm sure," he said. "Since you are determined to have your party, I'll do everything to make it a success."

"You?" Madame's expression was no longer joyful, but amused, her suspicions confirmed.

"Of course, Momanm. It will be all that the young people will talk about, from the west bank to the east," he said. "Only" — and Madame nodded, waiting for the other shoe to drop — "I would like to invite my guests. If you would be kind enough to write one more invitation, I'll deliver it myself."

Madame's amused smirk flattened. "Who do you invite? It is for the young people only."

"I assure you. I am inviting young people."

Madame put her pen down. "Who are these young people you know?"

"Don't you worry, my mother, my life. Don't you worry."

"Now, I worry."

"This is the problem. You say I hasten you to the grave, but it's you, Momanm. It is your constant worry. You make too much of everything."

"I worry for what you put me through."

"Worry does not care," Lucien said. "I care. I provide the seamstress for Jane, but you don't care the girl must be fitted in public. Or in the quarter among the Negroes. You should write to Juliette Chatham about that."

Madame was silent. He seized upon the moment.

"Mother, you exaggerate," he said, clearly enjoying himself. "We will fit her on Sunday. Go to church, then. Worship your patroness. Rosalie will fit her early. It will be done. She will be gone."

Madame was cornered. "You should

have let Eugénie take Jane to New Orleans for a real fitting and outfit."

"If Jane ate more like Eugénie, then we would have money enough to buy her riding outfits to tear on her horse and money enough for ballroom gowns she'll never wear. As it is, we're close to serving potatoes and roux."

Rosalie didn't expect to see her father a second time that day, so when she saw him approach, she put the cashbook on the counter for his review. Nothing had changed, but it was generally what he wanted to see. Even if there was only one paying customer for the day.

"Yes, Mon Pè?"

Lucien pushed the cashbook aside. He then took a square of linen paper from his breast pocket and placed it with some care on the counter along with a bottle of ink and a fountain pen.

"Leave this," he said of the book of accounts. "I'm sure there's nothing there."

"I'm afraid you're right, sir," she said.

"You've written me many letters from school," he began.

521

"Yes, Mon Pè." Her face now brightened with curiosity. She couldn't imagine the direction of his inquiry.

"I didn't read all, but I took note of the penmanship. The sisters did teach you something."

"Yes, Mon Pè."

"This is what I want you to do," he said, pushing the ink, plume, and paper toward her. "Write . . ." He scurried inward for recollection. "How did she word it? You are invited to a dance at Le Petit Cottage, St. James Parish, to bid Byron Guilbert farewell and bon voyage." He rattled the date. "Write as if the nuns stood over you with rulers to smack your hand. But with flourish. Style. Proper spellings. We don't want to be laughed at."

She felt him breathing as she wrote. He stood close.

Rosalie's mind raced with questions, but she held on to them for now. It was enough that he counted on her to write the invitation.

"Good girl! Good girl! Not a blob of ink! Not a misspelling!"

Now that she had pleased him, she felt her opportunity.

"The fitting?" she asked.

"It is arranged. In the meanwhile, ready your own gown."

"My gown?"

"The one I bought for you. My dear, there is much to do to prepare for Byron's farewell dance. I'm sure young Laurent dances the quadrille and the cotillon. I'll send your brother and his friend to teach you the dances."

Rosalie surprised herself and squealed with joy. She tried to contain herself but couldn't. "My grandmother? I am invited? Inside the house? As a guest?" She hadn't meant to question him, but each inquiry spilled out.

"So many questions," Lucien said. "So many. Worry about your gown. And your waltz."

II

Rosalie carried the garment, pins, and a pair of scissors, along with a hope to see her grandmother and to have her grandmother see her. The last time she was close to the house the woman had screamed at her, "Go away, nigger!" Her grandmother's words were hurtful and expected, but she still wanted her place in the house, and now there was this hope. She would enter the house as a dressmaker, but there was also an invitation to the house as a guest. And how else could they introduce her, but as the daughter of Lucien Guilbert? Wouldn't it follow that she would be publicly known as the granddaughter of Madame Sylvie Guilbert? Wouldn't the guests assume the Guilbert name was hers as well? Wouldn't her father have to draw up freedom papers for her if she was to be the wife of the accomplished, proud Laurent Tournier?

She did as she was instructed by her father and came to the back entrance. Marie and Louise greeted her.

"Bon matin, bon matin," the two said.

"Bon matin, mesdames," she answered their Creole.

The three exchanged more pleasantries, having remembered one another from childhood, although the twin sisters were eighteen, a year older than Rosalie. Marie and Louise complimented her hair, how long and straight, but scolded Rosalie that she was too skinny to get a husband. At this, they all laughed.

"I am to see Mademoiselle Jane to fit her." Rosalie gestured to the outfit.

"We show you to her room," Marie said. But first they had to pet the fabric and embroidery.

"Is Madame there?"

The two looked at each other before answering. They'd heard Madame's rantings when the quadroon was mentioned by name. They'd heard Madame Sylvie's arguments with Lucien.

Marie spoke first. "The maîtresse is at Mass." She and Louise crossed themselves.

"Of course," Rosalie said. Mass. She wished to do nothing but forget her time with the nuns. The holy days and feast days, where there was no feasting.

"The maîtresse will return at two. You are done by then, please."

Marie and Louise saw the disappointment in the girl and thought, *Pitié fille.* They sought to cheer her. "This dress will be marvelous, no?" Louise said.

"No doubt. The fabric, so rich," Marie said.

While the sisters admired the indigo-colored fabric, Rosalie took in as much of the house as she could and found it ironic that she had been in the Tournier home before having been inside her father's home. Compared to the Tournier home, the Guilbert home was humble. There were good pieces of furniture placed in the salons. Good, but not grand. A small gasolier hung in the dining room. Fading wallpaper and Persian rugs. Moldings decorated with fleur-de-lis patterns. Still, the home was quaint. Well kept. In a word, comfortable.

Rosalie loved her father more now that she understood his intention to install her in a setting of luxury in the Tournier home, to live better than he lived. She took this to heart. This pride in having a value.

She sniffed and turned to the west parlor.

"No, no. The painter is there," Marie said.

"We don't disturb his work, please," Louise said.

Unbeknownst to Marie, Louise, and Rosalie, they had already disturbed the painter's work. Through an angle of the doorless parlor room, he saw the slight figure of the young lady holding the dark cloth. After having studied his current subject for hours, he knew in a glance, and after a quick study of build and manner, who this young lady was. The likeness was undeniable.

Meanwhile, the two sisters tried to hurry Rosalie along, but her eyes lingered

on every corner, every piece of furnish-
ing — staying clear of the noxious odor
— until finally, the three climbed the
stairs.

Once upstairs, Rosalie stood before the
first room, large and open, colored in
mostly pink, gold, and white. At the
center, the rose-colored Queen Anne
chair. The room divider that separated
the bed from the public space. The vanity and mirror. Her grandmother's salon.
"Come," Marie said to move her along.
"Come, come."

Rosalie followed. But the next room
stopped her. Unlike the other rooms,
with opened doors and shutters, this
room was closed. A white rosette and ribbon hung from the doorknob.

"Come," Louise said to Rosalie. "Please
come."

She wouldn't move. "Whose room is
this?" Rosalie asked.

"We don't go in this room," Marie said.
"Not even to clean."

Rosalie nodded. "I see." But instead of
following Marie, she put her hand on the
doorknob, turned it, and entered the

room of her dead aunt. The aunt whose doll she possessed but wasn't allowed to hold during the time she had it.

"No, no, Mademoiselle Rosalie!" Marie said. "Mademoiselle Jane is this way." It didn't matter. Rosalie walked inside with all the swagger of an overseer inspecting field hands down a row of cane. Marie and Louise stayed on the other side of the now open door and pleaded with her. "Come back! Come back!" As though she were in the ocean and they on shore. "Come back! Come back!"

Rosalie continued to walk about the room, inspecting the bed, with its white and pink roses embroidered on the duvet, a doll resting on the pillow, shielded by mosquito netting. Rosalie promenaded about the room, taking in the vanity, the books, the child's Bible, and then back to the bed and the doll, identical to the one her father had given her for Christmas.

"Please! Please!" the two begged in concert. "Please, mademoiselle. Please!"

Finally, Rosalie turned and exited the room.

"Please," Marie said. "Please close it

for us, please."

A strange request, Rosalie thought. The two feared the doorknob as if it were a serpent.

Rosalie knew this fear. She had this fear where her father was concerned. She forgot herself momentarily, and then found her sense: The two were not to touch the knob or the ribbon, or enter the room. If they were asked about touching or entering, they could maintain their innocence. *No, Madame Sylvie, we didn't enter the room of the sainted one.* And then they could cross themselves on the Virgin upon mentioning the dead girl's name.

"Please, Mademoiselle Rosalie," Louise said. "Don't make trouble for us."

Rosalie took instant pity on the two. Her anger was at her grandmother. And the room. The room that should have been hers. A life that should have been hers.

The sisters ushered her to Jane's room and stood outside the open door. Any other person inside the room would have noticed the presence of the three and given a greeting or a command to enter.

Jane sat on her bed, still, engaged in nothing.

"Mademoiselle Jane," Marie said to the girl. "Rosalie is here to fit you."

"Bonjour, Mademoiselle Jane," Rosalie said as she entered the room.

"Jane," the girl said. "And English. Speak English."

"Of course, Miss Jane," Rosalie said.

"We go now," Marie said, although Louise had to be tugged by the apron. "The maîtresse, she comes at two."

"Please be gone before dat," Louise added, if her sister wasn't clear. They left. And talked fast between them. "White, colored, white," one said. The other disagreed. "Colored, white, colored." This meant the Master's daughter entered the house colored, became white-acting, and then reverted to being colored before the white girl.

"Miss Jane," Rosalie said. "This is your jacket. I will put the buttons on after I see how it fits you. Please stand."

Jane stood while Rosalie carefully slipped Jane's arms through one sleeve and then the other. Jane stood soldier straight, chin up, chest out, while Rosalie brought the two front flaps of the jacket together over Jane's chest. She placed pins along the left edge for the buttons, stood back and looked at the jacket, and then carefully removed it.

Of the bottom half of the outfit, she said, "I sewed the riding suit in big stitches first. In case I must make changes. Let me help you take off your skirt."

Jane stood still while Rosalie unhooked her skirt. She was surprised to find Jane nude and unaware.

"You wear no crinoline? No pantaloons, Miss Jane?"

"No," Jane said. "I don't wear them. My mother didn't say I had to wear them."

Rosalie didn't know what to make of her reply. "I could make pantaloons for this outfit."

"I won't wear them," she said. "Only the riding suit."

Rosalie hid her shock. She thought, this was the girl who emerged out of the pond naked, carrying Madame's servant. She seemed to need Byron's fiancée to speak for her. Rosalie decided it did no good to stand about showing her shock at the girl's behavior. After all, it was because of this unabashed girl that she was allowed in the house. It was easier to take the girl as she was.

"Step in here and here," Rosalie said, holding open the wide, skirtlike legs of the garment. "I will pull it up."

Jane did as she was told.

Rosalie pulled at the garment to make it fit properly on Jane. She studied the outfit on the girl, and then circled Jane instead of having the girl turn. She added more pins to reflect changes to the sizing.

"How do they feel, Miss Jane?"

"They don't feel like my father's pants," Jane said. "But I'll wear them."

"Very good, Miss Jane," Rosalie said. "Very good. Let me help you out of them." Rosalie was careful with the outfit to avoid sticking Jane with the pins. "I'll sew them in small stitches, so you can wear them riding."

"I'm riding my Virginia Wilder at two o'clock, when Madame returns from Mass."

"Oh! Miss Jane, the outfit won't be ready for three days at the least. Four days."

"I'm riding my Virginia Wilder at two o'clock, when Madame returns from Mass."

Rosalie was struck by how exactly she repeated herself.

"Yes, Miss Jane. Yes." Now there was a hint of apprehension in her voice and eyes. She had boldly walked though Madame's house. Entered the forbidden room. Allowed the feelings of hurt and entitlement to embolden her. Forgotten the reality of things. But now, her inability to make the girl understand brought her back to her true circumstances. Jane, no matter how unusual, was a white planter's daughter, and she herself was an enslaved woman without a proper last name. She had to be careful with this girl. How she wished her brother's snooty fiancée was there to intercede. Or even the Creole housemaids. Rosalie gathered that Marie and Louise had made themselves scarce and were probably laughing at her predicament.

Finally, she said, "I'll bring the outfit to you as soon as it's ready. I'm afraid the suit must be sturdy for riding, and I don't have a Singer machine."

"My father said I was sturdy."

Rosalie breathed. The predicament turned out to be nothing, or perhaps her mother whispering in her ear from afar, to not get ahead of herself.

She smiled and said, "Yes, Miss Jane."

"Go, then," Jane said. "Make the outfit sturdy for riding."

"Yes, Miss Jane."

III

That morning, the saints were with Byron and Pearce, who had fallen asleep in no suggestive arrangement, Byron using a textbook for a pillow.

When Lucien marched up the stairway of the garçonnière, loud as a newly shod horse, yet with gait dragging, not fully aware of his reason for hesitation, it all came down upon him in unbounding relief when he reached the bed chamber and found both boys asleep, one at the head, the other at the foot, cramped, but each one oblivious to the other body. He stood witnessing, and thought, *Yes. West Point has done for the boy what prostitutes couldn't. The discipline and close camaraderie among men has set him right.* What little cause for worry Lucien harbored over the years, he would push farther and farther away.

Now, Lucien could react appropriately to the sight of two young men asleep on a farm at half past six, an hour that found house servants and field hands undertaking their daily toil.

"Byron!"

Byron rolled over, saw his father, and stretched before he sat up. Pearce slept in spite of Byron stretching and kicking him.

"Up! Up! There's no time for sleep. Go to the commissary and make yourself useful."

"Sir?" he managed, although he wasn't awake.

"Your sister must learn the dances for the waltz. You and your Pearce fellow should pay her a visit. Show her your military dancing skill."

Lucien then left, his steps light and jaunty down the cedar-plank steps.

Byron returned to his sleeping position, except now with his arms wrapped around Pearce's leg, his head nuzzled against Pearce's warm calf.

■ ■ ■ ■

Rosalie didn't know which she enjoyed more. Whirling around with her brother in the commissary, as small a space as it was, or Pearce clapping and singing West Point drinking songs that served as their music. There was no space to cross and turn, but they managed. The singing, just passable. But this amiable time with her brother! She didn't want it to end but couldn't keep up with Byron's tireless drilling or Pearce's enthusiasm for merrymaking. Rosalie curtseyed and waved "no more" to Byron, to catch her breath.

"How will I repay you?" she said, still breathless from the turns. "We don't have the other couples to make this dance complete, but I'm sure I have the timing for the handoffs."

"I'll miss you, Rosalie," Byron said, also catching his breath.

"How can you miss me so, Byron?" she said, feeling it safe to remove the formality of title with her brother. "You've been so busy with Mr. Pearce here, I doubt you notice me."

"Impossible," Pearce said. "How can anyone not notice you?"

"Don't listen to him," Byron objected. "He's full of molasses for all the ladies."

"And full of serenades for them too, I'm sure," Rosalie said.

"What chance have I against both brother and sister? I thought you Southern born are known for your warm Southern hearts. Your hospitality."

"Please don't change your opinion of us, Mr. Pearce," Rosalie said.

"Pearce. Just Pearce."

"Don't change your opinion of us, sir," Rosalie said, refusing the informality that he offered. "We are truly warm and hospitable."

"But Southerners will close ranks and fight with all that we have," Byron said.

"I've been forewarned," Pearce said. "I prefer to dance than fight. Miss Rosalie, may I have a turn?"

"Once I start to breathe again," she said. "My absolute pleasure."

"You have no need to worry about the dancing," Byron told Rosalie. "You dance like a lady."

"As opposed to a bullfrog," Pearce said. "Of course she dances like a lady!"

"Thank you. Thank you both!" Rosalie said. "It's been years. The nuns didn't allow dancing, let alone the tunes for dancing."

"A crime to the Southern soul," Byron said.

"We Northerners are handy in the ballroom. Rhythm isn't confined to the lower states," Pearce said.

"Sister, we've ruffled Yankee feathers," Byron teased.

"I am outnumbered but never ruffled."

Rosalie clasped her hands together. "You are truly the best of friends to be able to tease each other. How wonderful that must be."

"Why, sister. You make me sad. Not by what you say, but by what you don't say."

"Oh! No! Don't let me dampen our spirits!" Rosalie said, now embarrassed.

"It would be your brother to dampen the mood. He sees dark clouds where there are blue skies. How sad to be this way."

"I like my brother, just as he is."

"As do I," Pearce said. "This way, he can be the dark fellow and I can be the fun one."

They all laughed.

After the laughter subsided, Byron said thoughtfully, "Rosalie —"

"I feel the darkness!" Pearce interjected.

"Do you not have a friend of your own?"

"Besides us?" Pearce added.

"Mr. Pearce, I would never intrude on something meant for you two alone. I have been away, but I know the meaning of 'three is a crowd.' "

"Three, a crowd?" Byron said. "We get on, we three."

"Agreed," Pearce said. "Three is a merry party."

"I couldn't be happier than this day," she told them. "I only hope I don't ruin the rhythm with the handoffs at the dance."

"I would have never believed in Grandmère's lifetime you'd enter the

541

house as a guest."

"I can barely believe it, myself," she said cautiously.

"I, for one, am glad," Pearce said. "All of this poking and hushing and saying 'Don't speak Rosalie's name in Grandmère's presence.' It's exhausting to keep this up."

"Indeed," Byron said. "I'm astonished but glad to see Grandmère has had a change of heart."

"No one is more astonished than I," Rosalie said. "I'm only pleased to be invited."

"I don't understand you Southerners," Pearce said.

"And I don't understand what's happening," Byron said. "But I feel a shift in the wind. My sister, at last, a guest in my grandmother's house." Then he said to Pearce, "This isn't an issue in most planters' homes. The Southern life is the Southern life and my grandmother is . . . well . . . my grandmother. It's only, poor Rosalie —"

"Don't be sad for me," Rosalie said. "Our father has thought of my future."

"What?" Byron was genuinely surprised. "Is there more to this than welcoming my sister into Le Petit Cottage?"

Her face darkened a bit. "Will you forgive me if I leave it at that? I don't mean to tease, but I won't count my chicks."

"Whatever your future, Miss Rosalie, we will drink to you tonight," Pearce said. "Three cheers before tattoo!"

Before she could ask, Byron anticipated the need for translation. "West Point slang to stop carousing and prepare for bed and battle."

IV

In the meantime, Lucien had his own interests to secure. With an invitation penned in Rosalie's hand, he took the smaller single-horse buggy to the church frequented by the gens de couleur libres, the church where Rosalie received the rites of baptism, reconciliation, and communion. There was a time when those sacraments alone were enough to guarantee a free Black person some protections under the law, but that was when the Louisiana Territory was young, and diverse people commingled freely. While it was within Lucien's power to free his daughter from bondage and give her the right to the Guilbert name, it was his duty first to look out for the Guilbert family.

■ ■ ■ ■

Lucien spotted Alphonse Tournier right away. He tipped his hat and made small talk among parishioners who welcomed him back, as Lucien had been a favorite in this parish. He happily reunited with most, and ducked others who knew his business status.

Lucien engineered his movements toward Alphonse and Laurent. He put some effort into not appearing too anxious, so as not to cause them to flee from the pushy father of an unmarried daughter. As he made his way across the church, he couldn't help but notice the Black, mulatto, quadroon, and octoroon eligible young ladies in abundance, accompanied by their white and colored fathers.

Laurent rocked on his heels, trying to disguise that he was searching for someone else, upon spotting Lucien Guilbert. Once the greetings were exchanged, he took it upon himself to ask, "Is Rosalie not well, Monsieur Guilbert?" Rosalie had always accompanied her father to Mass when they were children. Now that she was home from boarding school, Laurent couldn't imagine a reason, short of illness, for her absence.

"I'm afraid she has another engagement. Thank you for asking, young man." *Engagement.* This was said purposely.

"Please send my wishes," Laurent said.

"Which are?" Lucien replied right away. Although Lucien was in no position to play with Laurent, he couldn't resist putting the young man on the spot as he had done to his daughter but one week ago. Now, with the shoe on the other foot, the young man stammered before finding the words, "That I wish her a . . . pleasant day."

The older Tournier, not blind to the fun being had at his son's expense, slapped Guilbert's jacket shoulder playfully with his gloves.

"Show a little mercy," the older Tournier said. "You see the boy turning his head in search of the young lady."

Laurent respectfully objected to his father's remark, but neither Tournier nor Lucien took his protest seriously.

"I can do better than mercy," Lucien

said. How he relished being on the verge of making a grand gesture. If he could only hold on to the moment longer!

"We are hosting a small dance this Saturday for Byron, who's soon to return to West Point. Accept this invitation and convey your wishes in person."

He held out the envelope to Laurent, who took it and couldn't contain his gladness.

Alphonse Tournier wagged his finger at Lucien. "Nothing is settled, Guilbert," he said to Lucien. But Laurent's elation gave Lucien much confidence.

"I beg to differ, Tournier."

The thickness in the air was broken by a sudden storm. The dirt road was muddied, but the fresh air sweetened by fragrances released from the storm made Madame feel hopeful. She enjoyed being out and about less and less. Attending Mass weekly and on feast days was now her only social outing. She had been looking forward to doling out her handwritten invitations since the ink had dried on the linen parchment.

■ ■ ■ ■

"I was beginning to think I had dreamed of this dance," Madame Pierpont said at Mass that Sunday, six days before the dance. "I made no more of it. The girls get so little social exercise. Why dwell on these forgotten things?"

"Oh, Lucille! So comical!" Madame managed to be upbeat, laughing, even. "Nothing and no one was forgotten! Of course there will be a ball, with men enough for quadrilles to fill the salon. Your daughters must come! I will think your daughters poorly educated if they don't come. Why, they'll disappoint Byron's many male companions. And you, Lucille. I will blame you."

Lucille Pierpont laughed at Madame Sylvie's jokes. "We hope to be available Saturday. Such short notice," the woman added as a dig at Madame's planning. "And if we are free, we would love to make your party."

"Nothing formal," Madame said. "A farewell for Byron and his friend — I did tell you that young man manages all his family's properties? They are well known in Yorktown Heights, I believe Byron said. Did I mention this? And we will also have the unveiling."

"Unveiling?"

"Did I not mention this too? My portrait. Yes. The painter is from France."

"The portrait painter came from France to paint your portrait?"

Madame found Lucille Pierpont's surprise delicious. She was tempted to lie, but wouldn't do so on a Sunday.

"He is on loan to me from the countess. I myself don't claim to know the countess personally. But she is connected to my soon daughter-in-law. Family, so important! It's good to have these connections."

Lucille Pierpont's face made various pulls of incredulity and Madame enjoyed it so. She thought, that would teach Lucille Pierpont to cast aspersions on her grandson's ability to marry.

"Do come. Do come. We live simply, but we hope to give the young people a good time." Yes, Madame thought. Better to underplay than to inflate the affair beyond expectations.

"We won't miss it," Lucille Pierpont promised.

The two women kissed and parted, and Sylvie Guilbert fluttered to the next person and then the next, hoping to attract planters' sons and daughters while boasting of Byron's friends, when in reality, Robinson Pearce seemed to be his only friend. She announced the unveiling of her portrait by the artist who was of the Le Brun family line. *Yes, you know Elisabeth Louise Vigée Le Brun. Portrait painter to Marie Antoinette, the queen.*

Of course they would be there to dance and drink and gobble up the refreshments, as humble as the spread might be. Young people cared to dance and drink punch. It was their parents who noted what was missing from the menu and the decor. What did Madame care? Her portrait was to be unveiled.

One boy of about seventeen approached Madame and Thisbe. "Will you be there to take a turn?" His intensity was aimed at Thisbe, who looked to Madame. Sylvie promptly said, "She will be at my side, in service."

The boy, broodish, tall, easy to speak

his mind without consideration for the aged, said, "If 'n I caint dance with this here gal, I'll stay at home. Good day, Madame. Mad'mazelle."

Thisbe couldn't help herself. She laughed. Madame rolled her eyes rather than chastise her.

"I save you from these men. Be grateful."

"Yes, Madame Sylvie." Thisbe's cheeks were still high and rounded from laughter. Madame attributed this to her exposure to the painter.

Except for this rude and unsolicited interjection of the common boy, Madame was quite pleased with her accomplishments for the day. She gave thanks to the Holy Mother, took communion, and bestowed her good charity on her neighbors. With the portrait as a constant reminder, she would be remembered among her neighbors as a good-hearted, well-thought-of pillar of motherhood.

V

Thisbe was the first to feel this odd thing. The thing out of place. Both Madame and Master Guilbert had left the house separately, arrived at different destinations, but both returned to Le Petit Cottage in the highest spirits. Lucien hummed without drink — as far as Thisbe had observed — and twirled on his heel, for no one in particular. Madame Guilbert sang a nursery rhyme and trimmed the floral arrangements, a task she had left for Marie and Louise. She often scolded them if their floral sprays were too ornate or too plain.

Mother and son. Both pleasant. Both happy.

Thisbe worried. What could it mean?

She kept her eyes open and her breath shallow.

"Join me in a glass of claret, Mother?"

"Of course, my son."

Lucien didn't order Thisbe. That was his mother's pleasure. She had only to nod and Thisbe went to the sideboard to bring to them the decanter of claret on a tray with two glasses. She poured, set the decanter down, and found her standing place, her eyes lowered, her ears open.

"How was your day, my dear?"

"My day, son? What could I hope for on this holy day, but to give honor and praise to the mother of our Lord?"

Lucien found that amusing. "My mother giving praise to the mother of our Lord." He chuckled. "I hope it pleases you to know, I did the same."

"Impossible! I would have seen you."

"That is because you don't attend the Church of the Holy Child."

Upon hearing the name of the church attended by mainly free people of color and mixed-race families, Madame pursed her lips and rolled her eyes.

"I take it you didn't attend alone."

"My mother. One false leap so quickly follows the other!" He raised his glass and drank. "Devout son that I am —"

To this Madame scoffed.

"I went to give honor and glory to the Holy Mother on my own."

"Even worse," Madame said. "The attachment of your daughter would explain your attendance. Attend this church alone, and our neighbors will think you've lost yourself." Then she stopped. "Or are you picking through the mulattoes for a new interest?"

Lucien expected her barbs and enjoyed them. "You redeem yourself! I was there for my interests, Mother. But not as you think."

Madame waited for Lucien to continue.

"You see, *mô shè* Momanm," he said, purposely using Creole terms.

Thisbe flashed her eyes at Lucien and was almost brought to a snicker. She had already laughed once in Madame's presence. She wouldn't risk it again.

554

"See what?" Madame snapped.

"I have extended an invitation to Alphonse Tournier and his son, Laurent, to our dance this Saturday."

Madame was shaking her head long before he finished his announcement.

"No," she said flatly. "It can't be."

"It is."

"I tell you, Lucien, it can't be." She spoke clearly and plainly, as if this would make certain he heard her and that hearing her was all that was needed.

"And I tell you, Momanm," he said equally clearly, "the Tourniers will be here as guests, so the son can properly and publicly court my daughter. Now what have you to say to that?"

"Get in your carriage, ride to the Tourniers, and make your apologies in person. That is the gentlemanly way to handle it. They will understand. The colored son cannot be a guest in our home and eat with our forks and dance with the guests. Tournier respects the law. He will accept your apology and wonder what had gotten into you in the first place."

Madame was calm. So calm.

Lucien was also calm. "The only way I will refuse Tournier and his son is if I have the means to refuse them. Do you think I do this for my daughter alone? Do you think I do this to humiliate us? To cast us out of society — what small place we hold?"

"I think all of those reasons possible."

"We are in peril, Mother. Peril beyond your imagining. Why? Because I do what I can so you and the boy don't feel the true state of things. But as it is, we are overextended with the bank. I don't mean overextended like every other planter down the river road dodging the banker's sickle and scythe. I mean, the vultures fly overhead. I've done what I could with the money from Juliette, but we have no means to fully repay. All I have is the harvest to look forward to. And the girl. My daughter."

"My son. Even you are not that good an actor," she said, unmoved.

"I promise you, Mother. I don't exaggerate."

This time, Thisbe heard Mère, the

556

proper French, and not the Creole. Madame must have heard it as well. She took a drink and a moment to respond.

"And if you had the gold, your father's money, you could save our lives? And you would not need Tournier or his colored son?"

Lucien put his glass down and spoke in earnest. "With the gold in hand to save us, I'll ride to La Fleur Blanche on Zuk in the storm and dismiss the Tourniers, father and son."

Madame took another drink and looked into Lucien's eyes. "Then it's done, my son. When night falls, I will take you to the place. We will dig."

VI

Thisbe's form didn't make a shadow when she entered the west parlor carrying the bucket of water from the cistern. She found Le Brun at work, painting Madame's hair, his palette blotted with light brown, gray, and white. Thisbe watched as he glanced at a sketch of Madame, a sketch so detailed, it occurred to her that Le Brun had what he needed in the drawing. She wondered if Madame needed to sit for him to complete the portrait. Then, for herself, she wondered if she had to bring Madame's chair down the stairs and to the studio.

Le Brun didn't look up or turn to acknowledge her presence. He worked with the thickest of the smaller brushes, on the light-brown streaks of Madame's hair. Without stopping, he said, "Wash for me these brushes." He pointed his chin at the brushes on the table. "We won't need these big brushes. Only this big one for the final varnish and those smaller brushes for the face and the white and gray in the hair. And for the eyes, I have something special!"

She heard the change, something mischievous in those last words, but delivered her droll "Yes, Monsieur Le Brun." From his tone, she gathered that the less she knew about "something special," the better, for her sake.

She set the bucket down on the drop cloth, filled the smaller bowls with water, and then took the brushes, one by one, and waited for Le Brun to correct her if necessary. He continued with the work on the hair.

She scooped a cup of water, where she placed each brush, working and wringing the bristles to remove the paint. She didn't like the paints mixing with her skin or the linseed oil and turpentine, or their smells. She laid the brushes to dry after steeping them and went to empty the cup of water.

"Leave that for now," Le Brun said.

"Come. You must see this to do what I need."

When she was close enough to him, he said, "You will finish the hair, the crucifix, and the hands."

"No, Monsieur Le Brun," she said, stepping away. "No, monsieur!"

He looked at her pointedly. "Tell me your name."

"Thisbe, monsieur."

"This is not your name."

"Thisbe, monsieur," she said. "Please, monsieur. You're making trouble for me. They will make me pay for it."

He didn't give her sympathy, and instead looked at her in a way no one had looked at her. It was personal. For Thisbe, too personal. She looked away.

She said, "Why do you want to see me injured so? Why, if I might ask? I cannot stop you, monsieur. I cannot disobey you. But please, tell me why you do the things that will bring trouble on me. You will leave, monsieur, when the painting is finished. And I will be here."

"At last!" he said. "At last I hear your

voice and what you think."

Thisbe said nothing at first. Perhaps because she was angry. While she might have a right to her anger, she didn't have the right to express it. "If I might speak . . ." She lowered her voice, afraid to be overheard. "As it is, I cannot stop my own laughter when I try. It is you, Monsieur Le Brun. The time I spend with you. Madame said to not engage me with ideas, and yet you do it every day."

"Didn't you have ideas before I hired you? I saw it in your eyes." He shrugged. "This is what an artist, a painter of portraits, knows. Not the color of the eyes. How beautiful or dull. But what lies behind them."

Again, Thisbe struggled with how to answer. She had given away too much to the Frenchman for his amusement. Madame was right. Monsieur Le Brun meddled with her and now she would have to work hard to remain Madame's servant. To be as Madame had trained her.

Then he laughed as if he was reading her.

"Why do you laugh, Monsieur Le Brun?"

561

"Claude."

She shook her head no. She would not call him Claude. And yet, she was looking at him in the way she dared not look at any white person. Eye to eye.

He might have felt badly for carrying this as far as he did, but his eyes smiled when he looked at her.

And then it occurred to her. The flash in his eyes. Maybe he was joking with her. He seemed to wait for something. Perhaps for her to catch on. She asked, "I don't have to finish the painting, monsieur? This was your way to open my mouth?"

"Well said." He couldn't help himself and laughed softly. "No. You will have to finish painting Madame Sylvie's portrait. Not in the way you thought I meant. But I will need you to do the final part."

"It can't be, Monsieur Le Brun."

He put his hand up to stop her from speaking. She covered her face instinctively. Even in this quiet moment, her reflexes wouldn't let her forget his right to chastise her for her refusal.

"Mademoiselle," he said tenderly. "My

assistant. I will need you to apply the varnish to seal the painting. Had you let me finish, you could have held on to your silence and then said simply, *Yes, Monsieur Le Brun,* like always."

She said nothing. There it was. The impulse to laugh. Her face broke a little, but she didn't allow the laughter to follow through.

"Madame's portrait will never be as good as it can be," he said. "It is too hastily done. But I will leave soon, before the final layers of varnish are applied. You'll see the portrait and make sure it is dry. Then apply the varnish once, and let it dry. Then once more. If you apply the brushstrokes as I show you, you cannot ruin the portrait. Even if you apply too thick, too thin, I doubt your Madame or her son will know the difference."

"Yes, Monsieur Le Brun."

He smiled a little. "I will leave you with varnish and a brush to apply the varnish over the face. I cannot wait for Madame's face to dry."

"Yes, Monsieur Le Brun."

"Don't you think we are beyond 'Yes,

Monsieur Le Brun'?"

"No, Monsieur Le Brun."

He looked directly at her. She, for the first time, didn't demur, but looked back. If he slapped her, she would better understand her place with him.

He only returned her gaze.

"Well, my assistant. Take this brush. Look at the grain. If you turn your head so, you'll see it better, now that the sun is rising. Let me show you on this dry part. Dip the brush so. Yes. Here. Not so much. Now, turn your head slightly. See the pattern?"

She nodded.

"Good," he said. "Then follow."

Lily had enough to do to occupy her that morning. And yet she stopped her motion of busy arms and hands to draw out the quiet girl, seated before a full plate of biscuits and gravy.

"What that painter man put on you?"

"Miss Lily?"

"That's some good gravy gone to harden like my heart."

"Said what, Miss Lily?"

Lily did something in the cookhouse she had no time for. She pulled a stool from under the table and sat down beside Thisbe. "Yo' mistress be turning any minute. Y'aint got time for staring at the moon."

There was something sobering about taking Madame Sylvie into account that got Thisbe to sopping her biscuit in the gravy and chewing.

Lily said in the same way she said everything, "If a child's coming, let him come."

Thisbe's mouth was full, but she dropped her biscuit, chewed fast, and raised and waved her hands to protest.

Lily wouldn't hear it and talked over Thisbe's gestures and feeble squawking. "I had a child. He dead now. Ten years gone."

Lily never spoke about her dead child. She chopped hard. Yanked husks unmercifully. Cracked bones with bare hands. Pounded knuckles into tough meat. But she never spoke about her child.

Thisbe had pity and answered her. "I'm

not big, Miss Lily. That ain't my trouble."

Lily said, "Best eat, Dis Be. You don't need to know trouble, but I 'speck you know trouble. I 'speck you do."

VII

Madame looked up from her solitaire to find Marie and Louise standing before her. There was no need for their presence. She hadn't called for them. "Well?" she asked.

"Please, Madanm Sylvie," Marie said. "We need more hands to manage the party."

"Please, Madanm Sylvie," Louise said. "Let Cook help us serve."

Madame's face tensed. "Certainly not! Cook stays in the cookhouse." The request seemed too much for Madame, and Thisbe waved the fan over her until Madame fussed at her to stop. "No. No. Certainly not. Cook has no proper serving dress. No! She will ruin my party."

This meant defeat to Marie and Louise. They knew Cook had the stamina to

butcher, chop, fry, and bake in the cookhouse. She could stand on her feet and
sweat and had never been sick a day and
had no children and no man to care for.
(She had once been given a helper, who
fainted several times from being enclosed
in the hot brick room. The helper was
sent back to the cane field.)

Cook didn't have what Marie or Louise had. Or Thisbe, for that matter. She
didn't have the proper respect for class.
Gentility. She couldn't be made to serve
quietly, pleasantly, and most important,
invisibly. The thought of the large woman
serving the matrons of Madame's society,
and saying, "Heah, mah damn," made
Madame shudder. No amount of beating
or coaching could change Cook's demeanor. Better to keep Cook in the
cookhouse where she sweat over the food.

"Certainly not."

"Please, Madanm Sylvie. Let Thisbe
help," Marie said. "She does nothing all
day."

Thisbe made no expression. For this,
among other things, Marie and Louise
despised Thisbe. The sisters passed eyes
to Thisbe. *At least swat when the horsefly*

buzzes your ear.

Thisbe read them well and answered silently, with the slightest spread of her lips: *Better the horsefly than a hornet.*

"Certainly not!" Madame said, oblivious to their silent exchange. "You waste my time and yours. Think of all you could have done in the time you spent complaining."

"Yes, Madanm Sylvie," they both said. Marie turned to go, but Louise eyed Thisbe with her utmost scorn. Thisbe smiled.

When they left, Madame scolded. "You see what happens because of the painter? They see you cleaning his things, carrying his water, and they forget you are my servant."

"Please pardon, Madame Sylvie," Thisbe said.

"I told Le Brun to use your hands and legs to assist him in the work for my portrait. I told Le Brun to not put ideas in your mind, and he has you looking at me. Then looking at my portrait. *You see this, my assistant? You see that?*" she said, mimicking him. "And you! You dare to show your teeth and laugh in public. No, Thisbe. This is not good. Even my house servants forget themselves to tell me what I should do, because they see you."

"Pardon, Madame. Have pity."

Madame's face was stone. "Fetch me the brush."

"Yes, Madame Sylvie." Thisbe hurried to the vanity and retrieved the sterling silver brush, knowing its intended use.

"The brush, Madame Sylvie."

Madame took the brush. "You are a body," Madame said. "Not a whole person, so I must punish your body with what strength I have. Now, hold out your hand. Not the palm. Turn it over. The black side."

(Dear reader, if you must know, but cannot imagine, the answer is rage. The girl called "Thisbe" felt silent, jailed-up rage behind her mask as she did as her mistress commanded.)

VIII

Patience. Compassion and patience. For if the body is bound by enslavement, wouldn't the mind also succumb to the rules of bondage?

A rational person would respond with gladness if their jailer let them be. But that night, the top of her left hand still sore from the brush beating, Thisbe couldn't help but ask repeatedly, "Pardon, Madame Sylvie?" She didn't question Madame often. Or at all. It had been years since Madame gave the instruction, "I won't need you," leaving Thisbe free to visit her family or to sit. While she, Thisbe, had been on her own charge for the past seven mornings, working with the painter, leaving Madame alone, Madame had been asleep in her bed and not yet in need of her. This time was dif-

571

ferent. She had heard Madame and Lucien's plan, that they would wait for nightfall to carry out their digging. It didn't occur to Thisbe that her mistress didn't require her help or to accompany her. For the past ten years, her well-being depended on her understanding and performance of her duty as Madame's hands, feet, arms, and legs. She needed clarification. "Pardon, Madame Sylvie?"

"I won't repeat myself," Madame snapped. "I have my son to see to me."

"Yes, Madame Sylvie," she said. Still, out of habit, Thisbe knew no other command from Madame but to come, get, and stand. She followed Madame.

Surely Madame heard Thisbe's shoes padding behind her. "Stay," she said firmly.

Thisbe stayed and watched her mistress walk away determined, proud, under her own power. She was amused and puzzled. When Thisbe stood long enough, she returned to the low bed where she slept and slowly removed her shoes, glad Marie and Louise hadn't witnessed Madame ordering her to stay like a mistress commands her dog.

Lucien extended his arm in a curve and Madame hooked her arm around it. He escorted her through the large parlors and the dining room and out of the pantry and around to the carriage, as if to lead her on a ballroom floor. They would need the lantern on a night like this. The grounds were dark and quiet, with only the occasional rustle of leaves from the live oak and the intermittent song of the zozo monpè.

Lucien helped his mother up to the seat in the small buggy, as if they were riding to church. When both were inside, he took the reins and said, "Lead us, Mother."

"If this is what it takes, you can have your gold. It's but a day sooner than you would have it." Sylvie's resignation at having lost a long battle was clear in her voice, but she was not without pride. "To the monuments!"

"Mother. The monuments? But —"

She stopped him. "You have turned over your father's statue. I know, my son.

573

And to my horror, you dug up your sister's statue. Don't think I don't know about that. I do. But you say our situation is bad. And for once, I believe you, so we will let those desecrations go. Just do as I say, and you will see."

The monuments to Bayard Guilbert and Charlotte Thérèse stood three hundred feet away. The trip didn't require the horse and buggy, but it was late, and Lucien didn't know how far his mother could walk. He also anticipated a hefty weight in gold to carry.

When they arrived, Madame told Lucien where to stop, and to help her out of the buggy. He then took the shovel and oil lantern that he had stowed on the buggy's floor. "Where?" he asked.

He had stopped, but she said, "Not here. First, we stand at this point, between your father's stone and your sister's statue." The tall obelisk, molded from cheaply mixed cement, marked with Bayard Guilbert's name. A young girl sculpted in Italian marble stood as a tribute to Charlotte Thérèse's memory. Madame had put a good sum of her husband's gold on commissioning Charlotte Thérèse's statue.

"Now," she said, "the gold stands between father and daughter."

"Still, Mother. I have excavated this area thoroughly . . ."

"And may Jesus Christ have mercy on your sins."

He raised his shovel.

"Stop!" Madame said. "This is not where to dig. First we stand here. Then we look to the star." She pointed up to the brightest speck of the Little Dipper and then straight ahead to the landscape before them, grassy and flat — but then there was cane. Rows and rows of cane.

"Why there, Mother?"

"It was field when we buried it. I didn't dream you would plant over it."

"You could have told me not to plant over it."

"Had I told you, we would have nothing to uncover today. We walk straight. Leave the buggy. We walk straight." She looked up at the sky. "Don't make me lose my count," she scolded. "We must walk two thousand steps, straight."

575

"We need the cane knife," he said.

Lucien held the shovel and lantern and walked slowly for his mother's sake. He could hear her counting, counting. They walked in silence for more than ten minutes. At last, he had won. At last! The triumph almost at hand and the ridiculousness of the hunt made him smile, then chuckle, which caught Madame's attention.

"One thousand and eighty," she said, and stopped walking. "What is funny, son?"

"Besides us in the cane at midnight? It is all funny, don't you think? I am profoundly relieved, Mère, that we are at last saved. But one question I must ask. Whose two thousand steps do you count? Yours? You alone buried my father's gold?"

"Henri helped me bury it," she said simply.

Lucien's laughing face froze, and then gave way to the expression of a hopeful child. "My brother Henri?"

"Don't call him that," she snapped. "Your brothers are there," she said, pointing upward, to the heavens.

"Henri . . ." Lucien's voice was wistful, full of memory. Again, he said, "Henri."

"Stop it! You didn't ask about him all these years."

"You said he ran away."

"He is away," she sang without remorse, and began to once again walk and count. He followed.

"What does that mean?" he asked.

"He works somewhere. Away. Cuba, I think."

He stopped walking. She said, "One thousand ninety-five. Ninety-six?" aloud, and then she stopped walking. She looked up at the stars. "You made me lose my count."

"What happened to Henri?"

"You are like your father. Can't leave the Blacks alone."

"You sold him," Lucien accused. "My brother hides your gold and you sold him. Down the river."

"Do you want the gold? Your father's gold, or do you want to cry about Henri?"

"When this is over, Mother, I won't

forget who you are."

"Who I am? I am the one who thought about you before you were born. If not for me, we would have nothing. Now, I walk. One thousand ninety-seven. Ninety-eight. Ninety-nine. One thousand one hundred. And don't talk. Don't make me lose my place." She stopped. Looked directly up at the indigo sky to find her star and continued with her walking and counting.

Now that they were into the cane, deep into the cane, the blades, a tough, wicked fiber, scratched all the way. She no longer lifted her skirt to avoid the dirt, as she had taught Jane to do. Instead, she covered her face to avoid the slap of each cane blade in her path. Each step was met with the constant whip of leaves. Mother and son continued the trek into the punishing blades of cane, her cheeks and hands stinging.

"Finally," Madame said, shivering in the cold, her face and hands beaten. "We stop here."

"How do you know?"

"I counted two thousand steps, and I

looked up!" she said, pointing to Polaris, the one constant, unchanging star. "Henri's steps and my steps are different. But we walked to my pace."

Lucien set the lantern down. He removed his jacket and draped it over his mother's shoulders, then removed his hat and placed it on her head, against her objections. He took the shovel, traced a rectangle around the area of soil and cane stalks. He used the edge of the shovel to chop down the cane. The stalks were well rooted to the earth. With the area cleared as best as he could, he told his mother to stand back. She didn't move. He shook his head and began to dig, throwing the dirt to one side of the area and then the other, managing to hit Madame as the clumps of dirt flew. It took Lucien less than an hour to dig half his height. Madame urged him on while he dug.

"I believe," he said, out of breath, "this is a clever plot to have me dig my own" — he exhaled — "plot."

"Don't be ridiculous," she said. "Dig."

"I'm sure to find my brother's bones." He deliberately threw dirt on her. "Poor Henri."

Madame spat out the dirt that hit her on the mouth. "Yes. Poor Henri." She refused to step back.

"Are you certain, Mother? It's been more than thirty years. Stars" — he exhaled — "might change."

"One star never moves," she told her son flatly. "You are directly under the right star. Keep digging."

Lucien dug. With every other heave, he recited a line from Edgar Allan Poe's "Eldorado." This frustrated his mother, who implored him to dig faster, but to no avail.

"And, as his strength
Failed him at length,
He met a pilgrim shadow —
'Shadow,' said he,
'Where can it be —
This land of Eldorado?' "

Suddenly, Lucien's shovel produced a different and dull sound when he plunged it into the earth. He stopped digging. "At last, Mother. We come upon Eldorado!"

Madame clasped her dirty hands with expectation. Her acrimony and frustration fell away with this discovery. This progress.

Lucien threw the shovel up and was patting the surface where he stopped digging. He looked up at her. She looked down. He knelt and dug using his hands to free the object, and then brushed off the dirt from its leather. Lucien lifted the sack up out of its burial spot. The bag gave too easily.

He stopped brushing. And for a moment, he stopped breathing. He knew. Like buckshot to a boar, the realization hit him cleanly, instantly. The satchel. Not swollen with gold, but sunken in at its belly. There was too little resistance, no profound weight when he lifted it, not even an inch out of the earth. He shit on himself, not wholly, but did it matter? Dignity? Control? What were these trifles to Lucien Guilbert? He threw the satchel onto the ground near his mother's feet and heaved himself up out of the pit. He knew. He knew. He knew. The Guilberts, Le Petit Cottage, their generations, were finished.

"Open it!" she cried, impatient and yet proud that she had guided them correctly. "Open it!"

Instead, her son grabbed her by the shoulders, shook her until she screamed for mercy. Sylvie was shocked by his attack and wrestled in his grip. His strength, his fury, overwhelmed her. She didn't see her son but a madman with mad eyes. The memory of the same mad eyes she had buried beneath a cement obelisk some thirty years ago.

Lucien couldn't stop shaking her. His blood-raged face close, his spit relentless. "Foolish! Foolish! Stupid woman!"

"Lucien! Lucien! Stop! Please stop!" Perhaps it was the dark. She had not caught on to what was clear to Lucien at first sight of the satchel.

Finally, he pushed her away and then she fell. For that moment, he didn't care. *Let her rot in dirt,* the only thought he could articulate amid his cussing and damnation. "All these years. All these years!" he managed to say as he paced. Then kicked air. He turned to his mother, still on the ground. "And you — the instrument of our downfall. The cause of our ruin. Our complete ruin."

"No! No!" She squatted on the ground,

covering her ears with her hands.

"Yes! Oh, yes!" he said. He dropped, grabbed the satchel, and slit the cords that had bound it, toughened and melded into one another by determined hands and some thirty years of burial.

He didn't have to look down into the goat hide. Instead, he looked at his mother's face. Her face, crumbling and broken, upon seeing, finally seeing, what the lamp revealed under the indigo night: a handful of gold coins.

"Where?" she asked. "How?"

He looked down and surveyed the fifteen-odd coins. "About two hundred dollars in gold."

"I don't . . . I don't . . . I counted the steps," she went on, clouded by her disbelief. "I counted the steps. My steps. I counted the gold."

A howl came from her first. A howl so low, so animal-like, Lucien couldn't believe it came from his mother. She beat the ground with her fists.

When he couldn't bear her howling, then the choking in her throat, and last, the sobbing, her face in the dirt, Lucien picked her up. In her horrible sobs he heard the defeat of his mother's life and saw her for who she was. A woman. An old ignorant woman. He sighed. In his thinking, that should have been enough to forewarn him of this outcome.

"Gone" was all she could say. "Gone."

He cursed her. He cursed himself. And he forgave her. "Yes, my love. Thousands upon thousands, gone. All gone." At this point he didn't refer to the gold, but everything he had worked to save. Gone. Their lives. Gone.

Lucien dropped the pieces of gold into his pockets. He left the shovel, the lamp, and the goatskin satchel in the dirt, and began the walk, carrying his mother to the monuments where the horse and buggy stood. He said to her, although she had passed out, "Tomorrow, we will act the performance of a lifetime. We will lay out the ham and cakes and welcome the guests. And we will treat the Tourniers like French kings."

As for the gold, the sum worth sixty-three thousand dollars. The gold missing from the goat hide . . . *Patience. Once more, patience.*

Although Thisbe had long retired to her bed, she refused to fall into a deep sleep. She lay on the bed, her eyes closed, but her mind restless. In three hours she was to awaken, clean herself, dress, and apply more varnish to the dried background of the portrait. She needed her sleep but couldn't truly sleep without seeing her mistress.

She heard one set of footsteps, slow in their climb up the stairs. She opened her eyes and saw Monsieur Lucien carrying a limp and unconscious Madame Sylvie into the salon. Thisbe leaped to her feet when he approached the bed.

"Monsieur Guilbert! Oh, Monsieur Guilbert! Is my Madame Sylvie dead?"

"No, Thisbe. God can be cruel, but this time he let her live."

Lucien kissed his mother on the forehead; her face, to Thisbe's horror, was covered in dirt. He waited for her to stir. When she didn't, he turned and left his mother with her servant.

Thisbe went about undressing Madame

Sylvie, removing her shoes, brushing the dirt from her. She cleaned Madame as best she could, which was when Madame began to stir and murmur. Thisbe felt the scratches on Madame's hands and face. She knew these scratches. Her mother, father, and sisters wore them from the cane.

IX

Lucien didn't enter the cookhouse as a rule, but when the work bell rang that morning, he stuck his head in the door and told Cook to slaughter and smoke the female pig for the party. The blessing was that the sow's litter was now rooting around on their own, and not dependent on the sow for nourishment. Lucien had hoped to save the pig for winter, but he had no choice but to use it for the party, as the Guilberts must put out enough of a spread to keep the guests cheerful and dancing.

Since no hand could be spared to kill and butcher the pig, Lily went to the pen, got the sow, the last adult pig, killed it, and scraped off the hair with scalding water and a razor. She went to work removing the hooves and knuckles. She cut and yanked out the richest pieces of pig fat the sow had to offer for lard that would be rendered later. Lily fired up the pit and left the sow in the smokehouse to crackle and smoke for the good part of the day. There were still fifty biscuits to make.

Madame had sent Thisbe with a pass for the stable boy to ride to flag a river-boat for some ice for Cook to churn with milk and orange peel and vanilla bean. Thisbe went to Lily first, and then back to Madame.

"Cook said we have no vanilla bean or enough milk."

Madame abandoned that idea. Biscuits would have to do.

It was during this time that Madame remembered her old friend Marcelle, the gift from her husband shortly after the death of her twin sons. She remembered Marcelle's consommés. Desserts. Sauces. Their talks about Marcelle's adventures in grand palaces and chalets throughout Europe, the cuisine, the fashions. Marcelle, who could turn water, a handful of root vegetables, and sauces into fine dining. She thought of how she had overlooked Marcelle's color, and the two became close, until the day Marcelle overstepped her bounds and gave her the news she had a granddaughter. Marcelle had taken it upon herself to see the child, pick her up, and report to Madame, "It is early yet, but she is a beauty. She looks like you and Charlotte Thérèse. This Rosalie." And that was that.

"Ah! If only Marcelle were here to spoil the guests with her magic." Madame sighed. "We cannot cry over what could have been a social triumph. The guests will eat the slices of ham, the little cakes, and get drunk on punch. It will be enough."

X

Byron and Pearce rose early to exhaust themselves on each other one last time on the day of the dance and before they prepared to leave the following morning. They had dispensed with their private word game days before. The end of their summer, their idyllic furlough, had passed swiftly. There was nothing to do to stop the gallop of time. So, they lay together, kissed, and coupled to store up what they would miss once they reentered cadet life. Would there be another moment for a deep kiss between the two once they left the garçonnière for the party? Byron seemed to accept that every aspect of their furlough had ended. His travel bag was packed. Pearce, on the other hand, had put away very little. He arranged his shirts, pants, drawers, and personal items on the bed and studied them.

Neither Byron nor Pearce had much to take for the journey. Both had rented storage for their footlockers and supplies with families in Highland Falls before leaving the Academy, rather than hauling their wardrobes and paraphernalia to their homes, or in Pearce's case, to various stops and ultimately down to Le Petit Cottage in St. James, Louisiana. This made travel and packing for the steamboat ride less of a concern. But now it was time to get ready for the trip upriver, and Byron and Pearce agreed that they weren't reliable to assemble themselves after a night of drinking and dancing. The party would go on until the morning, and from there, they would leave St. James Parish. There was no need to return to their happy little fortress.

"I will miss this place and my time here," Byron said.

"You are not alone in that, my friend. What memories. What words!" Pearce sought to get a grin out of Byron, but Byron's mood was reflective and somber.

"I won't return to the garçonnière. This

happy place will be for my sons."

Pearce was folding a shirt. He stopped folding and sat down on the bed. "So, you'll do it. You'll marry Eugénie after graduation."

Byron seemed genuinely perplexed by the question.

"Of course I'll marry her. Why do you ask, and ask in that way?"

"You'll marry this girl? Is it fair to her? To expect marriage when you give your best vows to me? Could you do it? Could you, Byron?"

"I'm touched you care so much for my fiancée," Byron said dryly. So dryly, this is perhaps what hurt his friend terribly. "But let me ask you, is it fair to hold me to what we cry out in the heat of battle?"

Pearce gave a muffled but ironic laugh. "How it's all changed. In your letters you swore you'd die slowly if I didn't come to you. Silly me. Perhaps the ink was smudged, and I misread the urgency. Your meaning."

"What are we to do? Flee far, far away and set up house like a pair of spinster

592

hens? What can come of us, Pearce? Tell me."

"I see," Pearce said soberly. "I see." He went back to folding.

"Doesn't it mean anything to you that I asked you here to see the things that I love? My home. My way of life."

"Your fiancée. Lovely young lady."

The quarter that had been so cozy was now too cramped. Byron turned on his heel and left the garçonnière for a walk and some air. He marched down the aisle of live oaks, kicking stones along the way. He stopped at the place where he had stood in the early days of his furlough, the grand live oak, and wished day after day until his wish had come true.

While Pearce was tempted, he didn't perch at the window to spy on his love. He did throw a balled sock at the dresser. It was impossible to share his heart and hold on to his dignity, so the tears came.

When Byron returned, Pearce had packed his bag, except for a few items for grooming.

Pearce said, "I'll take your razor."

Byron crossed his arms. "Is that your

answer? The ultimate reminder or keepsake? To do away with yourself in the bed we shared?"

"Do away with myself? You ass," Pearce said. "Tonight we dance and tomorrow we make our way to the Academy. Unlike you, I must shave and police my locks to pass the commandant's inspection. Through no fault of my own or of my kin, I am a cursed reminder of your P. G. T. Beauregard of New Orleans."

Byron studied his friend. Pearce's face, slightly reddened. Byron came closer. "Only about the eyes. And mouth. Here. The lips."

Later, after what both swore was their last kiss, Pearce said, "I want to make peace and nothing more."

Byron laughed. "There is no more. We have spent it all."

"Maybe you're not so cold to quit us now. Maybe it's best to know how everything is."

"I can't call you friend and brother, and not honor our friendship. I can't lie to you."

Pearce said, "Maybe, friend, you shouldn't speak. Each word, especially 'friend,' makes it worse."

"It means everything to me that you know what I cherish deeply, and that you know that I'd die for it. This land is everything to me and my family. I have no choice but to keep it going."

"Let's pray it doesn't come to war."

"But if it does, my dear f—"

Pearce placed his finger over Byron's lips to stop him from saying the word.

Byron kissed it away and continued. "If it comes to war, let's both rest in confidence that we are cadets. We are prepared."

"Why do I love you so, Byron? You are the essence of melancholy. I come bearing a peace offering. You beat the war drum."

Byron exhaled and began to straighten himself up. "Then give me your peace offering so we can be merry gentlemen for Grandmère's dance."

Pearce took a small cloth-bound book from his bag and held it out to Byron.

"*Leaves of Grass,*" Byron said, taking

the book. "I will cherish it."

"You can read it to Eugénie on your wedding night."

Byron smiled at his friend. "And there's the bayonet."

XI

Eugénie arrived early, along with her regrets for her father, who couldn't make the short trip. Her chaperone and grand-aunt, Agnes, however, was at her side, spilling a stream of caution and chastisements in French Creole that her grand-niece's place was at her father's bedside and not at a waltz.

Madame would have enjoyed the aunt's constant rants and pecking over the impropriety if only to revel in her future granddaughter-in-law's upbringing. Comforted by what the family would gain in Eugénie Duhon, Madame would have borne the elder Duhon woman's rebukes with pleasure from within, all the while portraying a well-acted remorseful exterior. The family's attachment to Colonel Duhon and his sister-in-law, the countess, would be the Guilberts' salvation. Not the alliance between her son's quadroon daughter and the Tournier father's colored son.

The Duhon–Guilbert union would produce heirs to bring the family forward without destroying blood and birthright. But Madame, underneath the heavily made-up face she put on with Thisbe's help, thought about the current state of the family's affairs. And her portrait.

Eugénie was too distracted to listen to her aunt's words of caution. She greeted the family. Allowed Monsieur Lucien Guilbert to kiss her hand over the lace green gloves that matched her traveling dress. Her grandaunt raised objections to this paternal kiss, but Eugénie wouldn't hear them.

"Have a girl bring my dress up," Eugénie said, and ran upstairs to find Jane.

Lucien leaned over to his mother and said, "There goes the future Madame Guilbert."

Aunt Agnes wagged her finger at Lucien and said in French, "No, no. You are too hasty."

■ ■ ■ ■

Jane stood up immediately upon seeing Eugénie, and the two embraced as though they had been separated by more than nine days.

Eugénie couldn't contain herself. "Jane! My Jane, I've missed you!"

"I've missed you, Eugénie."

"Don't say it if you don't mean it," she said, pouting.

"I've missed you, Eugénie."

"Of course you have!" Eugénie squealed. "Oh! We are closer than sisters."

"We are," Jane said. "I didn't like my sisters."

"Oh, my Jane. They didn't know how to love you."

They kissed on both cheeks and then briefly on the lips.

Marie, looking older than her eighteen years, entered the room carrying the gown and a small suitcase.

Eugénie stepped away from Jane to direct the servant. "Hang the dress in the wardrobe. Set my bag here." She pointed. "And come up before the party to steam the wrinkles from my gown."

"Oui, mademoiselle," Marie said without hesitation. She left the room.

Eugénie turned back to Jane. "What will you wear to the waltz?"

Jane turned to the outfit on her bed.

"Is this the riding outfit?" Eugénie went to the bed where the blue-black outfit lay and traced with her fingers the embroidered cording sewn along the sides of the pantaloons. She examined the jacket, its embroidery, the shoulders adorned with gold epaulets, and last, the gold buttons from Jane's father's war jacket. Although Jane hadn't asked for drawers, a pair of open drawers had been sewn to match the loose fit of the pantaloons.

Eugénie was stunned to the point of gasps upon seeing the outfit. "I must see you wearing it!"

"I'd like to go riding, but I didn't have my lesson with Madame Guilbert today."

"Lessons! Pooh!" Eugénie said. "You are lady enough."

"I'm not a lady," Jane said. "But I want

to go riding."

"Then we'll go riding, Jane. But tomorrow," Eugénie said. "There is no time today with the party only hours away. Oh, Jane! The party will be just right. A few friends. Not too grand like the countess's balls. No dancing with every proud parent's son! Only one, or two."

"I don't dance. I won't dance," Jane said.

"Not even with me?"

Jane didn't know how to answer.

"Besides Byron," Eugénie said, "you are my closest, dearest friend. How can I enjoy this party without you at my side?"

"You are my closest, dearest friend," Jane said. "I don't dance."

Eugénie hugged Jane and kissed her face and lips. "Hold on to me and we will waltz, you and I. You see? One, two, three." But Jane didn't move.

"Will you kiss me?" Jane asked.

"Of course, my dear Jane. Of course." She planted little kisses on Jane's face and lips again.

Jane giggled, then asked for more kisses.

"Only if you dance with me," Eugénie insisted. She placed Jane's left hand on her shoulder and took her right hand in hers. "Please, Jane. Come. Come. One, two, three. Follow me."

Jane took the awkward steps.

XII

Patience, finally. The night of enchantment and revelation is at hand.

The west parlor had been returned to its original sunny purposes. The drop cloths, paint boxes with paints, palette, chemicals, tin cups, and brushes had all been put away. The curtains were pulled back, the door, shutters, and windows open to fill the room with fresh air and give it the full benefit of sunlight. The room desperately needed the open air to blow through the house, from the naturally sunny parlor, the larger salons, and out through the doors and windows of the east parlor. Even with the open doors, shutters, and windows, the odor of paint and chemicals lay heavy.

Two days had passed since Madame last

sat for her portrait. Surely two days was enough time for the oils to dry, she thought. It was now time to see this thing she had made a deal with the devil to have done.

She, with Thisbe, entered the west parlor room where the painting and her chair sat. She intended to be seated on her rose brocade throne for her first viewing of the portrait, whether Claude Le Brun was ready to show it or not. Given the ordeal and disappointment that she had endured the night before, Madame found her resolve and the realization that she was much stronger than she looked. She should get what she wanted.

She found Claude Le Brun standing next to the easel, the portrait covered by a drape that had been bound around the legs of the easel to prevent a stolen glance.

Madame was insulted and enraged by the implication. She didn't bother with a greeting. "How can it dry with the cloth over it?" Madame asked.

"It will take time to dry, Madame Guilbert," Le Brun said coolly. "But it will dry."

"I would like to see it before my guests, if you please." She spoke cordially enough, but the command was undeniable.

"Of course, Madame Guilbert. Of course." Le Brun met and bested her cordial notes. "As soon as I am paid, then I will untie and lift the draping."

Madame gathered herself. She couldn't scream at the man, although she felt her control ebbing away. In the past twelve hours, she had been through so much. She said, "Lucien will see you to finish our business. In the meantime, you must dress and enjoy our party."

"But, Madame Guilbert. I have plans to leave as soon as I am paid. I am anxious to join my retreat. The journey is long."

Madame put on the appearance of being taken aback. "What man asks to be excused from dancing with young ladies and drinking? But you must stay to enjoy this final act of our hospitality."

"Madame," he said firmly.

"How can the couples dance the quadrille without enough men? Monsieur Le

Brun . . ."

He wasn't so green that he couldn't see the sudden shift in mood, from indignation to good will. He heard her out.

". . . how can I entice you to stay?"

Le Brun said nothing for a while.

Madame waited for Le Brun to offer her some hope, but she refused to plead with the tradesman.

He asked, "Will Mademoiselle attend this party?"

Madame was dumbfounded. "Mademoiselle?"

He looked at Thisbe. "If Mademoiselle Assistant will attend, then I will stay for your party. But I will leave promptly in the morning. And your stable must accommodate the carriage that will come for me, and its coachman."

Madame allowed herself to be shocked. "My *servant*? Oh, Monsieur Le Brun. This mixing is impossible. It isn't done. In the big cities, New Orleans, yes. But in these small circles? Impossible."

Le Brun sighed. "Then I will see your son for my payment and be on my way."

"Not so hasty, Monsieur Le Brun. Thisbe will attend." She even smiled in defeat. To herself, she thought, *Of course Thisbe will attend the party, as a servant. Not as a guest.*

She said to Thisbe, "I try to save you and you drop your scent like a deer in the woods."

Thisbe followed Madame to Lucien's office.

Even with his mother conveying her impatience and urgency, Lucien looked at Thisbe, winked, and said, "Your master leaves for two years. How will you bear it?"

Thisbe, already chastised by her mistress for possessing a modicum of womanliness, dared not speak, even if to respect the Master or to deny his claim.

Madame didn't have time for this foolishness. She would let her son think the boy had meddled with her servant for his sake, but this was not the matter at hand. "My son, we have trouble with the painter."

"How so?"

"He won't show the painting without payment. He wants to leave as soon as possible."

"Let him and his painting go. The end of our immediate troubles."

"No," Madame said. "No. I sat for my portrait. It is mine."

Lucien put down his pen. "Mother, what can we do?"

"We must pay. Can you imagine? Suppose word reaches the countess that we have treated her painter poorly? Think, son. She will end the engagement between Eugénie and Byron. The scandal! How will I face Lucille Pierpont? We will be ruined."

"Mother. Dear Mother. You have controlled our living all these years. Look at us. We are in ruin because you hold on to the reins. We are in this ruin because we must have a sitting in St. James, when no one sits for portraits. But rest assured, Mother. We will be famous throughout St. James Parish. Maybe throughout this Louisiana."

"If you went to France so many years ago —"

"We are beyond France and so many years ago, Mother."

Thisbe remained in her servant's pose. Head and eyes downcast. Ears open.

"Now, more than ever, we need everything to orchestrate in our favor. We need Laurent Tournier to fall so much in love with Rosalie that there's nothing he and his father will deny us. Yes, Mother. It has come to this. As humiliating as it will be, I will ask Tournier for a loan. I would much rather use the liaison with the Tourniers to better the farm, but here we are. The carriages will soon arrive. I will escort my daughter into the waltz. Into our home."

He waited for her to object to Rosalie or the Tourniers.

Madame turned, and Thisbe followed.

XIII

Marie and Louise rolled up the carpet and moved the tables and large chairs out onto the gallery on the side of the house. The floors were swept. The vases put away. Ladder-back chairs were placed in a row in the main salon for parents to sit and watch their children navigate on the small dance floor. Smaller tables were moved into the east parlor and quickly set up with the punch bowl, cups, small plates, dessert forks, pickle forks, and linen napkins.

Next, the sisters carried buckets of water from the well to fill large clay jars for punch. Then they carried buckets of water from the cistern into the room where the barrels were housed for washing clothes. The room was cool. Ideal to mix the punch, but most important, this water would keep a steady stream of silverware, dishes, and cups washed and rinsed before they were dried and brought back out to the sideboard and tables for reuse.

The fiddlers, a father and young son, had been inspected by Marie and Louise. They were told to wear shoes, their best jackets and pants. They were told, No straw hats in Madame's house. No talking to the white people. Then Louise remembered that there would be two colored people in attendance. And Thisbe. The sisters then said, "No talking to guests." They scolded the musicians that there would be no American reels. No hopping music. No Irish jig music. No German music. No Cajun music. No Black music. "Make the rhythm for white Creoles." The waltz, the cotillon, and the quadrille. This would be no hard task for the fiddlers. Both father and son earned themselves and Lucien Guilbert a pretty penny, as they were often rented out to other planters. It gave Marie and Louise pleasure to scold and to order someone. The fiddlers, both promised a dollar each, took the twin sisters' fussing in stride.

Marie's and Louise's demeanor changed when they entered the cook-house. There were no orders to be given to Cook. Every "order" spoken to Cook in English was tempered with, "Madame Sylvie said," along with its necessary companion, "if you please." Miss Lily didn't suffer taking orders from Marie or Louise.

XIV

When the commissary closed early for the day, Camille watched to see which direction Rosalie walked. To the big house or to the cottage. She had heard from the gossiping twins that her daughter was a troublemaker, traipsing through Madame's house like a planter's white daughter. She had also heard that Rosalie would go to the big house as a guest to Madame's soiree. This, after Camille had spent the early years of Rosalie's life keeping her from the maîtresse's sight. The twins gossiped like woodpeckers, but for the bits of information they dispensed to Camille, they had their uses.

Without her husband's knowledge, Camille carried a dish of cooked rice, red beans, cornbread, and smoked ham fat to her daughter's cottage. Meat and even its renderings were hard to come by, and her husband would have beaten her if he had seen the amount of food she had taken from their meager larder. She praised and thanked Santa Maria and the saints for her protector, John-John, as she hurried to the cottage. She worried the girl was too thin, and that her daughter hadn't the cooking skills to keep her and any family she would have well fed on a plantation. She was relieved to see that in the three weeks that Rosalie had been back, Rosalie had had sense enough to break ground and start a garden. Beans had already begun to sprout out of the newly turned soil.

The visit was a surprise and wholly welcomed by Rosalie, who hung on to her mother until Camille pushed her away. Rosalie led Camille inside the cottage that she was certain her mother had cleaned and prepared for her when she returned home. She was pleased to see her mother but was even more anxious to show her mother the ball gown that she would wear to the waltz. She held it up to her neck and preened to show off the dress.

"Mother, do you like it? I fixed it. The bodice now fits, and the sleeves fall just below the shoulder." Rosalie spoke in Creole, the language forbidden in her stepfather's house. To win her mother's smile would mean so much. Rosalie not only wanted her mother's approval; she wanted her mother's forgiveness.

Camille made a face of reserved approval. She smiled and said, "When I worked in the house with Madame Lucille, I helped her and her sisters dress for parties. That was long ago."

It amazed Rosalie that her mother could look both happy and sad — although she herself was filled with expectation and nervousness.

"Monsieur Lucien hopes this night will end in engagement between Laurent Tournier and me. You remember Laurent Tournier?" She watched her mother's face while she shared her news. Camille gave her too slight a reaction. Rosalie had to know what her mother thought. "This is good, no?"

Camille said, "Your soul has wings that fly over your head," to Rosalie's disappointment. "And as for the party," she

615

said. "The engagement. The grand-mother's house . . . The gombo is stirred, my love. But who is the cook?"

And she was gone.

Her mother filled her belly and then put weight on her feet. Feet meant to dance that night.

This is what Rosalie heard repeatedly as she readied herself for the waltz: *Who is the cook?*

Lucien had the coachman drive him to Rosalie's cottage in the rockaway, instead of taking the buggy himself to pick up his daughter. The walk from the house to the cottage was not long, but Lucien didn't want his daughter to walk the distance. While some of the other plant-ers' daughters might have a bit of dirt on the edge of their hems, his daughter couldn't have a visible speck of dirt on her gown. The invited mesdemoiselles would be there to frolic as freely as they pleased, but Rosalie had to be beyond reproach in every way. He would inspect her before she entered his mother's house.

He knocked on the cottage door. Before

the door opened, he removed his hat.

She stood before him, a vision. More than he had hoped for.

"My dear," he said. "If we don't toast Byron and Eugénie, we will toast the Guilbert–Tournier engagement."

"Do you believe so, Mon Pè?"

"What have I told you about fishing for compliments?"

She smiled demurely.

He stepped back to look at her. "But, how is this the gown from the dressmaker in New Orleans?"

She turned slowly to show the modifications she had made. He was astonished and took her hand and turned her as if she were his dancing partner.

"I've altered it to better fit me," she said.

"You've done more than alter it. Why, this is magnificent. How will your future sister-in-law love you if you outshine her on her day?"

"Thank you, Mon Pè."

"Between you and me, I exaggerated your sewing talent to the ladies to keep from spending cash on Jane Chatham. But, lo and behold! I didn't exaggerate at all!"

"Do you think Madame will like it?"

"My mother will like the dress. But she won't say that. I won't lie to you. She doesn't truly welcome you. Know this so that you don't behave like a child when she doesn't embrace you."

"Yes, Mon Pè."

"Stay close to your brother and his company. I will make all of the introductions."

"Yes, Mon Pè."

"You are there for Alphonse and Laurent Tournier. When his father sees you two gliding across the floor, he must be sold. Our very lives depend on you."

"In other words, Mon Pè, do all that I can to win the Tourniers. And avoid Madame."

"No, my daughter. In those words. Now, your arm."

XV

Byron and Pearce, both with clean-shaven faces, hair newly cut, and wearing gray cadet uniforms and black boots, marched down the stairs from their furlough tower and made the two-hundred-foot walk to the house, their strides in step. They carried their travel bags with them, as they planned to leave the party and go straight to meet the steamboat for the trip upriver, especially if the party went on until four or five o'clock in the morning.

Madame made a fuss when she saw the cadets. This took her mind off things momentarily. "How splendid! Even you, Monsieur Pearce, look impressive. What a uniform can do!"

"Bonjour, Madame. You embarrass me with your compliments," Pearce said.

"Good! Good!" Madame said. "Be full of these charms when the young ladies arrive." To Byron she said, "Make sure he dances with both Pierpont sisters."

"But, Madame," Pearce said, "I hope to spend my time with Mademoiselle Jane." He raised an eyebrow, rather than remind her what she had told him one evening.

"We are few men tonight," Madame said. "You must dance with every girl. The Pierponts more than the others."

"I am at your service, Madame Guilbert."

"Yes, yes," Madame said. "Please excuse us a moment," she said, leading her grandson a few steps away from Pearce.

"Yes, Grandmère?" Byron asked.

"The signet ring," she said. "Do you have it?"

"I do," he said.

"You will give the ring to the girl. But you will tell her away from the others, away from her chaperone, the meaning of the ring."

"The meaning?"

620

Now Madame was exasperated. "How can you forget what I told you? That the ring is the inheritance for your children. The Bernardin de Maret vineyard. The convent. The contract."

"Yes, yes, Grandmère. Yes. I will tell her."

"It is very important," she said. "She must know who you are. Who we are."

Byron had his eye on Pearce while he gave his assurances to his grandmother. He noted Pearce's attentions turning to the stairs. He and then Madame followed suit. Both Eugénie and Jane, trailed by Aunt Agnes, descended the stairs. Eugénie, floating carefully in her light-blue satin ball gown. Jane, in her indigo riding suit.

"Lovely," Byron said, holding out his arm for Eugénie. "Absolutely lovely."

"Two fair enchantments," Pearce said.

"Merci," Eugénie said. "And you are both near gentlemen perfection."

"Thank you, Eugénie," Byron said. To Pearce, he said, "Near perfection. She keeps us on our toes."

Pearce agreed.

Madame seemed both pleased and stunned at the sight of Eugénie and Jane. "Jane. What is that you're wearing? Where is your gown?"

"I'm wearing my riding outfit."

"But . . . but . . ."

Eugénie came eagerly to Jane's defense. "Oh, Madame. Doesn't she look magnificent? So proud. So regal?"

"I couldn't agree more," Pearce said. He held out his arm to Jane. Jane wouldn't take it.

Madame Sylvie was inconsolable. "But . . . the girls wear ball gowns. Oh, poor Madame Chatham!"

"I like Jane's riding outfit. Why, she will cause a sensation," Eugénie said. "And her dancing is coming along."

"In that case, I look forward to a dance with you," Pearce said to Jane.

Jane ignored Pearce.

"Dance?" Madame asked. "Oh, Eugénie. Is this so? Our Jane dancing? Why, we hadn't progressed that far in our lessons."

"I dance, Madame Guilbert," Jane said.

"I only dance with Eugénie."

"For now," Eugénie said quickly. "You can change your mind, Jane." She turned to Madame. "Can your maid show my auntie where to sit?"

Madame made a motion and Thisbe led the older woman to the chairs meant for the parents.

"We are short on men. Perhaps Jane can help fill in," Byron said.

"Don't be ridiculous," Madame said.

"I must say, she is quite handsome," Pearce said. "Why, she looks like an Argentinian gaucho. All she needs is a sword."

"I have a sword," Jane said. Then she turned and dashed up the stairs.

"Jane," Eugénie called. "Jane."

It was too late. Jane now had purpose.

"See what you've done," Madame said to Pearce.

It couldn't get worse, or so Madame thought.

It was at this moment that Lucien Guilbert strolled into the transformed ballroom, his daughter Rosalie on his arm.

Byron, filled with joy and surprise, was the first to rush to them.

"My sister. Who knew you would turn out to be exquisite and truly beyond compare?"

"Careful, boy. Your fiancée looks on with concern," Lucien teased.

"Thank you, Byron," Rosalie said. "You're too generous in your compliments."

Byron said to Lucien, "Allow me to introduce Rosalie to Eugénie."

Rosalie didn't say she already had had that pleasure. She took her brother's arm and followed him across the room.

It was with this movement that the room began to move like an orchestrated dance. Madame walked away, while Byron escorted his sister to his fiancée and Pearce, while Lucien went after his mother.

"You won't greet her?" Lucien asked. "Even you see how lovely she is."

"I don't see anything," Madame said. "So I don't greet."

"We need her, Mother."

"Then let her do what she is here to do. But I am not a part of it. I keep my hands clean of it and my eyes won't see any of it."

In the meanwhile, Rosalie and Eugénie made the best of an awkward introduction, neither betraying they had previously met.

That was when Jane returned, sword in belt.

XVI

Of all the statements describing the good people of St. James Parish, two rang especially true: spirited music paired with food and drink would draw them out, and there was no one better to enjoy these with than their fellow St. James denizens. While the Guilbert party was by invitation, Madame was desperate for young people to attend. No sons or daughters of white planters hearing the fiddlers' call, even from across the mighty river on the east side, were turned away.

This presented problems for Marie and Louise, who begged Lily, "If you please, fifty more sponge cakes. Please. Please. And the pig is almost finished. Some cooked squabs, if you please."

Lily's answer was, "I don't climb ladders and I got no eggs." This meant Lily wouldn't climb the ladder in the pigeonnier to cook up a quick pigeon dish, and that she had no eggs to make more sponge cakes. There were no children for the sisters to order to get the eggs or to kill and stuff pigeons into a basket. It was settled. Marie ran to the henhouse with one basket for eggs and Louise ran to the pigeonnier with the larger basket and climbed the ladder to get the pigeons.

Within the hour the mood of the party rose. Guests called out requests for polkas and a cakewalk. Couples high-stepped across the floor and Jane marched. Pearce marched beside her and then turned his attention to the Pierpont sisters, who seemed out of place among the younger revelers. Pearce went about charming them, bringing them cups of punch and coaxing one and then the other onto the dance floor.

"Sylvie," Madame Pierpont gushed, "I cannot wait any longer. I must see your portrait!"

"In time, Lucille!" Madame said playfully. "In time." She looked over at Le Brun, who stood sentry by the parlor, his hands behind his back. She tugged Thisbe's skirt. Thisbe bent down to give Madame her ear.

"Bring Monsieur Le Brun a cup of punch and when he finishes it, bring him another. Let him talk to you. And if you must talk back to keep him talking, then talk. Now, go!" She all but pushed the girl on her way.

Thisbe went to the refreshment table in the east parlor. When she reached for the punch ladle, Marie was there to stop her.

"Who is that for? For Madame?" Marie asked in Creole.

"It's for Monsieur Le Brun," Thisbe answered, also in Creole.

"I'll pour it," Marie said, taking the ladle.

"Mèsi," Thisbe said, and took the crystal cup.

Marie watched Thisbe as she walked carefully around the dancers in the main salon and made her way to the west parlor.

Thisbe was certain Marie's eyes followed her. Once she was closer to Le

Brun, her concerns shifted to him. Le Brun was already acknowledging her approach with a smile.

"Bonsoir, my assistant," he said.

"Bonsoir, Monsieur Le Brun."

He looked her over, from her hair pulled up in a bun to her dress. "No apron, I see."

"No apron for now," she said. "This is my Sunday dress, for when I ride to church with Madame Sylvie."

He didn't compliment her. He just said, "Hmph," and nodded.

She offered him the cup, but he raised his hand.

"I cannot," he said. "Unless you have one with me."

"No, no, Monsieur Le Brun. None for me, thank you."

"Then none for me," he said. He took the glass, tapped the shoulder of a nearby guest, and handed him the cup of punch.

"Aren't you thirsty, Monsieur Le Brun?" she asked.

"If you are."

Thisbe glanced nervously to where

Madame sat. "Madame sent me to bring you refreshment. Why do you make trouble? Why don't you take the drink?"

"Because the cup doesn't come from you. It comes from your madame, who would like me to drink not one drink but six."

His reply caught her off guard. She laughed, surprising herself and Le Brun. Then she covered her mouth.

Lucien anticipated they would run low on rum and that the punch would lose its spirit. It wasn't so much the enjoyment of his mother's guests that concerned him, but that of his own guests. He kept a flask of his best bourbon in his breast pocket, and three shot glasses for himself and the Tourniers. When father and son arrived, Lucien was quick to fill the three shot glasses and march over to welcome Alphonse and Laurent, the glasses in one hand. He offered each a shot glass and said, "Drink up! Drink up!"

Alphonse obliged, but Laurent declined. His father took the glass and gulped it down.

"You must drink like a man," Lucien told Laurent, patting him on the back.

Laurent smiled but was obviously embarrassed. "Thank you, Monsieur Guilbert. But it is early."

"And he wouldn't want to step on the mademoiselle's toes," his father added.

Through his side vision, and a cursory survey, Lucien saw the discomfort and lingering stares of a few of his guests. He saw these same guests leave, no doubt when they realized the colored man, Tournier's son, was among them as an invited guest. Lucien put on his best indifference and brought the two men over to where he perched. The guests, invited or not, meant nothing to him. Tournier and Laurent meant everything.

Laurent searched the room. He saw Rosalie, standing close to her brother. From where he stood, he greatly admired her, but also envied her. Her complexion, hair, and features were such that they called little, if any, attention to her Negro blood. However, he, a commanding figure, a man of deep-golden complexion, and outfitted as a gentleman with no equal, escaped no one's notice.

631

Laurent excused himself from his father and his host and wove himself around the dancers to reach Rosalie.

Byron was the first to see Laurent advancing. He tapped Pearce's shoulder, a signal to follow his lead. But also to point out the handsome man approaching — they would talk about him later in private company. Byron left Eugénie and stepped in front of Rosalie. Pearce flanked Byron. What a sight! Two men in gray uniforms standing as one tower.

"What is this?" Laurent said in good humor. "A military blockade?"

"Intruder! Who goes there?" Byron asked.

"Byron!" Rosalie was horrified.

"Laurent Tournier. Request permission to approach."

"Approach?" Byron asked. "State your purpose."

"Byron!"

"Permission to compliment Mademoiselle's beauty." Laurent played along.

Byron stepped closer as if to inspect the man, older and taller than he. "Aren't you the same Laurent Tournier who pulled my sister's hair and called her names?"

"Byron! Please stop!"

Laurent said, "Didn't you do the same?"

To that, Pearce said, "He struck fast. He struck well."

"I am hit," Byron said. "Mortally hit."

"Not mortally," Pearce said, "but on target."

"Good to see you, Byron," Laurent said. He turned to Pearce.

Rosalie came forward. "I am embarrassed and apologize to you for my brother."

"No need for apologies," Laurent said. "Only for introductions?"

"My Creole manners!" Byron said. "Laurent Tournier, this is my fellow cadet —"

"I gather from the uniform," Laurent interjected.

"— and classmate Robinson Pearce, from Yorktown Heights, New York."

Laurent bowed first.

"You know my sister, Rosalie."

"I thought I knew her," Laurent said. "But the Rosalie I knew was far from this enchanting lady. May I?" He extended his hand.

Rosalie looked first to Byron, who acquiesced with a nod. She gave a discreet smile and lifted her hand. Laurent took it and kissed it, barely.

"Careful," Byron warned, although it was clear Laurent was well coached in social manners and propriety. Still, Byron enjoyed playing his role as Rosalie's older brother. He turned to Eugénie and Jane. "And these lovely ladies are our family friend and guest, Mademoiselle Jane Chatham of the Lavender Plantation, and Mademoiselle Eugénie Duhon of the Duhon Plantation. Mesdemoiselles, Laurent Tournier of La Fleur Blanche Plantation."

"Miss Jane Chatham," Jane corrected. "My uncles are colored."

"No, Jane," Eugénie said. "We don't say these things."

"They are," Jane insisted.

What could be done with the awkwardness? Laurent bowed to each lady, rather than attempting to take their hands. "A pleasure to meet you both."

As the introductions were made, Madame kept her eyes on the couples to watch Laurent's actions. She exhaled when the colored man bowed and didn't take Eugénie's or Jane's hands.

The fiddlers now played a waltz. Laurent, with Byron's permission, led Rosalie to the dance floor where their fathers could observe.

Byron turned to Eugénie and extended his hand. "My dear?"

Eugénie surprised him by not taking his hand. "I refuse you!" she said and turned her back to him. "Dance with Pearce."

Pearce, in good spirits, held out his hand. "Or should you lead?"

Eugénie took Jane by the arm. "Will you dance with me?" she asked.

"I will dance with you," Jane said. "Only you."

"First, please tuck your sword in your belt, Jane."

Jane had grown quite happy to have her sword in her hand. Her face went grim.

"Please, Jane. With kisses."

Reluctantly, Jane slid her sword down between her belt and waist. She held up her hands the way Eugénie taught her, placing one hand on Eugénie's shoulder as she began to count, "One, two, three . . . one, two, three."

"How do you like these waltzing couples?" If Byron was wounded by Eugénie's refusal and preference, the wound was clearly shallow.

"I like them fine, but not as much as that pair," Pearce said, looking toward Rosalie and Laurent.

"Or half that pair."

"Forgive me, but —"

"No forgiveness needed. The Tournier fellow is quite —"

"Quite!"

"To the Pierpont Sisters," Byron said with resignation. "They'll dance with us sad fellows."

Byron and Pearce went to persuade the older sisters off the chairs meant for parents, Lucille Pierpont urging them on.

Eugénie and Jane were one step, maybe two, behind the fiddlers. Eugénie was gracious enough to accommodate Jane's awkward rhythm. She whispered to Jane, "Byron would rather protect his sister from the Negro than protect me." Jane responded, "I will protect you." Eugénie whispered, "My Jane. My sweet, brave Jane."

XVII

Madame tried to watch all, but everything around her demanded her attention, seemingly at the same time. Marie and Louise didn't move fast enough to gather, wash, and refill the punch cups. And where was the food? They were out of sponge cakes. And the ham was now mere strips, bones, and fat on the platter. There was nothing to stab with a fork. These were the least of her worries. The portrait painter held their social event hostage with his smug demands for payment. Her servant was growing more and more at ease with showing her teeth when her invisibility was called for. Did it matter that the painter's interest in the girl bought them time? And if that weren't enough, the house was besieged with colored people — one being her son's daughter, whom she was forced to acknowledge with extraordinary civility. Madame kept a watch on Lucien as he talked to the colored boy's father: if anything was to come of it, this man of twenty-five hundred acres would step forward as their savior and make her endless suffering and humiliation bearable. Even when Madame Sylvie tried to distract herself with some gaiety, the music, which had taken a turn for the worse, made it impossible. Next, she thought, they would play Irish jigs. And then Irish ditchdiggers would come demanding entry. She would tell Lucien not to pay the fiddlers their two dollars. They were told to play waltzes, cotillons, and quadrilles only.

She clung to one happy thought: her letter to Juliette Chatham would swell in the envelope like a pregnant sow. First, Pearce, the scorned suitor. Then, the friendship with a respectable young lady whose family she was already acquainted with. And the most improbable — her Jane danced at the waltz. She would omit the parts about Jane's interesting frock, that she carried her father's sword, and that she danced with a girl. And, she thought, she must tactfully find a way to say that Jane grew robust with all the pigeon, pork, and beef she had been eating. Surely an envelope of cash from one of Jane's sisters would arrive.

And now, Madame thought of Byron, and why Eugénie refused Byron's hand. She did see that, although Eugénie's grandaunt Agnes was becoming drowsy, less watchful, and had missed the slight between the couple. Even with the music joyful and loud, Grandaunt Agnes didn't revive for most of the evening once she had fallen asleep. Madame Pierpont, however, remained alert and didn't tire of inquiring about the portrait and when it would be shown.

Thisbe excused herself from Claude Le Brun and navigated to Madame.

"Take me to my son," Madame said, anxious to get away from Lucille Pierpont. "What did Le Brun have to say?"

"That he was anxious to leave, Madame Sylvie."

"How many drinks did you give him?"

"He wouldn't drink, Madame."

"Would not drink? At a party?" She couldn't believe it. "You were to get him to drink. Make him merry. Agreeable."

"I gave him the punch, Madame. He would not drink."

"Useless!" Madame said. "You are useless to me." Madame looked at Le Brun, who stood sentry over the parlor room and shooed away anyone who might wander near the entrance.

Madame witnessed it and was disgusted. This behavior, by a tradesman, at a party in a small house, was unforgivable.

Lucien saw his mother. He sought to head her off, and exclaimed, "Mother! My mother! You remember Alphonse Tournier? Alphonse, I am certain you've met my mother, Madame Sylvie Guilbert."

"I am Sylvie Bernardin de Maret Dacier Guilbert," Madame said.

"We met at my daughter's baptismal. She is now married."

"But of course!" Madame said, although her recollection was vague.

Alphonse took Madame's hand and kissed it lightly. "I appreciate greatly the invitation you extend to my son and me."

"No, no, Monsieur Tournier. It is our pleasure."

"Alphonse," he said immediately.

"No, no, Alphonse. It is we who are honored that you visit our humble home."

Lucien, who had been holding his breath, exhaled.

"My compliments to your most exquisite granddaughter. However, I have one complaint."

"Complaint?" mother and son said.

"It is unfair the hosts' granddaughter," he said to Madame, "and daughter," he then said to Lucien, "outshines the other young ladies. And that gown! I've not seen one like it."

Madame was forced to look the way of Laurent and Rosalie. She couldn't bring herself to let her eyes rest on the young couple. She, slender and graceful; he, tall, with the strong features of his French Creole father. She glanced slightly, turned to her guest, and smiled. "You are kind."

"I have eyes," Alphonse said.

Lucien knew the extent of the performance his mother had given. He was moved to pity and gratitude and didn't wish to tax her any further. "Mother, is all well? Can I help you?" he asked.

"Yes, my son."

Lucien turned to Tournier. "Pardon, my friend."

Tournier excused them and gazed in his son's direction. His was the look of a father who saw his son happy and resigned himself to deal with the family his son chose to align himself with. Such as they were.

Out of earshot, Madame said, "It is a wonder *all* the guests haven't left."

Lucien glanced over at Rosalie and Laurent.

"Is this why you pulled me from Tournier? I was in the midst of securing —"

Madame spoke over him. "Le Brun

won't show the painting. He won't move from the parlor or let anyone enter."

"We'll have Byron and his Pearce fellow throw him out."

"And we'll have the countess end the engagement," Madame snapped. "You must talk to the painter, son. Get him to show the painting. Madame Pierpont won't let me rest. And believe me. She would enjoy my humiliation like she would enjoy standing over my grave."

"There is a lot I could say about that painting, Mother."

"We need to show this painting."

With Thisbe at Madame's side, mother and son made their way to Le Brun.

He folded his arms, waiting for them.

"Monsieur Le Brun. Are you enjoying yourself?"

"Not truly enjoyment," Le Brun said. "But it is a merry party. Your guests are happy."

"But you don't dance," Madame said. "You don't drink. We need men to dance with the ladies."

"One cannot dance or drink until our

business is complete. Then, I can join the merriment."

"But I ask you, as a friend of Elisabeth Louise Vigée Le Brun herself, to show the painting to my guests."

Le Brun lowered his voice. "Here is what I know of my relative and her great patroness. The queen treated her well. She provided for her lodging and saw that she didn't want for comfort. When my kinswoman dropped her paint supplies to the ground, the queen stooped to gather the supplies that had spilled out from her paint box. Before the paints were dry on the portrait, the queen promptly paid Madame Elisabeth Louise Vigée Le Brun for the sitting. Madame Guilbert, take care in using my kinswoman's name."

The rebuke was soft-spoken but went straight to the place where Madame Guilbert lived: her pride in her intimate royal association. He wiped it away. Madame felt herself failing and unable to recover. She held on to her son's arm.

"See here, Le Brun," Lucien said. "You will receive payment."

"And I will show the painting then," he said.

Madame looked to be on the verge of tears.

Le Brun was not moved.

"Monsieur Le Brun," Thisbe said.

Lucien, Madame, and Le Brun turned to Thisbe.

"Quiet, Thisbe," Madame said.

Lucien was of a different opinion. "Quiet, Mother."

"Monsieur Le Brun," Thisbe continued. "You asked me what I thought of the portrait."

Even he was shocked that she spoke up. He smiled, genuinely intrigued. "Tell me, my assistant. What did you think?"

With the following words, Thisbe stepped out from her shroud and was wholly visible, her head uplifted, her eyes focused: "I will tell you what I think. And I will answer the one question you put to me every morning" — here, she paused slightly — "if you show the picture tonight." Her words were clear and pointed, but without the haughtiness that would have been answered later by the whip. Instead, she spoke with the resolute possession of a young woman who knew her abilities and the value of what she had to offer.

Le Brun was taken aback, but he didn't think too long. "You make a hard bargain," he told his former assistant. Much more, to his surprise and delight, she didn't demur.

To the Guilberts he said, "I will show it, but I will only *show* the portrait. If I am not paid, it will be as if the painting didn't exist. If I leave in the morning without payment, my patroness, the countess, will make good use of your planters' newspapers with the story. And then, I will sue you for injury and recovery."

Madame said, "Monsieur! You are a gentleman. You wouldn't!"

Lucien said, "The business of art. So ruthless."

"The business of business," Le Brun said, "is simply business."

Lucien bowed. "We accept these terms."

Madame said, "We don't!"

"Come, Mother," Lucien said, leading her away. "You see, Momanm. Your servant has powers even you can't imagine. He is not the only one to fall for her charms."

Lucien thought of Thisbe's "tryst" with Byron.

His mother knew better but held her tongue.

XVIII

"Fresh air, my dear?" Byron asked Eugénie. He held out his arm and hoped she would take it.

Eugénie was still cross and didn't take his arm. "I shouldn't be seen with you. Not when you treat me poorly and so publicly."

Byron knew she was upset, but he couldn't imagine the part he had played in her displeasure. "Only minutes ago, we were dancing, having a wonderful time. How did things get so serious? Please tell me."

"You rushed to protect Rosalie, but you neglected me."

He took her hands. "Oh, my love. I was performing my brotherly duties. And surely you could see it was all in jest."

She pulled her hands away. "Byron

Guilbert, you don't take me seriously. Suppose the Negro asked me to dance? Would you protect me then?"

"Eugénie, try to understand. As much as this is a happy occasion, there is business at hand. Business I'd rather not bother you with. But Alphonse Tournier" — he looked at his father and Tournier — "is the largest planter among us. That we invite his son to the party is important to my father. But rest assured, Laurent Tournier is of great value to us all, according to my father. We must, *must* placate Alphonse Tournier. We must."

Eugénie still pouted, but Byron was able to lead her outside into the cool air.

"Eugénie," Byron said. "How can you send me back to the Academy with only your cross face to remember? I will worry and do poorly in my classes and exercises, wondering if you'll await my return."

Byron had hoped to soften Eugénie with his words, but instead, she turned farther away from him.

"Eugénie, if I've done anything to hurt you, I apologize sincerely. Please tell me your forgiveness is not pursued in vain."

Finally, she faced him, with tears

streaming down her cheeks. "Byron. It is I who beg your forgiveness."

"How can that be possible?"

"I have been dishonest, Byron."

He laughed. "Dishonesty and Eugénie. In geometry we call that an incongruence. The terms simply don't agree." He tried to lighten her mood but couldn't stop her tears. He took his handkerchief from his pocket and lightly dabbed her face with it.

She let him blot her tears, but she then stepped away. "I wish to unburden my soul and to make amends, but you speak as if you're writing me one of your letters about geology and Spanish verb conjugations."

"Eugénie," Byron said, changing his tone. "You are serious. I won't tease you. Please, tell me."

"I have accused you of seeking to break our engagement when I have something on my soul."

Byron became quiet. Ready to hear what she would say. Why she found him unsuitable. She would say aloud what polite company whispered.

"Yes, Eugénie."

"I cannot go through with the marriage."

"I see." He felt his fears becoming realized.

How could he face her? He hoped to not see her disgust and disdain when he looked into her eyes. And he hoped that her accusation would not be done publicly. He thought if she saw what was in him, what he couldn't remove from himself, then perhaps it was true. That he couldn't want as he wanted, love as he loved, and also be the master of Le Petit Cottage in every way. He was no stranger to snickers and suspicious looks. But out of a silent courtesy from a civil society, he would not be called out. And now, this inevitable but mercifully private refusal.

Byron inhaled and exhaled.

"Now that I see how much your family welcomes me," Eugénie said, "I must be truthful with you. To give you the opportunity to find your mistress for Le Petit Cottage."

None of the words were what he expected. He stopped to reassess. Had he been saved?

"What, dear Eugénie, burdens you so? We are friends."

"I hope you will call me friend after I release you from the engagement."

"There is no other lady I hold in as high regard."

She closed her eyes to gather herself. She opened them and said, "I believe I can make a good home. Manage the servants as I do for my father, as long as our lives are simple. I can be content and be a good mistress."

"I see no problems between us."

"There is one duty I cannot perform."

"And that is?"

"You'll have me say it? Even now, I can't suggest it, let alone say it. Of all things, Byron, I thought you a gentleman."

It occurred to him. The subject so abhorrent to her innocence. That it had nothing to do with him, his fears, but everything to do with her own fears and discomfort. Elation and compassion overwhelmed him. He took both of her hands once again. This time she didn't pull them away. "You need not say a word."

Still, she said, "My mother died in horrible, horrible childbirth —"

"Don't relive those unkind memories," Byron said. "If that is the burden, then let me unburden you, sweet girl," he said. "My Eugénie, I will give you the life you desire. We will have the most cordial friendship a man and woman can have and still be the envy of all who gaze on us. We do have a responsibility to our families. We must produce an heir. You see that, don't you, my dear? But I promise you, my sweet, after that, we will love and be affectionate in the most chaste manner. We will live like sister and brother, without the quarreling. I don't care for quarrels. Do you?" He was already wiping her face.

He took from his breast pocket the signet ring, with the initials *BdM* in the center, a small cluster of grapes etched below the initials. Then he took her left hand.

"You are worth the precious gemstones

that engaged ladies wear, but I offer this simple token. It has been in my mother's family for centuries. If you'll have me, we will visit the vineyard of my ancestors and reclaim it with this ring."

Now she wept uncontrollably. "Byron. How can you accept me under those terms?"

"Easily, my dear," he said, slipping the ring on her finger. "We are perfect for one another. We are a pair."

The ring hung loosely on Eugénie's finger, but she tearfully promised she would guard it well.

XIX

Lucien did all he could to settle his mother's nerves. He refreshed her cup of weak punch with bourbon from his flask and told her to "knock it back." Then he sat her with her company and returned to Alphonse Tournier.

"Is everything all right?" Tournier asked. "Is your mother well?"

Monsieur Lucien sighed. "It's the portrait artist we engaged. My mother insisted on this sitting, I suspect to remind her of her days as a young girl at court in France." He shook his head. "This Le Brun fellow . . ." He pointed his chin to the east parlor. "It pains me to admit it, but Le Brun can't wait for payment. He is holding my mother's portrait for ransom."

"Is this your trouble? Perhaps I can help."

"Oh, no, Tournier. It's too large a debt. Thank you, but we will make an arrangement. He can take my note for a thousand dollars, which of course I'll make good with the harvest. It's a pity it's so dark outside. The cane looks exceptional. Nothing like the miles of cane at La Fleur Blanche . . ."

"Let me help you, Guilbert. It is a small thing. And to see your mother disturbed at her own party. I can't bear it."

"I won't say no," Lucien said. "Let's have another drink." He reached for his flask.

From across the room, Rosalie said, "Look at our fathers."

"As thick as thieves," Laurent said. He turned to the fiddlers and then to Rosalie. The fiddlers changed the music to a rhythm for a quadrille, a dance for at least four couples. Rather than place Rosalie in the dilemma of being rejected as a dancing couple, he said, "I could use fresh air. Can you?"

"Yes, but let me get you a cup of

punch."

"Rosalie." His voice dropped to something grave. "Is your life so charmed?"

She didn't answer. They went outside and strolled down the lane of live oak trees. Rosalie didn't pretend to be ignorant of Laurent's meaning. Even she hadn't quenched her thirst with a cup of punch.

When they were far enough away from view of the house, Laurent reached inside his breast pocket and pulled out a flask. "I have my own fork and napkin as well."

"I'm so sorry," she said.

"Don't pity me, Rosalie," he said tersely. "Don't ever pity me." He instantly regretted his harsh delivery and said, "It's orange water. No alcohol. May I offer you a sip?"

"Just a sip," she said. She removed her glove, cupped her hand. "I can't imagine you wouldn't think less of me if I raised a flask to my lips."

He smiled and poured a few drops into her hand. She sipped. They both laughed. He took a full swallow from the flask.

"I've solved problems for many a

planter in this parish, Rosalie," he said. "I've improved their planting manifold. My father can buy and sell them all. Yet I don't enter their homes when I come to consult. The cook might offer a pan of food to eat outside with my hands, but no drink."

"Laurent," she began, "at the risk of your opinion of us, your opinion of me, I must tell you that this party, this night, is the first time I've entered my grandmother's house as an invited guest. And family member. Mine is the overseer's cottage."

She could see it in his eyes, even in the dark with no candlelight. He was astonished. She had miscalculated and wanted to kick herself. It was that when he spoke, she was certain he had removed his mask in revealing his torment. Now, as he looked at her, and from his lack of response, she realized that by removing her mask prematurely, she had gone too far, when what she sought was to affirm a common bond. There was no way that he could want her now.

"I see."

She spoke up quickly. "With this

known, we can return to the party as friends, I hope. After all, what else is there?" She took a deep breath. *"Spira, spera."*

"Say again?" he asked.

Now she acted, feigning ignorance. "After all —"

"No. What did you say after that?"

"Oh!" she said. *"Spira, spera.* Breath, hope. It's from —"

"Hunchback of Notre-Dame." He could only look at her in disbelief.

"Do you know it?" she asked. "Do you read Victor Hugo?"

"It's not among my favorites, but I saw it staged in Paris."

"Paris, France. I'm told my mother's father is from a town outside of Paris. A relative of the Pierpont family."

"A man could live in Paris and do well," he said. His look was far-away.

"You miss Paris," she said.

"I don't carry a cup, flask, or fork with me in Paris," he said. "My mother is in Paris. She won't return to Louisiana."

"You must miss her terribly." At the

same time she said this to him, she spoke also for herself. Every moment with her mother was a moment stolen.

"Laurent, would you like to return to the party?"

"I prefer the air, Rosalie. It's refreshing."

The sponge cakes and the squab drowned in claret were devoured as fast as Marie and Louise set them out for the guests. The sisters were without refreshments to serve and went to the cookhouse to see what they could bring to the party. The embers in the hearth had long cooled. The floor had been swept of any flour and feathers. The eggs and butter were in clay jars to keep cool. Pots, knives, mixing spoons, were in their places. In fact, everything had been put away. It seemed that Miss Lily had dismissed herself for the evening.

Lucien gave the fiddlers the signal to rest their bows. Dancing ceased; murmurs now filled the room. He tapped a crystal punch cup with a fork, and slowly the guests assembled around him.

"Friends," Lucien called out. "I won't hold up the festivities with speeches."

To that, Byron and Pearce shouted, "Hear, hear!"

"I only want to thank you for coming to wish Byron and his fellow cadet Robinson Pearce *bonne chance* and Godspeed on their journey upriver to West Point. We wish that they prepare in excellence and be ready to defend their friends and family and their country. And by that, I mean these Louisiana parishes, the gulf, and waterways, and our way of life."

The crowd hooted with glee.

"I want to welcome Mademoiselle Eugénie Duhon, daughter of our good friend Colonel Étienne Duhon of the Duhon Plantation, into our home and in time into our family."

At this, Aunt Agnes, now awake, said, "No, no! No, monsieur, no!" The guests for the most part saw her outburst as levity and laughed heartily, for the crowd was young and was not concerned with proprieties. Only Madame and the other matrons understood that the hint of engagement was improper without the representation of the Duhon patriarch.

Lucien spoke over the chaperone and the quieting laughter. "Last, I invite you to see the portrait of the mistress of this plantation, by the artist from a lineage of artists, Claude Le Brun."

Lucien took his mother by the arm and brought her to the threshold of the west parlor. He looked to Le Brun with a plea. Le Brun answered with a curt nod and a low bow to Lucien and Madame. This gesture was clearly for show. With Lucien's plea acknowledged, he escorted his mother into the parlor and helped her onto her throne.

Le Brun had already untied the cords wrapped around the cover and easel that kept the painting a mystery. "Messieurs, mesdames, and mesdemoiselles, please form a line to enter and view," he said. "With no further delay, I present Madame Sylvie Bernardin de Maret Dacier Guilbert of Le Petit Cottage, St. James Parish." With that, he slowly and carefully lifted the cloth, up and over the canvas.

Upon the complete unveiling of the portrait, the fiddlers, at Lucien's direction, played two notes. *Voi-là!*

Although only Madame and Lucien were able to see the portrait first, the guests applauded the moment of the reveal.

Madame was speechless at the sight of herself. Her likeness. She didn't expect the background to be darkened with splotches of a café coloring, but she grew used to the hair melding, almost fading, into the background. But it was the face. Something pert about the mouth. And the eyes. Perhaps Le Brun was kind after all, she thought. For the eyes were brighter than the eyes that looked back at her from the vanity mirror. And then she clasped her hands in recognition! Of course! He had brought out the expression of her much younger self from when she had posed with her friend Marie-Thérèse Charlotte, painted by none other than Madame Vigée Le Brun.

Madame Pierpont removed her spectacles from her drawstring purse and slipped them on her nose. She peered closely to study the painting.

Lucien cocked his head and examined the portrait. He looked at Le Brun. Then at his mother. He asked, "Mother? Mother? Are you . . . pleased?"

Madame Sylvie remained speechless. Even she didn't know how to explain what she saw.

Lucien then gave the signal to the fiddlers to play. Most of the dancers fled the line to return to dancing.

With a small congratulatory crowd clustered around Madame, Le Brun called to Thisbe. She went to him without looking to her mistress.

"So?"

Thisbe knew what he wanted, and this time, she didn't put on a pretense and ask for clarification. She had let her voice and quick mind out of their vault, and couldn't return them, even under the threat of every possible consequence from the onlooking Guilberts. "I watched every day while you painted. I think you wanted the picture to talk to whoever sees it. To say more than 'There is Madame Sylvie.' "

"How so?" Le Brun asked.

"Madame is old, but you made something young about her."

He nodded his approval. "There is a portrait," he said, "of two girls. My relative painted it. One is the queen's daughter. The other, I believe, is your Madame. I looked for that face within Madame Sylvie. So, you see her years, but also her spark."

"But, Monsieur Le Brun, there is something else. Something about the face that is Madame Sylvie, but it's not Madame Sylvie," Thisbe said. "It confuses me."

He smiled at her but didn't reply.

"I'm sorry, Monsieur Le Brun," Thisbe said. "I didn't mean to insult your painting of Madame Sylvie."

"I will tell you a secret," he said, dismissing her apology.

She looked around to see if anyone noticed them. When she turned to him, he was still smiling.

"I used Mademoiselle Rosalie for some features, and I put a few touches for age."

The party would go on for about an hour despite the scant refreshments. Except

667

for the few minutes that Lucien made his announcement, the fiddlers played without a rest or refreshments. They had been told not to set out their hats for tips, but they did so anyway in the final hour.

Byron and Pearce commended Le Brun and stepped back into the main salon, leaving Madame to enjoy the compliments of her admirers and to revel in the sight of the signet ring on Eugénie's slender finger. Soon, the fiddlers would head back to the quarter and the guests would leave. As tempting as it would be to lie with each other in the garçonnière for a few hours before dawn, Byron and Pearce agreed that the time to completely button up and prepare for caution and abstinence was upon them. They planned to rest on the cool lower porch and say their final goodbyes to family and host and be on their way.

They stood with their backs to the parlor and faced the direction of the fiddlers.

"I'm glad for this party," Pearce said. "Your father's speech was a success: short and sincere. Your grandmother's portrait, elegant."

"All is right," Byron said.

"And I congratulate you," Pearce said. "Truly."

"It will be two years yet. Graduation first, of course."

The tail end of these words is what Eugénie heard when she and Jane approached from behind. She remained quiet with Jane at her side, perhaps hoping to hear more of the congratulations. As Eugénie was about to tap her beloved's shoulder, she heard the second part of Pearce's congratulatory speech:

"Say the word, and I will be at your side, my saber stiff and in hand to thrust open the bridal gate, should you find yourself unable on your wedding night."

From there, the room spun. At first, the high pitch was thought to come from one of the fiddlers' bows. Screams followed. Then the young lady, Eugénie, fell to the floor, her gown and crinoline billowing around her. Byron went to take her arms and uplift her, but she wrestled in his arms, her skin bright pink. Aunt Agnes did all she could to pry Byron from Eugénie, but he wouldn't release her.

Jane pulled out her sword and held it over her head. She swung it at Pearce. He ducked. She raised the sword high once again and swung. Pearce ducked again. Lucien came from behind Jane and yanked the sword from her grip.

No one could make sense of the actions playing out before them, least of all Pearce. The room filled with sounds of astonishment. But the loudest cries came from Eugénie, who screamed, "My honor! My honor!" Pearce could only see and feel the Guilberts, his beloved's fiancée, and people of St. James Parish bearing down on him.

Byron, unable to comfort Eugénie, released her. He knew who he was and what was expected of him. The people of St. James gathered around him, calling him to do what he must. Byron rose. Walked to Pearce, who still reeled from escaping Jane and her sword. Byron removed his gloves from his belt. He slapped Pearce hard enough to turn his face.

"Robinson Pearce, you have insulted my fiancée. Her family and mine. There is but one word that can restore those injuries: honor." He seemed to breathe between each word.

Pearce's face went completely white. He had no words. But he tried. "Byron." He was again slapped.

"Well done," Lucien told his son.

"You see," Madame said to Eugénie. "Byron will restore your honor. He will kill his friend."

Jane added, "If Pearce kills Byron, I will kill Pearce."

"Byron won't be shot, silly girl," Madame said. "He will do the shooting."

Lucien took control of what would happen next. "Pearce, you'll stay in the garçonnière. Byron, in the house with the family." He said to Pearce, "Your second will get you at five thirty. I suggest you sleep."

"This is madness," Pearce said. "Byron. End this. We don't have to do this."

"This is tradition!" Madame exclaimed.

Le Brun, who had been watching, spoke up. "This old tradition is no longer carried out. No one in polite society follows these practices. And when they do it, it's all for show."

"I apologize with all of my soul," Pearce said, turning as he spoke to Byron, Lucien, Madame, and Eugénie. "What can I do to make amends?"

At the utterance of the apology, a few guests shrugged and left. *It is over,* they thought, for these days, the sincere apology was all that was needed to fix things between gentlemen. And while people enjoyed a good scandal, no one wanted to have to be called as a witness, should the need arise.

Unfortunately, Eugénie could only sob, "My honor, my honor."

Lucien, still holding Jane's sword, saw Tournier walking toward the door with hat and cane. He rushed to him.

"Alphonse!" he called.

"It's late, monsieur," Tournier said. "You have affairs to sort."

Lucien tried to speak, but Tournier would hear no more. He put up his hand and called for the stable boy. Within minutes Tournier was seated and at the gate in his carriage.

"We have overstayed," Tournier called

to the couple, who hadn't rejoined the party. "Good evening, Mademoiselle Guilbert."

Rosalie and Laurent appeared to be awakened from their blissful melancholy, although it was clear from the elder Tournier that things had changed.

Laurent turned to Rosalie, but she spoke first, to his father. "Thank you for your presence, Monsieur Tournier." To Laurent, who was still holding her hand, she said, "Good success to you, Laurent."

"Is this goodbye?"

She looked at Laurent's father. "I'm afraid so."

"But —"

She kissed his hands, something ill-advised for a young lady to do. At this point, it didn't matter. "I don't know what happened in the house," Rosalie said, "but I know when something cannot be mended."

"Laurent!" his father called.

"I'll see her to the house, Father," he said.

"Good Laurent," Rosalie said, "my

house is there." She pointed in the direction of the quarter. "Perhaps it's best, Laurent. Bonne chance, my dream." Yes, she did a cruel thing. She left him with *spira, spera,* two words from Victor Hugo, her well wishes, and a life with her at his side that he would miss and ponder for days, if not years.

Tournier's tone grew terse. The younger man climbed into the carriage. This time, Rosalie stood and watched the Tournier carriage disappear into the dark.

XXI

Lily slept hard, minutes after she laid her head on her pallet. The sun would rise and rise again. And rise again. And again. What did that matter to her without her boy?

Marie and Louise put the dishes in the barrel of water and lye soap to wash in the morning. They returned the rugs and furniture to the main salons. There was more to do to restore the house, but they walked to their shared cabin in the quarter and woke their children and husbands to feed them. The sisters looked forward to three hours of sleep, which was better than no hours of sleep, but they remained on their feet to tend to their home, and for a time on their backs, both attending to their husbands' needs.

675

Marie and Louise knew well the dangers of separation between married field and house servants and the danger of husbands being fed from the pots of other women.

Rosalie walked past her grandmother's house, down to the quarter past her stepfather's cabin, and finally to her cottage. She didn't have to know the details of what had happened in the house to know she had lost everything the evening promised. Everything within her grasp: if not the acceptance of her grandmother, then at the least a public claim to the Guilbert name and a life of her own without the stigma and reality of enslavement. And there was Laurent Tournier and the possibility of a life beyond what her father could give her. She had played her part to the end in securing the interest of Laurent, but to her surprise, she hadn't calculated the ache of the sudden loss of him. It wasn't quite love between them. They didn't know each other. The bereavement was the loss of what she had gained with him, a kindred spirit, and the moments they allowed their masks to

676

fall away. That night she cried for the loss of him in spite of herself.

Madame fussed while Thisbe removed the gold-wired emerald earrings from each ear. She sat still while her servant dipped a towel into the basin and rubbed the rouge from her cheeks. When she was dressed for bed, Madame ordered Thisbe to kneel at the prie-dieu and pray that Pearce's sins be forgiven and that he be spared the worst levels of hell when he was shot and killed in a few hours. After the prayers were said, Madame told Thisbe, "I've not forgotten. I'm only tired."

Thisbe gathered Madame referred to how she spoke up at the party during the business between Madame, Lucien, and Le Brun, but she didn't fret over what was to come. She too was tired.

Lucien sat on a stool in the well of the garçonnière to guard Pearce, the flask in his hands, the bottle at his foot. Jane's father's unsheathed sword stood against the railing.

■ ■ ■ ■

Pearce sat upstairs in the room of the garçonnière for an hour, his bag packed. The turn of events was so uncontrollably swift he couldn't grasp them or harness his sheer disbelief over the certainty of what was to transpire.

Byron removed his uniform, laid the gray pants inside the jacket, and rolled them to fit inside his traveling bag. He said his prayers, gave his confession to his Lord, and put on his trousers, shirt, vest, and jacket. This was a family matter. To duel as a gentleman was respectful, and in the cause of his fiancée's honor, expected. To shoot another cadet while in uniform, however, was to dishonor the uniform and surely earn him a discharge from the Academy. He would do what was expected and righteous. He would use the family pistol.

■ ■ ■ ■

When he could sit no longer, Pearce paced diagonally from one side of the room to the other, crossed over, and repeated the drill in the other direction. He attempted to write a brief letter to the widow Stewart to explain his circumstance and fate but couldn't make sense of the events. He kicked the bedpost. He had read about duels but could scarcely believe that he would be engaged in one. With his love. And wasn't he to have a second to handle his affairs, or to check and hold his pistol? He had no true friend besides Byron to act on his behalf. At that realization, he laughed.

The portrait artist was right, he thought. In any other part of the country, of the world, both gentlemen would turn and take aim at the dark clouds overhead. Apologies would be given and accepted. But not here, where pride, even false pride, overruled sense. He didn't know this South. This Louisiana. He was a stranger among people who clung to their practices for no other reason than it upheld who they were and how they lived. And now, they expected him to sleep peacefully, rise, aim a pistol at his love, and shoot.

How could he love a man so bound by this pride? A man who could kiss his mouth so deeply, and yet aim for his heart?

At five twenty-five a.m., Byron loaded one bullet only. He would give his pistol to his father, to inspect and hold. He walked the two hundred feet to the garçonnière.

He entered the well of the tower and found his father at his post, bottle and flask emptied and at his boot. Jane's sword remained faithful through the night, propped up against the bottom staircase.

"Father, Father."

Lucien snored.

Byron bent and tapped him on the shoulder. "Father, Father."

"What? Who?" Lucien peeled himself out of sleep, yawning, stretching, his son getting the full brunt of his breath fouled by tobacco and bourbon.

"Father, wake up. It's time."

"Yes! Yes! It's time!" Lucien rose, was overcome by his own unsteadiness, and fell back down onto the stool. He wiped his eyes, looked around, perhaps recounting to himself what events had brought him to sit guard through the final hours of the night. "Yes," he said, in a moment of clarity. "Oh, yes." His next attempt to find his footing was successful.

"I'll see you both under the grand live oak." Byron left his father. He walked to the prominent tree. *Live oak,* he thought. He had sat under that tree and laid his head in his beloved's lap, while Pearce read poems by Lord Byron, for whom his father named him.

Lucien staggered up the steps to retrieve Pearce. He found the room tidy. Empty. He looked for a note, but there was no note on the desk or bed. As far as Lucien could see, in his foggy state, there was no Pearce.

He made his way down the stairs and then to where Byron stood stiffly, soberly, under the live oak.

Byron saw that his father was alone. As

much as he didn't want to meet his friend, he had pushed himself in this unstoppable forward motion. And now, he didn't know what to make of the absence of his friend.

"Pearce?"

"Gone."

"Gone?"

His father nodded.

The two men stared at each other. Wordless. Finally, Byron, who wasn't aware that he had been holding his breath, exhaled fully, then inhaled. "I didn't want to shoot at my friend. Not even in ceremony." Then the other outcome occurred to him. "Or be shot."

"But Eugénie Duhon. Colonel Duhon."

"Father . . ."

"Tell me the insult, son. Did she hear something, something so distasteful, so vulgar? We are both men. You need not spare me."

"She did hear something entirely distasteful."

"And what was said? What was it?"

Byron knew what his father asked. It

was the question that had never really gone away, like the memory of his long-lost Jesse. He could put his father's mind to rest. He had become expert in doing that.

"I won't repeat Pearce's unfortunate words."

"I deserve to know."

"Father, you do know."

"What does this mean?"

"It means I must go."

"But you must set things right. For the Guilbert name. For the Duhons."

Byron gave his father the family pistol. If his father found him an abomination to God and to the Guilbert name, he had one bullet to prune his orchard. And who would convict a father for doing what he must do?

Once he had turned away from his father, Byron would not turn around. He walked the paces as he would have walked if he and Pearce carried out their business. He waited to hear the click. When he didn't hear it, he continued on until he was inside his grandmother's house.

XXII

Byron meant to see his grandmother
first, but he went to the room where Eugénie and Jane slept. He stood at their
bedside, afraid he might awaken them,
afraid he might frighten Eugénie. He
couldn't imagine a frightened Jane under
any circumstance. That thought and seeing Eugénie nestled in Jane's possession
about the waist made him smile a little.
He hadn't seen Eugénie so serene. So
well protected.

Mercifully, he found Eugénie's hand
free of Jane's embrace. He looked at Eugénie. And at the ring, dull but visible
beneath the mosquito netting. He asked
himself if he could do it. Not the mere
feat of removing the ring without disturbing Eugénie, but that final act of breaking the engagement in a cowardly fash-

ion, without giving her the opportunity to cast her rightful incriminations. This much-wronged girl deserved the chance to hurl her worst at him. But the ring so near, and loosely committed to the sleeping girl's finger, came to him easily, a willing accomplice, when he breached the netted barrier and slid it off her finger.

Eugénie remained undisturbed in Jane's embrace. Perhaps the two shared a dream. He found Eugénie's peace remarkable.

It was the boots. The sound of boots that had awakened Thisbe. She thought it was Monsieur Lucien, but she saw Byron. She laid her head down, closed her eyes, and kept her ears open.

Byron pulled the mosquito netting away, knelt, and kissed his grandmother several times on her forehead until she awakened.

"Grandmère, Grandmère," he said.

"Did you kill your friend? I heard no shots."

"I love Pearce," he said tenderly. "I couldn't kill him."

Now she was fully awake. She sat up. "No, no. You love your family. And the girl. Think, Byron. What will become of us?"

"I don't know, but I must leave."

"To the Academy?" she asked.

"I don't know," he said. "I don't know if I can return there."

"Will you return to us?"

Byron shook his head while she spoke. "I only know, I must go, Grandmère."

"This cannot be. It cannot."

"It is, Grandmère. And I return to you this." He held the ring out to her.

"She gave it back to you? She rejected you?"

"I took it," he said.

"Thief," Madame said. "You steal my grandfather's legacy. My great-grandchildren's legacy."

"I return to you what is yours."

She began to sob. "No. It can't be."

"I must go, Grandmère. I can't be here."

She wiped her face, then pushed the

ring back to him. "The Bernardin de Maret vineyard is just outside of Paris. I was young and had no one to negotiate for me, but I knew to put my name, my parents' name, and the vineyard on the contract. My gift to my children and grandchildren. It was all I knew to do to keep my parents alive. My grandfather alive."

"Oh, Grandmère."

"If you don't marry the Duhon girl, go to France. Make the claim."

"I will."

"In the drawer, in the small box, are the good pieces of jewelry your grandfather gave me. Take them. They can be pawned for your passage."

Byron wept at his grandmother's bed. "Tell Eugénie . . . tell her —"

"My sweet boy, what is there to say?"

Byron went to the cottage last. Rosalie had yet to put on her shoes, but she was dressed to go to the commissary.

"What happened?" she asked. "Where is Pearce?"

"My sister, my sister. It is all a lifetime away."

"I'm afraid to ask."

"The short answer is, I can't marry Eugénie. It seems I love my friend more. I could never harm him. Not even for my family. And yet I would have, simply because it's done."

"Byron, none of this makes sense."

"Exactly," he said. "None of it."

"Where is Pearce?"

"I pray he's up the river on his way to the Hudson. I pray I can catch him."

"Oh, Byron. You look so sad."

"As do you. Is there no good news for any of us?"

"I'm afraid for us there's only spoiled pumpkins and mice," she said.

"I will miss you, Rosalie. I will miss this life and everyone I love."

"But you'll come back, won't you?"

"I don't know. I might write."

"Please. If you write, send a letter to me, so I can know how you are. And address it to the commissary. Not your grandmother's house."

He didn't protest her choice of words. "I will." Then he hugged his sister.

There was no escaping the inevitable. Le Brun was packed and standing impatiently in the great room. He waited for payment. "Please tell them," he said to Marie and Louise. Marie went up to Madame's salon while Louise went to Lucien's office.

Lucien entered the house from the front. Marie and Louise made note of the mud on his boots. They would have to beat the rugs. Again.

With Lucien in the house, Madame felt safe to come down to meet Le Brun, Thisbe at her side.

"Madame Guilbert. Monsieur Guilbert," Le Brun said. "I heard no shot this morning. Good."

"If you say so," Madame said.

"I've painted the portrait. I've shown the portrait. My payment, if you please, and I'll leave your home and your hospitality. I've held up my carriage and must pay extra, as it is."

Madame looked to Lucien.

Lucien said, "What I have is a note of promise for one thousand dollars." He produced a slip of paper that Le Brun didn't look at.

"I cannot accept that note," Le Brun said.

"But why not?" Madame asked. "We are people of our word. Respected people. You saw the people who came to our party last night. Would such people come to the house of poor people?"

Le Brun spoke calmly. Plainly. "I didn't make a promise with you; I made a contract. An agreement. I painted a portrait and gave you my time when I had better use for it."

Madame was indignant. "Better use?"

"Mother, please climb down," Lucien said, referring to her figurative high horse. He turned to Le Brun. "We are all on equal footing here, Monsieur Le Brun. What can we do to satisfy this debt?"

"To satisfy the debt?" Le Brun asked.

"Yes, Monsieur Le Brun," he said, but by tone it was clear they were not on equal footing. "What can we do to erase the debt?"

Claude Le Brun turned to Thisbe. "I will take your female servant as a free woman. If she is willing."

"No!" Madame said. "No! She is my property. She is mine. I am owed her."

Le Brun looked to Thisbe. "Are you willing to come with me?"

Lucien said, "Speak."

Madame said, "I lose too much! I lose too much!"

Thisbe said, "Monsieur Le Brun, what will I be? What will I do?"

Madame said, "How dare you ask?" She raised her hand to slap Thisbe, but Lucien took his mother's wrist, stopping her.

Le Brun answered. "Assistant."

"She cannot decide," Madame objected, her hand bound by her son. "She cannot decide. We decide."

"Assistant," Thisbe said. "But first, a contract."

"A contract?" Le Brun asked.

"A contract with my name. My mother's name. My father's name. This place.

This day. The terms. One thousand dollars. Assistant to Le Brun. Free woman."

Madame moaned and howled. Lucien clapped and hopped from one foot to the other, wobbly as his balance was. This brought Marie and Louise running into the room to see the commotion.

Madame sank completely to the floor.

Thisbe stood at Le Brun's side.

Marie and Louise looked at each other. What did it all mean?

"For the contract," Le Brun said to Thisbe, "a proper name is needed."

She smiled. Very small, but apparent in her eyes, a trace on her lips. "My mother named me Marguerite. Marguerite Carver. My grandfather carved the bedposts in the house. My grandfather came to this plantation from Africa. This is what I know."

While Thisbe spoke, Madame screamed for Thisbe to shut her mouth. "Be quiet. Say nothing."

Lucien said calmly, "I will send for Rosalie. She writes well. I, Monsieur, am unable at present. My mother misspells."

"Please, with haste," Le Brun said. "I

would like to leave."

"Monsieur Le Brun," Thisbe said, "may I run to my parents?"

"Of course," he said.

No one had helped Madame up. She was on her knees. "You will run away? After all that I've done for you? The life I've given you? What I've spared you from?"

Thisbe thought before she spoke. And when she did, her words were simple, but delivered in her best French. "I have learned everything from you, Madame Guilbert, and I am grateful. I know the important things of being a lady. I know which books are good although I cannot read them. I know many things because I listen. But this was a gift as given to me by the Holy Mother herself. I had no cards of my own, but I still played the hand dealt me. Thank you very much, Madame Guilbert. Thank you."

Marguerite Carver removed her shoes and first ran to the cookhouse.

"I'm gone, Miss Lily. I'm gone."

"French painter? Figured so."

"Yes'm, Miss Lily!"

She wrapped her arms around Lily, but Lily was always hard to get a grip on.

"Well, go on, Dis Be. Go on."

It was the last time anyone called her Thisbe or any name resembling Thisbe.

She ran barefoot to the cane to find her mother, father, aunties, and sisters.

EPILOGUE

At last! Patience rewarded. While this, dear reader, is not the precise order of what happened next, this is what happened to all concerned.

The Duhon carriage arrived for Eugénie. She took with her her chaperone, Jane, and Virginia Wilder. Eugénie and Jane found happiness on the Duhon property, even after Colonel Duhon and Grand-aunt Agnes died, one first, and the other shortly after. Eugénie cared for rebels in gray while Jane proudly wore her father's war jacket minus the buttons and defended the Duhon Plantation against the Union soldiers. After the war Eugénie and Jane remained on the property. Eugénie refused all suitors. She had no need of them. She had her Jane.

That October, as cane swelled and begged for harvest, the banks and assorted creditors bore down on Lucien Guilbert with the swiftness of knife wielders in the cane. *Two months more,* he asked. *Two months more.* They wouldn't wait for Christmas. Le Petit Cottage was the property of the bank. (However, in November, with the presidential election and win of the "Kentucky Baboon," as he had been referred to in the quaint dining room, the affairs of Le Petit Cottage and its debt were forgotten. The talk of secession rumbled and then flourished. Banks had other matters to attend to, starting with the issue of Confederate tender.)

The harvest went on, under the October sun. The field hands hacked and stripped cane, loaded the stalks onto carts that went to the sugarhouse. Even with the antiquated presser and boiling pans, the men and women pressed the cane into juice, which was boiled and crystallized to yield molasses, rum, and sugar. The

enslaved but unsupervised people continued on in anticipation of the new owner
who never came forward to claim Le
Petit Cottage.

When Miss Lily first realized she cooked
for no one but herself, she brought the
stews to the quarter to feed those who
were there. And when she realized the
house was free of its white masters, even
if temporarily, Lily decided it was time to
enter the house. If anything, to see how
the Guilberts lived. One Guilbert she had
nursed, the other had murdered her
child. Those Guilberts she had fed all
those years.

Lily was drawn to the sunny room on
the west side where the family laid out
their dead. The faded pink chair in the
middle of the small room. With no white
people in the house, no masters or mistresses, only the Creole twins who continued to dust and scrub, Miss Lily sat
down on the pink throne. Surprisingly,
the chair took her weight, and in doing
so, it became her chair. She looked at and
then through the portrait of the old white
lady, Miss Silvee Gilbert, who once tried

to tell her something about cooking with love.

As for Master and Mistress Guilbert, it was a gorgeous night in October of 1860 when Lucien loaded the rockaway with what belongings of value he could. Once upon a time, that harvest moon was a blessing that allowed the field hands to work well into the night. This time, Lucien cursed that moon. It shone so bright the Guilberts could be seen fleeing for shame at their fall from society. He cursed the painting, the downfall of them all, and refused his mother's pleas to bring it with them. He would destroy it before he allowed it to hang in their next home. He did, however, carefully place the Singer sewing machine that Rosalie persuaded him to buy so that it would travel securely. "This will be our fortune, Father," his daughter had said with great optimism. He listened to his daughter these days and surrendered the reins of their fate to her. And wisely so. Within four months, she received a contract from the Confederate secretary of war to sew uniforms for the foot soldiers. She followed the practice of the grandfather she had never known, to change legal tender to hard coins and gold. It was her father's confidence in the Confederacy that urged her to question its stability.

The Guilberts settled in a townhouse in East Baton Rouge. Madame, in her remaining years, refused to look at Rosalie, even as Rosalie cared for her. Madame Sylvie soon stopped going out in public, as she couldn't escape townspeople who reminded her how much her enterprising granddaughter favored her. Rosalie, who could have easily escaped her mixed-blood heritage by having children with a white man, brought home instead the darkest man she could find and sat him at the dining room table for supper. Madame Guilbert died on the spot.

Lucien retired from any and all authority and was given a monthly allowance by his daughter. Even though his years were numbered, no one thought of him as dying, but as reciting Homer and Lord Byron, among others, and fading away, pining for his son, and at times for his closest half brother, Henri.

As for Henri, he proved to possess an attribute of his father, the one the Creoles called "Vié Pè" and the Africans called "Ol' Pap." He knew how to talk to people, especially to those on the lower rungs of society. As his captors took him away that fateful night that he had helped his father's wife bury Bayard Guilbert's gold, he struck up a proposition with the men. "For me, what do I care?" he said to them. "Take it all, but a few pieces of gold. Then ship me to the hardest cane boss in Cuba. I will work every day and laugh, just to imagine the face of my tormentor when she sees what is left to her." So, the men, guided by Henri, circled back to the plantation. In the dead of night, they returned to the burial place of Vié Pè's gold and dug up the goatskin satchel, leaving a few pieces to be found. His captors had quickly grown to like this poor devil, and let him off in Mexico, where he, like his father, made himself new in a new place, and he became Enrique Gilberto, fisherman. His descendants in Mexico and St. James continue to thrive.

On his journey, Byron found Pearce upriver. Pearce tried with great effort to be unforgiving to Byron for almost taking his life. For choosing his family and Eugénie over his life. But it wasn't in Pearce's nature to be unforgiving. Once the fear for his life was over, the depths of a broken heart took its place. Byron vowed to live foremost to mend Pearce's trust and his heart. Pearce held him to his pledge and made him suffer for as long as he could hold out.

The two sailed past the Hudson that guarded West Point Academy, and then they joined a ship bound for France.

It took some doing, but Byron was able to prove himself the heir to the Bernardin de Maret vineyard. He worked with the convent so they would continue to receive a profit. But with the vineyard returned to him, he was free to put the Bernardin de Maret signet ring on Pearce's finger. Snug, but a fit, nonetheless. The vineyard never achieved the esteem of the great vineyards of France, but it was old, and it was charming. He and Pearce lived quietly, happily, into the next century at La Maison Bernardin de Maret.

Claude Le Brun gave Marguerite her contract immediately and bought her a pair of moccasins before they left St. James. Once in Maine, Marguerite studied painting and gave Claude her thoughts on many subjects while at the retreat. As they engaged more in conversation, she told him outright that she had little interest in painting, but she would like to use her graphite and inks for words. In her sixteen years she had already gained a collection of words. Creole, English, and French words. Claude and Marguerite settled in Paris, France. She held on to her contract that proclaimed her free, but she never married Claude. Their son carried the name Claude Le Brun.

In her leisure, she thought of her life before France. Before Maine. Before Le Brun. The faces of her family, Miss Lily, more and more a memory. She wrote their names. She thought of Madame. There were kind thoughts. And rage. But she never forgot the education. It was much, much later in her own life that she would know Madame's pain. Miss Lily's pain. The pain of mother losing child. An only child. Perhaps this saved her from purely hating Madame — knowing about the babies that came from Madame's womb only to die. By her count, eight? Nine? More? Even though Marguerite had her son until he himself was a great-grandfather at seventy-three, she yearned for her time to be reunited with her Claude, who always seemed little. Her little Claude. For her grandchildren, greats and great-greats, she wrote her story. They didn't cherish this journal, written in Creole, French, and English. For who wanted to know of or be reminded of slavery? That old institution. Marguerite's journal lies somewhere inside the Carver–Le Brun home, waiting to be found. One day, her descendants would read and cherish her life and remembrances. That was Marguerite's hope, as she lived to see France come out from under a second great war. In spite of all that she had seen and lived through, Marguerite never grew out of

the habit of waving to airplanes, the great
marvels of the sky.

A NOTE FROM THE AUTHOR

My maternal great-grandparents, Dean and Mariah Edwards, were both born into enslavement. My paternal three times great-grandfather, Alexander Lloyd, fought and died as a soldier in the segregated Union Army in the Civil War. My paternal grandmother, Edith King Lloyd Williams, often shared memories of "Gamma," Mahalia Lloyd, who raised her and received a monthly Civil War widow's pension. So, why, why, *why* would I choose to write mainly about a white slaveholding family instead of about the people who closely reflect my own ancestry?

As a young writer I was frustrated by the lack of contemporary Black YA novels and vowed to never write about slavery or the Civil Rights era. My vow fell away decades later when I wrote *One Crazy Summer,* set in the post–Civil Rights era. In the years following, three impressions — two dreams and the other very much real — would challenge my resolve to never write about slavery. First, while at a Vermont College of Fine Arts residency, I daydreamed of a young white West Point cadet grooming his horse. I realized his sensual brush strokes were about his longing for his love, a fellow cadet. I let this go. At yet another residency, I awakened from a dream in which I heard singing and drumming and saw a West African woman throwing her baby into the ocean; the singing and drumming were joyous, the woman's act and tears were a victory. These sounds and images, along with the feeling of immense joy, as incongruous as they might seem, stayed with me. I knew I would do something with this second impression. Yet it was the third incident that compelled me to envision and write *A Sitting in St. James.* I was on a panel for a screening of the documentary *The Black Panthers: Vanguard of the Revolution.* A boy no older than twelve stood in the back of the theater sobbing before the microphone. He asked, "Why do they hate us?" *They* being white people and specifically the white police officers in the documentary. The panelist next to me poked me and said, "You're here for the children. Answer." I scrambled for words and said, "When they see us, they don't see human beings." I tried to explain myself, but I knew I had nowhere else to go but to talk about the roots of racism in the so-called justification for all forms of disregard for Black humanity: slavery.

I was plagued by my jumbled and uninspired answer long after the boy had asked the question. I saw his face and heard his voice with every killing of an unarmed Black person at the hands of police or those acting as vigilantes. "Why do they hate us?" I knew I would attempt to answer in story, about the source of disregard for our lives. I heard drumming, singing, and pleading in a language I couldn't make out. I only knew that the woman who threw her child into the ocean as an act of liberation would help me tell it. Even with her presence near, I struggled to focus wholly on the free and enslaved Black people. That was when the West Point cadet from the planter class stopped grooming his horse and spoke to me. He said he loved the land and his way of life, and that he would fight, even die, to protect it. This and other connecting thoughts brought to mind Toni Morrison's interview on the *Charlie Rose* show. When asked about racism, Morrison posed the question to white people: "What are you without racism?" She broke it down and concluded, "White people have a very, very serious problem, and they should start thinking about what they can do about it. Take me out of it." Yes! I thought. Take Thisbe out of it. And Hannah, Lily, Jesse, Marie, Louise, Marcelle, Georgie, the Carvers, Rosalie, Laurent, John, Camille, Jack, Selma, Henri, and the grandson Henri never saw. Take the free and enslaved Black people out of it. While they would be present in the story, I wouldn't task them to answer the boy's question or to prove themselves extraordinary or human. Instead, I would look at a family whose livelihood insisted on slavery, and the enduring legacy of racism handed down to their heirs, regardless of their connection to an antebellum past.

The backstory of the cadet's family took me to the French and the Haitian Revolutions, and ultimately to the Louisiana Territory, as I figured out the family's lives and viewpoints along this timeline. What would they think and believe, and why? I knew I couldn't write from my ancestral understanding, and that I had to also resist an American understanding of history as well.

I had already been a fan of the diverse Louisiana culture, but my journey into the research gave me an even deeper appreciation for a history and culture that had been taught to me through an American lens. I was surprised to learn that the term "Creole" in the Louisiana Territory in the early eighteenth century initially applied to white Catholic French-speaking people born in the colony, descendants of French and Spanish settlers. A Code Noir was established in 1724 by the French government to control the interactions between the white colonists and free and enslaved Black people and Native Americans.

These laws were concerned with religious practice and rights (and the lack thereof for people of color), criminal justice, interrelations — particularly a prohibition on interracial marriage — and establishing plantation work standards between the enslaved and their slaveholder. For example, slaveholders were not to punish enslaved people, but were to instead bring the offending person before the Superior Council to be adjudicated and punished. (When the territory came under Spanish rule, the Code Noir was replaced with the Código Negro.) Even with the codes in place in the territory, they weren't always adhered to or enforced. For example, while marriage between white men and Black or Native American women was outlawed, interracial marriages were illegally performed by clergy. For more information on the 1724 Code Noir, and to see images of the original document, I recommend Michael T. Pasquier's article: www.64par ishes.org/entry/code-noir-of-louisiana.

In spite of the Code Noir, a vibrant Creole culture was born of free and enslaved Africans and Caribbeans, Native Americans, French, and Spanish, who came together to socialize, engage in commerce, and practice Catholicism. Race was not a qualifier; they all identified as Louisiana Creoles. (For more detailed background on the Louisiana Creole identity, I further recommend www.louisianaperspectives.wordpress.com/2018/02/13/a-primer-on-the-evolution-of-creole-identity-in-louisiana/.) The burgeoning culture was facilitated in the 1740s by the Kouri-Vini language, or Louisiana Creole, a French-based language with African, Caribbean, Native American, and Spanish influences, not to be confused with Louisiana French spoken by French and Acadians. Kouri-Vini, so infused into the history and culture of Louisiana, is now endangered, as currently fewer than 10,000 people speak it today. In *The Story of French New Orleans,* Dianne Guenin-Lelle points out that many a white Creole child spoke Kouri-Vini taught to them by the Black Creole women who raised them. Lucien's use of Louisiana Creole is a nod to the language he learned as a child but is also spoken to irritate his

French-born, royalist mother.

Although *A Sitting in St. James* would take place generations later, in the mid-nineteenth century, I had to understand and then create the social, political, and personal points of view of the characters in the Guilbert family. Roger W. Shugg's *Origins of Class Struggle in Louisiana 1840-1875* was instrumental in helping me pin down the Guilberts' social standing and their attitudes toward other groups and classes of whites within and outside of their own planter class. While I had been taught about the Louisiana Purchase as a positive part of the nation's expansion, this view was not shared by Louisiana Creoles, leery of the encroaching Americans who came from outside states to take advantage of land grants that were available. The whiteness of Americans was irrelevant to the Louisiana planter class. The differences that threatened the Creole way of life included French versus American, French- and francophone-speaking versus English-speaking, Catholicism versus Protestantism, old landowners versus new landowners, socializing with free people of color versus little to no tolerance of free — and relatively mobile — people of color. These were far from the only clashes in culture within Louisiana. An outside gaze might unite Black Louisianans under the banner of race; however, conflicts between African Americans and Black Creoles tempered the working and social relationships between the two groups, divided along linguistic, religious, cultural, and economic lines. While there were free African Americans in Louisiana, they were outnumbered by free Creole people of color, who often proved a resource for their enslaved relations. This difference alone was rife with implications for how enslaved Black people thought of one another from the antebellum period to the present day.

As much as I needed to get a sense of the differences that divided cultural groups, I also needed to convey class differences among a diversity of white Louisianans, especially with the story set just before the Civil War. All through school and up until now, I had always worked with an American history shorthand of the Civil War: North against

South, and that Southerners were pro-slavery. But while that might generally be true, Shugg gave me much more to consider. The political scene within early-to mid-nineteenth-century Louisiana was anything but clear cut along party lines. The call to secede from the Union and to fight was met with differing arguments and interests. On the pro-secessionist side, the large slaveholding planter class (that also included slaveholding free people of color) was powerful but was outnumbered by various white socioeconomic groups and the small planters and farmers who held fewer than twenty enslaved people. Among the array of those groups, I posited, what would motivate white small and subsistence farmers, nonlandowners, and nonslaveholders to fight for a cause that provided them with little to no economic gain or social advancement, should the South prevail? Imagine the alternative outcome: Black people declared emancipated *and* equal. (The Civil War didn't pronounce Black people equal; that fight is ongoing.) But imagine the conscious and subconscious fear of those pronouncements to white Louisianans on the lower rungs of class! Shugg states that poor whites who almost fared no better than enslaved people economically feared becoming their equal, if the enslaved people became emancipated. Shugg then notes that many of the former white slave patrollers who hunted runaway Black people were now armed with a zeal to serve in a Confederate army to preserve the notion of white superiority. The ring of this familiarity wasn't at all lost on me.

When the cadet, Byron Guilbert, spoke to me about his "way of life," it was with a natural pride and expectation, minus the animus I imagined in the voices of his lesser-well-off white counterparts. I could see how these different classes could find their own causes to fight for and unite under an overruling belief: Black people do not exist on the same human plane as white people and are therefore not afforded the same rights or considerations as a human being. These beliefs of race-based inferiority and supremacy, whether conscious or subconscious, carry forward today and seep into every functioning social, economic, and legislative system in America. These beliefs that promote systemic racism are at the root of the continued fight for social justice for and equal treatment of Black people in America.

The questions resound:

"Who were you without enslaved people and slavery?"

"What are you without racism?"

"Why do they hate us?"

BIBLIOGRAPHICAL NOTE

A Sitting in St. James is a work of fiction whose plot and characters took shape from my day and night dreams with prods from voices in my head. This story would not have come to life without my reliance on period newspapers, literature, articles, narratives of formerly enslaved people, diaries of slaveholders, countless websites, blogs, videos, and photographs covering a variety of subjects that appear in this book. However, not a day went by during the writing that I didn't refer to one or more of the following books:

Michael Bronski, *A Queer History of the United States;* George Washington Cable, "The Battle of New Orleans" in *The Creoles of Louisiana;* Kate Chopin, *Kate Chopin: Complete Novels & Stories;* Malcolm Crook, *Revolutionary France 1788–*

1880 (Short Oxford History of France); Sue Daley, Steve Gross, photographers; John H. Lawrence, commentary, *Creole Houses: Traditional Homes of Old Louisiana;* David Deitcher, *Dear Friends: American Photographs of Men Together, 1840–1918;* James H. Dormon, editor, *Creoles of Color of the Gulf South;* Laurent DuBois and John D. Garrigus, *Slave Revolution in the Caribbean, 1789–1804: A Brief History with Documents;* Henry Ossian Flipper, *The Colored Cadet at West Point;* Richard Follett, *The Sugar Masters: Planters and Slaves in Louisiana's Cane World, 1820–1860;* Antonia Fraser, *Marie Antoinette: The Journey;* Dianne Guenin-Lelle, *The Story of French New Orleans: History of a Creole City;* Lafcadio Hearn, *Gombo Zhèbes: Little Dictionary of Creole Proverbs;* Grace Elizabeth King, *Creole Families of New Orleans (1921);* Denise Labrie, *Parle Creole French: Southern Louisiana Dialect;* Juanita Leisch, *Who Wore What?: Women's Wear 1861–1865;* Sister Dorothea Olga McCants, translator; Rodolphe Lucien Desdunes, author, *Our People and Our History: Fifty Creole Portraits;* Graham Robb, *Strangers: Ho-*

718

mosexual Love in the Nineteenth Century; Charles P. Roland, Louisiana Sugar Plantations During the Civil War; Richard Sexton, text; Alex S. MacLean, photographer, Vestiges of Grandeur: The Plantations of Louisiana's River Road; Roger W. Shugg, Origins of Class Struggle in Louisiana: A Social History of White Farmers and Laborers During Slavery and After, 1840–1875; Lalita Tademy, Cane River; Elizabeth Tate and Hazel Harrington, American Artist Guide to Painting Techniques; Albert Valdman, editor, et al., Dictionary of Louisiana French: As Spoken in Cajun, Creole, and American Indian Communities; Michael J. Varhola, Everyday Life During the Civil War: A Guide for Writers, Students and Historians; The Magnolia Mound Plantation Kitchen Book: Being a Compendium of Foodways and Customs of Early Louisiana, 1795–1841; Arie Wallert, Erma Hermens and Marja Peek, editors, Historical Painting Techniques, Materials, and Studio Practice; www.warpaths2peacepipes.com/history-of-native-americans/history-of-louisiana-indians.htm.

ACKNOWLEDGMENTS

The narrator repeatedly asks her reader for patience as she reveals the story. Throughout the writing and revising of *A Sitting in St. James,* I repeatedly asked my editor, Rosemary Brosnan, for patience. Thank you, Rosemary, for indulging my every plea but, most dear to me, for standing in for me when I couldn't be there for parts of this work. I also send big thanks and love to Courtney Stevenson and the rest of my HarperCollins family for patiently awaiting my delivery.

Any authenticity that the work achieves in its depiction of details of domesticity is largely due to my virtual and in-person visits in Louisiana to the Laura Plantation, the Magnolia Mound Plantation, the Old Governor's Mansion in Baton Rouge, and the Whitney Plantation, and to the Shirley Plantation in Richmond, Virginia. I send a special note of appreciation to the staff at the Magnolia Mound Plantation for the unscheduled but detailed personal tour of the Main House and grounds. Thank you for keeping the on-site gift shop open past closing time while I purchased books that ultimately gave life to my work, and while I asked yet more questions. Having my own copy of *The Magnolia Mound Plantation Kitchen Book* kept Marcelle and Lily's kitchen real to me long after my visit.

I began my initial attempts at Louisiana Creole translations by consulting the online Louisiana Creole Dictionary on Facebook and the online site www.louisianacreoledictionary.com. While these online resources kept me going, I needed my own reference tools and found the invaluable *Parle Creole French: Southern Louisiana Dialect* by Denise Labrie, and the *Dictionary of Louisiana French,* compiled by Senior Editor Albert Valdman, Associate Editor Kevin J. Rottet, et al. I am forever grateful to Thomas A. Klingler, also an associate editor on the *Dic-*

tionary of Louisiana French, who answered my SOS and generously provided translations and recommendations.

My respect and appreciation for Kouri-Vini (Louisiana Creole) has increased manifold as I sought to capture the voices of its speakers and rose even higher as I received additional translations and invaluable cultural and historical insights from Adrien Guillory-Chatman, a Lafayette-born Kouri-Vini linguist and activist, and contributing author of the book *Ti Liv Kréyòl: A Learner's Guide to Louisiana Creole, 2nd Edition.* During a time of profound personal loss, Adrien read and vetted the manuscript and gave commentary that would allow this work to more accurately represent its speakers. It pained me greatly to not be able to include all of Adrien translations — particularly the dialogue between Rosalie and Camille as Rosalie prepares to attend the soiree at her grandmother's house. It was an especially difficult choice to maintain the English text when Kouri-Vini, a language nearly three hundred years old, is endangered and not taught or spoken in schools. I deeply admire

Adrien's activism to keep this rich part of her culture alive through her educational resources and her Kouri-Vini practice tables in the Chicago area, where she currently resides. For being a blessing to this work, *mési,* Adrien.

I am grateful to the Writers Room in the Village for providing me with an alternative space and peace while I plowed through a rough and tough third draft. It was at the Writers Room where a chance meeting with author and New Orleans native Fatima Shaik proved to be more than I could hope for. Fatima offered her time as a reader and introduced me to scholars Adrien Guillory-Chatman and Joseph Dunn.

When I needed to go south without getting on a plane, the Linden Row Inn in Richmond, Virginia, with its large parlor rooms and nineteenth-century decor, and also the Hotel Indigo in Baltimore, provided me with the necessary retreats to connect with my work.

I am tremendously grateful to my readers, authors Kathi Appelt, Ryan Douglass, Cheryl Willis Hudson, Olugbemisola Rhuday-Perkovitch, and Tim Wynne-

Jones, who graciously took in this unwieldy child and gave feedback to get me ready for the next round of revisions.

I am wholly indebted to Joseph Dunn, of the Laura Plantation and former director of the Council for the Development of French in Louisiana, for vetting this work. For me, Joseph is that walking treasure of Louisiana Creole history and culture, who cares for the memories of the free and enslaved people on the Laura Plantation as he cares for his own ancestors. I was the grateful beneficiary of his essays, articles, information, and stories that spring from his fierce advocacy of the French and Francophone language and Louisiana culture, and his roots in Louisiana that date back to the 1740s. I cannot begin to convey my gratitude, and I'm counting the days to my train ride down to Louisiana to enjoy that bowl of gombo!

To the boy who asked the question that forced this book out in the open, I thank you for your bravery and your tears.

I pray every morning before I open my eyes, and then I thank Dean and Mariah Edwards, Alexander and Mahalia Lloyd, and all of my ancestors who endured, sacrificed, and, above all, who loved.

Coretta Scott King Honor Book. Rita

ABOUT THE AUTHOR

Rita Williams-Garcia's Newbery
Honor Book, *One Crazy Summer,* was a
winner of the Coretta Scott King Author
Award, a National Book Award finalist,
the recipient of the Scott O'Dell Award
for Historical Fiction, and a *New York
Times* bestseller. The two sequels, *P.S.
Be Eleven* and *Gone Crazy in Alabama,*
were both Coretta Scott King Author
Award winners and ALA Notable Chil-
dren's Books. She is also the author of
National Book Award finalist *Clayton
Byrd Goes Underground* and six distin-
guished novels for young adults: *Jumped,*
a National Book Award finalist; *No
Laughter Here; Every Time a Rainbow Dies*
(a *Publishers Weekly* Best Children's
Book); *Fast Talk on a Slow Track* (all ALA
Best Books for Young Adults); *Blue Tights;*

and *Like Sisters on the Homefront,* a Coretta Scott King Honor Book. Rita Williams-Garcia lives in Jamaica, New York. You can visit her online at www .ritawg.com.

The employees of Thorndike Press hope you have enjoyed this Large Print book. All our Thorndike, Wheeler, and Kennebec Large Print titles are designed for easy reading, and all our books are made to last. Other Thorndike Press Large Print books are available at your library, through selected bookstores, or directly from us.

For information about titles, please call:
  (800) 223-1244

or visit our website at:
  gale.com/thorndike

To share your comments, please write:
  Publisher
  Thorndike Press
  10 Water St., Suite 310
  Waterville, ME 04901